Fabrications

Johns Hopkins: Poetry and Fiction

Wyatt Prunty, General Editor

by Pamela Painter

Fabrications

new and selected stories

 Johns Hopkins University Press   Baltimore

This book has been brought to publication with the generous assistance of the John T. Irwin Poetry and Fiction Endowed Fund.

Johns Hopkins University Press
2715 North Charles Street
Baltimore, Maryland 21218-4363
www.press.jhu.edu

Library of Congress Cataloging-in-Publication Data

Names: Painter, Pamela, author.
Title: Fabrications / by Pamela Painter.
Description: Baltimore : Johns Hopkins University Press, [2020] |
    Series: Johns Hopkins: poetry and fiction
Identifiers: LCCN 2019059865 | ISBN 9781421438924 (paperback) |
    ISBN 9781421438931 (ebook)
Classification: LCC PS3566.A36 A6 2020 | DDC 813/.54—dc23
LC record available at https://lccn.loc.gov/2019059865

A catalog record for this book is available from the British Library.

In "Reading in His Wake," the Patrick O'Brian quotations that appear on pp. 257 and 258 are from *Master and Commander*, first published by W. W. Norton (New York/London), copyright © 1970 by Patrick O'Brian. The O'Brian quotation that appears on p. 261 is taken from *The Wine-Dark Sea*, first published by W. W. Norton (New York/London), copyright © 1993 by Patrick O'Brian. The Dave Barry excerpt is from "Don't Forget to Flush," © 1994 by *The Miami Herald*, distributed by Tribune Media Services, Inc.

Special discounts are available for bulk purchases of this book. For more information, please contact Special Sales at specialsales@press.jhu.edu.

Johns Hopkins University Press uses environmentally friendly book materials, including recycled text paper that is composed of at least 30 percent post-consumer waste, whenever possible.

For: Derek

      Kate

           Wayne

               Cameron

Contents

Fabrications

New Stories

Her Elvis Presley Wedding

The year was 1999, a time of strange foreboding. Newscasters made serious and wild predictions about what would happen when the clocks rolled over into 2000. Banking systems could collapse, nuclear power plants could shut down, the locks and dikes of the Netherlands could fail to keep the country's coastline above water.

It was also the summer that Noose made his first road trip with his friend Drum. Their nicknames—"Noose" and "Drum"—went with that trip and disappeared as soon as it was over. Though now, years later, when he thinks about those days, the names return.

Back then, Noose had been working for a lawn service, cutting grass with an old lawnmower he had to ride out of the flatbed of a rusting truck while Drum—his real name was Bobby—pruned hedges into walls. One July evening, the breeze alive with the cicadas' longing, his father took him out for barbeque, ordered up two tall beers, and told him he was "untying the knot." Noose supplied "for the third time." He felt like saying he'd not be around for the next one, and he never considered that someday the knot might be his own. When he asked how Darlene was taking it, his father confirmed his suspicion that no, he hadn't told her yet, though she probably saw it coming. Noose had mostly ignored their arguments and left the house to hang out with Drum and his older brother at

Jackson's apartment downtown. His girlfriend, Pres, was usually there.

"You'll see when you get married," his father said

"So where do I come in?" he asked.

That's when his father said, "We'll be moving out. Selling the house. I got us a great apartment over past the watch factory, a swimming pool. New friends." But Noose was pissed that his senior year would be happening at a new school across town. Space Cranks, the band he and Drum had put together two years ago, was catching on, though he suspected that to varying degrees they were in it for the girls. What girls?

It had taken the band a while to settle on their name. Some of the suggestions were *Dese Dazed Days*, *Spunk*, and *Fire and Vice*. Drum complained that Space Cranks was too close to Ryan Landry's Space Pussy, but he'd been outvoted, with Noose saying maybe a little of Space Pussy's fame would rub off on them.

Two days later, while throwing rakes and lawn bags into the truck, Drum asked Noose if he'd be able to borrow a car, told him that Jackson and Pres were getting married. "They already have a reservation at the Graceland Wedding Chapel in Vegas." Drum said this with a straight face.

When Noose asked, "Why my car?" Drum said Jackson's car wasn't up for the trip and reminded Noose that he'd mentioned his father and Darlene were splitting up. Noose didn't let him finish. Their second car legally belonged to Darlene, though Drum knew it mostly sat unused because she jogged to her work at the insurance agency.

"Shit, man, I can't just give you Darlene's car," Noose said.

"But you can borrow it, right?" Drum said. "I'm going 'cause I'm the best man." He motioned for Noose to drive the lawnmower up the ramp and into the truck bed. "And I need you to help me drive. You can't say no."

That night his father and Darlene had another fight, so Noose and his sax ended up at Jackson's place making plans. First, Noose had to wrap his mind around the unlikely reason for the trip. Shit, the Graceland Wedding Chapel. Who knew such a thing existed?

Pres had discovered it. As plans got underway, she made them sit through a promotional video of "Elvis" conducting a wedding ceremony. Sure enough, the impostor looked almost exactly like photographs Noose had seen of the older Elvis: silky paunch, long, curved sideburns, seductive sneer.

When Elvis launched into "Love Me Tender," Noose played air guitar till Jackson took a swat at him.

Transfixed by the video, Pres sat on the arm of the couch, the remote hanging from her hand, wondering aloud if it was a lip-synch. Noose felt slightly ashamed to see tears in her eyes. Then Jackson declared that with two great chauffeurs along he wasn't going to do any of the driving. Noose was relieved. He couldn't see himself sitting in the back seat with Pres, tongue-tied, thinking about her knees. She was four years older than Noose and Drum. When she was head cheerleader, the boys in the bleachers felt permitted to stare at her tight sweater, hope for a glimpse of lace panties, and jerk off on game nights. For two entire basketball seasons, her blonde hair whipped around her face and her legs kicked impossibly high, and then she was gone—taking courses at Community and going steady with Jackson. And now, damn, a road trip with Pres—and Jackson. Helplessly, he agreed to borrow Darlene's car.

When he got home that night, his father was snoring in the guest room, and Darlene, her hands in the air to dry a glistening coat of nail polish, was deep into a bottle of wine in front of a black-and-white movie. Two cars in the driveway, and soon there would be none. He considered telling his father about the trip but decided not to take a chance his father would object—though on what grounds Noose couldn't imagine.

Departure day, he waited till Darlene had left the house, then he cleaned the car of her stuff—red umbrella, sunglasses, gum, tissues, red change purse full of dimes for meters—and left it all inside the garage. As planned, his note said he was borrowing the Corolla and he'd be back in good time. Let his father deal with her when he gave her his own big news.

An hour later, the four of them were on the road, with eight days to get from the silver arch of St. Louis to the Vegas strip.

The minute they left the outskirts of the city and were coasting down the interstate, Pres had leaned over from the back seat, blonde hair swinging against Noose's right shoulder, and announced that they all needed new names. "I'm tired of Kathleen," she said, "and I hate 'Kathy.'" So she was going to be "Pres" in honor of Elvis's last name. She made everyone say it—"Pres." Noose liked the percussive quality of "Pressssss."

She tapped Bobby's shoulder, saying he was next. It didn't take him long to say that he'd be "Drum." They all laughed because they'd forbidden Bobby to drum on the dashboard, though Noose could tell that he was dying to back up the new Morphine CD. Hands twitching on his knees, he'd been as jumpy as Roy Haynes, added that year to *Modern Drummer*'s Hall of Fame. Noose admired how Haynes, his hands as floppy as wings and hard as anvils, could turn everything into a drum.

"You're next," Pres said, tapping his shoulder.

Shit, if he had to play this game, he wanted something edgy, something *disjunctive*—a word his English teacher used. Five miles later, he said, "You ready? I'm Noose," and they all laughed a bit nervously.

"You got it," Pres said. She leaned back against Jackson and tucked her head under his bristly chin. "You're next," she said. Jackson's deep-set eyes seemed to look into his future and approve. But for once, he refused to humor her. Rubbing his chin on her hair, he said he was cool with just being Jackson.

Two hundred miles out of St. Louis, Noose allowed himself to think that stealing Darlene's car might have been a bad idea. What if she put out an alert? He told Drum, who was taking a turn at driving, to ratchet down the cruise control. "Getting pulled over could screw up the wedding."

"Relax," Drum said, his voice lazy, but his hands were tight on the wheel.

"Hey, you two. It's Noose's car. So take it down to maybe 75," Jackson ordered from the back seat. Pres said, "Second that," and the car brakes squealed.

As if to ease the tension, Jackson said, "Okay, guys. Time for show and tell." He handed Noose his case of CDs, and balanced Drum's on the armrest.

The guys had agreed on fifteen CDs each and now they screamed and yelled, giving every CD a thumbs up or down. Noose was proud as hell that his CDs got the most votes. Pres said she only listened to Elvis. For her ninth birthday, she'd been given her mother's Elvis collection of vinyl—singles and albums with gushing liner notes. Noose suspected they were all grateful that she couldn't travel with a turntable. He and Drum exchanged eye rolls until Jackson kicked the back of their seats.

When they settled into adjacent Motel 6 rooms that night, Drum gave Noose grief about his choice of a name. "Jesus. 'Noose?' What about 'Crank Up' or 'Saxman?'" Drum wanted to know. He had his practice pad and drumsticks out and was already doing a downbeat roll, his floppy bangs keeping rhythm with his sticks. A can of peanuts sat in as symbols. Ta ta ta. Ta ta ta. It made Noose miss his alto sax. His hands felt empty; his lip was getting soft.

"So, give. What's with 'Noose?'" Drum asked.

Noose shrugged and said it probably had something to do with Jackson and Pres tying the knot. "You know. Knot. Noose." He hadn't told anyone but Drum that his father was untying a knot for the third time. The first divorce had happened when Noose was seven, and his memory of his father dim. His dad came and mostly went, leaving behind Noose, his mother, a huge black Lab named Furze. Two years later, when Noose's mother died suddenly, his father moved back home trailing a second wife and another black Lab, this one named Bruiser. The two dogs did not get along, which was almost all that Noose remembered about Janet. After being bitten several times by both dogs, she locked them out in the yard in the dead of winter when his father went to work. Three years after moving in, she left, scattering kibble around the entire downstairs—inside cabinets, the closets, the shower, the dishwasher. It was a mess, with the summer humidity and two dogs vying for the choicest morsels as if one corner of a room had barbequed chicken and the other filet mignon. The house still smelled like dog shit and dog kibble. About the dog bites, his father said, "Those dogs knew something about that woman that we didn't know." By then both dogs were hiding from Noose's practice sessions on the sax. Darlene came along a year later and Noose remembers her asking "What's that smell?" She painted every room in the house a pastel color. He told her, "Not my room," but she had an obstinate streak and Noose's room was pale gray though you couldn't see it with all the band posters. Now she could paint the whole house pink if she wanted to.

They stopped for gas, restrooms, and snacks, diner dinners of gray meatloaf and mashed potatoes, sometimes ribs, and crashed in Motel 6s and once in a Holiday Inn. They alternated between talking a lot and talking little. They lamented the disbanding of the 'Mats—the Replacements to Pres—and wondered if they'd ever get back together. Years later, that long-awaited reunion would happen, but only after most things in their lives had fallen apart. Jackson described his fellow workers at the bank, and the strategically placed foot buttons on the floor that the tellers were supposed to use in case of a hold-up. Twice, with his size 14 shoe, he'd set off the alarm.

More than once on the trip Pres opened her diary to read a passage she'd copied whole from Greil Marcus's *Mystery Train*. "'Elvis has emerged as a great *artist,* a great *rocker,* a great *purveyor of schlock,* a great *heart throb,* a great *bore,* a great *symbol of potency,* a great *ham,* a great *nice person,* and, yes, a great American.'

"So there," she said. "And those words I emphasized, well, it was Marcus who put them in italics." The first time she read it, Drum had sniggered and Noose had sputtered into his Coke till Jackson sent a fierce look at them from the back seat.

Soon, every time she read it, they joined in to bawl, "Yes, a great American," while Pres looked at them, suspicious of their ardor. But she was unstoppable, and seemed to know everything there was to know about Elvis. She pretended shock at Drum and Noose's ignorance, so she filled them in on his war record, his courtship of the fourteen-year-old Priscilla, his life-long support of his adored mother, his gifts of Cadillacs to friends, his lost (stillborn) brother Jessie, his slide into a drug-ridden life, his women, his death at Graceland, the vigils people still held for him.

Once Jackson asked Drum and then Noose if there were any women in their sorry lives. They both said "No," which was the truth back then.

"You'll have roadies soon enough," Pres said, ruffling Drum's hair from the back seat. He ducked so fast his nose almost hit the steering wheel. Noose's own scalp shivered with anticipation, but Pres only patted his shoulder as if in sympathy that it hadn't happened yet. But Pres, Pres was in his car.

The miles continued to unravel across the dry, flat planes of Missouri, Oklahoma, into the low dry hills of Texas. Interstates allowed them to bypass bit cities that rose in the distance like mirages and were hard to fathom. Once, when he knew his father's cell would be off, he'd left the message "not to worry" and given him an ETA. Hours later he got a text back saying, "Just get your ass home." He sent two more texts but got the same response. "Home" was a mystery. Pres was a mystery, but inspired a different kind of wonder.

Every so often Noose would insist that they clean the car of rumpled chip bags, beer cans, candy wrappers, and since things got left behind, they often had to walk deodorant sticks and tubes of Crest from one motel room to the other. When they stopped to do laundry outside of Amarillo, Pres's colorful bikini panties—furled like exotic flowers—sometimes showed up in the folds of their T-shirts and jeans. Several times, late at night, Noose got off just thinking about them.

Somewhere past Albuquerque, they exited at Interstate 40 and headed into a town that looked abandoned. Out here you could buy a whole town for the price of a house in St. Louis. Jackson shook Pres awake and as usual handed everyone a twenty for whatever. Noose pulled in behind a jacked-up long-haul trailer that hid his car from view. Staring at his license plate, he saw how a little duct tape would make his three into an eight pretty damn easy. He wondered if Darlene had put out a call for the car, or if his dad had sweet-talked her out of it. His dad always bragged about his way with women, but if he was that good, why didn't any last? Besides, what was a "way with women"—Jackson just *was*. Noose liked Pres and Jackson's easy way of being together. How they petted each other, smoothing down this or that. Sort of the way his father was with his dogs.

Back in the car, Noose drove while Drum went into navigator mode with the map. "Hey, guys," he said, slapping it with the back of his hand. "Since we're driving all this way we ought to take a detour to the Grand Canyon."

Jackson leaned forward to see where they were. Drum said they were probably fifty miles from Flagstaff, and a little past Flagstaff, at Williams, was the turnoff for the Grand Canyon. He pointed to a brown spot and held the map up for Noose to see.

Jackson peered a little closer over his brother's shoulder and whistled. "That's a serious detour," he said. "Way serious."

Pres stopped braiding her hair—hair that Noose knew he would never get to touch—and leaned in to look. "Fabulous idea." She turned and gave Jackson a loud kiss. "We'll go there on the way back. It'll be our honeymoon."

Then she was leaning over the seat again, her hand on Noose's shoulder, asking Noose how long they had the car for. Noose resisted shrugging that he didn't know, just to keep her hand in place. He tried to imagine what his father said to Darlene, how he'd made the announcement that they were through. Noose felt as if they were two people he didn't really know, and perhaps that's what they'd come to think too. Surely by now she'd ranted and raved to his father about the missing car? Showed him Noose's scrawled note. He imagined her ripping down his posters, taking one of her fancy boots to his CDs. He didn't know her well enough to know if she would or wouldn't, which surprised him. Belatedly.

Once, near Flagstaff, a cop bore down on them, blue lights flashing, siren blaring. Noose felt like puking.

"Cool. Stay cool," Jackson said. He and Pres each had a hand on his shoulder as he pulled over to the gravelly side of the road. Then just as quickly, the cop car, doing at least 90, sped past them to some more serious crime or accident. Not a wedding.

The next day the neon lights of Las Vegas vied with the desert's sun. To Noose, it felt like an atmosphere of desperation hung over the city, but Pres and Jackson were not daunted. They seemed so charmed by it that Noose felt like an usher at a sold-out Phish concert. Even Drum took off his sunglasses to see the real dazzle of the gambler's row.

Pres insisted that she sit up front for their parade down Las Vegas Boulevard, and shrieked at every name she recognized: the Riviera, the Venetian, the Mirage, Casino Royale, Caesar's Palace, the Bellagio, the Monte Carlo, MGM Grand, Excalibur, Mandalay Bay. "Who gets to design and name these places?" she asked. Noose was driving indulgently slow. Even he could see that these hotels were all competing for an exotic, seductive glamour. It was a glamour that just two decades in the future would look quaint, when corporate gambling money from somewhere like Dubai came to town.

The windows were down even though it was 93 degrees. Twice Noose pulled over to let people pass so he could keep up the snail's pace decreed by an enthralled Pres. She had insisted they stay at LVH on Paradise Road because Elvis had lived on the thirtieth floor when it used to be the International Hotel, where, she said, "He did a record-breaking fifty-eight consecutive shows." Space Cranks had never covered an Elvis song and Noose knew they never would. Pres had come to see them several times with Jackson and said she forgave them this oversight. Barely.

The honeymoon suite—actually one of many, of course—at LVH was conferred on Pres and Jackson with bows and nods at the registration desk. Jackson had called two days ago, given his card info, announced their hurried wedding plans, and said her daddy's private jet had been delayed in Anchorage but he'd be along to party big later in the week and, by the way, could LVH arrange a private poker game. Noose could tell that the concierge knew their car and clothes didn't support their earlier story of big money, but it turned out the LVH had everything Pres wanted.

Noose and Drum's room was a discreet six doors away, but they all gathered in the wedding suite to admire the heart-shaped bathtub with its retractable ceiling, the bedroom's mirrored walls, the patio that was larger than Jackson's apartment. Pres took a flying leap to land in the middle of the heart-shaped bed and Jackson followed, nuzzling her hair. Noose blushed at the thought that the bed could have held all four of them. They left to unpack. "Take a nap," Pres called. "This isn't the Heartbreak Hotel. We'll do the bars and casinos later."

The wedding was scheduled for 8:00 p.m. Noose knew he'd have to rein in his smirks, not even look at Drum, but he actually felt nervous as he shaved and dressed. Kneeling in front of the tiny fridge, Drum called out the name brands of the various alcoholic beverages at their disposal. Quickly, they disposed of two beers—toasting their luck at evading tickets and efficient cops.

Pres knocked on their door and soon they were walking to the chapel in hot, dry air. Noose's armpits felt like sponges. He and Drum wore jackets from a thrift shop that had more jeans, boots, and string ties than anything suitable for a wedding. Jackson's job at the bank required a suit, so his actually fit. Pres smelled like an exotic flower, or maybe it was the roses she was carrying, heads down as if to let them rest. She was wearing the lacy white dress she'd made from two dozen fancy napkins she'd bought at a flea market. Holding Jackson's arm, she minced past glittering fountains, riptide canals, and lush tropical gardens like a bride. Her back was straight and her giggles wouldn't stop. At least four couples whispered and pointed at her and Jackson. Noose suspected that their little group had "wedding" written all over them. Drum was carrying a cold bottle of champagne wrapped in a hotel pillowcase. Noose's fingers were threaded with four plastic flutes. "Flutes" was a new word for him.

They arrived at the chapel at 7:50. Palms together, a hostess—maybe a receptionist—wearing Priscilla's sixties bouffant hairdo greeted them and said that Pres was going to make a beautiful bride. They would surely use the couple's photograph in their promotional materials—with permission, of course. "If it's with Elvis," Pres said, and the hostess winked at her. Noose hung back; he sure as shit didn't want to be in any such photograph. The hostess ushered them down a mirrored hallway to a tiny chapel that looked exactly as it had on the video. Except that now they really were inside this wedding cake. The hostess said she would put their lovely bottle of champagne on ice and unthreaded the flutes from Noose's fingers. Then she asked only Pres to follow her. Pres kissed all three of them on the cheek and left to don the veil she had been waving at passersby.

Minutes later, the hostess led them through French doors and into the chapel. It was icing white, with low cozy ceilings, white satin walls, glowing wall sconces, and ten rows of white pews on either side of a short aisle. They were all instructed to go to the front, where she asked, "And who is the lucky groom?" Jackson stepped forward and took a little bow. Noose felt pleased with himself that she had to ask.

"Elvis" emerged from behind a white curtain, solemnly nodded at them, and then stood with his head bowed. His ringed hands clasped a burnished guitar in front of a wide silver belt. His shirt was dark with sequins or spangles stitched in circles, and open in a deep V above bell-bottoms that flared like a skirt from the knees down—not even the thrift shop had carried any.

Noose stared. He couldn't help himself. He had to admit that "Elvis" did look like Elvis. He'd probably won some Elvis look-alike contest back when it mattered. The thought of a room full of wannabe Elvises almost made Noose laugh.

A camera was set up behind them, Noose knew from the video. It was trained on Elvis and the aisle that Pres would soon walk down.

"Here Comes the Bride" suddenly spilled from Elvis's guitar. It was a startling combination, but the sound was so good Noose figured he must be playing a Martin or a Collings. This march was the only "real wedding thing" Pres had asked for when she sent in her musical requests.

Elvis motioned for everyone to face the aisle, and then he sauntered down its length, still playing, his legs doing the Elvis-the-Pelvis moves that Pres said had once titillated the entire Western world. Tame now, Noose thought, after Prince, Bowie, Mick Jagger's antics, Kiss.

When Pres came through the double doors, her eyes were glistening. Still strumming, Elvis held out his right elbow and Pres tucked her hand in its crook, as if they had rehearsed this gesture. Together, they strolled up the aisle. Her bouquet of four long-stemmed red roses, minus thorns, had been plucked from the huge arrangement in their suite. "One for each of my boys," she had said. "And one for Elvis." She was beautiful, and Noose could almost forget what was going on back home, that a marriage was unraveling, that his father was leaving his third wife, whose wedding was the last time Noose had heard "Here Comes the Bride."

Pres arrived at the—the what—the Elvis altar, where Elvis put his guitar aside to take her fingers and press his lips to the back of her trembling hand, which he then passed to Jackson. Drum was tapping his fingers against his leg, and Noose's own fingers tingled.

Elvis strung together a few silly lyrics from songs that Pres had picked for him about "a hunk, a hunk of burning love," his hips and pelvis still gently gyrating, and how "It's now or never." Then, moving to one side, he played "Love Me Tender" in velvety tones that matched the surprising richness of his voice. Pres and Jackson were bathed in a pink cameo light for ten seconds of pure joy. Drum and Noose did not laugh. Noose didn't even feel like laughing as he found himself almost succumbing to the mystery that was Elvis.

Then Elvis joined the light, and his deep voice asked all the right questions: "Do you take this woman . . . ? Do you take this man. . . . ?" "In sickness and health . . . ?" Finally, he came to "With this ring—" and looked expectantly at Drum, who slid his hand from his pocket and handed the ring to Jackson, "—I thee wed." Noose had heard it all twice before, at eight and thirteen, but he was suddenly choked up

with feelings of sadness and hope. Hope for himself? He would return Darlene's car when he got home—not home. Maybe leave a
note of apology, but he'd omit the reason for the trip.

Jackson and Pres gazed into each other's eyes, more solemn than
Noose had ever seen them, and they assured Elvis of their eternal
loyalty and love.

"Now kiss your beautiful bride," he told Jackson, and in the three
seconds they kissed Noose wanted to hold and kiss a girl just like
that. It wouldn't happen for him, though, for another year. Then
they received the final Elvis blessing as he declared they should "go
out into the world as husband and wife."

Magically, Elvis's guitar appeared again, and he strummed the
lead into "Can't Help Falling in Love." Doors opened at the end of
the aisle.

The ceremony was over.

Jackson turned to leave, but Pres hung back and patted Jackson's
arm before she let it go. Carefully, she separated one rose from her
bouquet and held it out to Elvis. "Thank you," she said.

Elvis looked startled, and then he had his first genuine expression of grace. He smiled, his own smile, and at that moment, as he
tucked the rose into his belt, Noose could imagine that he looked
exactly like the young, vulnerable Elvis that Pres had described, the
Elvis who became a star and went to war and fell in love with his
child bride.

He returned to strumming the opening bars of "Can't Help Falling in Love," apparently himself a little bit in love with Pres.

Jackson shook first Drum's hand and then Noose's. More hugs.
In an adjoining white room meant to efficiently collect them from
the chapel where Elvis would soon perform again, they found their
bottle of champagne on ice in a silver bucket. Standing beside it, already developed, was a white-framed photograph of the smiling

couple facing each other, an angelic Elvis in the center. Pres picked it up and hugged it.

Drum popped the cork and poured bubbles into four plastic glasses that Noose passed around. It was real. At the time.

Drum raised his glass in a toast "to the perfect wedding and the perfect bride and groom."

Noose said, "Hear, hear." When he was five he'd thought people were saying "Here, here." And he had looked around to locate "here." Things change. But he was looking forward to being Zack again, bending with his sax, playing out a hard line in front of Bobby's drums.

* * *

Fifteen years later, after the new century was underway, after Noose's own wedding on a Lake Erie beach, after Jackson and Pres's divorce, after Ryan Landry broke up Space Pussy and the 'Mats had a comeback tour, after Noose put his sax away for good, he sometimes thought about this trip. He remembered his father's news that he was leaving Darlene, that they would be moving out. Next came Drum's announcement that Jackson needed to borrow a car. Noose remembered the names they chose, though only Pres kept hers. And he remembered the four of them standing on the rim of the South Canyon's wall on the impromptu honeymoon, all of them unprepared for the grandeur of sheer copper rock, the distant silver ribbon of Bright Angel River, and the wide open sky.

Through the years that trip took on a meaning that Noose felt but didn't examine. Maybe those days spent with Jackson and Pres made him believe in the possibility of love. Maybe he saw that trip as an antidote to his father's own multiple uncouplings that had also left Noose untethered to a family and place. Maybe he returned home more open to the unfolding of his teenage years and the mystery that was college and women. He still kept his CDs from the trip in a frayed black CD case.

Then one day, after fifteen years had passed, when Noose was in his lawyer's office signing his own divorce papers, he was stung with a different memory from that trip. After the wedding at the Graceland Wedding Chapel, they had indeed taken the honeymoon detour to the Grand Canyon. They had followed the South Rim for miles; then he and Pres had ended up sitting on a picnic table waiting for Jackson and Drum, who were off booking a hotel for the night. With the canyon's wide skies growing a deep blue, he remembered that he had asked Pres—and maybe it was only his shy self making conversation—he had asked her why she had insisted on getting married by "Elvis" in Las Vegas. She had laughed and tossed her golden hair in wondrous amusement. "Oh, Noose. Don't you know? That way we won't take it too seriously. Seriously."

Brochures

"It says that the porch we're sitting on is one eighth of a mile long." Gordon gave the inn's brochure a little wave, but didn't pass it to his wife, even though Dora was holding out her hand. "That's about the length of porch of the Grand Hotel on Mackinac Island," he said. He'd always admired porches—the Old French word *porche*.

When she waved her hand again, he wondered how many seconds would pass before she simply reached over and snatched the brochure from him. He had been playing this game, hiding brochures from her, since they'd arrived. Little games like this had amused and sometimes aroused him in the first months of his retirement last year, but now less so. He had persuaded her to go on this trip two months ago. Finally she'd allowed him to make the reservation for a room, if it had a water view.

He read on: *"The Inn was built in 1923 and rebuilt in 1956 after a fire destroyed the main building. During the renovation, the original French windows were moved from the south wing to capture the spectacular views of the dramatic cliff walk that made the original Inn so famous."* He glanced over to see if she was listening. She was. *"Charlie Chaplin said it was the closest thing to his beloved Swiss landscape that America could offer."*

"There's a photograph of the cliff walk?" his wife asked, finishing her martini's third lurid olive. He himself tolerated only a wisp of lemon peel. They were awaiting the grand dining room's noonday Sunday dinner. *"In the European tradition,"* the brochure read.

"One photo of the cliff walk. It looks very manicured. No doubt for old people like us," he said. Ha. He liked to remind her that they were the same age, though oddly his retirement had made him feel older. He set his white wicker rocking chair to rocking. Dora's chair did not rock. He put out his foot and abruptly stopped. He longed for the afternoon's cheerful dose of sun.

"The hotel is so empty," Dora complained. "Who would have thought that 'off-season' meant there would be only one other couple? I mean, at a famous hotel that"—here Dora's dismissive gesture took in the vast empty porch—*"in season plays host to one hundred guests."*

"Now, how do you know that?" he asked.

"Oh," she said. "Here." She swooped into the string bag she always carried and came up with an identical brochure, waving it just out of his reach.

So, she'd had a brochure all this time. Unnerved, he said, "Shall we dine?"

His own martini finished, he lurched from his rocking chair. Lately, he'd begun comparing which of them was fastest out of the starting gate, so to speak—rising from couches, dining chairs, the BMW's low bucket seats—and was dismayed that he always lost, though Dora seemed unaware of the competition. Before he retired, he hadn't noticed that she went to the gym two days a week, leaving the house in shiny, tight leggings and returning in totally different outfits—a suit or sundress. There was a lot he hadn't known— her book club meetings (though he did remember seeing various frivolous-looking novels with Booker Prize stickers on their covers), her appointment to the town's Parks Board, her Zumba lessons. How luncheon hostesses at better restaurants seemed to know her. It was disconcerting.

He tucked his brochure into his seersucker pocket; he considered his seersucker suits a charming idiosyncrasy, though Dora had pronounced them merely out of style.

"Come along, Gordie," she called over her gray silk shoulder. It was the name from their long-ago courtship days, but it didn't conjure up the same excitement it once had. Now, he thought "Lordy, Gordie," every time she said it.

"Wait up, Dora," he called after her. His right knee was stiff, but he'd be damned if he was going to take up golf or fishing as his doctor had prescribed. Golf was silly. Fishing more so. Besides, he was still a consultant to the company he'd sold, though calls for his advice were few and far between and the office he was supposed to retain had been given to a new vice president who came to work in multipocket hiking shorts.

"Good afternoon, Madame," Gordon heard the maitre d' say as he bowed Dora to her seat.

He wished they could dine on the porch, with the ocean's breezes riffling the pages of the eclectic wine list. He liked the Doric columns, the white wooden floors dotted about with huge ceramic planters. Here, white tablecloths bristled and gleamed with unused silver and empty wine glasses. Characteristically, Dora rearranged the table's fall flowers in their tiny vase while he perused the menu. He ignored the greetings she exchanged with the Solwits, who glided by, he leading her by the hand. The only other guests at the inn, they were a frail couple at least ten years older than Gordon and Dora—retired lawyers who had worked for the ACLU. When they had asked Dora and Gordon about themselves, Gordon had let them know that, though retired, he still kept his hand in and just last week had written a blistering letter to the publisher of *The Iconic Building* decrying the omission of Louis Kahn. They had nodded in unison, though Edith Solwit had added mildly that Louis Kahn was a monster. "Oh, but a genius," Gordon had said, thinking surely that made up for almost everything Kahn had put his son and clients through. Gordon was grateful that he and Dora had never had a child.

The Solwits had listened attentively to Dora's description of the house he'd designed with its soaring wings, where they each had a study—she'd omitted the fact of their separate bedrooms—and showed a mild interest in Gordon's final projects: the building for the city's busiest dental practice, the branch bank kiosks that dotted the suburbs, and the two methadone clinics. Dora hadn't chimed in with her own interests. After all, he was the architect and she was merely a housewife, a poet-housewife, to be sure, whose little poems appeared in obscure magazines like *Poetry*. When they entertained, which they seldom did now, he tucked her journals underneath his own *Architectural Review*s and Italy's influential *Domus*.

"I overheard them say they were leaving tomorrow," Dora whispered, leaning forward above a shallow cleavage, still attractive in spite of her sour personality.

"The Nitwits," he said, briefly raising his eyes from the menu.

"Hush. I'm going to invite them to join us for dessert."

She didn't wait to quiet his protestations, but rose and went to their table, her solid form a silhouette against the noonday's yellow light. As she bent to Edith Solwit's ear, she smiled back at him.

He silently consumed appetizers and entree, finally conceding a few sentences over salad. Not that Dora noticed, entranced as she seemed to be by the inn's landscape murals, the hawk swooping in among the trees and lifting off with a chipmunk or squirrel in its beak. As they finished a bottle of Sancerre, she instructed the waiter to bring the dessert cart to their table. To Gordon's mind, the displayed pastries looked so sweet he half-believed they might mask a lethal poison.

When the Solwits had settled themselves, Dora gaily held forth, describing Gordon's fascination with the old inn as she placed her hand over his. The gesture was so unexpected, so unlike Dora, that he felt as if they were on stage and the Solwits were the audience. During the scabrous chocolate dessert, he continued to tolerate Dora's puzzling pastiche of their marriage. "Tomorrow we're kayaking to the caves," she said.

"So energetic of you," Alan Solwit said, clearly relieved that they had eschewed this activity. He and his wife were sharing a sliver of key lime pie.

"And exciting, paddling into the mouth of a dark cave," Edith Solwit said, taking a tiny, glistening bite. "Fingal's Cave in the Inner Hebrides was our last."

"We did manage the famous cliff walk," Alan Solwit said, pushing the last bit of pie toward his wife.

"Oh, how was it?" Dora asked. They were taking that walk later today, she added. Alan held forth about the views, the winding path with stations here and there. "Not to be missed."

Gordon nodded in deference to such a feat at their greater age. He'd wait until tomorrow to tell Dora that she'd be kayaking alone. He would stay behind to lounge on the long porch and play solitaire, though he knew what Dora would say: Why had he dragged them to this inn when he could have played Scrabble at home? "Solitaire," he would correct her. He refused to play computer Scrabble. The computer version exacted no penalties for a wrong word, merely deemed it "unacceptable." Penalties made the world go round.

Chairs being pushed away from the table brought him back to the Solwits and their impending departure. Ah, he and Dora would have the inn with its stunning long porch, its firm wicker couches and reassuring railings, all to themselves. A fleeting warmth touched and circled his girth but receded as quickly as it had appeared, like a tiny wave lapping the shore.

"I hope we see each other when we're back in Boston," Dora said as they exchanged farewells. Unexpectedly, as the two couples threaded their way through the tables, she took his arm. She'd last done that at *La Traviata* six years ago. She'd been wearing a midnight blue velvet cloak—cape. Now why had he remembered that?

"Enjoy the kayaking," Alan Solwit said. "And don't miss the cliff walk."

Not likely, Gordon thought. His cheek twitched in anticipation: once again he'd have the opportunity to feign a migraine. Since retirement, he'd perfected the gargoyle of a grimace that signaled one was coming on. He'd taken a lesson from Dora, who sometimes stood attentively in front of a mirror and recited lines of poetry as she touched up her makeup before going out. Or sat at her desk, reading her work out loud.

When Dora rang the silver bell in the lobby to inquire about the kayaks, the owners were abjectly apologetic. The boats had been put away for the winter, the husband explained. This was their last week at the inn before they closed for the season. In three weeks they would be leaving for St. Barts, where they owned a smaller boutique hotel. The wife, attractive in the high-color way that had once appealed to Gordon in secretaries and assistants, offered Dora a new brochure sprinkled with French words.

Oddly, Dora, too, looked apologetic—almost stricken. Gordon reached past her to accept the St. Barts brochure, and tucked it into the inside pocket of his jacket.

"Might you have walking sticks for the cliff walk?" Dora asked, her voice a bit pinched. "We can catch the afternoon's breeze and I want to take some photographs."

"That we do have," the husband said, and flung open paneled doors behind the lobby's registration desk. While Dora exclaimed delightedly over the antique collection of canes—one with a hidden, tightly furled umbrella—Gordon imagined just how he would thwart plans for the cliff walk, though doing so had nothing to do with the steepness of the cliffs or the narrowness of the path, as described in the brochure. It was merely another game. Dining with the Solwits had thrown him off a bit, but he was determined to wrest the upper hand from Dora—who seemed not ever to know when she had it.

Lately, it had occurred to Gordon that retirement would be more interesting if Dora were competitive, more dead-on with her preferences. Instead, she merely went on her merry way, ignoring Gordon's wishes, disappearing into her poetic study, dressing for the gym in grotesque regalia, serving soup at that dreadful soup kitchen. She wasn't at all curious about his days. They seemed not to exist for her. Which is why he had insisted on this two-week stay at the inn. Here, he could not be ignored, and was gratified to note her mild surprise that he was seated across from her at every breakfast, lunch, and dinner or beside her on the long porch instead of her gym mates or poet friends. He napped when he wanted. He entered into conversation—or not. He ordered their martinis for the dot of five. When they had arrived at the inn, the owner had suggested various things for them to do: no, Gordon told him, he did not want to attend Shakespeare in the Park; he thought the library's lecture series pedestrian and thin; and he did not want to visit the Vulture Conservancy. The inn itself, Gordon had said, was "everything I'd wished for."

And now, he told Dora, it was time for his nap. In a few days, they would return to Boston and he would immediately research the hotel in St. Barts, where, as here, he would gleefully determine their activities and schedule.

"Another nap," she said. "You napped all morning on the porch."

He ignored this, saying she could do what she wanted and he'd meet up with her for their customary martinis. "And please shut the drapes." He glanced at the brochure for the St. Barts hotel, admiring its wrought iron balconies, noting the activities he'd choose not to do—snorkeling in clear waters, deep-sea fishing, shopping for rare shells and native art. Then he drifted off.

An hour later, he woke with a start to find the drapes flung open to the late-afternoon sun and Dora standing over him. What on earth was she thinking?

Startled, he realized this was a new thought for him.

With a theatrical gesture, she brandished a silver-headed walking stick, declaring that he should change into the appropriate shoes because they were going on the cliff walk or she was going home. She picked up each shoe with the tip of the walking stick and deposited everything at his side of the bed.

When he sat up, protesting and bleary-eyed, she threw the walking stick onto the bed and methodically began sweeping her makeup from the dressing table into her traveling vanity case.

For once, this minor defeat felt sweet. "Fine. Fine. Let's do the cliff walk. But," he cautioned, "I will only do the first mile."

"It *is* only one mile," she said, as she pulled another of the inn's brochures from her case and waved it at him. "Here's the map."

At that, she stepped out onto what he'd decided was a balcony too rickety to hold two adults, and pointed to the cliffs below, jagged and beautiful in the languorous light. "The views will be unforgettable."

"I meant I will do only the first *half* mile," he said, picking up the walking stick and poking her in the back. She turned, eyes narrowed, and looked through him to some silly poem she was no doubt thinking up as though he wasn't there.

And that is where he found himself an hour later—on the first half-mile of the cliff walk, its narrow path solid and free of rubble, clearly groomed, and not as narrow as it looked from their balcony, or from the long porch. "Be careful. Enjoy your walk," the owners had called out. "Your martinis will be ready at the dot of five."

Dora and he could have walked side by side if they had chosen to, but she had forged ahead—dragging him along with a will he resented but also admired. The sea far below the cliff was a plate of steel, so beautiful that he was almost tempted to continue for the entire luminous mile. Secluded sections of the walk sported ornate wrought iron benches set in bowers of flowering vines and leaves— Gordon guessed for lovers.

Minutes later, they rounded a bend and came upon another isolated bower nestled beneath a trellis whose trumpet vine was overflowing with heavy orange blossoms. The bench underneath was really a chaise—hard, but inviting. He imagined the wizened Solwits exchanging a chaste, but to them exciting, embrace. Should he mention this to Dora? Probably not.

He felt jaunty with his silver-headed cane and determined that he would buy one for their trip to St. Barts. He relished swinging it out in front of him, then stabbing it into the path.

When Dora stopped abruptly in front of another lush, secluded bower, he joined her. Had they reached the half-mile mark?

As if reading his mind, she said, "This is as far as you wanted to go." There was a lilt in her voice, but lower than usual.

"Yes, well, it is as far as I wanted to go." In the interests of the game, he must refuse to continue on the walk. "I'll just rest here and read the brochure about St. Barts."

He turned to face the darkening sea, the walking stick a slender post to lean on. Oddly he felt like describing this melancholy light to Dora before she left him—its spirit of flatness, of weight, like a hand closing one's eyes slowly. It was then that she stepped behind him as if to adjust his collar. In these final seconds, he wondered if it was too late to start over, too late to retire in a peaceful truce, too late to regret that an accident might prevent the owners of the inn from leaving for St. Barts. It was certainly too late to appreciate her touch, now firm on his shoulders for the last time.

A Fabricated Life

Where on earth was Grace's email congratulating Trixie on getting a cat? She was certain she'd told her sister that she'd gotten a cat— probably wrote about a cat six or seven months ago when Grace pointedly asked if Trixie was still living alone. In fact, she needed to track down all her emails to Grace, emails about her life—or rather her fabricated life—since her niece, Grace's daughter, Bianca, would be arriving any day now expecting a cat, a boyfriend, and a sober Aunt Trixie with a paying job.

What had she said about a job?

She scrolled back through her emails to Grace in which she described a new apartment that allowed cats, the new job, her new friends. She paused at the one in which she had described "Nerdboy," who *is always hanging around my desk at work, complimenting my new fluffy hairstyle. The guy has an enormous tie collection that he must pet and groom like a cat.* Now that was a coincidence—that she'd had grooming cats on her mind. Though he was no candidate for her usual in boyfriends. She resumed scrolling past the JOB email where she'd talked about her position as an executive assistant. *My boss said he didn't know what he'd done before he hired me.*

Yep, the subject line said CAT: *I went to the SPCA Shelter and adopted a two-year-old feline. Her name is Granite, for her elegant gray fur.*

Lordy, she must have been buzzed when she wrote "elegant gray fur." So, she would have to adopt a cat fast. A gray cat. It seemed the easiest thing to fake. How smart were ten-year-olds? Maybe Bianca was twelve? Did she like her Peruvian name?

When Trixie looked up cat houses—ha—she discovered a shelter in Boston's South End totally devoted to black cats. It seemed that numerous cat owners were superstitious about black cats. As a result, mewling black kittens arrived in boxes on the shelter's doorstep. She was tempted. But she'd told her sister gray. She couldn't remember ever having typed the word "elegant" before or since.

She put a different shelter's address into her GPS and got lost anyway. South meant beyond the Back Bay. Rain made it hard to see street signs. Her wiper blade was shredded. Weeping, she pulled in front of a dumpster. Feeling desolate, she wondered if she could get away with a story about the gray cat's demise. Fuck. Her flask only had a whiff of vodka left. For old times' sake, she breathed deeply, practicing: "Granite flashed out the door when—when UPS rang for a signature. No. When my neighbor showed up to complain about her late night Zumba. When Charlie's Liquors was delivering a case of vodka." She put her tongue in the neck of the flask and was rewarded with a heavenly drop.

But a cat would be good for a ten-year-old. Lord save her from a snarky preadolescent. Bianca had been snarky already when Trixie last saw her several years ago. Trixie remembered a long-legged, skinny kid whose nose was glued to her phone when her ear was not. And now, Bianca would be arriving on Trixie's doorstep and, as Grace had promised, staying for the fall, and "only the fall." Grace's husband, Drake, had tumbled into a test pit on his dig in Ecuador and broken both legs. He'd been moved to Quito, but he didn't want to leave the country. Tenure depended on this research, and he desperately needed Grace to keep the natives in line. Not quite Grace's words. Trixie had countered with, "Why can't you take Bianca? Homeschool her?"

Grace's voice was tight as she said that Bianca refused to go. Then Trixie again: "What about Bianca's friends? Her babysitter? Your sister-in-law?" She felt chastened when she was told that they'd thought of those avenues, but they hadn't worked out, and a prep school was way too expensive. "So, I'm the last resort," Trixie had said. "You're her aunt," Grace said. "And you're sober, right?"

"Right," Trixie said. "You want me to resend my email about AA?" At least she hadn't lied about that. She said she'd been to two meetings, which was true, and then quit because it was too soaked in God stuff. Also true. She'd written, "Every time they said the word 'God' I pictured being ushered into this black hole with Stephen Hawking as MC." Not true, but she liked the sound of it. He'd given the world only a hundred more years before it killed itself with pollution, plastic, and new viruses. She'd watched a YouTube interview with him when she was looking up her astrology chart. Amazing what appeared for sale in the right column of each screen. "I'm doing it without AA," she said.

There was a pause, and then Gracie said, "Besides, Bianca loves cats, and Drake's allergic." The clincher.

"It has to be a gray cat?" the young man with a long, almost-orange beard asked. The shelter was alive with murmurings and howls. Surely cats didn't howl? "How gray? I have a cat in the third row that is partly white and partly gray. A real sweetheart."

Trixie was tempted to take home "Sweetheart" but, remembering what she told her sister, conjured up another story for the shelter volunteer. She told him about Greystoke, her childhood cat, whose seven gray kittens had been—sure, why not—gathered into a basmati rice sack and drowned by her grandfather. "Ever since then . . ." She let her words trail off as if grief-stricken by this memory rather than horrified at her vilification of her beloved Grandpa.

The young man's beard quivered with sympathy. She imagined him petting it, or letting a cat nestle in its neck warmth. She followed his orange beard out past rows and rows of stacked silver cages filled with young cats with suspicious gazes and hopeful twitching noses, older cats curled in on their sad and lonely past lives.

"A docile cat," she told him, describing her three-year-old terror of a niece who liked to pull tails.

He nodded and moved ahead more slowly, reading cat descriptions. *"Likes to dine on your table." "Watches cat TV." "A good mouser, but not a ratter."* He peered into each cage for a docile cat that seemed as if it would only eat and sleep—preferably, Trixie thought, curled up and purring on Bianca's bed.

It was $100 for spaying and defleaing. A month ago she would have thought, *There go my next three bottles of gin.* But the cat was totally gray. Was she really going to call it "Granite"?

When the young man asked, "Name?" she said "Granite," then corrected herself when he said, "No, *your* name."

Cat food, a litter box, bags of litter, and a spiffy new cat carrier were nestled on the back seat, along with a gray cat that began meowing and panting the minute Trixie started the car. The panting surprised her. Huge lungfuls of air. At a red light she turned and aimed her empty flask at the cat carrier. The cat shut up. She hoped it would forget that little gesture later when she got out the catnip. She wouldn't mind a hit of something, a mind-embracing sweetheart of a line, maybe two, but she had sworn off that for sure.

The ten- or twelve-year-old Bianca was due in two weeks. Trixie was too embarrassed to ask her age.

The cat settled in. She liked the old radiator for naps, and people ambling by in the busy street below the window. Food disappeared— and reappeared, transformed into what she'd forgotten: piss and shit in the litter box. Trixie learned to sift the sand and smooth it out with fresh litter. Mornings there was a warm lump at the bottom of her bed, the first guest since a month ago, when she'd unadvisedly brought home a guy hanging onto the barstool next to her who designed tattoos. The next morning, she'd declined his offer of half a free tattoo. The other half he'd said he'd take out in trade, so to speak. She avoided that bar for weeks, grateful that she could remember which one it was. He certainly wasn't the imaginary boyfriend from work that she'd written Grace about four months earlier. *He's sweet. Has mom's sense of humor and Dad's lack of hair. He brings cookies to the office that I thought his mother must have baked, but no, he likes doing "pastries."* Oh, how could she acquire the boyfriend she'd bragged about to Grace as easily as she'd acquired a cat? Did she want a boyfriend? She'd forgotten what a real boyfriend was like. Real breakfasts. Birthday presents. Real conversation. A shared addiction to reruns of *Seinfeld*. Someone sober.

She shopped for flowered sheets and a plush rug to put by Bianca's bed in the second bedroom, where she'd been hoarding liquor bottles, pizza boxes, and dry-cleaning hangers—those black wire ones that breed in the night. On the nightstand, she placed a spiffy new red diary with a tiny gold key. She bought a gift certificate for a place that sold posters of boy bands. They looked so young and callow in their torn jeans and mussed hair; not a one wore a tie.

That week at work, Trixie answered the phone, somewhat abashed at her coworkers' compliments on her new look—blouses and sweaters instead of her usual roadie T-shirts. *Southside Johnny and the Asbury Jukes. Big Head Todd. Queen.* Trixie's job was really that of a glorified receptionist rather than the executive assistant position she'd made it out to be. The boss didn't actually know her name, and barely greeted her when he strode past her desk, but at least it was a job with a regular paycheck to supplement Grace's grudging monthly dispensation from their parents' trust fund. She remembered sitting in the lawyer's office when the will was read after their father's slow dying and their mother's quick accident. Expecting a tidy sum, she'd been horrified at hearing the conditions of their will: that her sister was to write Trixie a monthly check on condition that she get sober and hold a job. How she would be monitored was not spelled out. It reminded her of Gracie doling out carrots and cookies when they played safari or explorers as kids. Hey, answering the phone at work—"Hello, Immortal Electronics"—*was* a job, though she sure as hell wasn't going to bring Bianca to work on Bring Your Child to Work Day.

Trixie's snoopy next-door neighbor had seen her arrive home with Granite. He showed up at her door two days later. His tattooed right arm was waving—waving what? "It's a FURminator," he told her, after asking if she owned one. Her first thought was that he was coming on to her about some strange instrument of eros—had she ever used that word before?—then she remembered that he had three cats. "It is the Rolls Royce of cat combs," he told her as he captured Granite and brushed her till she was purring like a drum. Trixie squinted at him, taking in his old-fashioned mullet, his sleeveless undershirt, the cigar he'd parked on her porch railing. No, he wouldn't do.

She could make up another story. *Jackson and I broke up last month; he didn't like cats.* Or, *Fitzbag got a job offer from the dot-com crowd in San Francisco and no way was I going to be part of dismantling the entire Mission District.* No, a name like "Fitzbag" would give it away. Or, closer to the truth: *Joey's doing a bit of time in the penal system.* Nope, no need to go there. Besides, he was three men removed.

At work the next week, she found herself squinting at Nerd-boy. Once she could forget the sheer number of his ties, she actually liked his taste in patterns, fabrics, and knots. She imagined standing behind him, her arms around his waist as he tied a Windsor knot by rote, his gaze locked on hers in the mirror. She could imagine finding the small tug at the end of the exercise rather sexy, together with the downward stroke of smoothing the tie in place. Surely men must be aware of how all ties pointed south.

Two days later, when Nerd-boy came hanging around her desk again, she was ready for him. His tie was a march of spring petunias and hummingbirds. Almost a Windsor knot. Norm—his name was Norm, not Fixer, or Lefty—went into his spiel, asking her out for coffee for the millionth time—coffee!!!!—but she surprised him by suggesting that instead he should come over to her place for dinner. "Bring dessert," she told him. "One of those pastries you told me about." Little did he know that if he were going to be her boyfriend they'd have to move along fast. Grace would be leaving for Peru, her phrasebook in hand for saying "Dust every shard well" or "Nothing is too small to catalogue." Or, to Drake's doctor, "How much longer before the casts come off?"

Norm surprised her with a bouquet of forsythia, a taste for jazz, a mild allergy to alcohol, and a penchant for cats. Granite coated his pants legs with a layer of fur Norm didn't mind. Eyes narrowed, Trixie described the niece, soon to arrive for the entire fall. Turned out he had nieces of his own—"In the next town over. I take them to Red Sox games." The evening lingered along, though Trixie had imagined "limped."

A year later, after their engagement party guests left, and Bianca, who wailed when she said goodbye to Trixie and Granite, was safely on her way to her own home, they would look back at this dinner and Norman would tell her that he had known from the beginning that they were meant for each other: their cats and nieces were compatible, they both liked jazz, books, both were foodies, "and you liked my ties." She buried her face in his tie, also remembering that first dinner, when she hadn't planned a minute, never mind a life, past acquiring him for several dates so she could introduce a "boyfriend" to her niece. At that first meal, she hadn't known how to say good night. She'd been so used to falling into bed with anyone she met at a bar that she had forgotten how to act on a first date. Turns out the night of their first date was almost the same—falling into bed—though the morning after was totally different.

Off Stage

The first day of Playwriting 320, I open the door to the classroom and nod hello to fourteen students with expectant faces, weird garb, new tattoos. Earlier today, I considered asking my TA to pass out my syllabi, make introductions, assign homework. I considered not leaving my sister's hospital room where any day or week now she will surely die. But a professor herself, she insisted that everything flows from a first class. "Annie, go. You need to be there," she said. "Get the fuck out of my room and give them grief," then she coughed a laugh I couldn't echo. When the meds again pulled her under, I made sure the nurse had my cell, then I headed to campus three miles away, the mobile of glass birds for her birthday next week chirping in the back seat. I'm thinking of giving it to her later today.

We do introductions: where everyone's from, the roles they've played, and one unusual fact. Most facts are too common, except that the girl with black, black hair is a triplet. The short young man is a bungee jumper; a student with a neat blond beard says he was almost kidnapped when he was seven, and the students all murmur "Wow." I can't stop myself from thinking *My sister is being kidnapped*.

I drag myself back from that precipice.

It is time to explain the exercise I always do the first day. I tell them we're going to start a play—now. Eyes widen, eyebrows rise.

Dutifully they get out notebooks, pens. Their cell phones rest in front of them, quarantined in envelopes I provide. It takes the pressure off.

"I'm going to do some improvising." I close my eyes, tell them to close their eyes to see. "Setting: Kitchen/dining area. Table with four, no, five chairs. Maybe Ikea or used furniture from the alley. The wall clock says 8:30. You decide a.m. or p.m." I open my eyes to watch them conjure up tables and chairs and decide the virtue of night or day.

"Now we need characters. I'm going to come up with a cast for our play. You'll do your own next week. First character is—female, early thirties." I refrain from saying around my age. "The script says: 'Woman enters from stage door left. She is holding a small box. She drops the box and looks—looks horrified.'" Some students nod. I enjoy creating worlds that come alive for them. For any audience, which in my own modest career as a playwright is a new production every three or four years. Right now I'm stalled, and I know my sister blames herself.

"Let's add another character. Script says: 'A young man'—I'll make him about twenty-two—'enters from door stage right. He takes off his wet T-shirt and throws it over the back of a chair in disgust.' One more character: Script says: 'Seconds later, another young man enters from door stage left. He looks surprised.' So, we have three characters. You can open your eyes."

They hurriedly set to taking notes.

When I ask what the emotional cues are, one student with an eyebrow piercing calls out, "Well, the woman is horrified when she drops the box. So maybe 'horrified.'"

"'Disgust.' The guy throws his T-shirt down—in disgust," a student in a Cowboys T-shirt says. I remember he's the bungee jumper.

"Yeah, and the second guy is 'surprised.'" They got it. So I explain how every professional actor, first thing, crosses out the emotional cues put in the script by the playwright. "Horrified," "disgusted," and "surprised" get blacked out. Black permanent marker. Actors only go with the dialogue, which is why dialogue has to convey everything.

Here I ask, "How many of you have seen a play?" I'm pleased that most of their hands go up. Someone asks if Shakespeare in the Park counts. Absolutely. How many have acted in a play. Again, most hands go up, so I switch to high gear. I ask, "What's off stage, what's behind those doors, or curtains, or walls? The wings. What is in the wings?" There's a catch in my throat that I cough to hide. More fidgeting.

"What's in the wings?" I ask again. One student tentatively says, "Costumes," and I nod. Another says, "Props, like the box the woman is carrying. Maybe more kitchen chairs." When I tell them to keep going, a student says, "Sound equipment. A fog machine."

Another student says, "Water—hopefully beer." Everybody laughs.

When a young man in red glasses says "Lights," a girl with a star tattoo on her cheek says, "No. Lights are done above the balcony, if there is one. But somewhere across from the stage."

They wind down with "Roadies who move the furniture around."

So, I step in. "You are all wrong." I love this moment: they shrug and look at each other, then back at me.

Now I'm standing in front of them, near the door. "Here's the magic of theatre," I say, looking each student in the eye. "Every character's entrance on to the stage is really an exit from somewhere that matters to their individual story. Every entrance is an exit from somewhere else."

A student in the front row repeats "Somewhere else." And I hope their stage is expanding with the possibilities of what is happening in the wings. I move on. "Now what I want you to do is give every character their first line, and add a clue about that 'somewhere else'—begin to decide what the play is about."

"With one line?" a student says.

It's the first day, I remind myself. They need coaching and I need to hurry things along. "Okay, here's the woman's opening line. Remember, she is carrying a box. What if she comes on stage and says, 'Help. I just passed the 7-Eleven and some guy with a nylon stocking over his head ran out, handed me this box, and dashed away, calling not to worry, that he'd find me later.'" They get this story with hoots and whistles. "Give our woman some other possible lines, other scenarios," I say.

"I'll give it a try," the girl with the star tattoos says. "The woman comes in and says, 'I expected my husband's ashes to weigh more than this.'" She lifts her hands palms up as if weighing something. That quiets them down. Me, too.

Another student says, "The woman comes in and says, 'Tomorrow's our sister's birthday and I splurged and spent way too much money on her present.'"

It's a bit tame, and I can't stop my frown.

"In my fiction workshop, we learned to raise the stakes," says another student. "What about this? 'Tomorrow's our sister's birthday, and I spent way too much money on her present. We have to pretend she isn't dying.'"

The students gasp. "Shit," the cowboy says. They are alarmed and gratified by what has been set in motion—somewhere else. Do they see the hospital room I see, smell the disinfectant, stand by a sister's hospital bed?

My cell phone vibrates in my pocket. A text from the nurse to say my sister is awake. If I give her my gift early—the mobile of colorful glass songbirds to sing above her bed—she'll know why I didn't wait a week. Can we handle this? The sterile stage she'll never leave alive.

Hurriedly gathering up my papers, I tell them that's all for today. I tell them to set a stage and give me two characters for the next class. A great first line. They sit there, slightly stunned, then they, too, begin to gather up their books and backpacks, pull out phones. Next week, I'll tell them more, how when the play says "Exit" that means the character is returning to the story they came in with. How, even today, we're each in a play of our own.

I don't say I'll see them in a week because my voice fails. I wave as I take my leave. A little puzzled, to a one they wave back as if they almost understand my exit, how I am going somewhere else.

Doors

His wife had closed another door. It must have happened while he was taking his afternoon nap. All fall, as the days nipped into dusk at an earlier hour, throwing shadows deep into the long second-floor hallway, Franklin had walked past the closed doors without really thinking about them, without thinking *closed*. Until today, when he noticed that the light in the hallway had changed once again, that there was less of it. Now, of all the various bedrooms, adjacent bathrooms, and the attic, their bedroom and his wife's sewing room were the only rooms whose doors were still open.

Tonight, his wife was out, meeting with the library board to plan the town's Halloween events. "Children are so difficult to scare these days," she said as she was leaving. "They think ghosts retired with the horse and buggy." Old red draperies were folded over her arm.

"How about slipping a few sinister elements into the school's drinking water?" he'd joked, anxious for her to go so he could snoop around the house. He needed to know what she was up to here at home.

When he was sure that she wouldn't return for some forgotten item, he'd climbed the stairs to the second floor followed by a panting Zeus, their aging setter.

The doors—tall and narrow with molded panels and faceted glass doorknobs—had particularly pleased his wife when they were looking for a house thirty years ago. She had scraped and painted them with a creamy high gloss lacquer, and they had gleamed in the hallway like windows. With age, they'd acquired a dull patina, and now their glow was the quavering of candlelight.

Tentatively, he put his hand on the cool glass knob of the first door his wife had closed—their oldest daughter's room, with pink-ribboned wallpaper and a pink vanity table. Of course he was defeating his wife's purpose by opening it now, but he resented the authority of her purpose anyway.

He turned the knob. When the door didn't yield, he twisted it back and forth, then rattled it. Surely it couldn't be locked?

He gripped the doorknob harder and pushed against it with his shoulder as Zeus looked on in bored disbelief. Six months ago, when his wife had closed the first door, Zeus lay on the carpet outside, his scraggly head between his paws, eyes mournful, and whined all night. "Just let him in for a minute so he can see that Alessa isn't there," Franklin said from his side of the bed. "Oh, I don't want to do that," his wife had said. "He'll just have to learn that the room isn't there." Well, Franklin would see about that soon enough. Except clearly the door was locked. This possibility had never occurred to him. He hadn't even known the bedroom doors had locks, though of course that special sharp-waisted opening beneath the knob was a keyhole. Where was the key? He pictured it dangling from a chain attached to a belt circling his wife's ample waist. Surely not. Annoyance gnawed in his chest like a caged rodent he might have operated on at the lab—one of those hapless creatures he sometimes named, which he later regretted doing.

Ever since their youngest daughter had married, he had talked of moving to a smaller house: less yard to mow and protect from moles, closer to his work. "Leave? Leave our home?" his wife said the first time he brought it up. He had tracked her down in the kitchen, where she was drying herbs. Abruptly, she stopped stripping the thin twigs of dried sage and thyme and stared at him. "How could you even think of leaving our gardens, selling this house?"

Perhaps his response—that he could leave it quite easily, and that maybe he'd call in a real estate agent for an estimate—had been a bit hasty. She'd gone on to say that they'd reared their three children here, that four cats, three dogs, and two gerbils were buried in the field beyond the barn, and that her greenhouse was a second home, not to mention home to her extensive orchid collection and herb garden. Impatiently, he waited several months before he'd asked the realtor to stop by.

"You have a gem of a gold mine," the realtor said, his small eyes promising huge profits he would no doubt share. "Classy old farmhouses with architectural detail are hard to come by. Just enough land. Good location."

"We'll let you know," his wife said, ushering the realtor and his paperwork toward the door. When he'd gone, she turned to Franklin. "Gold mine!" The next day she closed the first door and announced at dinner: "I've closed the door to Alessa's room. Don't go in there anymore. You'll see. Pretty soon the house will seem smaller."

A month later, he brought home spec sheets for the apartments in the new block of condominiums near his lab. The next day, she closed the second door. "It won't just seem smaller," she said. "It *is* smaller."

When the realtor returned with two eager people from his office and papers awarding his firm an exclusive listing for the first two months, his wife retreated to the greenhouse till they were gone, and then she set about clearing out the attic. She hired the teenage son of the neighbor who farmed their land and together they unpacked and repacked boxes and sent it all off to the three children or Goodwill. Franklin took it as a hopeful sign that she'd come round to his point of view, but when the last box was disposed of, she didn't acknowledge his talk of summer as a good time to sell at all. She merely and firmly closed the attic door. Looking back, he suspected she'd emptied out the attic so she could close that door, too.

Now, with Zeus padding behind him, he moved to the second closed door. The room belonged to their son, who was overseeing the installation of a colossal oil rig he'd designed for Australian waters. The walls of his room were covered with posters of the world's tallest buildings, drawings of the most improbable bridges. Franklin had sometimes wondered if they'd ever been built or not.

He tried the knob. Locked, too.

He moved along the hallway, surprised to find the door to their younger daughter's bedroom was also locked, its shelves of delicate music boxes now silent and still. His wife used to go in there of an evening and set two or three music boxes going. "They miss singing," she'd say, getting into bed. And he'd turn his back to her, his head deep in a pillow, grumbling that he didn't miss their puny tinkling at all. Just as he admitted to himself that he didn't really miss the children. But actually locking their rooms was going too far. He now pictured six keys dangling and clanking on his wife's belt, above stiff black skirts and tightly laced shoes that only a nun would wear.

Once again, he gripped the glass knob of his daughter's room and tried in vain to force the lock, an old-fashioned cast-iron rectangle. "God damn it," he said, kicking the bottom panel hard. A slight tinkling came from inside the room, then silence. "Be damned." Another kick to the door sent Zeus panting to the top of the stairs, clearly hoping the fuss would not flush a rabbit he'd be obliged to track. Frustrated, Franklin nudged the dog down the stairs ahead of him and waited for his wife in his study. Damn it, this was his house.

He'd never liked closed doors anyway. He could vaguely remember, as a child of three or four, watching his parents open the front door and disappear into the dark night. "For an evening out," his mother would say, waving cheerily to Franklin and the sitter, then she'd pull shut the door. For years he'd thought that "out" meant they were just outside on the porch, on the other side of the door, standing still, breathing quietly, until a whim would bring them back long after he'd cried himself to sleep.

He must have dozed off because he woke with a start at hearing his wife's merry voice in the entryway, murmuring the praises of her prize orchids. Soon she set the teakettle on, then looked into the study where he'd been working the *Times* daily crossword. "Tea, Franklin?" she asked brightly. "The library is almost ready for Halloween. Just a bit more atmosphere—cobwebs, infrared lights in the stacks, the carrels closed off into tiny hidden rooms—the kids will love it." She bent to the fireplace and reached up to open the damper. "I think I'll build us a fire—the first of the fall." Zeus padded over and nudged her shoulder.

"Locked," Franklin croaked, his jaw so locked itself that it was all he could manage to say.

"Ah, the doors," she said, scratching Zeus behind the ears.

"Why? Why did you lock the doors?"

She looked up, surely in genuine surprise. "So you wouldn't open them."

"Why shouldn't I open them?"

"But you want a smaller house, Franklin. How can I make the house smaller if you insist on keeping it large?"

How had their children survived her logic? "There are only a few condominiums left," he said. "I'm stopping by for floor plans tomorrow. If you won't go look at them, I'll bring them home to you." The teakettle began to whistle.

"Oh, dear," she said, patting Zeus's head, then rising. "Please, Franklin. It feels like such a loss. Just give us a little more time."

"Loss," he said, throwing the uncooperative crossword into the fire. "Don't be so melodramatic. We're merely downscaling our living arrangements."

The next day, unbelievably, the door to her sewing room was closed, the place where, long ago, she'd sewn curtains for the forty-four windows he cursed each spring and fall as he prepared to put up or take down the summer screens. Wisely, he'd hired someone to do this job the last ten years. This fall, as he'd followed the hired man around from window to window, calling instructions from the bottom of the long aluminum ladder, the task oddly had seemed to take less time. But her sewing room—how could she abandon it! Now only their bedroom was left.

He felt so queasy that it took him fifteen minutes to find the right kind of chisel to open the sewing room lock. Zeus lumbered after him to the basement and then back upstairs to the sewing room, where Franklin knelt in front of the door. He imagined dust settling on the long oak table where his wife cut out patterns and on the white cloth torso of the wire mannequin she fitted and pinned the fabric to. Years ago, he'd had erotic dreams about that shapely padded torso, and now it was as if he were going to visit a woman he'd once flirted with at a party. Didn't his wife miss the whir and sputter of the sewing machine? When was the last time she had sewed something for their home?

Finally, the door swung open.

Still on his knees, he had to grip the doorframe to keep from falling into the night. Zeus whimpered at his side.

The room was gone.

There was at least a twenty-foot sheer drop to the lawn below. Franklin could smell the fertilizer from the back paddock, and the harvest moon showed golden on the horizon. A chill wind blew against his face. Breathless, he pulled closed the door and leaned against the wall. It couldn't be. When he recovered, he set the chisel against the lock on the attic door.

Absurdly, the attic, too, seemed to be gone.

Where there had once been a steep curving staircase, the door to the attic now opened onto a view of his wife's slumbering greenhouse and the gnarled orchard, which stretched as far as the eye could see. The same chill wind, this time carrying the scent of marjoram, made his chest ache. What had she done with the rooms? The furniture?

Frantically, he peered around for something, anything, to throw through the open doorway—Zeus obliged by dropping a slobbery fake bone at his feet. He held Zeus tightly by the collar and threw the bone, glistening, out into the night, where it landed with a soft plop on the wet grass. Real grass.

He hadn't the courage to open the other doors. Instead he put new batteries in the flashlight, pulled on a heavy sweater, and went outside, feeling oddly safer there. Crickets sawed in the dewy grass. A coyote howled a mating call. Slowly, Franklin prowled the perimeter of the house, squinting up at the flashlight's beam playing over the white clapboards as he located each child's bedroom, identified the corner windows of his wife's sewing room. The house's dimensions were unchanged.

"Where's your bone?" he whispered to Zeus beneath the attic window. He stood there shivering in the cool night while Zeus reluctantly zigzagged back and forth, sniffing the wet grass. "Find your bone," he called again. But Zeus returned without it, tail drooping. "What are you good for?" Franklin said, but after five minutes of pacing back and forth, he, too, failed to find the bone. A cloud passed over the moon, and Franklin gave up. He didn't know if he was more frightened or relieved.

On the way back to the house he stopped by the car for the condominium plans. He'd been patient long enough.

In wide swipes, he spread the rolled pages on the long table in his study and secured the corners with heavy books. The architectural drawings glowed eerily in the dim light of the moon. Zeus came by to rest his head on the table and slobber over them, but Franklin pushed him away. Franklin knew exactly which apartment he wanted—four rooms with a balcony for his wife's herbs and a generous storage room in the basement. Bringing the plans home for his wife's approval was only a formality. They'd move sometime after the new year. Sadly, condominium rules decreed that Zeus would not be able to make the move with them.

Franklin sat in the deep shadows of the corner near the fireplace, in his old leather chair, and waited, his eye on the door, too angry to turn on a light. About ten he heard his wife's foolish murmuring in the hall, flattering her orchids, then her solid footsteps on the kitchen tiles, where she set the teakettle to boil. Finally, she retraced her steps down the hallway and entered the study, squinting into the dim light. Zeus stood and noisily stretched; when she said his name, he ambled over to her, his tail swishing loyal and low.

Franklin smiled furtively to himself. Let her turn on the light, let her find the plans for herself.

The room remained dark. Zeus padded past Franklin's wife out into the hall and, after a moment's hesitation, she followed him. Seemingly as an afterthought, she turned and closed the door. Then she locked it.

Blood-Red Moon

Mid-afternoon heat sent Cramer outdoors for his daily walk to the bay, a shimmering silver platter a quarter mile from his summer house on the Cape. He needed a breeze to tickle his beard and dry his sweaty skin, to make him forget that he was not in love with anyone, except with Lily, his wife, who had died five years ago. Grief deepens, it doesn't fade.

He sauntered down his usual path, the long sandy lane to the main road of pressed dirt and sand, past gray-green marshes, empty now with the bay at low tide emitting its sulfurous smell. Come fall, after he'd closed up the house and returned to Boston's reassuring claustrophobia, this was a walk he would often take in his mind. With pleasure, he'd recall each step and curve of the road in photographic detail—it was a practice he'd learned from four years in the army visualizing infantry maneuvers.

Halfway to the water's edge, a silver Honda rumbled toward him, swerving to avoid the road's ruts and potholes. It was his daughter Julie's husband—his son-in-law, Dane, with four-year-old Benjy. After lunch, Julie had gone to her welding studio a hundred yards from the house, and Dane and Benjy had left on another "boys' adventure" to search for tadpoles and frogs in Duck Pond. Cramer had been invited but lamented that he had to review a friend's proxy and sent them on their way to learn the mysteries of "how tadpoles grow up."

When Dane slowed to a stop, Cramer saw that, in spite of his stern warning a year ago, Benjy was sitting on Dane's lap once again pretending to drive. What the fuck? Benjy's pudgy hands gripped the steering wheel at 4 and 8.

"Grampa, look at me." Benjy thumped the wheel, fingers splayed flat. His head with its wet curls was tucked tightly under Dane's unshaven chin. As Benjy hit the horn with his fist, Dane grinned proudly. "Isn't he something?"

Ignoring Dane, Cramer nodded at Benjy, saying, "When I get back from my walk I want to hear all about the tadpoles."

"All gone," Benjy said, his mouth folded into a frown. "Now there's only little frogs with little legs."

"Not gone," Dane corrected, in the patient teaching voice Cramer reluctantly admired. "Remember, those tadpoles we saw a few weeks ago are now little frogs."

"Let's go," Benjy said, bouncing on Dane's lap.

Cramer avoided looking Dane in the eye, though he knew his disapproval was visible. The car lurched forward. Dane probably suspected that Cramer's wave wasn't the end of it. Dane's field was finance, managing a hedge fund. Cramer had never trusted those practices, but he appreciated Dane's knowledge of the natural world, which he diligently passed along to Benjy. Benjy already knew the names of constellations, the birds that visited the front deck's feeders, and how to pitch a tent—all lessons from an engaged father, a role which had certainly been missing in Julie's life. Cramer belatedly regretted his long hours writing trusts and wills or reading military histories instead of teaching Julie how to tie flies, or play tennis, or run rapids in an almost stable raft. Ruefully, he remembered family dinners where he told how the Great Wall of China had once been an important fortification but was now a tourist site, or described the elaborate military decoys of World War II. How they had a double for General Patton, and even for his dog, Willie. "Your father is a hero," Lily would tell Julie, as a coda to these dinner ramblings. She had particularly liked the story of Patton's "Willie," which is where their golden setter, now long gone, had acquired its name. Though Cramer never described his deployment to Korea, he wondered if Julie remembered her fascination with the letters DMZ, how she loved saying it—DMZ, DMZ. Cramer hadn't been a hands-on father, and he could imagine this was something his daughter loved about Dane.

The Cape house, which he and Lily had bought twenty-six years ago, was where Lily and Julie, mother and daughter, had spent their summers. Back then, Cramer arrived every Thursday, briefcase in hand, and left on Sunday afternoon, except for his three weeks off in August. Here, Julie learned to swim, water ski, kayak, and grow weed. By the age of eighteen she had worked at every crab shack and lobster joint in town.

The spring Lily died, Cramer had been retired for three years. His grief became more pronounced when, that first summer, he moved to the Cape alone. Yes, he had a cadre of friends in town, but for the first months he actually considered selling. Then, with Julie and Dane's first long visit, he realized how much the house was enlivened by their presence. He put up gates when Benjy started to crawl, then toddle, and though they had been taken down, he would put them up again for Julie and Dane's next child, expected in September. When they were in residence, the house once again bustled with messy preparations for breakfast, lunch, and dinner. Sand everywhere. Ragged beach towels hung on the railings of all three decks. Toys squawked underfoot. They argued over legitimate two-letter words for Scrabble and the King's Knight's Gambit in chess. But now, the question Cramer had to consider was whether another confrontation with Dane might put all this in jeopardy. He no longer felt like telling Dane about the rare occurrence of tonight's blood-red moon. Seething, Cramer cut short his walk, unable to forget last summer's prickly encounter with his son-in-law.

* * *

On that humid August day a year ago, Cramer and his daughter had been outside going over plans for a new well when they heard a car roaring down the long sandy lane to the house. His baseball hat and Julie's sun hat turned in unison to watch the Honda swing round the tall stand of scrub pines and stop in the parking space of glittering, crushed oyster shells. Dane had pulled the car's nose right up to one of Julie's six-foot metal sculptures and beeped the horn. To Cramer's dismay, Benjy was seated on Dane's lap, energetically turning the wheel.

Dane dislodged Benjy's small hands and pivoted in his seat to set Benjy on the ground. Then Dane announced in his proud father's voice that soon they better lock their cars, because Benjy clearly thought he knew how to drive. Giggling, Benjy tried to climb back into the car. Julie laughed as she picked Benjy up, then carried him off to "scrounge for the dinner's lettuce."

Cramer stayed behind. He tried to keep his voice neutral as he told Dane, "Letting Benjy pretend to drive on this lane is not a good idea."

Dane cocked his head respectfully—or at least what had seemed to Cramer at the time to be respect. "No? Why?"

Cramer was grateful when Dane pushed his mirrored sunglasses up onto his shaved scalp, a military haircut that to Cramer's mind he hadn't earned.

"Because," Cramer said. In his days as a master sergeant, that would have ended their exchange. But now he felt obliged to elaborate. Pointing back to the narrow lane, he described how the blind curve at the top was a trap lying in wait for a head-on collision, that there was no way to see around the lane's curve, and how it bore ruts the depth of a clam bucket. He recalled being on the lane in broad daylight a year ago and colliding head-on with his neighbor's rusted pickup. "We were both going ten miles per hour tops, and sort of slid into each other with a thud." Dane was nodding, listening. But learning? Cramer said they got out to see what damage and there wasn't a scratch on either vehicle. "Good we were both going at a snail's pace," his neighbor said, then backed up to let Cramer pass.

"A slow-mo crash," Dane said, laughing. His glasses came down. "Damn lucky." Then he set to gathering up the fishing nets, slamming shut the trunk.

"I'm not finished," Cramer said in what Lily had called his "command voice." He knew he sounded cranky, a fusty military man-*cum*-lawyer making a point. Then he reminded himself that the previous year Benjy had come within inches of falling down the steep outdoor steps because Dane had forgotten to latch the screen door. A month later, Benjy had been rushed to the ER with a badly dislocated shoulder because, as Julie put it, "Benjy went one way and Dane went the other."

Dane stopped, clearly irritated, and leaned back against his car, cradling the small nets.

Cramer went on to say that hours later his "slow-mo crash" had made him break out in a cold sweat remembering how often he'd hurried down this lane to reach the post office or liquor store before it closed. "But you," he said to Dane, unable to alter his accusatory tone, "you must do thirty-five, forty around that curve. And if you ever had a head-on it would be more than enough to release the Honda's air bags."

"So? Air bags are good," Dane said, squinting.

"Not always," Cramer said, annoyed. This was something Dane should know. That the force of a deployed air bag was deadly for young children, that it can snap their necks, cause a fatal concussion, sever a spine. Dane's expression was noncommittal. "So, please,"

Cramer said, irritated at the need for "please," "Don't let Benjy pretend to drive. When he asks to drive, say 'no.' He'll soon forget about it." To Cramer's mind this was an order.

"Hey, Cramer, no problem." Dane nodded, then moved off to stow the nets and buckets in the workroom. "Got it," he called over his shoulder.

Later that afternoon, when Benjy was napping and Dane was sanding a kayak, Cramer left to find Julie and tell her about his talk with Dane. She was in her studio on the edge of the marsh, thirty yards from the house. Her door was latched, her welder's mask on, so Cramer gave it a mighty whack so she would hear. She turned the flame down to a glow and pulled off her mask. He knew enough not to ask what she was working on. It would eventually reveal itself, like the other pieces rusting among the pines. Quickly, he told Julie about his encounter with Dane, saying she wouldn't dream of letting Benjy near her welding studio, so why was it unreasonable to keep Benjy out of the driver's seat of a car? After listening with an inscrutable expression, she said, "Hey, Dad, haven't you noticed that Dane does what he wants?" Her hands in their hard welder's gloves rested on the pliant curve of her belly. "What he wants could kill Benjy," Cramer said. Julie sighed, then pulled her mask back on. Her voice was muffled. "Look, I'm glad you talked to him, but, well, good luck. Hope he heard you." Her response was in the careful voice of six years as Dane's wife. He supposed his daughter still loved her husband, but maybe she was relieved Dane's actions were being given more scrutiny? That was last summer.

*   *   *

Today, after his encounter with Dane and Benjy—Benjy once again seated on Dane's lap, pretending to drive—Cramer returned from his walk, troubled and pissed off. Letting the screen door bang shut, he was met by the smell of caramelized onions and roasting garlic. Al Green was playing on the Bose. Julie was unloading the dishwasher and Dane's hips were tapping against the counter, where he was chopping cilantro on a wooden board. At his side, Benjy was perched on the counter's edge, his legs dangling down, corn chips in each hand. It was another thing Cramer had warned Dane against. A fall onto the kitchen's slate floor could split open a toddler's delicate head like a melon. He mentally calculated Dane's young reflexes, including time to drop the knife in his hand.

"Want to shower before dinner, Dad?" Julia asked, her back still turned to them as she put wine glasses away. "There's time. Benjy's next."

Cramer said "Sure" just as Benjy, hearing his name, swung around, teetering, almost falling, to offer Cramer a corn chip. "Here, Grampa."

With his elbow, Dane nudged Benjy to what he must have considered a safer spot on the counter, ordering him to "Hold onto my sleeve, little man."

"Jesus, Dane," Cramer said. "He's not safe up there."

Julie immediately stopped unloading dishes and, without looking at Cramer, scooped Benjy off the counter. "Hey, Dane, Dad said he didn't want Benjy sitting on the counter," Julie said, her voice neutral.

Dane rolled his eyes as Julie plunked Benjy into Cramer's arms. He heard her tone again that saddened him. "He's all yours. Why don't you entertain him while we do dinner?" Not only that, clearly, Cramer thought, she was getting him out of the way.

Benjy smelled like sand and sweat and muddy water and Cramer held him tightly. Lord, how he adored this child. How dare that jerk put Benjy in harm's way, and with another child expected. Dane would surely be the same, or worse—distracted by the chaos of the new baby.

Benjy led Cramer to the couch, to his rubbery assortment of fish and lurid, gelatinous sea creatures from the aquarium's gift shop, where Dane took Benjy at least every other month. Methodically, Benjy introduced his menagerie. He told Cramer that the great white shark was very dangerous. "And this is Octopus. It can get long and skinny and crawl through a soup can. Here, you be the octopus."

"Hey, Benjy, let's give you a bath in your swimming pool," Cramer said, and Benjy immediately gathered up the floppy sharks, the octopus, crabs, and misshapen dolphins, and headed out through the sliding doors to the deck. A furry animal leapt from the railing onto the roof and disappeared. "Squee-erl," Benjy shouted. Cramer thought it might be a large chipmunk, but Benjy was surely right.

Julie had heard the change in Benjy's bathing plans, and soon appeared with the first of several buckets of water. "No, you sit with Benjy, Dad," she commanded when he rose to help her, eyeing her rounded stomach. Benjy lifted his arms for Cramer to pull off his T-shirt, then shrugged out of his shorts and stepped into the blue plastic pool. "Grampa, put your feet in, too," he ordered, splashing Cramer's legs. "Take off your shoes."

Cramer scooted his deck chair over to the pool and slipped off his sneakers. As always, Benjy was only squeamish for a second as he bent over to stare at Cramer's right foot, the shiny scar tissue of its missing big toe. Then he swam a shark over to the empty space, demanding the story Cramer called "The Tiny Land Mine." Belatedly, Cramer had realized he should have come up with a rusty rake, a slammed door, or a runaway wheelbarrow. But dutifully, Cramer described the below-zero temperatures, his men by his side, the incoming mortar, and the boom.

"Uh, Dad. Let's cut that story short," Julie said, dumping in the third bucket of water, saving the last drops for Benjy's curly hair. She was good at giving Cramer orders, pushing him around with her mother's voice. Why not send a few orders Dane's way?

"I know, I know," Cramer said. For the next few minutes, he guided the octopus around various reefs Benjy had created from stones and slithered away from Benjy's shark, keeping the octopus safe.

"I don't remember ever seeing your missing toe when Jason and I were little," Julie said, sinking into a chair, her eyes closed. Grinning to herself. "We missed that particular bedtime story."

Is that what it was? When the kids were little, he'd mostly gotten home after their baths and bedtime rituals. Often they were asleep with their favorite stuffed animals whose names he could never remember. And maybe he'd wanted to protect himself from the memory of his radio operator being blown to pieces by that same mortar. The sudden bloody deaths of war, as vivid still as Lily's slow decline. His new war with Dane now offered up different scenarios: Dane, alone, on the way to work some morning and disappearing in a blaze of upholstery, metal, and glass. But what if, on a boys' Saturday adventure, he wasn't alone? Cramer abruptly bent to scoop water onto his face, as if to quench a fire. Then, dripping, he rose from his chair and perched the octopus on Julie's knee. "Watch out for Benjy the shark," he said. "I'm going to talk with Dane."

Julie looked quizzically at Cramer but shrugged off her sandals and settled her feet in Benjy's pool, moving the rubber octopus to the round mountain of her stomach. Cramer stopped in the living room to put on his sandals. Just as he wouldn't ever go into a courtroom in sandals, he could not confront Dane in bare feet.

Dane was mixing up a rub for the swordfish when Cramer placed both hands flat on the countertop, elbows at hard right angles. He said, "Hey, Dane."

Dane looked up, wary, as if he knew what Cramer was going to say. "Yeah?"

When Cramer didn't speak right away, Dane stopped chopping garlic and said, "Okay. Out with it. About Benjy driving."

His "out with it" was something Cramer would not tolerate.

"You're pretty damn sure of yourself," Cramer said.

Dane's eyebrows rose. He probably thought he knew his father-in-law. And maybe he did, Cramer thought, but what Cramer said next shocked them both. He looked Dane in the eye. He said, "If anything—anything—ever happens to Benjy, I'll expect you to kill yourself."

Dane's laughter was an eruption, a roar of disbelief. "Whoa," he finally said, putting down his knife.

"Don't you fucking laugh at me," Cramer said.

They both heard the screen door to the deck slide open. "What are you two up to?" Julie called. Her arms were full of a wet naked Benjy, wriggling to be let down. When his feet hit the floor, he started pulling on Cramer's shorts, insisting they return to the pool. His tearful pleas filled the silence that Julie's raised eyebrows clearly did not trust as she looked first at Cramer, then at Dane.

Dane went back to chopping.

"Well," Julie said, waiting. Then, to Cramer, "Dad, I told Benjy he could have another ten minutes in the pool." Gleefully, Benjy led the way, his tousled hair and freckled back and butt in charge. When Cramer took off his shoes for a second time, Benjy kicked them to the other side of the deck, then handed Cramer the octopus. "There," he said. "There."

*   *   *

The next morning, by breakfast time, Cramer surmised that Dane had not told Julie what Cramer said. He didn't know what to make of this, if he was annoyed or relieved, though somewhere in the early dawn of a bad dream about a hurricane whisking away Julie's studio, he wondered if he'd gone too far. What if Dane insisted they leave today? Would Julie leave, too? Cramer's retreat to the deck to play with Benjy before dinner had been that—a retreat. Eventually, last night's dinner had been a desultory affair. Plans were made for later: put Benjy to bed, then Julie and Dane would drive to the beach to see what Cramer told them was predicted to be a rare, blood-red moon. Over the years, Cramer and Lily had seen several flaming discs rise from the ocean. "The otherworldly part of this amazing world," Lily had said. Cramer was reading in bed when they returned. He listened to their murmurings, checking on Benjy, their quiet retreat to the deck to finish the dinner's second bottle of wine.

The memory of his afternoon encounter with Dane, in hindsight, made Cramer break into a cold sweat over morning coffee as Julie described the exact color of the moon, "from blood-red to orange-red, finally fading to a deep ivory." Only her second sighting. Benjy quoting from *Goodnight Moon* and Dane nodding absently as he peered into the fridge to compile the grocery list. If it was a truce, was it meant to hold?

After breakfast, Julie went off to the farmer's market with Benjy, who was already planning a shark assault at the adjacent playground. Cramer waved them off, cleared away the dishes, then carried his latest history tome out to the deck, where Benjy's plastic pool was already breeding mosquitos. Stooping over, Cramer tried to lift one side to empty it, but it was way too heavy and noisily slapped back flat.

"Let me help," Dane called from the living room. Pulling on his sunglasses, he joined Cramer on the deck. Effortlessly, he lifted one side of the pool, and they both listened to the cascade of warm water land on the kayaks below. When the pool was upside down, Dane scooped up the sharks, crabs, and octopus and beached them on the railing to dry. He was helpful like that—had cleaned Cramer's gutters at the beginning of the summer and stacked a half cord of wood. Julie would say, "Let Dane do that." And Dane did it. No eye-rolling or rain checks. "Thanks," Cramer said.

Abruptly, with purpose, Dane dropped into a deck chair across from Cramer, who hadn't started reading his open book, but wished he had.

Dane's fingers tapped his chair's arm. "Look, Cramer. About what you said yesterday. You were way out of line."

This portrayal of what he'd said caught Cramer off guard.

Dane's sunglasses continued to point in Cramer's direction. "I mean I can't let what you said just go by."

Cramer found his usual voice. "I should hope not."

"You should hope not?" Dane repeated, and rose up, overturning his chair. He yanked off his sunglasses. The skin around his eyes was white and emphasized their angry glare. "You hope not? What the fuck does that mean?"

Cramer slowly closed his book. "It means you take too many chances with Benjy's life. You put him in harm's way—pretending to drive. You could kill him."

"Look," Dane said, "we can pack up our shit and leave this afternoon." He kicked at the fallen chair but didn't set it to rights.

What the hell. This dumb-ass son-in-law would drag Julie away from her studio. He'd take Benjy away from his tadpoles and turtles, his pond and marsh? A rage returned that Cramer hadn't felt since the war. Then just as suddenly, what he'd said to Dane the day before came back to him in all its obscene aggression.

"We can drive right back up your dangerous crappy lane," Dane said. "We can be gone today. Out of here."

"My dangerous crappy lane is also your dangerous crappy lane," Cramer said. A car door slammed. In minutes, the screen door to the deck slid open.

"Cool it. No one's going anywhere," Julie said, her eyes hidden by her hat until she took it off and threw it onto the table.

Dane stooped to right the fallen chair, banging it into place.

"No more orders. No more bullshit," Julie said, looking first Dane then Cramer in the eye. Then holding Cramer's gaze. "None." Cramer's lungs deflated; his breath allowed him no words. So Julie knew what Cramer had said to Dane. She needed nothing from either of them except a harshly bargained peace.

"Good. You emptied Benjy's pool," Julie said, turning the blue plastic pool over and pulling the aquarium's marooned inhabitants off the railing. "It needs fresh water, Dane. Too much traffic for the ponds today."

Just then Benjy ran through the doorway and flung himself into Cramer's lap, a prickly artichoke in his hand. "You're going to eat this," he said. "Not me."

"We all are," Julie said.

Some bird with a red ruff swooped low over the deck, then cantilevered off into the pines. Cramer watched Dane and Benjy and Julie track its flight. He felt stupid thinking "some bird."

"Scarlet Tanager," Dane said.

"Odd for this time of year," Julie said.

Dane turned to Cramer. "You and Julie were right. Last night's moon was otherworldly."

It was Lily who had said that; Cramer let it go. How far? Would he always be on lookout for what might happen next, a silent vigilance his burden? Maybe a burden to others, too.

"Blood-red moons are rare, but there will be more," Cramer said, his chin resting on Benjy's head, while Dane filled the pool right up to the brim.

In the coming years, Dane will stay on the lookout for the next blood-red moon, and for sure he will take Benjy to see it—and no doubt Julie and Cramer, too. Dane will drive too fast up the sandy lane, Benjy's car seat left behind in their other car. Ignoring signs posted at McGuire's landing, Dane will park in a restricted parking spot meant for wheelchairs. In the lead, he will bypass the marked paths and they will all slip and stumble down the steep, unstable dunes. At the bottom, Dane will reach for Benjy's hand as they plow through sand, too close to the ocean's crashing waves and dangerous riptides. Julie will turn to check on Cramer's progress, reassured by his brusque wave back. Finally, Dane will choose the spot where they will all stop. Out of breath, Cramer will catch up with what is beautiful but also dangerous. Transcendent. And together they will marvel at this blood-red moon.

Hitchhikers

Here's How It Went

Paige was on her bare knees, her hands planted in the scrabble of small rocks, peering down into the abyss of the Grand Canyon's south face. The striated walls of bronze and purple and gold shimmered in the afternoon light. If David were alive he'd be right beside Paige, a few inches closer to the edge. Where was Marcy? She was missing the show.

She heard footsteps approaching and called out, "Enough with the willies, Marcy, come look." When Marcy didn't answer Paige glanced over her shoulder and instead saw an older woman she didn't know a few feet away. The woman was holding out Paige's camera and trekking hat, which she'd foolishly left on a rock. Still on her hands and knees, Paige backed up, then lurched to her feet, her right knee giving her trouble.

She thanked the woman for looking after her stuff as she draped the camera back around her neck and planted her hat on her head. Then she yelled again, "Marcy, I'm over here." Hitching on the daypack she'd left a few feet away, Paige told the woman, whose splotched, tan skin made it look like she'd spent her life in the sun, "You should see that view." Paige was pleased to share it with someone, given that timorous Marcy hung back at every cliff, parapet, balcony, and beach. They were old college roommates, had been couple friends back in San Francisco, and were supportive of each other after their husbands' deaths—David's the most recent. Paige and Marcy had talked of buying a home together, if Paige could learn to tolerate Marcy's bossiness, her belief that she had a finger on the pulse of any world, made manifest in her ghostwritten books and predictions that needed no tarot deck.

Instead of Marcy, another stranger in a green vest sprouting a hundred busy pockets suddenly appeared on the path. David had owned a vest just like it, a pocket for everything, zippers here and there. Paige hadn't been able to give it away. The tanned woman pointed to Paige and said to the vest, "She's been telling me about the view," then to Paige, "This here's my daughter."

The daughter stopped short and snorted, saying, "Yeah, mom is always telling me what to look at."

Paige told them not to miss this view, and suggested they might want to do what she did—get down on their knees and creep forward since there were no viewing decks or guardrails so far off the designated paths.

The daughter snorted again—she had a narrow, long nose—but did as Paige suggested. The older woman followed, dropping her army backpack and crawling closer to the canyon's edge. Paige noted that their cowboy boots had ragged holes in their soles, bitten-down heels. Unaccountably, she imagined her foot on one of their backsides. How easy it would be to send someone right over the edge to the canyon's floor! Now where on earth did she get such thoughts? Must be from Marcy, whose vivid imagination made bestsellers of her ghostwritten books. Paige recalled the first time Marcy had delivered one of her stories. They all began *"Here's how it went."* Paige always heard these words in italics. In their senior year, Marcy had been to see their college dean, who noted her absence from two finals and a missing final paper. Marcy told him she was dropping out, but that it had been worth it: at least she'd made a best friend in Paige. *"Here's how it went:*

The dean says to me, 'You don't go to college for friends.'
I say, 'That's precisely what I got out of college.'"

Remembering this scenario always made Paige smile, though there were other Marcy-imagined scenarios about Paige's life that she did not want to remember just now.

When the women had backed up and were standing, Paige described the absent Marcy's short, curly red hair and freckles. "A largish woman," she said, thinking, *Understatement.* No, they hadn't seen her, though both women seemed alarmed as they looked around for her.

Minutes later, they watched Marcy huff up the last rise of the low-grade hill, clearly the lost friend. Per usual, she had no wish to see the precarious view from the cliff, though they all assured her it was safe on hands and knees. "Worth the detour," Paige said, quoting the slim green Michelin Guides that she and David had consulted on every trip. The tanned woman obligingly took a photo of Marcy and Paige, arm in arm, a safe distance from the cliff, then waved away Paige's offer to take their picture, saying both she and her daughter were camera shy.

Together, they trekked back to the park's designated path. There, they were led toward a rough-hewn concession stand by Marcy, who announced she was tired and suggested that surely it was time to stop for a bite and a cold drink. The mother heartily agreed, and she and Marcy hurried ahead to plunk themselves down at a wooden picnic table. Paige and the daughter followed. *Lordy,* Paige thought, glancing from mother to daughter. This mother must have been ten when her daughter with the bulging pockets was born. Paige had been thirty when she'd had Sean, and then they'd lost him. And now David was gone. Her spirits hit bottom at least twice a day and they were close to bottom now. If she hadn't been outnumbered she would have been able to talk Marcy into waiting for a real restaurant experience with cloth napkins and the right glass for a martini. The mother hesitated before ordering two Cokes—but changed her mind when Paige asked for two Coronas. Marcy treated them all from the tiny red purse that she and Paige took turns carrying. At the start of their trip they both put one hundred dollars into the purse and paid for incidentals from that fund. When it ran out, they added more. They had started this practice in college and it still served them well.

Eventually the four of them exchanged names—the mother was Vonnie and the daughter Dawn. Paige volunteered that she and Marcy lived in San Francisco and were headed to the international ceramics festival in New Orleans. The trunk of their car was partially filled with Paige's mugs and bowls and platters.

When the drinks appeared, Marcy said, "To happy travels," then bemoaned the fact that plastic does not clink. Dawn snorted and Vonnie grimaced.

"And you," Marcy asked Vonnie, "Where are you headed?"

Vonnie said they were on their way to Louisiana, which is when Paige and Marcy heard the sad story of their broken-down car.

"We left it at Ernie's Lube and Lift a while back. He was asking a god-awful price to fix it. He said we'd have to wait a week, maybe two, for a rebuilt part from Canada."

"It was pure junk," Dawn said, squinting through the Corona at her mother.

"So we decided to abandon it—Ernie got himself a parts car. And now we're sort of hitchhiking. Got one ride behind us already. A guy delivering supplies to these concession stands." Vonnie gave the stuffed backpack at her feet a kick. "We sent our suitcases and crap along to my brother by US Mail."

So they were all headed in the same direction, though once this became clear an awkward silence settled over them like the gray anvil of fog that often hung over San Francisco. Dawn's chair scraped back, and she patted at least three pockets—comb, lipstick, Tampax, what? maybe it was a tic—before she ambled off to use the ladies'. She had the fluid gait of a horsewoman to go with her worn boots.

As if exhausted by their tale of woe, Vonnie dropped her head down to rest on her skinny arms, the Corona still in one hand. The gray-white part in her dark hair looked skunk-like—Paige had always liked a faint whiff of skunk. She hoped Vonnie wasn't crying. She and David had sometimes given hitchhikers a ride, usually teenagers with backpacks, shaggy hair, and a witty cardboard sign. Any instrument—guitar, mandolin, banjo—was a sure ticket. Maybe they should offer these women a ride. Marcy wouldn't just wave goodbye and walk away, would she?

Just then Paige's eye was caught by Marcy slowly shaking her head, her red curls swaying, as if she knew what Paige was thinking. "No," Marcy silently mouthed, three mouth-puckering "No"s.

Catching on—but dismayed by Marcy's lack of generosity and moved by Vonnie's skinny, freckled arms, her willingness to crawl to see the view, a certain resourcefulness in her story—Paige nodded a definitive "Yes."

Dawn was on her way back. Their sign language stopped abruptly, except for Marcy's ample shrug. Later that evening, in their dingy motel room, Paige would admit that David had told her never to pick up hitchhikers unless he was in the car. Later still, Marcy would say, without at all knowing the future, "I guess we had to accept our fate."

Paige wasn't fond of fate. David had died a year ago and she sorely missed his meticulous travel arrangements and choice of luxury hotels, his cold feet in bed, the warmth of the rest of him a welcome haven, even his pissiness at her acquisition of their trips' art objects, ceramic bowls with unusual glazes, the statue of the Black Madonna from Rocamadour that he referred to as "cement." Two months ago, she'd gone on a group tour to study with a Chinese ceramicist famous for his glazes, but the people she'd been forced to travel with were too fussy about their pillows, or cheap about their wine, or talkative, or just plain dull as unbuttered toast. She needed to revive her friendship with Marcy, who admired Paige's ceramics in the same way Paige enjoyed Marcy's entertaining stories about her life as a ghostwriter of celebrity bios. Marcy's calls often started with: "Lord save me from aging celebrities who only want to talk about their house pets or the stars they've slept with. I have to trick them into fact-checking their own lives." Now, forty-five years after they first lived together as college roommates, Marcy and Paige were back to sharing a room, dividing up drawers, taking turns choosing a restaurant, and appreciating a bottle of good wine. And considering buying a house together, merging their cats. They couldn't share clothes because Paige was a skinny size 8 and Marcy was into the Xs— 1X, 2X. It was just as well because Paige disliked the colors that Marcy wore—purples, muddy mustard yellows, cerulean blues.

When Vonnie finally raised her head from the picnic table— expectantly, Marcy would say later—Paige generously offered her and Dawn a ride, "since we're going in the same direction."

Vonnie said, "You sure it wouldn't be putting you out?" Though it wasn't a question for even a nanosecond, but rather a statement she rolled right over into accepting their hospitality. She announced this turn of events to her daughter as soon as Dawn sat down, her pockets settling around her like small pets. On cue, Dawn snorted out her thanks. Paige wondered if she dared suggest snorting was a habit Dawn should consider breaking. Surely her mother was tired of it. Once, Paige had advised David that he should consider not grimacing when a dinner guest bored him through one too many courses. He'd been cranky for days. Hurt, she later heard from him.

Twenty minutes later, Paige pointed out the silver Honda in Lot G, Park 6. At this time of year there were very few cars in the lot, but Marcy had parked off a ways, beneath a tall tree for shade, though she really wasn't good at using the remote key chip.

"Ah, that *is* your car," Vonnie said, an odd inflection on the "is" which Paige didn't register till later. "Well, yes. It is," Paige replied in the moment.

"Bet you would have guessed it, right?" Marcy said. It wasn't a question.

They hoisted their backpacks and gear into the Honda's trunk, rearranging Paige's carefully wrapped ceramics. Then Vonnie and Dawn settled into the back seat with great sighs of relief and many thank-yous. It was still Marcy's turn to drive, so Paige studied the unfolded map—neither of them liked Siri or Waze or the map apps. How many miles, she wondered, would they be a foursome? She'd leave that calculation to Marcy. But would their hitchhikers appreciate any of their audiotapes? Munro. Saunders. Cheever. Joyce. Had they even heard of them?

As they drove away from the parking lot, Vonnie leaned forward behind Paige's seat and volunteered that they would both be looking for jobs once they reached home. They'd been away a long time, and neither of their employers had promised to hold any openings. "Dawn is a wizard with drinks. Give her a well-stocked bar and she can knock your socks off."

"Oh, Vonnie, leave it," Dawn said.

"It's true," Vonnie said. "A customer could name any candy, and Dawn can make a drink that tastes just like it—licorice, for example." Marcy, a purist about her dry martinis, was able to successfully cover her gag reflex with a sharp cough.

"Do you mind if we finish the Cheever story we were listening to?" Paige asked the hitchhikers. Soon they were all listening to Cheever's tale of cocktail party guests strolling manicured green lawns, men in white pants, ladies in light dresses with straps slipping off their shoulders. Betrayal lurking in empty glasses. When the story came to an end, Vonnie offered from the back seat, "Money can't buy everything." Feeling generous, Paige passed back the audio CDs for Vonnie to choose the next one. Paige could hear the shuffle as Vonnie flipped through them twice, then finally said she was feeling snoozy and would probably take a nap.

*   *   *

Paige must have fallen asleep. When she woke, her neck tingled. Her throat felt sanded. It was late afternoon, and it became apparent that they should stop somewhere for something to eat, and also eventually for the night. She imagined Marcy wondering if Paige had thought of that.

Marcy's hands on the wheel were 6 and 4, so she must be tired of driving. The back seat exuded a silence Paige didn't care to break. At the next rest stop, Marcy suggested they get sandwiches to go, and handed the red change purse to Paige. They took turns using the ladies', and Paige bought sandwiches and chips. While they ate at a nearby picnic table, Vonnie talked about their relatives. Uncle Shawn's cigar shop and his fancy clients with Ferraris and Benzes. Cousin Midge's hair salon, where the sheriff's wife gets her hair done; their forty-year-old cousin who was interviewed for *Sightings* after his experience with a UFO. She clearly hoped to appear respectable, trustworthy. But Marcy's narrowed eyes meant that, in her opinion, Vonnie lacked the ability to tell a story. And clearly Marcy didn't believe a word she said.

"Let's get back on the road," Marcy ordered. It was Paige's turn to drive. Hours later she pointed to a sign that read "Next Exit: $50 Rooms All Night." The mother-daughter pair had again dozed off in the back seat, Dawn's snorting had turned into a snuffle.

Paige parked near the "VAC NCY" sign, and Marcy heaved herself out of the car to check in. Dark clouds hung in the sky like giant gray rocks, solid looking and immoveable. The asphalt parking lot was empty except for three long-haul trucks, so surely, Paige thought, the motel had enough rooms for them. The "them" surprised her. Abruptly, she realized that she couldn't imagine abandoning their mother-daughter team to sleep in Paige's cramped car, filling it with unpleasant night smells. And what would happen when they took those boots off? And what about her ceramics?

When Marcy banged out of the office door, Vonnie and Dawn were awake and Vonnie was assuring Paige that sleeping in the car was no hardship for them, that the front seats probably tilted back. She began fussing with the lever on the side of Marcy's seat. Dawn was already balling up a gray sweatshirt around her backpack as a pillow.

"Maybe just a quick use of your facilities," Vonnie said, waving a toothbrush with curly brown bristles at Paige. "And borrow a bit of toothpaste."

"No need," Marcy said, leaning in the passenger door. She tossed Vonnie a key attached to a wooden Kokopelli. "We can spring for fifty bucks," she said. "They gave me a break on account of it being two rooms. You get the double; we get the twins."

Dawn giggled and her mother gave her a poke in the pockets.

* * *

Once in room 4, Paige said she was glad Marcy had gotten the hitch-hikers a room, too. "It was the friendly thing to do."

"You're joking," Marcy said, groaning as she tugged off her purple walking shoes. She looked up at Paige. "You *are* joking, right?"

"No." Paige didn't think so.

"Hell, I just didn't want our hitchhikers stealing the car for a measly fifty dollars," Marcy said. Her socks were next; then she aired out her toes.

Paige said that thought hadn't occurred to her. She was only thinking of their—their what? Comfort? She looked around. The room was a dead square with liver-colored ivy wallpaper and unlikely matching linoleum. The curtains looked like a cat had been held captive and wanted out.

"Paige, Paige. Wait. You do have the car keys, don't you?" Having been reassured, Marcy scrabbled around in her suitcase for the bottle of Knob Creek whose inch-a-night helped them sleep. "Because if they come around saying they need something from the car, we need to go get it for them." Soon she was pulling a sleep shirt festooned with purple hyacinths over her head. Her loose, heavy breasts rested on an ample stomach. Paige admired her unselfconscious attitude. Marcy had reported that once, when buying bras in a fancy lingerie department, the snooty saleswoman had exclaimed, "Is *that* where you wear them?!"

"You mean if they want something I need to go get it," Paige said, annoyed that she needed to stay in her walking shorts a bit longer. She looked suspiciously at the door, which Marcy had locked with the chain lock.

The bathroom had a cracked sink, no amenities, and only two musty bath towels. Paige washed her face with a towel end textured like a Brillo pad and then dug around in her make-up bag for an extra toothpaste. Waving it at Marcy, who was tucked into bed and sipping from a plastic glass, Paige said she was going to make a quick delivery.

When she knocked on the peeling door of room 9, she was surprised when a voice called, "Come in." The door was unlocked. It felt spooky to turn the knob. "It's me, Paige," she said.

Both women, mother and daughter, were sitting on the double bed, facing the glowing TV's garish weather report, sweatshirt and vest still on, backpacks at their feet. They looked ready to leave. Reluctantly, their heads swiveled toward her.

"Oh, thanks," Dawn said. "I was going to have to hunt through our stuff in the car." She held out her hand for the toothpaste, and tucked it into a vest pocket.

Paige was glad she'd made the delivery without car keys, though she wouldn't admit this to Marcy. Their room had the same wallpaper, the same cracked linoleum, the same TV. As she backed out of the door, Vonnie called out, "Hey, what's our departure time?"

"7:00 a.m.," Paige answered, making it up on the spot.

Back in room 4, Paige described the scene for Marcy: two women slumped on the double bed, still in hiking gear, transfixed by the TV. "They looked like they were in a movie theatre—or a police lineup," she said.

"Tomorrow, early, let's take off without them," Marcy said. She assured Paige there was no way the hitchhikers would be ready to leave that early. And she didn't want to hear more stories of their sad and sorry lives. Anyway, they had to be making the stories up. Cigar shop and hair salon. Ha.

"Why would they make up stories?" Paige asked.

Marcy rolled her eyes. "Besides, next time, closer to civilization, the motel would probably cost one hundred dollars or more."

"But how awful to be looking for a job in your sixtieth decade. Homeless," Paige said, changing into a T-shirt. Her twin bed felt more like a camp cot. She hadn't thought about camp in years. Bugs and burnt marshmallows and ghost stories that made her shiver.

As if reading her mind, Marcy began to concoct another story. "This very minute, they're probably plotting how to steal our car. I just hope they don't have any skill with starters."

"And do what with us?" Paige bunched up her pillow and reached for her inch of bourbon.

"Know what I think?" Marcy said, leaning forward over her flowers, pointing her glass at Paige. "Back at the canyon, when we got separated, I think Vonnie and Dawn followed you. They assumed the only car in the lot was yours. It sounded to me like they crept up on you. Maybe Vonnie was going to push you over the edge."

Paige sputtered out a laugh. "'Crept.' 'Crept.' Don't be silly." Though she was embarrassed that she'd had a similar thought of her own. "She had my backpack."

"Then maybe they wouldn't have had to kill you. Just take off with the car." Marcy was giggling, too, her stomach's hyacinths blooming with each breath.

"Wait, first they would have had to do something with you," Paige said.

Marcy thought a minute. "Over the edge, too," she said. "I mean, after a scuffle." She pumped her flabby arm.

"You make it sound easy. Or likely," Paige said, turning out the 60-watt bedside light. "Go to sleep. You're first to drive tomorrow." A good thing, because it took her an hour to finally drift into a dream about her and Marcy moving into a dilapidated house where Marcy discovered a secret room and began to make up one alarming story after another about what dire scenarios it had been used for. When Paige woke from this nightmare at 2:00 a.m., she recalled another of Marcy's stories. One about Paige's son, who had overdosed on some unnamed drug twenty years ago. She and David had known he was in trouble, and David had insisted on going to Vancouver alone to try and talk him into rehab. Paige would never forgive him for going alone. But Marcy told Paige she understood, that here's probably *what went on.*

"David doesn't want Paige to see how far Sean has fallen, how his rented room smells of vomit and piss. David offers to pay for rehab and reminds Sean of his success in the world of animation. But Sean is a lost and doomed soul. He refuses any help. David returns home, regretting that he insisted that he go alone." Marcy finishes by saying, *"But he is glad you didn't see the broken Sean. That's what went on."*

A month later, they received a call from the Vancouver sheriff about Sean's OD. David's sense of failure never abated. Paige was helpless with sorrow, and her forgiveness was weak. Now, after a fatal heart attack, David was gone, too. Paige is left with Marcy, her improbable stories, and two hitchhikers. "Improbable" because "probable" is too painful. Though history has proved them true.

At six thirty, Paige and Marcy crept from their motel room, and there they were—Vonnie and Dawn. Dawn waving the tiny tube of toothpaste as if to prove they'd brushed their teeth. Once they were settled in and on the road, Vonnie suggested they play the license plate game. Regretting the mean-spirited talk with Marcy the night before, Paige agreed. "So, you see who can spell a word that uses the first and last letter on the plate going by," Vonnie said. License M56G67 from Nevada flashed into the distance. "M and G—Mug."

Paige hated car games. Sean had been able to read while travelling, and David had preferred conversation or listening to audio books—the last was Ian McEwan's sinister novel set in a Venetian palazzo. And Marcy could always keep Paige entertained by tales of her most recent ghostwritten saga. "I call it 'filling in the blanks.' One star always played the ingénue's role, till suddenly her agent stopped calling. She didn't want that fact included in the book so I made up some wild roles she played as a villain and a witch, and she had a fit. Finally, she owned up to the mother-in-law roles." Then there was the famous director who went to Iceland and couldn't remember a thing, couldn't tell ice from cocaine. In that case, Marcy also had to fill in most of the blanks herself. Paige admired how Marcy could imagine anything. Though Marcy's suspicions were starting to make her fearful. Of their hitchhikers? Their two western gals?

Along about noon, Vonnie, calling the game quits, offered to drive. "To earn our keep," she said. Paige, knowing that Marcy would never allow it, was at a loss for words. Not Marcy. She said she loved to drive, loved feeling her hands on the wheel at 4 and 8—and Paige loved driving too. "We often toss a coin to see who gets the wheel first." Paige, who hated driving, felt her neck prickle with heat and hoped it wasn't a giveaway red. She patted the wheel in a friendly gesture. Vonnie settled back, nodding.

Out of nowhere, Marcy heaved herself sideways in the passenger seat to ask Vonnie and Dawn, "How did you two meet?"

"Meet?" Vonnie said. "What do you mean?"

Dawn nudged Vonnie and said, "You're on."

So, reluctantly, Paige could tell, Vonnie leaned forward to deliver her delivery room story complete with a sympathetic nurse who taught her how to push while doctors were preparing for a C-section. "I was young," she said. When Marcy rudely pressed, "How young?" Vonnie said sadly, "Thirteen. It was a neighbor boy who got me pregnant. Our babysitter. Hide-and-seek. Ha."

Paige could see in the rearview mirror that Dawn never once opened her eyes during her "mother's" account of how she entered the world. When Vonnie asked about Paige and Marcy's lives, Marcy offered up some cheerful fake facts. She said she wrote catalogue copy and designed brochures for an IT company. Paige followed her lead, saying she worked in an art supplies store. "Our husbands are off on a fishing trip together," Marcy said. "They can talk fishing for hours and are both expert fly tyers." It took Paige a moment to realize that Marcy had conjured up "husbands" to make her and Marcy seem less vulnerable. David had never fished in his life.

More sandwiches. Another game of license plate. Paige felt like playing "What's in that vest pocket?" They listened to a Cheever story. "So people really live like that?" Vonnie asked. "I'll bet Marcy does," Dawn said, surprising them all. "Paige, too."

*   *   *

The next evening, in their $100-a-night motel, Marcy returned from locking up the car as Paige was snapping on all the lights. Marcy poured their inch of bourbon, maybe a little more, and handed Paige a glass. Hands on her wide hips, she said ominously, "One of your bowls was broken. It was rattling around. But never mind. We need to talk."

It actually brought back their college days, when, hands on her hips even then, Marcy would announce enough of studying, they needed to find a party, and describe the fun and libations they were probably missing.

Paige suspected she knew the reason for a "talk." Sure enough, Marcy said, "I said this before: there's something wrong with their mother-daughter abandoned car/hitchhiking story. I can fill in some nasty blanks, I think. Like *what went on*."

"Please, please don't," Paige said, rubbing the back of her neck, growing tense with worry. Completely on her own, she'd imagined a scarf being flung around her neck from the back seat, a scarf pulled tight, tighter. Maybe at a rest stop, having sandwiches and sodas, Vonnie would do Marcy, and Dawn would do her. Those poor women?

"No way are they mother and daughter," Marcy said, pouring them a second tumbler of bourbon. "They don't look alike at all. Their noses—Vonnie's is wide, pug, and Dawn's is sharp like a bird. Their eyes, hairlines, body shape, necks, everything is different."

"Necks," Paige said, startled. "Who looks at necks except your aging stars?"

Marcy was back in her hyacinth nightgown. "Clearly, they are almost the same age—middle to late fifties."

"But why would they lie?" Paige was grateful that this motel's bathroom vanity sprouted shampoo and toothpaste. "They could have said they were friends. What's the matter with being friends?"

"Maybe they thought it made for a sweeter story—a mother and daughter travelling together. We'd feel sorry for them—sorrier. I bet they waited tables in the same sleazy bar and were fired for playing loose with the cash register. Or worked as dispatchers at some plant and were caught selling stuff that fell off the trucks. I wonder if they ever had a car."

"Now you're making me feel sorry for them."

"Hah. I noticed you only let Vonnie win the license plate game once."

Belatedly, Paige regretted all the unusual words she'd pulled out of the air: jute, plinth, berm. At least it had shut the game down.

"And I like how you said you wrote IT brochures for a living," Paige said. "Guess you didn't want to answer a million snoopy questions about your aging C-list stars." Her eyes filled with tears. What was happening? What were they holding off? Things were getting too testy between them. How could they ever live in the same house? She longed to feel a pliant, wet clay under her hands as she kicked her antiquated pottery wheel. *David, how dare you leave me behind when you went to visit Sean? How dare you die? Does anything good come of anger mixed with grief?*

"Could we just get past the hitchhikers, stop searching for their motives, stop assigning them criminal lives?" Paige said. "Could we just listen to a Handel symphony? Or the Mozart quartets?" Besides, she thought, if they aren't mother and daughter they must be friends. Friends matter. Especially when one doesn't have children—another thing that Paige and Marcy had in common. And isn't friendship ultimately what makes a good marriage—when husbands and wives are friends, as opposed to someone whose mind and tastes go sideways from yours? It always seemed to Paige that infidelity in couples she knew was a result of such distance rather than the other way round. Paige's cell phone ran out of charge for Mozart at 3:00 a.m.

*   *   *

Their $100-a-night motel served breakfast in the cherry-wallpapered dining room, where the four met with their bags and gear. Greetings were strained. Damp from showers, Paige and Marcy were barely talking. Vonnie's dark eyes rode identical smudged hammocks and Dawn's vest was shedding some sort of feather lining. Marcy rolled her eyes when the waitress called them all honey, acknowledging no distinctions. Fat. Thin. Clothes. Class.

Marcy said she wasn't hungry, and was going to see to the car. She held out her hand for Vonnie and Dawn's room key. She'd turn them in.

Fifteen minutes later, Marcy showed up in the dining room lobby with a man in tow. She and he exchanged a few words, and then she left him to approach their breakfast table. He looked uneasy in his rumpled suit and assigned role, *Whatever that is,* Paige thought. He wore a name tag, so he must be with the hotel.

Briskly, Marcy pulled out her chair and lowered herself into its skimpy seat. She had five or six twenty-dollar bills in her hand. She glanced back to ascertain that her man was still there, and he was, nodding at her. His right hand petted his tie, as if calming it down.

"I don't know who you are, but now it doesn't matter," Marcy said to Vonnie and Dawn.

She held up a hand as if to silence Vonnie, who had repeated, "Who we are?"

"For sure, you're not mother and daughter," Marcy said.

Vonnie's eyes narrowed above pursed lips. Her chin went up. She met Marcy's stare with one of her own. Dawn's hands went into her vest's side pockets. Her expression was blank, bleak.

"You're con men—rather, con women. Accomplices. Collaborators," Marcy said, looking from mother to daughter, from one con woman to another.

Paige's "Marcy, what—" was cut short as Marcy continued, mostly addressing Vonnie. "You two are up to no good, and I don't want to know how dangerous 'no good' can be." She slapped the twenties onto the table. Placed one on the restaurant bill.

Vonnie's gaze took in the man at the entrance, and her tanned glare wilted. Her daughter sat with closed eyes as if praying.

"You're con men, but I don't think you are killers," Marcy said. She stood up and motioned for Paige to follow her.

Paige couldn't move. She stared at Vonnie. "Well, are you? Killers?" she burst out. "Were we in danger?" Her heart wanted to know. Vonnie looked stricken. Dawn's eyes flew open as if also waiting for Vonnie to answer.

"Do not say a word. Nothing," Marcy instructed Vonnie and Dawn. "We might have saved ourselves—we might have saved you."

Her hand a vice on Paige's arm, she dragged Paige from her chair and out the door to the bright sun and new day. Marcy announced that she was driving. Paige turned to see the manager's stricken face in the motel lobby. He waved and backed into his office, clearly wary of all four women, no doubt relieved that he didn't have to take sides.

*　*　*

That night, in a more comfortable motel room with an ice bucket and a mini-bar, Marcy tells Paige, "I'll go in reverse. *Here's how it went on Day Three:*

'What went wrong?' Dawn asks, counting the twenties, then pushing them across the table to Vonnie. Marcy and Paige are gone. The manager hasn't come out of his office since they left.

'We got this far,' Vonnie says. 'Those twenties will get us to somewhere.'

'But how did she know?' Dawn asks.

'She didn't know for sure. We don't, either,' Vonnie says.

'Whatever that means,' Dawn said."

Paige is speechless, her throat tight with wonder, so Marcy goes on: "*Here's how it went on Day Two:*

'She's smart. Especially the thin one,' Vonnie says. 'Whoever heard of "plint"?'

'"Plinth,"' Dawn says. Though she doesn't know what it means either.

'If only I could have gotten the keys. If only the fat one had let me drive.'

'There's no way they both love driving.'

'I stole one of the skinny one's bowls. A tiny one. A stupid one,' Vonnie says. 'But it broke in my backpack so I put it back.'"

"So it's true about a broken bowl?" Paige asks. Marcy nods, "I told you that already. And finally, *here's how it went on Day One:*

'Would you have done it?' Dawn asks. They are slumped side by side on the double bed of room 9, backpacks at their feet. The weather report is dancing on the TV.

'In the moment, I thought so,' Vonnie says. 'That skinny backside just waiting for a boot.'

'There were two of them when the fat one showed up,' Dawn reminds her. 'So, maybe that's why not.'

'I'll say one thing,' Dawn says. 'I'll never forget that view.'"

"So, there. That's *how it went.* Probably." Marcy was mixing martinis in their $150-a-night hotel room. "I give you points for crawling to see the view." Their room had an espresso machine for morning coffee. Marcy's martini was very dry. Paige had one also. Actually, two. She suspected Marcy was right, or almost right, as she had been about the dean, and David's visit to Sean. And about their moving in together. "Just plain right. On the nose," Marcy said. "So, let's look at houses when we get back home," Paige said. "I need a place for my wheel—and you need a room for your writing." They both raised their glasses. Paige recalled the day's expansive feeling of appreciating the newly empty back seat, of honoring a friendship that had endured, and finally of driving the remaining miles to New Orleans companionably listening to Cheever's sad narrators and their tales of suburban misdemeanors and mild vice.

from *Getting to Know the Weather*
(1985)

The Next Time I Meet Buddy Rich

We pulled into town just as the sun was coming up, dropped stuff off at the rooms they gave us, and took the drums and other instruments over to the club. The debris of empty glasses, full ashtrays, disarranged chairs was still there from the night before, heavy with stale air. I unrolled my rug, set up my drums. Felt for the piece of gum Buddy Rich once gave me—now stuck at the bottom of the floor tom-tom. Vince hooked up the sound system and then we headed back to the hotel.

I carried in my practice set, calling to Gretel to open the door. Finally, I used my key. Sounds of the shower running droned from the bathroom. Her clothes were scattered over a chair, suitcases sprawled open on the floor. Then the water went off and Gretel appeared in the doorway with a towel around her, a folded rim keeping it in place, flattening her breasts. Her hair was piled on her head and held by one barrette. Beads of moisture gleamed on her shoulders, her legs.

"No more hot water," she said as she pulled the barrette from her hair, shaking it loose. "I'm getting tired of these places. This is too far away from the club considering we're going to be here two weeks."

"We can move. We have before."

"It's the whole scene," she said pointing to the suitcases. "Where's it going? I know what you want. But sometimes wanting isn't enough."

I lay down on the bed and closed my eyes. I saw her standing in the towel. I took the towel away and looked at her full breasts, her stomach, a different texture of hair.

"Sorry," she said. "You want to listen now or later?"

"Later." I put the towel back and opened my eyes. She was looking out the window. I felt sorry for her living this way, but the words to change it all, to take me back to Erie, just wouldn't come. "Let's have a nice dinner after the club run tonight. Chicago doesn't close down like Kansas." She shrugged her shoulders. She was right. If you weren't playing, it was hard to care what you did out here. One room after another. A hundred tables in a hundred towns. The bed slid as I got up. I licked some of the water off her right shoulder. She didn't move.

"OK, later," she said. And I understood that everything would have to wait. That was OK too. She had been traveling with me for the past year, ever since we decided we'd eventually get married. We never mentioned settling down, but I could tell she was tired of being on the road. The band probably wouldn't be together much longer anyway with Jack pulling toward hard rock. Then I'd take my uncle up on his offer of being a plumber for him again. *That* I didn't want to think about.

So I arranged my practice set, fitting it around my chair. Settling it into the sparse pile of the rug to make it steady. "Bring me back two ham on rye," I told Gretel when Jack and Vince knocked on the door.

Vince understood. Five years I've been breaking my ass to get the big break, trying to make it happen. One night in Columbus I was talking to a drummer who was almost there, would be in a few years—by thirty you have to be. That's what I asked him. "How do you get there?"

He wiped his hands under his arms and said, "You practice your ass off all your life and the better you get the worse you seem to yourself and you're ready to give up; and then one day when your hands aren't getting any faster you say the hell with it. When you next sit down at a set of drums after you haven't touched them for days, weeks, like a vow you'd made—suddenly you're doing all the things you've been trying to do for years—suddenly there is a 'before' and 'after' and it's the 'after' where you are now—and goddamn you don't know why, you just know that you're finally there. Then it's only a matter of time."

And now my time was running out. The band close to breaking up. Kids, pets, hard rock up against the slower stuff. I looked down at my hands. Clean, now. The prints clean, sensitive to the smooth surface of the sticks. I hated being a plumber, although I was good at it. All that grease, fitting pipes, welding. I straightened my back. Time enough for planning that later. Time to practice now. I pulled back the plastic curtains to let in the last of the hotel's sun. Then I started to play. Slow at first, just letting my wrists do the work, looking out past the sunken single beds, past the cheap print of some flower, using a little pressure, feeling how my wrists were somehow connected with the tension in my feet. Just feeling it happen like I was watching myself in the mirror. Trying for the sounds of Buddy Rich.

The next time I meet Buddy Rich it'll be at a 76 station in some crazy place, like Boone, Iowa, not at a concert, and he'll be all burnt out waiting for a cup of coffee and I'll go up to him and say—what I'll say I haven't worked out yet but it'll happen and I'll say it then.

I met Buddy Rich for the first time at Rainbow Gardens in Erie, Pennsylvania. I was playing a spot called The Embers and it was our night off. We went really early to get good seats up close so I could watch him play, watch his hands and feet and the way his body moves. He's a karate expert—once said that the martial arts apply to drumming; they key your mind up for getting into it, coordinate your hands and feet. I want to ask him about this when I meet him next.

The Rainbow Gardens is an oval-shaped arena, a stage at one end and a big wooden dance floor in the middle of a bunch of tables. Loads of people and glasses and cheap booze. It was during intermission, on my way back from the john, that I saw him. He was sitting off to the side, just happened to be there—probably after changing his shirt. Not drinking, just leaning back in his chair. Looking out as if to say, "OK, show me something intelligent."

I walked past thinking, "That can't be." Somehow you think of stars as either living on stage or in their dressing rooms. No real life, no tired hands. Then I walked past again and got enough nerve to say, "Buddy Rich?" and he didn't say "No," so I went on and said, "I'm Tony—I'm a drummer and I play with Circuit of Sound." The words kind of rushed at him like a spilled drink and were just as effective. "I think your band is really great," I said. He seemed to lean further back in his chair. He had on a long-sleeved gray shirt and gray pants. His fingers were tapping on the table, tapping like they were just doing it by themselves. I fumbled in my wallet for a card with the name of my band on it. "Would you autograph this for me?" I asked. I gave him a pen.

His first words were, "Who do you want it to?"

"Tony," I said, "and 'Good luck on the drums.'"

He looked at me kind of funny and then wrote, "Best Wishes." I nodded, disappointed. Then I thanked him and went back to my seat, knowing I had blown my chance. Where are the questions when it matters? I wished I could grab him by the collar and say, "Hey, I'm different. I'm not like all the rest of the people who don't understand what Buddy Rich is unless you're in solo. Who don't understand that you, Buddy Rich, are here for the band—while all these people are here for Buddy Rich." But I didn't say it. I drank down eight ounces of

Schlitz—chugging it to drown my embarrassment, and dying a second time because I finally realized that he thought I meant good luck to him on the drums. As if he needed it. Shit.

I let about ten minutes pass. Watching him just sitting there, wanting to know what was going through his mind, wanting to know what was keeping his hands moving or still. What's in his mind when he's playing. He had a back operation in July and a night later he was on the bandstand, behind the drums. Later, on a talk show, he said they should have done the operation while he was playing, then they wouldn't have needed anesthesia.

I hadn't talked to Gretel since I sat down and all I could do now was tap her under the chin—grateful that she understood.

Finally, I couldn't stand it anymore. I chugged another Schlitz, stood up, and went back to try again with Buddy Rich. "I talked to you a few minutes ago and nothing came out right—including asking for your autograph," I said. He seemed to appreciate my honesty because his eyes stayed on me longer and again I told him how great he and his band were and he said, "Sit down," so I pulled out a chair across the table from him. Then I started to pinpoint all the different songs that I really enjoyed off his albums—some of them almost unknown. I counted on that. Like "Goodbye Yesterday," how it talks to me instead of playing.

"It shows how close the musicians work—you know the music is in front of them, but no arranger, no charts could do it for you— it's the energy of the group that pulls it together, that makes it talk." I told him this and more about "Preach and Teach," and he was nodding his head and not leaning back anymore. Now he leaned forward on his table, looking at me. "You know," I said, "with you, it's not just jamming. It's structure pushed to the end in sound." We sat in silence for a few minutes thinking about it.

"Yeah, you do understand," he said. Then he kind of grinned that wide smile of his. "Hard to talk about, isn't it. Easier to play."

"If you're you," I said. "I'm still trying."

"You know," he said, "interviewers are always asking me about the future of music. Hell, I don't know about that. For me it's playing two hours here, then going down the road to Muncie, Indiana. It's the next night for me. Nothing more." His hands were still now and I saw them for the first time.

"You don't have any calluses," I said.

"Hell no, I don't." He grinned again, spreading his fingers on the table, palms up. "If the pressure's right the sticks don't rub." Smooth. Magic.

Just then I noticed kids standing off to the left of us waiting with their pencils and papers—finally having figured out who he was and who I wasn't. I stood up to give them their turn and he reached out and grabbed my wrist. "Don't go," he said. "I'm not done talking to you." So I sat down. My wrist was burning and I knew that the next time I played, the next time my right hand had to make itself heard, it wouldn't be the same. "Sit down," he said. "I got a few more minutes before I have to play to this airport hangar." He gestured around the arena, the high steel-beamed ceiling, the cold aluminum walls painted yellow, pink, blue. It would never be the same for me again.

He held out his hand for pencils and paper and a guy stepped forward, a couple more shuffling behind him. Wondering who I was, sitting there like a friend.

"I really like your 'Sing, Sing, Sing,'" he said to Rich. Rich looked up at me sideways and winked and told him, "I'm going to play 'SSS' and 'Wipeout' in a medley just for you." The dumb ass should have known it was Krupa's theme song. I suddenly had a feeling for what Buddy Rich had to deal with, wanting to be liked and understood and yet running into people who kill off any generosity you feel for the public out there. Like the ones who come to hear his band— they're all looking for the drum solo—you can see their eyes light up as if the stage lights suddenly got switched around. They don't understand the dynamics and togetherness. They know the finished product in a half-assed way, but not how it comes about. Even the critics in the early days would say he plays too loud, or throws rim shots in where they don't belong. *Now* they know what they're hearing.

We talked for a few more minutes—then he said he had to go. Gave me a stick of gum—Dentyne. He stood up and leaned over the table and did a quiet roll with his hands to my shoulder. "I think you'll make it," he said. "I'll be hearing you some day." And he was gone. I guess I heard the rest of the concert. But now being there meant something else to me. And when I hit home that night the stick of gum went into my drum. Was there now. A small pink lump. I look at it just before I begin to play.

Gretel still wasn't back so I practiced a while longer. Then I moved to the bed and lay there, still hearing the sounds, my own sounds this time, for one whole hour. Not sleeping but waiting for show time to come round. When she arrived with the sandwiches I ate them. When Vince called to check the program, I talked. But I was hearing other things, I was making my own program for tonight.

Finally, I must have slept for a few hours, because pretty soon Vince was pounding on the door yelling, "How we going to make it without our practice?" I knew what he meant. He plays a cool sax—sliding notes around like melted butter then pulling them together with a tension that tells in his back, in the way his arms move toward his sides when he gets up for his solo run. We might have made it, Vince and I; maybe he'll keep something together. "Meet you in the lobby," I yelled.

We all went in one van over to the club. Jack was driving, tapping the wheel. He's a good guitarist and up-front man. Can talk to anyone—sifting his smile out over the audience behind his velvety voice. Carol, the vocalist, and he were a good pair. She was filing her nails. Gretel was out shopping.

The stage loomed in the back of the place away from the bar and the lighting was OK. Bad was bad. OK was good. There were a few early drunks sitting around before going home to the wife and kids and mashed potatoes—they'd be moving along as soon as the sound built—it always happened. I took a run on my drums—did some rolls—soft then faster and faster. I hit each drum firm, getting that crisp beat, starting with the snare and ending up with the floor tom-tom and then one closing beat on the bass to cut it off sharp. I set out two sets of new sticks because I've been breaking one or two a night. Then I rolled up my pant legs and sat there sipping coffee. Vince was off talking to the waitresses, trying to line something up for later—much later. It's hard—you have fifteen minutes here and there to make contact, change clothes, and sound like you're not coming on too strong. He's good-looking in a seedy sort of way and even then he's about 90 percent unsuccessful. Sometimes classy groupies show up two, three nights in a row, and you know they want to be asked out. Sometimes they think you'll be a temporary drug source, but they got us all wrong. If we find it we use it, but we don't travel with the stuff. Or play. If cops are even a little suspicious in some of those one-horse towns they'll rip your van apart in the middle of a cornfield—drum sets, suitcases, instruments, speakers, music. It happened once when Jack had some coke from another musician at a gig. But it wasn't on us. Who the hell wanted to be looking for bail in Boone, Iowa.

We were about ready to play, so I changed into my high-heeled boots for a better angle. We started out with show songs, dance music—moving toward two shows a night. My solo is in the second. I usually start light, play something basic that people can tap their feet to. Then I build up by getting louder and faster, bringing it back down to nothing then building to a finale with a very fast single stroke roll. My sticks are moving so fast you can't see them. People relate to a set of drums before any other instrument—I guess because it's obvious what a drummer does; it's so physical.

We started playing and people began coming in. The usual crowd—single people needing movement and noise, countermen, clerks from the local record and sheet-music stores. Bored couples. And a drummer or two. I've met one or two in at least half the towns. Some I looked forward to seeing, some I hated running into again.

We didn't get any requests yet. That'd come later in the evening, after a show, after Carol went into her act. A few songs. Talking at the tables, telling women about the men they're with, always on their side. Gretel wasn't here yet. I missed her. But it wasn't reason enough to make her want to stay.

While we were playing "Preach and Teach," something felt different. I moved into a double stroke roll. Not too loud, just testing. It was a feeling. And then I was going faster and my sticks were almost floating across the drums, washing the high hat, the cymbal and snare, with rushes of sound. Solid sound. And suddenly I knew I had to stop. It was happening and I wasn't going to let it happen yet. Gretel still wasn't here. And I was afraid of what it meant for both of us. But I had to be sure so I changed into a quiet single stroke, hearing the sounds I've heard on my Buddy Rich albums, and my hands were going places they hadn't been before, moving to beats I'd dreamed of playing, sounds I'd played in my sleep, and tonight they were mine. They were in my muscles and fingers as if they'd always been there—even though I knew they hadn't, but this time I hoped they weren't ever going away.

I slowed way down as Jack went into his bass solo and then we took one more run at the chorus before ending. I felt my back relax and curve into a tighter arc as I sat there feeling the sticks in my hands, rolling them between my fingers like magic wands, marking that place and that time. The bar stretching off into the distance of lights and neon noise. Gretel now at our table center front. Gretel in her beaded Indian blouse. My brown coffee mug on the floor beside a bottle of Schlitz. Me at the drums, at twenty-six.

We took a break and I joined Gretel at the table. I wanted to tell her but first I wanted her to hear it—without words getting in the way. Anyway, she avoided my eyes, so I ordered a beer. The tables were filling up. Sounds, smells starting to multiply into that magic of late-night movement. A girl at the next table raised her glass to me. She had beautifully manicured nails—painted green. I nodded politely.

"I went to the bus station today. Checked out the fare home," Gretel said, finally turning to me. Her eyes were tired. She used to look more alive slaving in the Head Start program where she was working when we met. "But I didn't get the ticket yet."

"Is that what you want?" I asked. My stomach felt like a drum tuned too tight. I knew what she wanted but now I wasn't sure I'd ever get the whole thing together. I covered her hand with mine.

"I don't know what I want anymore," she said. "This just isn't enough even if we wanted the same thing. You big and famous on the drums. Us." She looked around the noisy room and I followed her glance to the stage, to the light glinting on the steel rims of the drums.

"We *are* us," I said but she didn't hear.

"I mean what makes someone give up. I feel like giving up and you're still out there playing." There were tears in her eyes and she blinked fast to spread them away.

"You want to know where being on the road ends for us?" I asked. She pulled her hand away, but I caught her fingers, could feel the turquoise ring I'd given her. "You're afraid I won't know." I knew she was because I had the same fear—living on a dream till the real end of everything. It was almost enough to walk me out of that club, my arm around her, the sticks and drums left behind. Almost enough.

She nodded. "And I know I'd keep asking. Wanting two things at once. Like I don't want to go now but I think I'm going anyway. For a while. Maybe I'll be back in a week. Round trip." She wiped her eyes and laughed up at me. It was a laugh too weakly struck to carry, but, God, I loved her for that smile. Then she clinked her glass with mine.

"I might get home before you do," I said. I missed her already. Her waiting for me at tables. Sleeping, turning when I turned. Her trivia games on the road as we zigzagged across Route 80 just to break the monotony, getting off onto the county roads for a while.

"Don't say that, Tony. I don't want to expect you."

She was right. There was nothing for me to say that I could say.

Vince and Jack were back on stage, tuning up. The others were coming back fast. I gave her hand a squeeze. "I have to play. We'll talk later."

"I'll be back for the last show," she said. Light glittered on the beads of her blouse as she sighed. Softer than drums. Her lips smiled. I kissed her fast. I loved her, but I left to play.

Close to the next break I peered out through the haze, the smoke now thick with words, perfume sprayed on too heavily in the ladies' room. Through the conversations, words going as much past the other person as our music, past people not used to listening to anything beyond their own pulse. And with the drums I had two. I looked out through this, searching for the few who made it all come together, for the one person alone, here for listening. The one who was watching my hands go to where they're supposed to be, craning his neck to watch my feet make the beat.

These people were the ones I leaned toward, the ones I played to. They knew it, and I knew they knew it. And sometimes during a break I would go and sit at their tables. I listened to things Buddy Rich must have heard a million times. But I wasn't tired of it yet, maybe because it wasn't true—that I was the greatest. But I liked to hear it and I talked back, I looked at them straight. It was the same way I played. Sometimes they couldn't handle it—me coming to them, my hand on the back of a chair ready to join them if asked. Maybe they didn't have the next three questions memorized—so I moved on. I loved them just the same, but I moved on, doing us both a favor. A time and a place and all that crap. I've been there.

That night I sat with Harry Ratch, an ex-drummer turned history teacher. He told me that once in St. Louis he sat in three nights for Earl Watkins when he had an emergency operation. Harry was the high school hero. History went down pretty easily for the next few months.

I ordered a beer, keeping my limit of two while playing. Harry Ratch was drinking beer, too. He was past the physical fitness of a drummer—it was hard to be overweight in this business—but I could tell by the way his arms moved, his shoulders moved, that he once sat behind a set. Suddenly I saw myself ten years from now sitting in The Embers in Erie, Pennsylvania. Talking to some young kid. Telling him about the time I talked to Buddy Rich. Pulling my back straight to hide the tire around my waist. Hoping he'll offer to let me take a turn at his drums. Wishing I hadn't had three drinks already.

It hadn't happened yet. I focused back on Harry Ratch. He told me that Earl Watkins said the thing for beginners is to always practice. "If you're right-handed, do it with your left. There's always practicing to be done when you're not behind the drums." Harry was passing this advice along to me. I accepted it graciously. It made sense. I told him I hoped to see him again in the next two weeks. Maybe he could sit in on a couple of numbers. For a moment his eyes lost their sad history.

"I'll be here," he said sitting back. "I'll be here." It felt good to make someone's night.

I broke my sticks in one of the first numbers and started working with a new pair. Then we began to play the medley that led into my solo. Again I just moved into the drums. I held off till the last moment, catching the beat at the last possible second, almost afraid to know if it stayed, afraid to trust my knowing. But man it was there.

I could feel it again and I listened to my wrists making music I was born to hear. I was loose and tight at the same time. My wrists were loose and my forearms were keeping the pressure under control. I was arching over the set. I looked for Gretel and she was watching. And she knew. I was playing the answer. Her eyes were sad and happy; her hands flat on the table, still. And I was moving back and forth toward the sounds I needed to make, toward the sound Vince heard, because he stood up, and—still playing—he turned and saluted me with his sax. I knew he was hearing what was happening to me as my legs were tight against my jeans and my feet were wearing shoes I didn't feel and I thought: this is what I always wanted to know from Buddy Rich. What do you feel? When I'm as fast as you are, will I feel what you feel, will I know?

These questions went through my head like lightning, their smell remained, and now it was what I knew that stopped me thinking. That pulled my sounds out of the forest of tables and noise like an ancient drum in some tribal ritual. It was my night. I heard the voices in the club lose their timbre, saw heads turn. There was no going back to Erie, only nights like these to keep me whole.

People were standing now. And Harry Ratch must have felt in his heart that he was helping me to what he never made. I was glad he was here to help me move, and then there were no more voices. One by one the band was dropping back and out, and only Vince and I were left—his fluid notes winding around the sticks I was moving but no longer felt. We were making circuits of sound. He turned, facing me, leaning into his sax, giving his pledge with the notes he made before he too dropped out and I was left. I was dripping wet and winging it. The spotlight hung before me like a suspended meteor. I played as if waiting for it to hit.

Intruders of Sleepless Nights

They own no dogs; the maid sleeps out. The catches on the windows are those old-fashioned brass ones, butterfly locks. No alarm system or fancy security. He memorized everything Nick had to tell about this job. He pulls on black cotton gloves, soft and close like ladies' gloves. He is no longer just a man out for a late-night walk as he enters this strange driveway wearing black gloves—if the cops come they would be hard to explain away. The porch is just like Nick described it, screened in, running the entire back length of the house. He mounts the brick steps slowly, slits the screen, and opens the door. Listens. These small pauses set him apart from other second-story guys he knows, take time away from the seven minute in-and-out rule. But he ain't never been caught. He pulls a roll of masking tape and a straight-edged knife from his jacket pocket. Nick said the easiest window opens into a bathroom off the front hall. Two over from the back door. Quickly the taped asterisk takes shape—corner to corner, up and down. He always varies the pattern, uses different width tape. As he hits the window sharply, once, in the center, it splinters and holds. He folds the sagging shards of glass outward toward him, loosens more from the caulking, and puts them on a wicker table. Once more he listens—not taking Nick's word for everything. He hopes the sound wasn't loud enough to wake the sleeping couple eleven rooms and two floors away.

*   *   *

Her husband is asleep—finally. His back is to her, his right shoulder high, and now his breathing has slowed to a steady pace like some temporarily regulated clock. She has been lying on her back, staring at the ceiling, her silence a lullaby for him. Now she lifts her arms lightly from the bed, readjusting the blankets, placing more folds between them. She thinks of her husband as the mountain range to her lower plain in their nightly landscape. She flexes her fingers, her toes, stretches her legs until her tightness leaves, absorbed by the bed. She feels an energy at night that she cannot use by day, moving around this house with too many rooms. If she were alone—in some other, smaller place—she would live at night. Who else is up at this time while her husband dreams of secretaries and waitresses? Should she buy twin beds, electric blankets, or a divorce attorney? Or new garbage cans to foil those damn raccoons!

*   *   *

His wife thinks he is sleeping. He knows this by the way she begins to move, adjusting the sheets almost gaily, like a puppet released to life. He dislikes being able to fool her so easily, and sometimes he varies his breathing just to feel her freeze—he hopes, into an awkward unnatural position that hurts. But usually the game bores him, he'd rather sleep. He sleeps better with his girlfriend, Nan, when they finally go to sleep after making love, after a last nightcap. "What an old-fashioned word," she said. Nan will be listening to NPR, propped up in bed with three or four books, cigarettes, ashtray, crackers, nail polish, cotton balls, a miniature magnetic chess set, a hair brush. Nan lives on crackers—Wheat Thins, water biscuits, ak-maks. She likes to brush her hair as she watches television though it makes him nervous. He is ahead of her in games won at chess. Barely. He hears a noise somewhere near the library or patio. Raccoons again. They have both heard it, he can tell.

*   *   *

Carefully, he removes the remaining shards of glass from the edge. Then he twists, first to put his head and arms through, then his shoulders. He can't see a thing. The room smells too sweet. His stomach heaves as he dives slow motion toward the sink. His belt pings softly against something, his hands find the sink's edge, the curve of the toilet seat. He balances unevenly for five seconds while he drags his legs across the windowsill. Finally he lowers himself to the floor, which he has taken for granted. He sits on the soft carpet, breathing hard, and lets his eyes adjust to the light. Then he pulls a nylon stocking over his head, stretching it out near his eyes, pushing back his hair, raising and lowering his eyebrows. He stands to squint into the mirror at a face even his own mother couldn't finger. Next, he locates the back door, leaving it open and ready for a fast exit.

*   *   *

What will Cola think if she buys twin beds? Or say to friends, trains of cleaning women going home to Chicago's South Side? Friends who pass the talk on to "their women," as they call them. She herself hears a lot of gossip this way, making Cola a sandwich for lunch in their particular reversal of roles. Cola has five children to her own two, and a husband she gives a weekly allowance of $10.00—to keep him coming round to see the kids. They both know, but don't say, what else for. She considers getting up to read, write letters to the children or an old roommate from college, but she never does. She is more aware of herself at these times than any other. It might have something to do with the thin nightgown she wears, her breasts loose and flat. Sometimes she lies perfectly still and tries to feel the silk against her stomach, her thighs. She regrets that her mind's eye has no picture of herself naked as a young woman. She sees herself dusting, running the vacuum cleaner, shopping for a china pattern. She would like to do her own cleaning again.

*   *   *

For the hundredth time he wonders where he will go if he leaves. What will he take from this house as perfectly arranged as a stage set? He has not yet said "when" even to himself. Nan has given him a deadline but he knows he'll let it pass. He stopped counting deadlines—they and the bright, cheerful women who make them after an elegant dinner or as he is about to turn off the bedside light are all gone. But the children are gone too, and that was the deadline he made himself when they were still in high school and he slept in spite of the Rolling Stones, or maybe because of. Then, the woman was Francine—he thinks? He doesn't know this woman next to him anymore. She reminds him of the sad, aging ladies who sell the perfume and lingerie he buys for Nan. She could be the owner of a smart mauve boutique, or an efficient travel agent, glasses dangling on a gold chain—should he suggest this? Sometimes he is surprised to see her across from him at breakfast, as if the maitre d' has doubled up on tables. He is having more and more trouble sleeping next to her. What *does* she want? As in, "What do *those* women want?"

*   *   *

He locates the silver in the dining room to retrieve on his way out. He pulls open the usual shallow drawer and the forks and knives gleam dully like rows of fresh dead trout. Then he returns to the pantry, where the maid's stairway opens onto an upper landing which leads to the second floor, to the master bedroom where the woman keeps her jewelry. He has memorized the floor plan sketched by a nervous Nick over a couple of beers at Tandy's. The other guys left them alone when they moved to a booth, carrying their beers and Nick's first sketch on a napkin. You can always tell when someone is planning a job, the way they lean together, taking the beer slower than usual, and you know to leave them alone. No one says this, it just happens. But he and Nick can't go on much longer, been four years already—Nick, the inside man giving inspections on insurance riders, sitting in living rooms of the rich, taking notes about rings and things while drawing the floor plan in his head. Shit—forgetting to mark the uncarpeted stairs. He'll have to take it slow up the sides.

*   *   *

What will she do? She feels divorce coming like unreported bad weather, even though her husband has been giving her cheery predictions each of the past eight years she brought it up. Divorces have left two friends with large empty malevolent houses, looking for work in a young woman's world of Olay. Could she get thin again? She isn't fat, but curves seem to have gone to the wrong places, like a badly designed traffic rotary. She has stopped hoping for airline crashes, car accidents, a coronary as her husband straddles his most recent girlfriend who, she knows, wears Chloé. It was the dream that did it—when they were selling the grand piano a year ago. Even now she shivers, sending ripples across the cover of the bed as she recalls that early morning dream before dawn. A man's voice, rough like some milkman or mailman's voice, said "I just killed your husband. You owe me ten thousand dollars." Finally, she woke sweating and wet to the shrill sound of the phone across her husband's empty side of the bed. She answered the seventh ring, terrified, hoping, her first thought—where would she get the money? But it was some early riser who wanted to make sure the piano was his. Her disappointment turned petulant: "You're too late." She was shaking as she hung up the phone—alone, still married to a man probably very much alive. That squeak—like Cola on the stairs.

*   *   *

He resents her relaxed movements when she thinks he's asleep. He himself lies there tense, missing Nan, finally drifting into a dense exhausted sleep where he dreams of moving into his first apartment, an orange U-Haul and four drinking friends to help. His wife—and Nan—are both waiting for him. The apartment has one bedroom but two kitchens, although neither woman cooks. He wakes with stomach cramps before he has to choose whose dinner he will eat. He practices saying, "I want a divorce." But he would have to turn to her. Even now, even thinking it, his back feels vulnerable. When he sleeps with Nan she curves around him, her knees behind his, her stomach breathing him to sleep. He pictures her large bed where she does everything, reads, eats, polishes her nails, studies chess books, talks to him on the telephone. During the first month he insisted on the formality of the couch for at least cocktails, but she sat so stiffly, as if she were still at her drafting board, that they were soon back on her bed, pillows propped against the quilted headboard, although he is never entirely comfortable. It's the only detail of their affair, this cave-bed, that he has kept from his shrink.

Cracker crumbs everywhere like a sandbox. Crunching—the springs like that squeak on the stairs.

*   *   *

Next, the landing and then another short set of stairs. Big houses amaze him, like living in a hotel—everything so far away from the kitchen, a room for this, a room for that. At last he stands at the entrance of the bedroom, adjusting to this new light, letting his face cool beneath his nylon mask, turning his head from side to side. He listens for sounds of breathing in sleep. Two figures on the bed— one turned toward the far wall, the man; one flat on its back, the wife, the dresser is long and low just inside the doorway wall, the jewelry box on the far side. Maybe some things in the middle drawer. "Put your purse away," he is always telling his own wife. He can hold his breath for one minute thirty-five seconds last time Nick timed him. He checks for shoes, junk in his path, and starts across, count- ing, as he moves past the threshold of his fear. He never uses a light.

*   *   *

She knows what she heard even before she sees a man appear in the doorway. She lowers her eyelids to slits, pulls air in and out of her lungs to mimic sleep. Her hand is within inches of her husband's buttocks but she can't move, or else she can't bring herself to touch him there. Slowly the shadow slides across the wall, its back to the bed, searching for her diamond ring. What else—her emerald brooch, the long rope of pearls from her mother's graduation. "No, not the pearls," she wants to cry out. "I was mother's little girl."

*   *   *

It was a slight change in the tone of light. He knows there is some-one else in the room. Sighting down the rifle of his legs he brings the man into view. His breathing practice of countless nights keeps his body under control. He wishes he had a gun. Should he call out, reach for a lamp or phone, alert his wife by groping for her hand? But she is awake, surely she sees the figure. If she knew he lies awake beside her, it would be more evidence of his cowardliness. Her jew-elry is only so much furniture anyway—just smaller.

*　*　*

They are both sleeping, he checked that, but there is something dif-ferent about the way they sleep that nags him. As if they have been forcibly tucked in, both coiled side by side, head to toe. He moves down the dresser searching for the box. Going after three pieces listed in the rider Nick copied from the office files. A big diamond—maybe three, four carats—an emerald pin, and pearls. The pearls are lying out as if they'd just been worn. He slips them into his pocket to waiting folds of cotton gauze to muffle sound. Next, the wooden box, wooden inlaid with three drawers. He bends slightly to see more clearly. Still counting—at ninety-five seconds he will have to leave to breathe. The pin. Into his pocket. The ring—should be in the jewel box 'cause she doesn't wear it much, Nick said. And there it is, must be four gorgeous carats. Ba–by. Into his glove, and he turns to go. "Kill him," a voice whispers. Slowly he turns to the bed, not believing his bad luck.

*　*　*

"It's OK," she whispers again, trying to keep her voice calm, persua-sive. "Kill my husband. I'll pay you tomorrow." The words come out as if they have been planned last week, last year, rehearsed for months. She can barely see the man turn toward her voice. Her body no longer feels attached to anything, sheets, bed. She cannot live through this moment, and then the next as he takes a step toward the bed. She breathes in, to rasp out again, "Ten thousand." He comes another step closer. His features are molded by a stocking into a grotesque vegetable shape. She is going to faint. His face is a dream. "Jesus," he says, his flat lips moving like dark red worms. Eyes like the sockets of a dead man. He makes no sound as he turns and goes, out the door, down the steps, not quiet now, and, she supposes wildly, keeps on going. Tears leak from her eyes, slide down to her ears, to the pillow. How would she have lived with that? She has to leave him. Why has she waited for her husband's move as a deserted warehouse begs for arson in the night? It really is the end. She has been saved.

*   *   *

He is disbelieving. *She said it twice.* She spoke to that dark shape as if her life depended on this one chance. He almost sees her real again, feels his heart warm to the heat of her desperation. It is the first time he has respected hate. Yet he's frozen into a target so still and ready that even now that the man is gone—although he could come back—he can't move. There could have been that stocking around his neck, his tongue as thick as now and dry, but hanging out. Or blood so deep it would have floated both of them to freedom. Would she have lain and watched? How could he have taken so much for granted—like her resignation to his lies, her days, her life. He will lie here till morning, stark awake, lie here for the last time, he knows that for certain, until some morning sound sets him free. Then he will surely leave; his staying he sees now unfair to both of them. They will call the police, so their last day together will be a public one. Questions from some officer with a dull pencil and yellow pad. Did either of them see him? They will both answer "no" with averted eyes. Hear anything? Only the valuables are gone.

*   *   *

He is out the door in ten seconds flat, not stopping for the silver. Thought he was a goner, sure as hell, but she wasn't talking to her old man lying there beside her. *She was talking to him.* He peels off stocking, gloves. The cotton fingers are sticky wet, but he ditches them before he reaches the street. Je–sus. He ought to go back and give it to *her*—except it ain't his thing. He doesn't carry a gun— professionals don't need them. The car parked two blocks away seems the next country. No sirens or flashing lights yet. Did she call the police, wake her husband? Or, Christ, kill her old man, laying blame. Nick'll have to fence the jewels way out of state—it's a losing proposition. And he'll have to keep an eye to the newspapers— he don't need a murder rap. The deserted streets tempt him to speed, but he drives careful. He is too old for this. Monday he'll call his uncle, get into the hardware business for once and all. Stay home nights. Be nicer to his wife.

Something to Do

One morning I wake up bored. I feel too connected with the threads of what I do, thin streamers that connect me to Boston Edison; the phone company; Saks; to the library where I have worked for four years since graduating from college; to friends who depend on me for company and who I depend on in turn; to old lovers wanting to be friends; to my current lover searching for a graceful way to stop seeing me—as if I didn't know things are over long before they end.

I decide to lie.

I call my lover at his office, which automatically limits his responses. I tell him I have found someone else. I have found someone who brushes my long blonde hair, someone who reads as I read instead of pacing till I stop, who cooks elaborate breakfasts while I give myself a pedicure until the tray is actually resting on the antique quilt covering my knees, someone who does not mix his laundry in with mine. My lover is necessarily speechless as I voice a few regrets. He hangs up, but I know he is torn between relief and surprise.

This has made me nervous. I always tell the truth and assume others do, too. At different times I have felt like the Statue of Liberty, the goddess Athena, Emma Goldman, and Queen Victoria, although I don't know what they thought of lying. Perhaps it is the strength of their arms, one always raised on high.

I call my boss at the library and tell him the distant aunt who welcomed me into her spinster home when my parents died in a fiery plane crash, that distant aunt is ill and asking for me in New Orleans, where I grew up. (It is a place I have always wanted to go.) I tell him I might be gone two weeks, that I won't know the length of my stay until I have consulted her doctor. I mention her quavering voice saying her paid companion of the past twelve years has run off with the silver and the handyman. I am expected to search for both. I humor her, I tell my boss, but I am really going in order to be near her when she dies. The last word makes him shy so he says he will wait to hear from me. I ask that my current project be put aside, my papers put in a drawer, that it is something I'd prefer to finish myself. I can't remember what is on my desk besides the clear nail polish I wish I now had.

As I am making myself a cup of strong tea someone calls and asks for "George." This time I do not apologize for the caller's mistake; it is a woman's voice, and it seems surprised by my own. I tell her George is in the shower, that he likes to take long, soapy showers. I take her number, repeat it back to her, but suggest that she call again in an hour.

The phone rings once more. A friend's husband is delighted he's caught me before I've left for work. He invites me to a surprise party for his wife's thirtieth birthday. He explains it will not be tacky as so many surprise parties are. We will not be required to spring from closets or emerge from behind a couch. We will not be led in cheery singing, or asked to shout "Surprise!" I tell him his taste verges on the profound, that until now no time seemed appropriate for saying so. I picture his bald head, his dome ridged like the one over the statehouse. Bald men have problems women cannot assuage. When he invites me to lunch later in the week, I accept. I name a tiny French restaurant, cozy, expensive, and so romantically lit I feel sure he will be unable to find me there. He breathes deeply, says good-bye. One always has friends one dislikes.

My best friend calls. (Not the wife of the surprise party.) She also works at the library. I take the phone and my tea into the bedroom and get comfortable. My stomach feels tight from the tension of my lies. My friend has heard "the story" about my aunt from our boss. She says "the story" because she thinks she recognizes a lie when she hears one. Maybe. I tell her I tried calling her last night. I say last week there had seemed no need to relay my worst fears to her. I tell her my lover and I are taking a trip that will include an abortion, that it will be a bond between us, perhaps leading to the marriage I have longed for. I am annoyed that she swallows this last remark. I hold white lingerie up to my breasts and imagine an unusual wedding.

I immediately call my father to set things right. He is surprised to hear from me in daytime hours, the rates between Ohio and Boston being what they are. He says he's just about to go to the Elks for some poker. Looking out over the faces at my mother's funeral I realized that the Elks had won. He says the raccoons kept him awake all night and now what? Why Dad, I tell him, I'm just calling to say hello. I never call to say hello. His deeply suspicious nature is unable to relax into small talk, so I am forced to admit reluctantly the true reason for my call. I am annoyed by his sudden intake of breath, his certainty that I haven't failed him yet. He has already constructed various scenarios for me. He suspects I live my life to embarrass him in front of his friends. How can I disappoint him? I tell him I've decided to keep the child. "What child?" does not occur to him. The child he has been prepared for—notwithstanding that I was probably the first valedictorian of my town to hold forth on birth control at slumber parties. No, I say, you'd better sit down before I tell you about the father. I hear a kitchen chair being scraped across to the wall phone by the refrigerator. I tell him we have decided not to marry, that our relationship has been ending anyway. I imagine him only half listening, already rehearsing his role in the tragedy when I arrive home on the train (he's never flown, so I'd have to come to him), a wet bundle in my arms. He asks who the father is— his voice dreading the wrong race or religion. That the father is unsuitable goes without saying. I feel him hoping the father is merely a married man, or an inmate of the minimum security prison he warned me against teaching furniture refinishing at, or that the father is an intelligent priest I have temporarily led astray. I announce that my lover is eschewing all legal rights to the child. I rephrase this to eliminate *eschewing*. I say that he has decided to return to the Punjab (let him look it up) and I am taking a two-week vacation to see him off. I tell my father I love him, wishing I did. The most he'll lose today is five or ten dollars. At the Elks the stakes aren't high.

My lover calls back as I am cleaning out the refrigerator, snacking on leftovers. Now he is huddled in a phone booth trying to talk above the noise of trucks going by, and full of questions too indiscreet to utter in his office. He wants to see me but I tell him I'm not well. There is a red mold on the green beans that is the brightest I've ever seen. He demands to see me, he will be over in half an hour, but I mention I changed my locks last week when my purse was stolen on the subway. He doesn't remember my telling him this. Surely I would have told him of such a terrible thing. Perhaps this accounts . . . I cut him off, lamenting his faulty memory; it is, in fact, one of the reasons I'm leaving him. "Who?" he asks. "Is it someone I know?" I realize he is behaving exactly as I might have had our places been reversed. He is behaving badly. This time I hang up, tempted to tell tales of pregnancy, but I refrain.

I do not call my sister in New York. She'll be hearing from our father tonight at 11:01. I'm grateful for the ten-hour reprieve. I'll send her the first postcard. The possibilities are endless as I locate my colored pens.

My landlady beams. She promises to take in my mail and water the plants, which I have gathered together in my bay window. She is so excited for me she wrings her hands in blessing. I'm the first person she knows to actually win something big like a trip, though her cousin used to enter all the contests and wrote jingles that were pure poetry.

I call to cancel my subscription to *Library Journal*. I tell them that somehow their computer has been sending me seventeen issues for the past three months. No doubt it is happening to others. I refrain from telling them of the new efficient filing system I have quietly instituted in the reference section of my library.

My next-door neighbor watches me pack after making us both Bloody Marys. She is sympathetic, though surprised, at my career change. She could never picture me a librarian, what with no glasses and all that blonde hair. She didn't know that Arizona State had the best veterinary school in the country. Wasn't it all snakes and bears in that area? Animals not in need of medicine? I magnanimously wave aside her lack of knowledge and show her a picture of my childhood cat. It is a photo I found last week marking someone's place in *The Annals of European Civilization*. As I fold clothes I tell her how "David Livingstone" got her name. She turns the photo over and reads "Muffy." "Oh," I say. "Only my crazy aunt called her that."

"Getting married in New Orleans." My travel agent smiles widely. "How absolutely romantic." I mention my hesitation at meeting his parents, since they are one of the prominent families always to be found at the head of the Mardi Gras parade. They live in a grand home in the disintegrating Garden District and are probably disappointed in what they've heard of me. "Not you," she says, "you'll knock them dead." I promise to try.

On the way to the airport, my cab driver practices for the Indianapolis 500. I tell him I feel queasy, that perhaps he should slow down, I hope I make it to a restroom. His foot jumps from the gas and he cleaves to the slow lane. "Hey, lady, just hold on." He has another six hours' work tonight, he says, glancing back at me. I relax and promise to mention him in my prayers that evening in Paris.

Finally, fifteen minutes before boarding time, I call the police, handkerchief over the phone. I explain slowly and carefully about the bombs I have placed in the Boston Public Library. I say I have had a change of heart—now they have a fighting chance with early warning. (These threats are always good for at least an hour coffee break.) I try to think of a signature to tip off my friends working there, to make them suspiciously thankful, but I don't want to stay on the phone. "Begin in Fiction," I say.

The plane seems to be waiting for me. The hostess smiles like one of my detested sorority sisters but I ignore her and incline my head to the handsome, silly pilot. The gentleman dressed like a banker is sympathetic to my claustrophobia and graciously offers his window seat. I settle back, remembering the day.

The Kidnappers

Her father had given her a new coloring book. He would only be in his lawyer's office a few minutes, he said. Ellie wanted to wait in the car and so he showed her how to push the button to lock it, how to pull the button up when he wanted back in. Not to open the door for anyone. He insisted they practice once. Then he stood looking at her for a moment through the window before he waved and jogged across the street.

It was a Wonder Woman coloring book. Ellie flipped through it, then turned back to the first page and started on the red and blue outfit Wonder Woman always wore. She was finishing the top that looked more like a bathing suit when a rapping on the window made her go way over the line. A woman in a green scarf and big sunglasses was calling her name: "Ellie, let me in."

"Mom," Ellie cried, before yanking up the button. They both were crying as Ellie's mother pulled her from the car and together they ran down the sidewalk toward a red station wagon belonging to Jane, her mother's writer-friend. Ellie scrambled across the front seat under the wheel and her mother followed and slammed the door. She slipped off the scarf and threw it into the back seat.

"God, Ellie." Their wet faces touched, then she started the car and pulled away, wheels scraping the sidewalk edge.

"We are going home," her mother said. Her voice trembled on "home." She drove with one hand, holding Ellie's with the other. Maps crunched under Ellie's feet.

"Right now?" Ellie said. To her room, her toys, her friends.

"Right, now. We're on our way." Her mother snapped her sunglasses off and put them on the seat. The buildings grew shorter beside piles of garbage as they drove faster than usual away from town, into the long curving miles of the highway that led to the interstate that led toward home.

Ellie had missed her mother. Had missed cuddling with her at night, their T-shirts touching, her mother's soft body curved around her for a short story about when she was a little girl, before sleep separated them. Ellie had missed her sitting hunched over her typewriter, looking into her head for a word. Sometimes Ellie held her breath until the typewriter began to beat again. Ellie had secretly hated the typewriter and sometimes pounded the top when she was alone with it. Until she had been given a smaller desk next to her mother's with a painted wooden sign that said "Sssssssssssh." Ten s's. Was it still there?

Soon the car slowed and her mother stopped watching the rearview mirror. She began telling Ellie about the new family on the block who had a little girl, eight years old, just like Ellie. Telling Ellie about her new book. "I'm not just typing," her mother said once when she read Ellie's five-sentence essay about her parents. "My mother tipes," the essay said.

"It's what I type that matters," her mother said.

"You type what you write," Ellie said.

"And you print what you write," her mother said.

"So what."

Ellie closed her eyes and leaned her head back against her mother's shoulder. What was her father doing now? Was he missing her, coming out of the lawyer's office to the empty car, and her and the coloring book gone?

*   *   *

Ellie woke just as they were pulling into the driveway. It was night. A small light on the porch hurt her eyes. Somebody finally must have replaced the bulb. Ellie's mother wiped her damp cheek and gave her a long hug. Ellie squeezed her harder than she ever had before. Then her mother began dumping stuff on the seat. The "key hunt," they called it. At least once a day.

Later, as Ellie slept on the couch with her head in her mother's lap, her mother and Mrs. Conway from next door talked. They thought she was sleeping, Ellie knew.

"He didn't follow you?"

"No. Anyway, all I had to do was cross the state line back into Illinois. I have custody here. I keep forgetting that after the horror of the last few months." She smoothed Ellie's hair as she talked. Her ring pulled, but not enough to hurt. "I feel like hell. Like a criminal," her mother said. "But I couldn't afford to go through the courts. 'Too much time and money,' my attorney said. And missing her all that time. 'You go get her, or I can get you someone,' he told me, 'but it's better if the parent goes along. Doesn't scare the kid as much.' So here we are back."

"Just get settled and it will seem like it never happened," Mrs. Conway said.

"But I had to do it," her mother said. "And anyway, he did it first."

She means he *took me* first, Ellie thought.

That was true. She remembered the day her father had picked her up for the weekend. It had been hot and he was wearing a green short-sleeved shirt that stuck to him, no jacket. They had gone to the same hotel with the slide into the swimming pool and the pinball machines. Getting him up Saturday morning was always slow. First, he sat on the edge of the bed blowing smoke all over the room and rubbing his eyes. Asking, "What's it doing outside?" Then he showered and shaved, farting a lot. She always used the bathroom before he got up. Finally, filled with pancakes and eggs, they went to the pool. He taught her how to turn somersaults—pushing off from the bottom at just the right time. Knowing when the time was right. Ellie's mother was afraid of water—learned to swim to graduate from college and forgot as soon as she passed. Ellie thought that was dumb.

Later they went to the zoo. The monkeys sat at the back of their cages, hot and cranky, too tired to play. Ellie's father kept looking for park benches. Ellie knew her father liked to sit a lot because Ellie's mother used to yell at him about it. Now the television was never on. Ellie missed it. The low buzz and glow from the family room. It had taken her a while to get used to the silence after school. Her mother always called "Ellie?" which helped. After the zoo, on the way back to the hotel, her father said he wanted her to live with him for a while. Started off just like that. His eyes hadn't moved from the street. He missed her terribly, he said, and it wasn't fair that he was being deprived of her just because he was a man. "You're going to live with me for a while," he said, "just like you lived with your mother." *Live where?* Ellie thought. He usually just appeared in the car at the front of the house. She remembered crying because she was going to Molly's birthday party the next day. Her father never kept Kleenex in the car like her mother did. Ellie wiped her nose with her hand and then wiped her hand on the seat. He didn't see.

"You'll be able to see your mother," he said. "Just as soon as the courts work things out."

"But my new dress for Molly's party. Mom just finished it. Can't we go back for my dress?" It was home on her bed all laid out for tomorrow, its plaid sash hanging down to the floor.

"We'll buy you all new clothes," he said. Ellie didn't think he had any idea of all the millions of things girls wear.

"I want to go home," she said. Her hands were sticky from cotton candy and she had to go to the bathroom.

"I know, I know, but 'home' is going to be with me for a while."

They drove through the night. Once stopping by the side of the road where Ellie squatted down. Again, no Kleenex. Once stopping for hamburgers and malts. Ellie ordered a big chocolate sundae that she couldn't finish. She hadn't looked at her father when she ordered it. The next day they bought shorts and halters that matched. And a canopy bed with a pink ruffle around the top that swayed in the breeze from her window. A jungle gym arrived two days later. Her father swore a lot when he worked, Ellie remembered. The neighborhood kids came around and watched. About laundry, "You're on your own," he told her. She learned to rummage in the still-dirty clothes for socks when she forgot to run the washer. Her father took her to his barber to have her hair "styled." "It's too short," she said. "That's what it is."

Her mother called. Finally she and Ellie talked while her father listened in. "I'll see you soon," her mother said. Ellie could hardly speak past her crying, and then her father came in and hung up the phone. They ate hot dogs with onions, mustard, and relish, hamburgers with ketchup, and heated-up TV dinners. His first girlfriend was Barbara, the second Jude, but he called them all "love," so when the third one came to visit, Ellie didn't bother to learn her name.

*   *   *

And now fall was here and she was back with her mother. Everything looked strange and new for the first five minutes. The softness of the curtains and tablecloths and pillows was comforting. Her desk was still in place. It had a new sign: "Let's Talk." Ellie liked the

"Sssssssssssh" better. She'd see Molly tomorrow, wear the new dress. She wondered if her father was angry. He would know she had opened the door because the window wasn't broken or anything. But she'd had to do it. She missed him, too.

Two days later a man came to change the locks on the front and back doors. Her mother's friends touched her lightly as if she weren't quite real. They'd all heard the story of the trip back home. Angry voices puffed smoke. "The bastard," Ellie heard before her mother told her to go watch TV for a while. Her mother's friends were a bore—all that talk.

Ellie's mother walked her and Molly to school. Holding hands with them, skipping partway. Ellie wore her new skirt. They looked for Mrs. Logan's room. Mrs. Logan squeezed her and later chose her to write the date and quotation on the blackboard. It had taken her a while to print: *September 10, 1982 "Nothing in life is to be feared. It is to be understood." Marie Curie.* She stood aside while Mrs. Logan explained it and told a story about Marie Curie. Ellie turned back and forth so her skirt swished against her legs. Molly wanted one like it, she could tell.

Ellie knew her mother had talked with the principal. Miss Woodson was to call the police if anyone came for Ellie. Even her father. It had to stop.

Ellie liked walking back and forth to school with her mother. Once her mother said, "I think it's OK now, Ellie," but Ellie had insisted she put her shoes on and go along. "You have to," she said, making the hole in the screen door larger.

*   *   *

Ellie's hair was "growing in," her mother said, looking up from her typewriter. She still hunted for words—more often now, and for money. Sometimes Ellie had a babysitter and her mother had dates.

They wore suits that looked alike and always asked Ellie the same questions. She did it back. "How many kids do you have? Where are they?" Some did, some didn't. Only one came now and stayed over sometimes. He wore jeans and a plaid shirt, often no shoes. His toothbrush was red and hung next to her mother's. Ellie used it to scrub her nails. She always put it back. Sometimes he played Monopoly with her on Sunday while he watched football and her mother was cooking things that took too much time and didn't taste worth it. She'd slam the dice in front of him to get his attention. He'd jump but he never said anything. His name was Jack something.

She missed her father sometimes. She was allowed to talk to him now. He told her he would see her soon. It was complicated, he said. She hoped nobody like Barbara or Jude was sleeping in her canopy bed.

*   *   *

Field trips weren't really much fun. Just got teachers out of teaching. The bus ride was always too long, and the driver made them stop singing at the twentieth verse of "99 Bottles of Beer." Allison, whose name was near Ellie's in the alphabet, usually threw up, so that was an extra stop—if they made it in time.

The trip to the museum wasn't any different. Allison barfed two seats away. Ellie giggled and held her nose high in the air. Windows crashed open. The driver would clean it up while they were gone. They were each given a pamphlet for a game called I Spy. You had to look at a detail, like a dog's face, and then find it in a painting. Afterwards, Mrs. Logan lined them up by twos like babies and went to find the bus. Ellie and Molly held hands. A fight began in the back of the line and Ellie stepped out to look just as a pretty woman with red bushy hair came over and said, "Ellie?"

Ellie said, "Yes," and it seemed to be enough because suddenly behind the woman was a tall man who bent down and scooped Ellie up. Her chest collapsed and he pulled her against him. She tried to scream but no air came. "Ellie," Molly's cry followed her, and she kicked her legs out but he was holding her too tight. Something was tearing open, cold air on her shoulder. He carried her down the steps two at a time, past the stone lions, carried her fast, making it difficult for the red-haired woman to keep up, telling Ellie that her father was waiting for her at the corner in the blue car over there and he wanted to see her very badly. The man's eyes were steamy red and he was panting like a dog into Ellie's face. "Put me down." She arched her back but it didn't work. "Hey, little girl," the man said, "in one minute now, OK."

"No." Ellie knew that somehow her father didn't want to just see her, like she wanted to just see him. And then they were in front of a car and her father was opening the door to the back seat. The man bent over and pushed her in. Her father held out his arms and they did feel good and big and he said, "Ellie, Ellie, Ellie," and then something about "your first ride in a little airplane, just like you always wanted." What did he know? The woman called, "Good-bye, Ellie"; she seemed about to say something more but turned away. The woman's voice, not like her mother's at all, made her cry harder. No Kleenex, just her father's rough suit, but she didn't care.

The airport was too small. They drove right up to the toy plane and the pilot led them up the steep steps, saying as soon as they got off the ground he would let her fly the plane. Had she ever flown a plane before? His teeth glistened. *The dumb shit,* Ellie thought. She could hear her father say just that.

But he told her he had a new sales job and that's where they were going. Her canopy bed was already there with a new pink quilt. All girls like pink.

"It sucks," Ellie said. "Sucks" was new at school; this was the first time Ellie had used it. It didn't make her feel better.

"Forget that talk." Her father patted her knee.

"Where we going?" she asked, but he couldn't tell her right now. A new place.

"Will we be there long?" she asked.

"We're going to live there. You know—cook and sleep there."

"And watch TV."

"Quit talking like your mother."

"I like TV," Ellie said, her eyes filling again. "How long are we going to live there? When will I see Mom?"

"Oh, Ellie, Ellie." He put his arm around her. "Not right away. I'm sorry it has to be like this—but the same thing would happen just like before. It has to end sometime."

The plane made Ellie sick, lurching into slides she felt inside her stomach. She didn't want to fly. Would she barf like Allison, make the pilot mad? She felt wet all over. Her father talked on about the new school, the teacher expecting her. Ellie wondered if the teacher knew she had a mother.

*   *   *

The teacher called her "Ellen." "Ellen, stop daydreaming," and Ellie tried. This school was smaller, just like her father said. The whole town seemed a smaller version of where she lived with her mother, except people were outside their houses more, planting things, chopping wood, waxing cars, cutting hair. She missed her mother, and this missing brought an ache that made it hard to eat. She hadn't seen or talked with her since the museum trip. She was sure her mother was still alive. Only grandmothers die. Her father said of course she'd see her mother again. But she didn't think she would see her mother here. Strange how the words "daddy" and "mom" had become "your father" and "your mother." They seemed to accuse her of something. "Your mother" was far away, she knew. At least three plane-hours away. When she thought about her mother she sometimes held her breath. She didn't know what to do.

She began to forget what clothes she had. Her father never separated the dirty laundry into piles and so her blouses grew gray and limp. One turned pink—at least she couldn't remember *buying* a pink blouse. She learned to throw a baseball. They took bike rides along roads with trucks that seemed to pull at her hair as they passed. She ate breakfast alone, trying to forget her dreams, but her throat was always sore. She woke screaming one night when she fell down three steps to the landing in the middle of the stairs. At home, at her mother's house, the bathroom was *that way* down the hall. She lay there until she realized where she was. Until her father told her, lifting her, "You must have been sleepwalking," as he tucked her into bed. Ellie felt such tightness in her chest that she couldn't feel the bed under her. Or the blanket above. Her teacher asked about the bruise and her explanation sounded silly.

She knew now where she lived because it was on signs in town. The grocery store was called "Granada's Largest Market for Fit Produce." *Where do they sell maps?* she wondered. *Wyoming?* Her father had more "loves" who probably had names. They smelled good and sometimes brought overnight bags with fun compartments. The latest cooked special breakfasts of very mushy eggs and crisp bacon. She put green things in the eggs and turned their orange juice pink with something from her father's liquor cabinet. She played cards with Ellie and fixed her hair as they all sat in front of the TV's glow.

Ellie's father became president of the PTA. "Men are usually just treasurers," her teacher said. "You should be proud."

After three months Ellie was allowed to walk home alone from school. Oh, not really alone, because her friend Juanita joined up with her after the fourth block going and up to the fourth block coming home. Home? One of them, anyway.

*   *   *

The car was on its third time around the block. She hadn't noticed it the first two times until the third and then she remembered all three. Did that make sense?

The car was going slower. She looked over at the driver. He was a man she didn't know. But she didn't know everyone in town yet. She put her lunch box down by a lamp post and kept on walking.

The car, it was green, not too new, speeded up to be a little ahead of her, then stopped. She kept on walking.

"Hello, little girl," he said. He raised his eyebrows, instead of smiling, she thought.

She was surprised he didn't know her name. She stopped.

"You don't know my name?"

"Uh, no," he said. His hair was shorter than her father's hair. It looked molded to his head like puppet's hair. "Do you want me to guess your name?" he asked softly, as if there were someone else around to hear.

"No," Ellie said.

"You know," he said. "I passed an ice-cream store a few blocks ago and I bet you like ice cream." He didn't seem to be asking her anything so she didn't reply. She looked back at her lunch box sitting by the lamp post.

"Why don't you come with me and we'll go get an ice-cream cone? I'll let you have double scoops."

"You don't know my father, do you," she said.

He hesitated, then adjusted his mirror.

"Or my mother," she said. "Do you know her?"

"No," he said shaking his head, "I don't believe I've met them."

A car came by and he watched it pass without speaking. He turned back to her, his eyebrows pulling up a smile this time.

"Can I have a triple scoop?" she asked. Did her father mind her having ice cream before dinner? She couldn't remember for sure. Maybe it was her mother?

"Sure," he said, patting the empty seat beside him. "Sure."

She walked around the front of the car and opened the door herself. Then she got in and closed the door. Herself. The radio was playing something fast and loud. He must have turned it on while she was walking around the car. She folded her hands in her lap.

"I thought we'd take a ride first," he said. He lit a cigarette. It smelled sweet.

Ellie closed her eyes and breathed deep. She felt the car speed up on its ride away from town. She wanted to go back but she didn't know where. Now, as her mom and dad both said, it simply had to end.

Getting to Know the Weather

She has been watching them for two weeks: women named Lou and Betty and Alice. Gert, Ellie, or Kay, or Irene—their names on plastic tags, in white stitching on a pocket or on gold pins holding a lacy handkerchief in place. She chooses a good seat at a different lunch counter each day. Droops her coat around her lap, the sleeves pulled across her stomach, and orders coffee, sometimes scrambled eggs or an English muffin when she can't resist the smell of melting butter as it foams. But her money is running out and even though she feels her training isn't quite complete, today is the day.

She sits and watches the women work. Her wrists feel the motions they make spreading chicken salad on a slice of toast, cutting Danish for the grill, or shaking a can of whipped cream. Each woman has distinctive flourishes—an extra swipe with the knife or a small flip that pings the silverware when it is set down. But Jessie knows it is people watching, even her own watching, that makes these women pull together such dramatic stage gestures—customers are more appreciative than any husband or kids. She needs to remember that deftness matters, to practice with peanut butter tonight. Jessie, at forty-five, knows without question that the men who manage lunch counters in these small midwestern towns can tell who's worked as a waitress before. She needs a job her first try—it will be her first real job, not counting selling the chickens she took to church fairs for twenty years in Irwin.

This town has three possibilities; Kresge's, where she now sits under a too-garish light, but she could get used to it. They have good hamburgers and the nicest cosmetic counter of things she wants to try—cream rouge, eyeliner, body powders called Evening in Paris and Wind Song. Then there is Woolworth's just like the one back home in Pennsylvania, with oiled dark floors and bolts of cloth too near the front doors. But their counters are bright red and clean and the waitresses wear little green aprons, starched and welcoming to tips. Today, Woolworth's put a sign in the window: COUNTER HELP WANTED. After her coffee she'll go over and apply. Finally there is the coffee counter at the bus station, but it is last choice. She went back twice after coming into town on the cross-country run from Pittsburgh. Too much noise from the jukebox and traveling radios against a lingering level of bus exhaust worse than a cloud of burned onions. The people come and go from too many places to ever see a familiar face again—some you wouldn't want to. She wants to know her customers—even the mean ones who only leave a quarter rather than dig deeper for an extra nickel or dime.

Marge is on the morning shift as Jessie slides into her seat beside the cash register. She's been practicing on Marge. Marge has the flair she wants. Marge's apricot hair is fluffed under a wispy net. Jessie has one in her pocket just like it. Marge's cheeks glitter more than usual—tiny specks of silver or gold floating on soft red ponds. Jessie never wears rouge and this has been hard to get used to. Now each night in her housekeeping room she applies it liberally to the "apples of her smile," as the counter girl put it. Her husband and kids wouldn't recognize her just because of the new color in her cheeks. But all waitresses wear it—Jessie can tell it is more important than lipstick although some waitresses keep a tube in their pockets and use the side of the coffee machine or toaster to reapply it just before their male customers come in.

"Morning. Coffee?" Marge pulls a white paper napkin out of the holder and swoops it down an instant before the spoon lands on it dead center, without a sound.

Jessie nods first, then says, "Hi, Marge. Coffee. Maybe a muffin today if you have any." She forces herself to say Marge's name even though she doesn't really know her.

Marge writes "cf" and "mf" on her tiny green pad, not keeping to the lines. The pencil is dull and leaves a trail of wide lead as 'mf' drifts off the page. Pad into her pocket and pencil into her hair. Jessie will have to let her hair grow.

"Still raining out there?" Marge asks, pouring a high dark steaming arc of coffee into a white mug.

"Rain?" Jessie never knows what the weather is. Showers or record heat waves always surprise her. Is it still raining? She's been looking at powder puffs and nail polish for the last five minutes. It is a question she'll have to learn to ask, sighing heavily over lingering storms, rolling her eyes at three inches of snow and her stuck at work without any boots, and the buses probably running late, or her ride not showing up. Or fanning herself with a plastic menu against the July heat or the air conditioning on the blink again.

Marge brings her muffin and pulls up a knife, a butter pat, and a tiny plastic container of jelly from under the counter. Jessie likes this miniature world.

"Muffins just come in," Marge says, giving the small round plate an extra twist in front of Jessie. "More coffee yet?" Jessie notes the "yet." It makes her feel cared for.

Like Mr. Arnold must feel. Once or twice a day he comes in from First National Bank. The shoulders of his coat are dark and he runs a hand over his thin wet hair.

"Morning, Mr. Arnold. Still raining, I can see." Marge pours him a black coffee and tempts him with the pastry tray. "Ten days straight. It don't quit we're going to have to dry out our money." Jessie marvels that Marge has actually counted days.

"Make it a grilled Danish today, Marge. I need something to lift my spirits," he says. But Jessie knows Marge already did that.

Next, Mrs. Penrose, a plump cashier from the grocery store, comes in for six coffees to go. As Marge fits their lids on tight, the woman hands across a picture of her new grandson. He is the most beautiful baby Marge has ever seen. She holds the picture carefully by the edges and steps down the counter to include Jessie and Mr. Arnold in the viewing of a scrawny yellow wrinkled face. "Look at that face," Marge says. She is serious.

The clock, red with fruity numbers, probably from Kresge's own kitchen department, says 10:30. Few customers come in so Jessie lingers. Marge works around her as if Jessie is an anchor. She wipes the surfaces of the counters, checks to see the salt lids are on tight, and marries the ketchup bottles, placing one on top of the other. The record department is playing "Raindrops Keep Fallin' on My Head," which makes Marge inexplicably roll her eyes. As Marge works she tells Jessie all about her daughter, who just had twins and already gave one of them a haircut. "Shaved his head is what it amounts to. Just so she could tell them apart."

Jessie sips her coffee sympathetically. She tells Marge teeth will do it. Marge should pass that along to her daughter. "No two people have identical teeth—like fingerprints—I know from my own son's twins," Jessie says.

Marge stops wiping. Her cloth, stationary, smells sour. "Imagine that. We both got twins in the family. It's a small world."

Jessie has imagined it. Her two kids are off working and not even thinking about having families. She'd like twins. But it might have been hard to leave grandchildren behind. "One's lost three baby teeth and the other five. Teeth do it."

Marge looks relieved. Jessie has come to realize that just saying things brightens someone's day. She always suspected this. Her own parents and sisters talked and talked. But George never got over their having to get married. "Just a little earlier than planned," she said to him, trying not to cry, back when they were both graduating from high school in a record class of seventeen. Today kids have it nice. Pills and women's magazines talking about real things instead of meat loaf recipes or thirty ways to make your husband happy. But George didn't have a reply and after they married he settled into an early silence that spread a pall on the kids even before they could talk. It sent her friends from the Fire Hall Ladies Aid away too. And now her question to herself is not what she ever saw in him, but what she ever heard from him.

*   *   *

Jessie planned her exit a long time. When the kids were in high school, she walked the mile and a half into town, past the neighbors' farms that were farms in name only, the chickens and cows long since sold off, the tractors dead in the overgrown fields, men in the mills making steel. In those days she sat at lunch counters to watch the counter girls cutting pies, cleaning coffee urns as big as the old milker in the barn. She admired their self-assurance, the perky hats they wore, their pockets gray and heavy with tips. The way they slid coins off the counter into their hands like men palming poker winnings. Talking back to sly managers, calling orders to sassy cooks. Ringing the register and catching the drawer with cushioned stomachs. She looked for wedding rings, signs of marriage or kids. Most were single with birthstones on their right hands, women who a generation ago would have been the resident spinster aunts. She imagined apartments or rooms where they put their feet up and complained about the hours, the sass, the tips, to the woman upstairs who heard them come in and wandered down to talk. She expected to find she was over the hill but her first visit reassured her that women her age, extra pounds around their middle, hadn't been pushed aside by the shrill teenagers who worked at the drive-in places and Dairy Queens. A few high school girls came to work the late Thursday and Saturday shifts but their hearts weren't on the weather or keeping the counters clean. Their friends lounged around learning to smoke, sneaking doughnuts, applying coats of fuchsia nail polish, waiting for closing time. But Jessie didn't want a job in Irwin anyway—too close to home.

Instead she saved money for a red collapsible suitcase which she kept folded in her pantry till she could also afford a one-way bus ticket to somewhere in Indiana and a place to stay for a month. She planned to go to a large city, say Indianapolis, and work her way out of town till she came to a place that suited her. She'd know it when she saw it. She chose Indiana because no one talked about it except for the top part cut through by 1–90 on the way to Chicago.

When her youngest, her daughter, was a senior, Jessie was already planning her own departure. She began to make lists of things she would take along. Long lists at first, her despair directly proportional to the size and number of items. Her heart lightened as she crossed things off. This was hard on her because she suspected George would begin selling her stuff as soon as he realized she was gone for good. When their children's departures seemed permanent George had carried Susie's canopy bed and Mike's aquarium out to the front lawn for a yard sale. Jessie can still see the pink eyelet canopy fluttering in the breeze, catching the eye of a passing motorist better than any sign could. A month later the children sulkily enumerated to her the lost items of their childhood, carting off remaining records and scrapbooks that Jessie had hidden from the sale. "I'm going to close them rooms off and save heat," George said.

Jessie's final list included: her mother's amber necklace, her mother's ivory hand mirror, pictures of the kids, one dress, one skirt, two blouses, underwear, one nightgown, comb and brush, the 1937 *World Atlas*—sure, she knew the world had changed, people had changed, but Indiana's geography hadn't—and the family Bible.

The last day, waiting to go for the one o'clock bus, Jessie packed in the pantry. Then she wandered around the house touching things she regretted leaving: her mother's cherry sideboard, the rocking chair she'd used for nursing Mike and Susie, the braided rug she made for the front room, her teacup collection used but once for the Ladies' Aid. She fretted about a note for George. What could she say that wouldn't run on into angry words? She simply couldn't think of a thing to say—considering it might be showed around. But she had to leave a sign—in all fairness, he had to know.

Suddenly it came to her. She went down to his tool room in the basement and returned with the tiny red circular stickers he had used for the yard sale. Then she set about pricing the sideboard, rug, teacups, dining room table, and other stuff he'd consider hers—fair prices in black ink with a little room for bargaining. This was information enough; she figured he'd know what to do.

She was nervous buying her ticket and might not have found her voice except for a radio blaring from someone's shoulder. "Speak up," the ticket man yelled. Selling tickets didn't appeal to Jessie. She studied other people's jobs. Grocery stores didn't allow time to visit with customers as clerks shoved lettuce and meat onto the bag boy. Bank clerks were too prissy, and maybe you needed college to take care of all that money. Factory jobs she didn't know about. Anyway, her mind was made up.

She got on the bus and settled into a seat to watch the landscapes go by the wide tinted window. This was her first trip in a direction other than north to Niagara Falls. When a sign welcomed her to Ohio she put her head back and said good-bye to Pennsylvania and George.

Jessie hopes her blouse isn't wrinkled. Last night she borrowed an iron from upstairs, from a retired couple who write letters to people whose books they read. They collect answers. Jessie takes out a new compact of rouge and lipstick and adds some color, glancing at Marge to see exactly where the red spots should be.

She leaves Marge thirty-five cents and says, as she puts on her coat, that maybe the rain is letting up.

Marge shrugs elaborately. "I'll keep your cup in place for a refill. Come back if it's too wet." Tears blur Jessie's eyes—it's all in what's said.

The rain has stopped. Jessie walks three blocks to Woolworth's, past a post office, a hardware store, a dress shop, and a bank and stops across the street. She wants this job. She can't remember wanting anything as bad ever before.

The "help wanted" sign is still in the center window near the display of lunch boxes shaped like houses landscaped with pink tennis shoes.

The pungent smell of grilled and rolling hot dogs provides a special warmth from wet streets. They have the best hot dogs in town. Jessie straightens her shoulders, taking five years off her age, according to *Women's Day*. Two people are sitting at the counter, a postman with his leather bag at his feet and a lady in a flat rain hat writing in her checkbook with a red pen. "Helen" is slicing a blueberry pie while the postman watches, tapping his foot. Jessie knows he will have a piece, maybe two.

Helen points her toward the manager's office, a tiny black room partitioned off from a display of wall lamps and frilly curtains. "Rain finally stopped?" Helen calls after her.

"For at least ten minutes," Jessie says, happy to have a sentence to propel her to the back of the store.

Mr. Martin looks up from his littered desk as she knocks on the door frame. Everything about him seems concave, his chest, his cheeks, his wide forehead.

She tells him she is looking for a job. He motions to a chair. "Any experience?" he asks. "I gotta have girls who already know what they're doing."

"I've been a waitress for the past fifteen years in Irwin, that's in Pennsylvania." The twins come to mind. "At a Woolworth's there, a counter almost identical to your setup." She cranes her neck to bring Helen and the pies into view as if to make absolutely certain of her comparisons. "Training new help can really be a pain," Jessie says, trying to make her eyes reflect broken dishes and lost revenues from people she has worked with in her fifteen years. At Woolworth's.

"Good. Then you probably still got a Woolworth's employee number on file." He picks up a pencil.

"Oh, that," Jessie says. "For the past two years I've been at Sun Drugs."

Mr. Martin says, "Oh." His gaze wanders back to his desk to diagrams of windows and screens. "That number would be nice. Saves paperwork. Don't suppose you have any old uniforms?"

"Lost too much weight," Jessie says. "A move does that to you. I moved out here to be near my married daughter."

"She got any kids? You wouldn't be taking time off for babysitting, nothing like that?"

No twins. "No kids. She don't want any." Jessie shrugs elaborately—like Marge. "Times have changed."

He agrees with her, heartily tapping his approval with his pencil. She admires his lunch box window, the bright lights of the counter. He tells her the hours, where she can get uniforms. When to come in. "Helen'll show you the ropes tomorrow morning, you can double on her shift the first two days." He swings around in his chair. "Still raining?"

Jessie rises. "Stopped, but not for long," she says. "Looks like it'll keep up through the week." He is cheered by this, as if she predicted tropical temperatures. He laughs and she laughs too.

"Tell Helen to take the sign out of the window," he says.

Helen gives her a cup of coffee and says to come in at nine. She has been working here ten years. "Nine," the mailman corrects, naming the year of the fire next door. Hand on her ample hip, Helen says some people just notice too much but her posture improves as she says it. The mailman heaves his bag up as if it were weightless and waves.

Jessie buys two uniforms and two aprons, both a trifle snug because she is going to lose weight. She buys a blue ceramic pitcher which she'll use later for flowers. That evening she tries on the uniforms, standing in front of her dresser mirror, her hairnet floating in place. She has to be convincing when Mr. Martin comes by for coffee. She practices her pour. Her arm lifts the blue pitcher at the same instant the water begins to pour forward into the sink.

The calendar hanging on the back of the door tells her she has been away twelve going on thirteen days. The calendar has fuzzy pictures of flowers whose names she doesn't know. Flowers that look like they grow indoors in small spaces. They give the room color—like her rouge. She isn't going to do any more in the way of furnishings for now. She likes not having one thing that needs to be picked up and dusted. She likes the silent TV in the corner of the room, its face to the wall. She has the bed to herself. Lord, is she tired. Not too tired for a hot bath and maybe a short visit with the couple upstairs. Letter to her daughter later. *It's a job*, she'll tell her. *Hard on the feet, but it's a job.*

from *The Long and Short of It*
(1999)

Feeding the Piranha

Our father waits till we've picked up our duffels and left the San Diego airport to ask if we've had our teeth cleaned lately. Josh? he asks me. I say no, not lately. Finny? My sister says she thinks she has a cavity in one of her back teeth either top right or bottom right. Her tongue visits the elected spots, probing for confirmation. Dad nods, satisfied that this will be a good visit. And doctors' checkups? I disappoint him with my required physical for football this fall, but Finny's shake of her head assures him that where our mother's neglect is concerned nothing has changed. Not that he's about to pay for any of this. Finny and I exchange glances as we pull into his apartment complex. It's all cement except for stunted palm trees in cracked clay pots and patches of bright green grass, one per apartment, each with its own sprinkler whirring away. Nothing else moves. The pool is smaller than it sounded on the phone.

Dad throws our duffels and books into his empty extra bedroom beside the sleeping bags he borrowed for us. I explore the tiny balcony baking in the California sun while Finny assesses the fridge. The balcony is 3 feet by 6 feet. A rusted hibachi sits on bricks at one end like an abandoned altar. Back inside, Finny slams the fridge. Guess we better go shopping, she says.

We gather back in the living room where Dad explains his temporary lack of employment and how he didn't want to ruin our first visit in a year by looking for a job. His time is ours, he says, spreading his arms expansively in a gesture I remember. So, Josh, how much money did your mother give you? he asks.

We pool our money on the old oak table from the Chicago family room. I have fifty dollars; Finny has thirty; Dad has twelve dollars and nineteen cents. As the coins plink down, the nineteen cents makes me feel guilty, but not guilty enough to mention the other fifty bucks in my back pocket or the twenty in Finny's new Madonna purse.

The money on the table comes to $92.19. Dad scoops it all into his hand and puts it in the pocket of his jogging pants. We head off to our first meal at Burger King—my favorite restaurant. There, Dad catches us up on his latest jobs and why they didn't work out. You have to be able to cut your losses, he says. Your mother's probably still teaching. Stuck in the same rut. Yeah, Finny says, she'll never quit. Later we shop for eggs, milk, ketchup, hamburger, and bread. Your mother still making that fancy food? he asks. I don't eat it, I tell him, rolling my eyes at the thought of shrimp curry, the coq au vin, the cold pasta salads that I'm gladly missing. I eat cereal, I say, and dump more ketchup on my fries.

Dad and I run three miles every morning while Finny stays in bed and reads *Playboy*. They have great interviews, Dad says. Before we run, he stretches out in front of a mirror, seriously bending, pulling, reaching. I do what he does right behind him in the mirror. He's in better shape than I am—except for losing a little hair. He asks if Mom is still fat and I say yes, that all her skirts have stretch waistbands. But, Finny says, expensive clothes hide it well. I add that her new husband probably doesn't notice because his nose is always in some book. Dad laughs; there are no books cluttering up his place.

Dad arranges for courts every day that his old club has extras—usually 6:00 a.m. or 11:00 at night. Dad plays Finny first, then me.

You keeping up your tennis? he asks. Pretty much, I say. Then I tell him about Mom's refusal to send me to tennis camp last summer, even though it would have guaranteed me first place on the team. Finny says that it's because she bought a new computer. Still got her priorities mixed up, Dad says.

We meet the girlfriends on different nights. Girlfriend Number One is closer to my age than his. She has great boobs and an overhead smash that in a couple of years would get me into college. We play doubles and go out for Burger King. Then we go to her place for a sleepover. Dad had packed our sleeping bags in the back of the car just in case. Girlfriend Number Two shows Finny how to make up her eyes with black eyeliner and colors like purple, plum, and apricot. She puts her lipstick on with a pencil. The next day they go out to the Hacienda Mall to have Finny's ears pierced. Finny comes back with two gold circles in each ear.

Girlfriend Number Three cooks real Chinese food and shows us how to use chopsticks. Her apartment complex has an exercise room next to the pool. We take turns jumping and falling and reclining and jumping up again. Working on our appetites, Dad says. We play hard and sleep late out here, Dad says. Your mom ever take time off? Just for Scrabble or chess, Finny says. But it's no fun 'cause she doesn't let anybody talk.

Dad has an invitation to move in with any of the three. So which one will it be? he asks later in the week when we are back at his place, sitting beside the empty pool that is being repainted. I vote for Number One and Finny votes for Number Two. But what do we do about Number Three? Dad asks. No doubt your mother would have some well-chosen words on the subject. Does she still talk most of the time with her hands on her hips? We both picture it and say yes.

Our grandmother calls from a little town north of LA. Finny figures out that the last time we saw Gram or Gramps was eight or nine years ago. I remember Skippy, their dog, a dachshund with scabby hair who wouldn't stop playing fetch. I remember the musical toilet seat that played "She'll Be Coming 'Round the Mountain."

Our grandmother tells Dad that she and Gramps won't be able to make it down from the mountains to see us this time but to say hello for them. We'll all get together at a big reunion next time for sure. He passes this along to us. To her he says: The kids are sooooo biggo. Mucho biggo. To us he says: Your grandmother wants to know if you get the letters and the cards she sends, or does your mother throw them away? I don't remember getting anything, Finny says. What's the name of the town they live in?

Before long it is time to pack. Finny searches the car for our plane tickets while I throw my clothes in a duffle, sniffing to decide what to wear home. It's time, because we have run out of clean clothes. There are a few things I can't find. Dad watches us pack. Can't your mother buy you enough clothes to make it through a week? Dad asks. He has an unending supply of jogging pants and tennis shoes. Mom makes us do laundry instead, I say. She goes nuts on Clorox, Spray 'n Wash, and Bounce. You name it and we learn to use it, Finny says.

We stop at Burger King on the way to the airport. I order double fries to get the football cards and pie. Hold it on the apple pie, Dad says, we're almost out of money. Finny keeps checking her makeup in her new Madonna compact. She's not so good with the pencil lipstick yet. I'm wearing a T-shirt from the Del Mar Tennis Club.

At the airport, Dad talks the woman at the security gate into letting him walk his only kids to the boarding area. She laughs us through. Dad's face is red, his voice husky. He asks if we missed our mother and we say no. He asks do you ever miss me and we say yes.

In Boston, it's raining and fog makes our plane late. We get a cab home. Mom is making curried shrimp and banana raita for dinner. She hugs us, and here it comes. Did you miss me? she asks. We say yes. She wipes Finny's lipstick off her cheek and steps back. What happened to your eyes? she asks Finny. You look like a raccoon. My stepfather glances up from his book and says Hello. He says Hello again, then goes back to where his finger marks his place.

Mom follows us to our bedrooms to collect the dirty clothes she is sure we came home with. So, how's your father doing? she asks. Finny tells her Dad is almost bald and wears jogging suits absolutely everywhere. He also wears his Princeton ring, I say. He lost the old ring at the beach last year and had to order another from Balfour.

So, what did you do in sunny California? Mom asks, hands on her hips. There isn't a book in the house, Finny says, just his old *Playboy*s. Went running, played tennis at cheap times like 6:00 a.m., I say. Did you see your grandparents? Mom asks. As usual they were too busy, Finny says. They're probably pissed we don't cash their piddly five-dollar Christmas and birthday checks, but I knew it was Grandma on the phone because Dad was talking baby talk. Mom giggles as if remembering. Any wedding plans? she asks. I say there seems to be more than one girlfriend, that one's only a few years older than me. Than I, Mom says. The other girlfriends are closer to your age, I tell her. He takes turns seeing them. It's Dad who calls them girls. Mom says, well, nothing's changed. My sister peers in the mirror at her earlobes and asks Mom to check them out. She's sure the holes are unevenly punched; one looks red and yucky. Mom goes close. "Jesus," she says. "You got a surgical procedure done at the mall."

Later Mom ladles out shrimp curry while I pour cereal into a bowl. Does your father have a job? she asks. Yeah, jogging's hard work, Finny says. She counts up the meals at Burger Kings, describes the fridge, empty except for ketchup. She tells Mom that once again we had to contribute our money to expenses because once again Dad doesn't have a job. But we didn't give him all the money this time, Finny says. If I can walk dogs, he can get a job. Fat chance, I say. I tell

Mom I didn't even ask him about sending me to tennis camp because I was afraid he'd suggest I leave my extra racquet there for him to use. Mom is putting two and two together with the past twenty years. Do you think we'll be able to count on any money for college? she asks. Not a chance, my sister says, but the next time we go out there we'll steal his car. I tell Mom, by then he probably won't even have a car.

Custody

The divorce lawyer tells me, "No problem." He doesn't mean there is no problem with my marriage and therefore I should stay married. He is smarter than that. He devotes the first five minutes of my appointment to letting me know how smart he is. He tells me he doesn't take on a woman client who wears a hat. Hats are trouble. That's how smart he is.

I do not ordinarily trust men so concerned with surface things, but he comes highly recommended. Moments before, on the sidewalk, just yards from his office, I lost my hat. It sailed across the avenue and I had to make a quick decision: How important is a hat? I let it go. Should I tell him?

Instead, we get down to particulars. I tell him my husband is a writer and we have been married two years. There are no children.

See. See what I mean? the lawyer says. No children: no problems with custody or visitation or child support, no messy false threats of child abuse. He says in terms of grounds, child abuse has replaced adultery. What we have to deal with here are assets, he says. He makes assets sound like a part of my anatomy. Make a list, he says. You know: the house, the car. He has a lined legal pad in front of him on his desk.

I am momentarily distracted to see a legal pad used for something legal.

So, what are the assets in question? he asks.

I tell him the house, the cars.

He breathes deeply as if gratifyingly dismayed that a writer with such a major minor reputation as my husband should have so few material possessions. It's simple, he says: You add the house, the car, your car, and divide by two. He openly looks at his watch.

Well, I tell him, it's not so simple. It's about my life, our lives. I include my husband's life to appear fair, though I don't envision it an asset. I tell the lawyer the last straw occurred two weeks ago. That's when I learned my husband wrote a story about the abortion I had when I was fourteen and published it in a prestigious journal that doesn't appear on newsstands. I explain how he read it at a reading before I knew it existed. That I could tell by his guilty look as he left the podium that he knew what he'd done.

What he'd done? the lawyer says.

In public, I say. He'd done it the same way a man might take a woman to a restaurant to break up with her and thereby avoid a scene involving her no-longer-seductive removal of clothes or her vengeful use of kitchen scissors.

The lawyer doodles to avoid a reply.

I say my husband was hoping to dazzle me with his images, his sensitive characterizations, his solicitous dedication. When all along he knew I was saving up the abortion story for when I write my own stories one day. Besides, I say, he wasn't the father. And since then I've found his notes for a story about the humane method my mother used to kill farm cats, a draft of a story about living in a house, my farmhouse, with not a single door, lists of my uncles' and cousins' names.

The lawyer isn't following this. I remember my hat. I might have saved us both trouble if I'd run after that hat and come here with it planted on my head.

Put yourself in my place, I say. Try to put yourself in my place.

At fourteen, the lawyer says, risking eye contact. OK. I'm pregnant at fourteen.

No, now, I say.

You're pregnant? the lawyer asks, his eyes skimming my waist.

No, I'm not pregnant, I say. It is amazing how dumb men can make you feel as vulnerable as smart men. I tell him, put yourself in my place; I say, pretend you are an aspiring writer.

OK. I'm an aspiring writer, the lawyer says, leaning back in his chair as if thanking the lord he is not. I'm an aspiring writer and I'm pregnant, he says.

I sigh. Let's start over, I say.

He turns the page on his legal pad.

Now, let's say you had a drug problem at fourteen.

I must have hit home because he looks uncomfortable and snaps to an upright posture.

Say you had a drug problem at fourteen and now you're forty-five. I give him the benefit of five years. You've kicked the drug problem, I say. You write stories, your wife writes stories, and one day she writes your story. It gets published in *Esquire*, the story of you at fourteen with a drug problem.

I get it. I get it, the lawyer says. But where does that leave us—or rather you, he asks. I don't see libel here. I don't see malicious intent.

He's stealing my life, I say. Don't you see? He's using something that belongs to me. After all, it's my material. "Assets" would be your word.

It's not exactly the family silver, the lawyer says.

Exactly, I say leaning forward. It's much more valuable. Listen to this: I was born in the South. I learned to read in our outhouse from a Sears catalogue. A mall was built across the road from our pig farm. I was one of the first people in this country to see a mall.

My mother worked at Kmart till 7-Eleven bought out the pig farm. When I was thirteen, we moved to New York City, where my father abandoned us for Seagram's Seven Crown and the counter girl at Chock full o'Nuts.

There's more, I say. I was the oldest of seven brothers and sisters named Mo, Fayjean, Fester, Wilmer, and Quinn. My twin sister was Star and I was Starlight. She and I used to take the subway to Greenwich Village and shoot up while wearing fingerless black wool gloves. I tell him, I know death. Star was buried in those gloves.

The lawyer is listening now.

I tell him an English teacher took an interest in me and taught me everything he knew in the high school supply room. He took credit for my SAT scores and scholarship to Radcliffe; I gave him credit for my first sexually transmitted disease.

I describe one of my brothers who is doing time for armed robbery and another brother who holds a chair at MIT and communicates only by computer. I tell him how I hit Europe so hard I skipped over it and landed in India. I tell him I've been a cab driver in Israel and a nun in Burma. I omit that my first husband was a count because Americans, especially lawyers, are so impressionable. I tell him I met my current husband on a tramp steamer out of Australia. It was the calmest two months of my life and, my husband later admitted, his most exciting. I say this should have been a clue. I lie to the lawyer a little, tone things down. Most lawyers have unfinished novels in their bottom drawers.

So he knows all this? the lawyer asks.

Most of it. You don't know someone until you know all about them, I say. It comes after "You show me yours and I'll show you mine."

Whatever happened to imagination? the lawyer asks.

I shrug and treat it as a rhetorical question.

So tell your husband to stick to his own life.

I tell him about my husband's life. I describe the intact happy marriage of his parents, Fred and Norma; his sister Jennifer and brother John, a teacher and a doctor, respectively; the dog, McDuff—Sam, the cat; the midwestern schools from kindergarten to Ohio State. Band practice. Debate team. Student government. I say, Lord knows why he became a writer. I say, I suspect my husband of marrying me for my life. And now he thinks he owns it.

So you want a divorce, the lawyer says.

I need protection, I say. When my husband and I first met, he'd say more, more, tell me more. Sooner or later, he'll know everything. I tell the lawyer, I've had it. I tell him I want custody. I want it all back. My life.

New Family Car

A snow day for Steffie's high school and my car's transmission problems have marooned us inside, unexpectedly together. Steff and her friends are sprawled on beanbag chairs in the adjacent dining room, which has no dining table, only audio equipment, an Exercycle, and books. I can see them—five in all—through the archway across from where I'm stretched out on the couch grading freshman comp papers. Two pizzas are baking in the oven. One with anchovies, one without.

I'm still in my bathrobe, no bra, even though it is late afternoon and soon I'll have to turn on a light. A cup of cold tea beside me on the floor makes me want a glass of white wine. The comp papers are weighing flat and heavy on my chest, along with the news that Andy is moving out. I haven't yet told Steffie, or her brother, Greg, a sophomore at Brown.

Their voices come to me like a radio at low volume—white noise—till I hear Zack ask Becka, "So, where are your parents?" Since when did kids care where their parents were—except to decide at whose house to throw the all-night party? Now I'm listening in.

"Mom's here. Dad's in LA," Becka tells him. She is the new drummer in the band Zack's putting together for the third time. Steffie

says their gigs have increased since she joined up. Zack is Steffie's
boyfriend.

"No shit! LA," he says.

"You can have it," Becka says. "It's mostly hot pavement, cars,
and smog."

"Don't you ever go back?" Taj asks. ("Taj as in Taj Mahal," Steffie
told me.) Taj is their songwriter and singer—vocalist, they call her.
Steffie is French braiding Taj's long blond hair, something she seldom does for me. I watch the fat braid curve slowly over the crown
of Taj's head. "You know," Taj prompts. "Go out to see your dad?"

Becka shakes her mowed head. She has a half-inch growth of
auburn hair under an equally short lawn of matte black. Not one of
her six earrings has a mate. She tells them her dad has this two-year-
old kid and treats Becka like a babysitter. "As soon as I arrive, he
and Vivian whip out a list of new restaurants they want to try. One
night they came back stoned and he told Vivian to drive me home
like I was some sitter from their neighborhood. I don't even know
how I'm related to the kid: first he married this woman—after di-
vorcing Mom—and they fought all the time. Then they got divorced.
Then they had a kid. They're still divorced, but now they're living
together again. You tell me."

"You have a half-sister," Zack says, cradling his guitar. "Thank
God my parents got divorced and stayed that way. But Dad still rants
and raves about Mom all the time. I agree to shut him up. He says
she buys purses like Marcos's wife bought shoes. Once he asked me
to actually count them."

"That's really sick," Steffie says. She goes over to Zack and kneads
her fingers in his curly hair. He reaches up and pulls her in close for
a kiss.

Please keep it light, I think, and turn my head to watch the snow
swirling heavily against the windows, no pattern to its falling. Andy

is probably in his new apartment assembling bookshelves, cutting shelf paper, and making room for his share of dishes, pots and pans.

"You gotta shut them down sometimes," Franco says. He's a lanky kid with a black Mohawk, the band's leader. "I hold up my hand and say, 'Hey, Mom. I've heard it before.'" He scratches his Mohawk with a pencil—it resembles Taj's braid. He says his father used to drink straight vodka from a brown coffee mug. "I give him credit for going off the booze, but now he's cheating on the new wife just like he did on Mom. She's dumb for sticking around. But, hey, I'm not going to get involved."

Involved, I think. *Franco, my boy, you are involved.* I remember crying to a friend that we're traumatizing our kids with all these divorces and recouplings, and he said, No, we're just giving them emotional information.

Becka is talking. She says the problem is you never know how to treat stepparents. "Vivian insists on playing serious makeup with me—waxing, mud packs, manicures. Last time there I told her what she really needs is a two-tone punk cut like mine. Now she doesn't bug me anymore."

Zack rolls his eyes in sympathy and says his father was living for a while with an old high school girlfriend named Jeanette who'd named her daughters Lynnette and Fayette. "I told her if she had a son she could name him Crockette. She didn't think it was funny. 'Funny' to them is this game they play at dinner." Zack puts down his guitar to demonstrate. "First night I'm there, Fayette burps and suddenly everbody's laughing and pointing at me. I look around the table and they're all sitting with a thumb poking into their foreheads. 'You're last,' Lynnette said. 'That means you have to eat it.'" Zack burps and I watch him smash his thumb against his forehead. "I refused to play," Zack says. "I 'ate' it every time. Dad finally smartened up and moved out."

"Gross." Steffie pauses in her braiding, her hands holding the blonde strands of Taj's hair like reins. She says she remembers when Andy moved in. I close my eyes, not sure I can take it. She says, "Suddenly there was this stranger in the bathroom trimming his toenails. I could hear it in my bedroom two doors away. His tennis shoes smell like rotten eggs."

She's right. Andy's tennis shoes reek. He used to count on me to tell him when to buy new ones. I haven't had the nerve to do that for a while. And he hasn't suggested I take off a little weight either. Unexpectedly, tears well up in my eyes and I need to blow my nose, but that would expose my couch-cover, so I turn my face into the cushion and sniff softly and fast.

"You think you got it bad," Franco says. "My mom's living in a humongous loft with this painter who's ten years younger. He listens to the Grateful Dead all day and cooks in an old black wok—it all tastes like fried shrimp. When I sleep over this guy borrows my clothes. I wake up late and there he is, painting in my shirt or jeans." He points to purple and black splotches on his Levis.

"At least you don't have to live there full time," Zack says. "Anyway, it probably won't last."

I force myself to read an essay on a pet raccoon for the third time. It's no competition for these kids.

"Trouble is those divorces really mess up the photograph albums," Steffie says. My pen freezes on the page and here it comes. "Mom butchered ours. There's only two pictures left of Dad in all twelve albums."

The albums are numbered and lined up on the shelf beside the fireplace. I'd always wondered if Steffie or Greg noticed—heads missing, hands emerging from uneven borders.

But Steffie isn't finished. She goes on to reveal how her father and I had to get married. Uncharacteristically, I'm speechless as she continues, "Dumb, but that's what you did in Mom's day if you got pregnant."

"No wonder they got divorced," Becka says. "Why didn't she get an abortion?"

"Wasn't legal. And anyway, you're talking about my brother, Greg. He's at school," Steffie says, giving Taj's head a hard push.

Taj's shoulders shrug. "My father could have arranged it—even back then."

What's he do, Becka wants to know. Me too.

"He was a dealer. Dead now," Taj says, her tone matter-of-fact as she describes his sudden heart attack in St. Bart's. Zack says to tell Becka the rest of it. He must have heard this story before because, having ushered it in, he leaves to check on the pizzas.

"When I was six, Dad got me every other weekend. Used to take me on drug deals—said I was good luck." Taj pats down the length of her braid to see how far it's done. Then she recounts how she helped him weigh stuff out on special scales—back then it was grass. "We put it in baggies and tied it with those wire things. He died before they invented Ziploc bags." She describes Saturdays, their big days, how first they checked in at the zoo to see the bears or lions, or a hallway of snakes—to give her something to tell her mother. Then they'd go make deliveries. 1 picture a little girl sobbing as she is dragged away from giraffes, elephants, monkeys. There's the song Taj should write.

Steffie winds a rubber band around the end of Taj's braid and flips it over her shoulder. Then she drops down next to Zack. The beans in the chair crunch and shift. "So who's the guy answering the phone in such a sexy voice?" she asks Taj.

"*Guys*. But Mom swears she's not getting married again. One moved in a week ago—the guy on the phone—I mean it's not exactly a revolving door or anything. They're OK. Once this guy came on to me and I told Mom and he was gone that same night."

"Pervert," Steffie and Becka say in unison.

"Mom's bottom line is they have to have a job. She says it keeps them busy."

"My dad's had seven jobs in the last three years," Steffie says. "They don't last longer than two weeks. You meet him and he mentions Yale in the first twenty minutes. Mom said it was all downhill after Yale. She said—"

"Stephanie! Goddamn it, that's enough," I yell, throwing the comp papers on the floor and sitting up. "At least I never told you how low that hill was to begin with."

No one says a word. But they're all looking at me like I'm the evening news. I tighten the belt to my bathrobe, wishing I'd put on underwear and combed my hair. Where did they think I was anyway? Taking a goddamn bubble bath? I search for my flip-flops and stand up. "You ought to be doing homework, or out there shoveling walks, not sitting around here—"

"Mo-om," Steffie says. She gives Zack a push and tells him to check out the pizzas again.

No one is looking at me now—the destroyer of photographs. What would they do if I announced, "Yeah, well, another thing: Andy and I are splitting up. He's taking his tennis shoes with him. We won't have Andy's old toenails to step on anymore." Would Franco shrug and say, "Hey, these things happen?" I mean, how cool can these kids be?

"Come and get it," Zack calls from the kitchen and slams the oven door. They exit fast. I marvel at their appetites.

*   *   *

At midnight, the comp papers are finished and I'm in bed with a book, waiting for Steffie to get back from Zack's house, where they fled after the pizza. Greg hasn't come in yet, so I missed the chance to rehearse my eleventh-hour news. I refuse to let my ears imagine what Steffie will tell her brother tomorrow.

Outside, the snow stopped as the temperature fell, and now, outlined with lacy frost, the small windowpanes have become black valentines. Boxes of Andy's books and papers, three overflowing duffels, and a mountain of shoes tug at my peripheral vision. He's coming early tomorrow to move his things out and say good-bye to Steffie. But I need to tell her first.

It's close to one when I hear her coming up the stairs. Angry with relief, I pull on my robe and go down the hall to her room.

"What are you doing up so late?" she asks. Expertly, she crosses her arms in front of her and pulls the red sweater over her head in one movement. Her long hair swings free.

I sit down on the other twin bed, and my first words surprise me. "Jesus. Did you need to tell them your father and I had to get married?"

"Yeah, you're right," Steffie says. "I guess I said too much, huh?" She turns her back to slide her bra around and pulls on a red nightshirt. Then she lifts her quilt and flops into bed. The wool quilt, made by my grandmother, is almost in tatters but she refuses to sleep with anything else. Her eyes are closed as she says, "I'm sorry, Mom." A little too easy. "They won't remember." And definitely too cool.

"Don't give me that shit," I say, reaching over to yank her pillow hard from under her head the way magicians separate tablecloths from plates.

Steffie jerks up onto her elbow and clutches the quilt to her chest. "What are you doing? What the fuck is wrong?"

"I'm trying to talk to you," I say.

"But it's one in the morning. Can't it wait? Where's Andy?"

I tell her then. In a calmer voice I say that last night Andy and I agreed to split up—that he'd be coming over tomorrow morning to officially move out. To say good-bye to her.

"Oh, shit," she says, rolling her glistening eyes.

"What do you mean 'Oh, shit?'"

"I mean I'll miss him," she says. Tears are running down her cheeks, darkening her freckles. "I mean he was OK."

"Give me a break," I yell. "First you complain about him and now he's a saint."

"That bad, huh?" she says.

I nod and hug the pillow I swiped from her. "You've probably overheard enough to know what happened."

"Yeah, I guess it's been coming."

My mouth quivers as I say, "But you don't have to make a big deal about it. I mean you don't have to announce it to your friends—'Hey guys, no more smelly tennis shoes,' like you did this afternoon."

Steffie points her finger at me. "You were spying on us."

"I was not. I was grading papers in the living room. I was hearing you talk—there's a difference. And 1 don't like my life paraded around in front of a bunch of kids."

"You forget. It's my life, too," Steffie says, lurching up. She grabs her pillow back and squashes it to her chest. "You ever think of that? Did you and Dad ever once think of that? Of me and Greg and what we were going through?" She buries her face in her pillow, and her hair cascades forward as I move across to sit on her bed. I hug her hard and soon her fingers are pressing and smoothing the soft chenille ridges of my robe where she holds my shoulders.

"Oh, Steffie, we agonized over what it would do to you and Greg. Endlessly. Andy and I talked about it, too. It isn't like we didn't try— for you." My voice is rising, catching as it soars, but I can't stop. "I know that's not what you and your friends think, complaining about half-sisters and boyfriends and stepparents. You think you'd be better off if your father and I had stayed together."

"What's the matter with that?" Steffie says, pulling back and glaring.

"Because it wouldn't have been true," I say.

"But that—doesn't—help!" she hiccoughs, her chin trembling. "Don't you see?"

"So why do you have to talk about it?" I ask.

"Oh. So that's it," she says. "You're still thinking 'What will people say?' Jesus, Mom. If you're going to listen in, you have to lighten up."

"But it's like—it's like you and your friends are playing games."

"Games!" Steffie's eyebrows, tiny arcs, rise.

"You're playing—I don't know." I shake my head—somehow it is all so familiar, and then I do know. "You're playing 'my-family's-more-fucked-up-than-your-family.'"

Steffie's shoulders quiver and suddenly she's laughing hysterically, wiping her face with both hands. "That's funny, Mom. That's really funny."

"It is not. It's how we used to one-up friends. Only we did it with the number of bathrooms we had, or who went on vacations to Niagara Falls—or whose family had a new car. No one ever had two cars."

"So what?" Steffie says. "So now it's fucked-up families." Then she grins. "You're lucky Greg and I don't flunk out of school, do crack or get a body piercing, or join the Hare Krishnas. Besides, some kids can't play—they have dumb happy homes. Their parents have been married for twenty-seven years and they go to church on Sunday and in summer they trot off to family reunions two states away. Like NOT having a new car was for you twenty-five years ago. I mean what are these kids going to say? Nothing. So they don't get to play." She tugs open the shallow drawer in her nightstand and fishes around. "Here. You want to see something?"

I can't imagine what.

She pulls out a smudged envelope and empties it onto the quilt between us. "See. I saved all those pieces of Dad. So that wasn't a big deal either." And there they are, ragged photographs of my first husband—small glossy heads, square torsos, bits of me. She stirs the pieces around with a wet finger.

"Oh, Steffie, I wish—"

"No. Stop. You're right. It's better this way." She scoops her dad up and dumps him back into the envelope. We're all still in pieces. "Andy, too," she says. "You going to operate on him?"

Our laughs are damp and giddy. Then I lean over her to smooth her shining eyebrows, kiss her wet cheeks and bangs. She puts her arms up to hold me for a moment, then she lets me go. I tell her I love her. When I turn off the light, her windows sparkle with the same black lacy valentines. They'll be white by morning.

"Hey, Mom," she calls out from the dark, her voice still offering too small, small comfort. "So maybe it is a game, so what? At least I didn't win."

The Real Story

It starts simply enough when the son, back home from a volunteer job with Vietnamese refugees, discovers that he has become a minor character in one of his father's novels. In Chapter Ten the "son" returns from the "Peace Corps," sleeps a lot, and makes exits and entrances talking of El Salvador rebels, not Vietnamese refugees.

"So this is how real people and places are transformed into fiction," the young man says to his father after reading the father's manuscript. They are in the father's downstairs study.

"Real? One never knows another human being that well," his father says. "Characters are always composites, acts of the author's imagination." He leans back in his chair, closing the subject.

Nevertheless, the son determines to read more of his parents' work.

*　*　*

His parents' library and files are illuminating. He discovers he has lived with them in fiction, in various permutations, for a long time. Perhaps he too is a writer. The cleaning woman seems cheered to have him home again and helps him clear out the storage space over the garage.

There he sets up shop.

The first story he writes is about a son who returns from the Vietnam War to discover that his parents, both writers, have used material from his letters, from his life—the mother in stories and the father in a novel.

"But we wouldn't do something like that," his parents say when he shows them his manuscript for comment. "How could you write such a thing?"

The parents follow the son to his study over the garage, where they all sit on orange crates. The son begins addressing SASEs.

"You wrote about a kid who thinks the laundry is washed in the laundry chute," he accuses the mother.

"But it was so funny," she says, trying not to smile.

"And there's a son in your latest novel who gets three graduate degrees before deciding he wants to be a garlic farmer."

"You're not a garlic farmer," his father says.

"Maybe you should be a poet," his mother says.

*   *   *

The mother's next story is about a brilliant young poet who writes mystically about nature and its life cycles, yet refuses to "examine" his two years in Vietnam. Critics wait expectantly for a decade. Finally, as the poet is dying of something related to Agent Orange, it is revealed that he has been writing about the Vietnam War ever since he returned. But he wrote only on the walls of buildings, the seats of subway trains, the tiles of public bathrooms.

Instantly, scholars find themselves with a new terrain. Bespectacled, bearded young men and lank-haired young women armed with Nikons begin the task of gathering his epic "graffiti" poem. Each "line" is numbered. He used black spray paint and a red magic marker. The scrawled lines are spotted in Albuquerque, Peoria, Memphis; he has been everywhere, even Bangor, Maine. His biographer waits at his bedside and not in vain. "I ended with number 352," are the poet's last words. The hunt intensifies. Female scholars claim discrimination and demand escorts into the men's johns. This indignity ends the mother's story.

The son is angry. "Just because I haven't written about Vietnam yet doesn't mean I'm not going to," he says to his mother in her study, where her black Underwood sits quaintly on an old sewing machine.

"Of course you will write about Vietnam," his mother says. "But you had such a normal childhood. My poet is an orphan."

*   *   *

"A Normal Childhood," the son's next story, tells of a young boy of nine who reads his mother's journals. One journal indirectly recounts a series of affairs she has while he is growing up, all with men closely associated with his father: his dissertation adviser, his squash partner, his dentist, his star graduate student. But the writing in her journal is so oblique that it isn't until the boy has his first sexual experience that he knows his mother's "friends" were actually her lovers. He has come of age.

The story is accepted immediately by his father's old editor.

His parents open a bottle of Veuve Clicquot to celebrate their son's first publication. Even the cleaning woman is given a glass. But later that night the son overhears the mother angrily assert that since she didn't have any affairs, their son must be writing about his father. She asks her husband if, in addition to having affairs, he also wrote about them in a journal for the scrutiny of future biographers.

"You know I think journal writing depletes creative energy," the husband says as he undresses.

"Affairs don't!" she says.

Her husband ignores this and, shaking his head, says, "That kid. Didn't he write a great sexual awakening scene."

* * *

So: the wife writes a story about a woman who understands her husband's sexual inadequacies only after she finally meets his mother, who chatters about the unusual methods of discipline she employed to stop her son from wetting his bed. The mother-in-law enjoys telling how she dressed him up as a little girl and sent him out on the front porch for all the neighbors to see (those she had also alerted by phone).

When the wife's story is published the husband storms into his wife's study, pounds on her Underwood. "I resent you using painful details from my childhood!"

"But after all the affairs you've had, no one could possibly think the man with the sexual problems is you," his wife says, already at work on another story. (She writes them in two to four hours, which makes both her husband and son nervous when they compare the day's output at dinner. But, she reminds them, she works on her stories for weeks, months after. Rewriting is writing.) "As for the details from your childhood. Your mother, thank God, lives in New Mexico and never reads a thing."

* * *

In the husband's next story, his first in several years, a man is married to a woman who suspects him of having affairs. He is innocent, of course, which the reader also knows, but the increasingly distraught and suspicious wife proceeds to become a master domestic spy. She draws up elaborate charts and graphs for his meetings, his conferences, his out-of-town trips. She charts gas receipts, restaurant checks, long distance calls. These "clues" are color-coded by both paper and ink and require long hours to assemble. Soon the wife begins to think of them as works of art. A select committee at the Museum of Contemporary Art actually admits a chart titled "Infidelity #4" to a juried exhibit. Finally, in the story's cataclysmic scene, the wife is confronted by a museum guard as she is adding another name, "Felicia," to the collage.

"Why don't you stick with novels," the wife says, barging into her husband's study, an open *New Yorker* in her hand. He whispers into the phone and quickly hangs up but she ignores this. She points to the thin shiny column of prose. "How dare you. Until I learned to tolerate your affairs, drawing up those charts kept me away from my work for two whole years."

"It was a detail I simply could not resist. There are such details I've discovered," the husband sheepishly admits. "Besides, friends know you're not crazy."

"Your affairs are real enough," the wife says.

"True," the husband says, "But only your psychiatrist saw your charts."

*   *   *

The psychiatrist is a closet writer with three novels in his bottom drawer. He plans to use a pseudonym, not because he might be breaking his Hippocratic Oath by revealing his patients' secrets (which he is), but because he doesn't want to disturb his patients' progress by introducing a personal side of himself into their lives. In fact, he has an irresistible temptation to write about a wife's— no, he changes it—a husband's elaborate system of charting the suspected course of his wife's affairs as if they were stock market fluctuations. It rings familiar. Commodities? No. He makes the husband an oil tycoon obsessed with fat phallic oil wells (now who designed them?). The oil wells appear as blue pushpins on his eight-color top-ographic map of Texas. Red pushpins represent his wife's gas receipts, her Platinum American Express bills, her extended visits to the ranches of rich Texan relatives. (Alliteration pleases the psychiatrist.) Finally he has his secretary type up a copy of his manuscript, then he calls a patient who is a writer (the free association of this escapes him) and asks for the name of her agent.

*   *   *

"Jesus, my shrink called me for an agent," the mother complains to a friend. "He says he's beginning to write fiction." She cancels future appointments, risking writer's block, but her anger has energy.

Consequently, her next story is about an analyst whose most stimulating patient is a writer of stories that appear in *Esquire*, the *Atlantic, Playboy*. Soon this writer realizes that the analyst is not treating him but rather his characters—the flat ones on some glossy page. In their sessions, the analyst asks the writer to explain: why a father reveals a daughter's real mother to be an aunt the daughter loathes; why a woman creates a second set of journals when she suspects her husband is reading the first; why a criminal, given a new identity through the government's Witness Protection Program, leaves clues as to who and where he is, even though it means certain death. "Where do these stories come from?" the analyst in the story asks. Bored, his writer-patient retaliates by writing a story about a patient who seduces her gullible analyst with her flair for silly plots and outrageous metaphors, bringing about his downfall. After "The Coaching Couch" appears, the writer and analyst agree to part ways.

The mother mails this story off to her agent. Writing is therapy!

*   *   *

The son's next stories are about: a mother who reveals a son's real father to be an uncle the son has always hated; a husband who keeps a second set of journals when he suspects his wife is reading the first; a woman spy who, given a new identity under the government's Witness Protection Program, leaves clues as to who and where she is, even though it means certain death.

"Those are my stories," his mother accuses.

In defense, the son says he read that a young Algerian woman recently wrote to Doris Lessing and asked if she could write Paul's novel, whose first line is given to him by Anna Wolfe in *The Golden Notebook*, and Lessing said yes.

"But you didn't ask me," the mother persists, although she is secretly mollified by his comparison of her with Lessing. She is even more pleased when the stories appear in a magazine that has been turning down her husband's latest work.

*   *   *

Flushed with success, the son buys a computer and gives his old typewriter away. Now the most prolific member of his family (he doesn't have children yet), he writes a story about an artist, a son of well-known artists, who finally confronts what it meant to grow up in their shadow, of needing to find his own light.

"Good image," his father says, "but I wonder if your artist's career would have taken off so smartly if he hadn't used the family name."

Furious, the son locks himself into his garret over the garage and pours out a story in which a dying composer accuses his son of trading on his father's name in order to get his own, less accomplished concertos performed.

"What will people think?" his father rants and raves. (Clichés are true, the son has discovered, but you still can't use them.) "I mean, what kind of father would say a thing like that?"

"You tell me," the son says.

"But you're the one who wrote it," the father says. "Stories demand motivation, consistent behavior. Real people aren't held accountable for what they say, but characters are. Besides, once this story comes out I'll be besieged by reporters' morbid phone calls, neighbors' discreet condolences for an illness you neglect to name."

"But the father has to be dying," the son says. "Why else would a father say a thing like that—accusing the son of using his name?" Suddenly he looks at his father with curiosity—and false enlightenment.

"No. I am not dying," his father says. "The answer is 'no.'"

*   *   *

But it makes the father think. In the next five weeks the father finds a new well of creative energy and begins to write brutally honest memoirs of his childhood, his teenage years, his marriage, and his lovers. He loves his son, his wife, but he loves immortality more. He will preempt the biographers, the biased memoirs of a wife and son, by telling more than any son or wife could ever imagine. All his life he wrote fiction in order to tell the truth, but now he will write the truth to avoid becoming a fiction.

He retreats to his study. He allows his latest affair to wither and instructs the cleaning woman to screen his calls. The son must do his own editing; his wife has stories of her own to write. Furthermore, he forbids the cleaning woman to disturb a thing. "Come to think of it," the husband tells her, "You needn't clean my study again at all."

*   *   *

The cleaning woman, of course, takes offense. She has also been taking notes for years, ever since she overheard some writer ask on *All*

Things Considered "Why aren't there any novels by cleaning women?" She's ready to quit. They have ceased to surprise her, this quasi-famous family (her vocabulary has improved while cleaning their toilets, changing their sheets, baking their casseroles). She has enough material: habits, plots, dialogue; the charts and graphs of adultery; the son's letters from Southeast Asia; the husband's wimpy affairs; the mother's line—"My shrink called me for an agent." She tells her new employer she wants to work part-time because she has other things to accomplish. Somehow, and truth is stranger than fiction, she finds a job with a psychiatrist who fancies himself a writer and has all the books on technique—books the famous family used to ridicule. She makes sure before taking the job that he never locks his files. There is an efficiency about all this the Missus used to accuse her of lacking. But she feels efficient now as she assembles her cast of characters. Heavily into symbols, she begins her saga by recalling a story Robert Graves told of the Scilly Isles, a place that had no industry and where the people had to make do by taking in each other's laundry. An island setting appeals to her. Three famous writers all live under one red-tiled roof, in a white stucco house overlooking a cerulean sea. Mother, father, son—and, of course, the cleaning woman. It will be a roman à clef. She types on an old typewriter the family gave her, gave her the way folks always give things to the help.

The Bridge

A bicycle whizzes past her from behind just as she steps onto the pedestrian walkway of the bridge. It startles her. It also startles a young woman who is walking slowly fifty feet ahead of her, cradling a bundle of something—a potted plant, flowers, a baby—she can't tell what. Belatedly, she has the impulse to call something nasty to the young man on the bicycle, but he is moving away too fast, head low, legs pumping hard. Anyway, the young woman must have said something to him, because he swings his head around to her, slowing down just slightly, before he zooms away, more dangerous than ever. He could have injured them both. The mother and the baby. Or crushed the flowers.

*   *   *

She carries her purse slung over her shoulder on a long strap and in her left hand a bag of groceries—no jars or cans to make it heavy. English muffins, tea, two lamb chops, a bottle of red wine, a ripe cantaloupe. The wind from the bay is brisk, cool. Below and behind the bridge, the ribbon of water reflects the fall's gray-white sky. She stops to button her jacket, wrap her scarf smartly around her neck.

The scarf matches her skirt, which pleases her. The young woman ahead has also stopped. She doesn't know why she says "young woman" because she might be a grandmother out for a stroll or a volunteer for the elderly on her way with bright flowers and a lot to say. Squinting the young woman into sharper focus brings no more illuminating details than a scarf that matches nothing else she wears. She has changed the bundle from her left to right arm.

If she catches up to the young woman, and if there is a child bundled into a blanket, perhaps they might talk for part of their trip across the long bridge. For instance, they might exclaim about the rudeness of the boy on the bicycle. Or she will smile at the baby, admire its hair or eyes or nose, or if nothing warrants, the charm of children. "How old?" she might ask. "Is it a boy or girl?" "The name?" Or perhaps "What lovely flowers," although she can imagine that people might not respond to this beyond a polite murmur of agreement and downcast eyes. Perhaps because they have nothing to do with making flowers.

*   *   *

Ahead of her the young woman stops again and leans over the heavy iron railing of the bridge. The young woman is looking down into the water as if something has caught her eye, something worth the pause. She, too, stops, torn between catching up to the young woman and wanting to see what holds her interest in the water. She sets her grocery bag down between her feet and peers over the shoulder-high railing into the river below the young woman. There are no barges or colorful sailing boats, no sightseeing cruises with loud speakers blaring the bored voice of a guide. So what can it be? As she looks back up again, in a graceful curve as of a ballet gesture, the young woman throws her bundle over the side of the bridge.

*   *   *

She strains against the railing and tries to guess the weight of it, the drift of flowers or the downward spiral of a helpless infant, but she cannot. It lands with a soft plop (like a tire puncture), floats an instant then disappears with tiny bubbles. Paper of the kind from a florist's long roll or a small square of blanket drifts past the original spot until it too has gathered enough water to sink. There has been no color, only white paper around flowers, or a baby's white blanket.

She screams, whirling around to passing cars, but they are traveling by too swiftly. She turns back to the young woman, turns toward the young woman whose coat is blowing open in the breeze. She realizes immediately that if it was—or rather—is a baby, what would be the difference? Would she throw down her groceries, tear off her jacket and scarf, leaving them draped over the railing, kick off her shoes? Would she call to anyone to witness her leap, even the young mother who now stands motionless, her arms withdrawn from the graceful arc of her throw? And then, after the climb onto the iron railing higher than it looks, the leap into the water? The cold, high shock of the water. Even now, half-believing, something has died in her. She does not jump.

*   *   *

She hurries toward the young woman, heels clicking like a mugger sure of his prey and silence no longer necessary. She half expects the young woman to hear her footsteps, turn toward her, and then run. Another bicycle passes and she wants to cry out, send for help, but she can't find the words. What can she tell even her husband later, as they sit with a glass of wine and watch the news? She glances again at the darkening river, scraping her elbow as she continues to run. Her scarf streams behind her. And below, a large camellia floats on the water where the bundle was dropped, or a small baby's bonnet, white and scalloped. She runs on, the sack of groceries banging against her legs, bruising the cantaloupe. "I was watching," she calls out to the young woman, breathless. "I was standing over there." Pointing, she tries to determine just how far away she was but can't identify her precise place along the stark railing of the bridge.

The young woman turns but doesn't run. Together they stare at the place where she stood on the bridge. The young woman's face is smooth and shiny like a plate and, yes, young. Her eyes are gray as the water and she raises them to the sky as if looking for signs of changing weather. Her hands fill her pockets, her arms are tight against her sides where a bundle was. Is she used to strangers talking to her, calling breathless from fifteen, ten feet away? She herself isn't used to watching babies being thrown into the river, or even flowers. There is a story in flowers, too, although a far different tale, probably romantic and full of meaningless gestures, predictable details. But what happened? There is a new emptiness inside her. What must there be in this young woman whose life has changed by the crossing of a bridge in fall. "I saw you throw something into the river," she tells her.

*   *   *

The young woman seems to consider everything, then says, "I heard you call out. Are you all right?" as she pulls her coat closer about her, ties up her scarf. The young woman continues, "I think it is going to rain again. It's ruined everything I planned." The grocery bag feels heavy and she sets it down as if it contains quarts of heavy, rich milk. "What was it?" she asks the young woman. "What did you throw into the river?" The young woman seems to think that the question does not refer to specific things like flowers or babies as she glances at the bag of groceries—perhaps wondering if she should offer to carry it, or making a list of what she herself needs from the store. "I must go," she says, putting her hands in her pockets again, and she goes.

She watches the young woman once more recede into the distance. In her wake, Cambridge neon begins to breathe above the gray water. The T thunders past her on its short sojourn across the bridge outside the tunnel. How much does a baby weigh? She stoops down and moves aside English muffins, the wine. Then she hefts the cantaloupe before lifting it out with both hands. She tries to palm it like a basketball but can't suspend it in one hand. And so, as she holds on with one hand to the railing of the bridge, she pulls her arm back over her shoulder, her hand under the ripe fruit. Lacking the grace of the young woman's motion, she heaves it like a catapult out into the river. She tries to remember the soft plop of entry, and failing that, she listens for a cry.

The Second Night
of a One-Night Stand

Margo Ainsley was hoping to find a place like Mercer's—a small-town bar where regulars drink cold beer on sweltering afternoons and the home team wins in the bottom of the ninth. Today the Pirates were striking out at low volume on a color TV angled high above a vintage jukebox. The bartender wore a blue work shirt with *Mercer's* stitched on the pocket, and his longish hair was combed straight back from a high forehead. Arms crossed like he owned the place, which he did, he leaned against a shelf of serious-looking bottles, talking to a man in a leather carpenter's belt, a hammer hanging straight down like a plumb line. Margo hitched up onto a stool a few seats away, put her elbows on the bar, and ordered a draft.

She had learned the etiquette of small-town bars while bartending during college. That was fifteen years ago, the early sixties, but the blinking Schlitz sign, two sagging pool tables, and oiled wooden floors assured her nothing had changed. You start slow, especially if you're a woman and reasonably good-looking. You hitch onto a stool not too near the other customers and order a draft with your money ready. Then you listen to the talk around you. If it's private they'll keep it down. But chances are it will be something you can be an audience to. Something to take your mind off your own troubles—an ailing muffler, warring kids, an unfaithful husband—like Ben, back home, three states away.

Afternoons in a small town are the best time to meet the bartender. Watch while he sets up for the evening—restocking bottles, installing kegs, ordering up the bar food, but always ready to stop and talk. Like now with the carpenter. Margo listened in.

It seems that an old man had hired the carpenter to repair his picket fence, instructing him to "Pound that in a little harder. Straighten that post a quarter inch." The carpenter shrugged. "After the old man paid me, he said to pull the damn thing up and haul it off."

"Nah," Mercer said, his amused glance including Margo and another customer in a Mobil shirt.

"I got it fencing in my wife's tomatoes now." The carpenter's receding hairline had left a happy sprinkle of freckles in its wake.

"What happens when the old man drives by?" Mercer asked.

"I painted it green. Looks like it's always been there." He turned to Margo and shrugged. She smiled at the carpenter's ingenuity, and the picture of a green fence guarding a patch of red tomatoes. When she got up to leave, the bartender glanced her way. "See you," Margo said, and sure enough, he nodded. The carpenter, too.

In the car, she spread an old towel on the sweltering seat and headed out of town on the lake road, windows wide open to her need for air. She felt grateful for the men's notice, and cursed Ben for making her feel so vulnerable. Easing up on the gas, she forced herself to take in the landscape she used to love to paint. The gray lake road winding parallel to the uneven shore line, spanned by fields of purple grapes whose slender rows flashed by on either side, narrowing abruptly, point after point, to infinity. Farm stands selling wheelbarrows of unshucked sweet corn from adjacent fields, homemade plum jellies with handwritten, dated labels, and tangy warm tomatoes she could never find back home. But this was her home now—at least for the summer.

For the past few years she and Ben had been seeing a marriage counselor who advised her "Don't take Ben's affairs personally," assigning probable cause to his father's alcoholism and his mother's long, irritable illness. What made her crazy, though, made her doubt her love for him, were Ben's denials that he was having yet another affair. "It's in your mind," he'd say, with unwavering eyes, the same even gaze she'd found so erotically persuasive the first time they'd undressed each other. Then, months later, he'd confess his most recently ended affair—the last with the substitute French teacher at the high school where he was assistant principal. Margo had foolishly called the woman to say she knew about their pet names for each other, the woman's fling with an uncle in the rug business. The indignant woman had countered with "Did your husband also tell you he's screwing your college roommate?" Heartsick, Margo sat with the phone in her hand but found she couldn't face a second call. Even sick, the heart still empties and fills, and so she'd gone outside to question Ben. He'd been teetering high on a ten-foot ladder, belatedly putting up the summer screens. His shirttails flapped in the wind above tanned legs as straight and solid as boat oars. Margo stepped onto the first rung to yell over the drone of the neighbor's lawnmower, "God damn you. What if I had an affair with your college roommate?"

He looked down at her for a long moment and then said, "That wouldn't solve anything."

"Don't be too sure." Then, advising him not to "take it personally," she told him she and the kids were leaving for her summer cottage. Thank God school had ended three weeks earlier and she'd already ordered next fall's art supplies. Tears in his eyes, Ben watched her pack their honeymoon suitcases, pleading that it had only happened a few times. Judy meant nothing to him. "She once meant something to me," Margo said. Polly, six, and Sam, four, were young enough to trust her cheery strained announcement of their surprise vacation. Stricken, Ben stood in the driveway beside the rest of the screens, waving and calling out for them to have a good time. Grateful for sunglasses, she'd driven eleven hours straight from Chicago, across three midwestern states, stopping for junk food after the bananas and apples gave out. She almost turned back when she found herself worrying about Ben high on the ladder, balancing screens, missing her. Missing him, she babbled on about the summer cottage, the beach, the stones she'd painted as a child. Soon the kids were squealing, "How long before we're there?"

*   *   *

Margo's cottage stood in a row of seven scruffy cottages on a low bluff overlooking a troubled Lake Erie. Five belonged to aunts and uncles and the rusted key on her Niagara Falls key chain opened the back door of each. Every summer her family had driven north from Pittsburgh to Erie then turned east where the chimney of Pennsylvania reaches up to claim its sixty miles of Lake Erie coastline. Her father told people visiting for the first time, "Head east till you see 'Welcome to New York,' throw your car into neutral, take your foot off the gas, and you'll coast to a stop at the turn onto our beach road, right over the state line." In June, the mothers scrubbed and cleaned while the cousins carried messages from cottage to cottage. Fathers arrived on weekends, horns honking, in time for Friday's dinner and Saturday's naps. Sundays, they headed home again, foil-wrapped leftovers on the seat beside them. Weekdays, with only the mothers in charge, consisted of daily communal dinners, hysterical laughter, and long hot nights when the cousins settled down at one cottage or another to sleep the sweet, exhausted sleep of their mothers' anarchy. Now, since she'd inherited her cottage from her widowed mother five years ago, two of the cottages had been sold, and the aunts and cousins had jobs that kept them in Pittsburgh.

Halfway through their long frantic trip, Margo had stopped to call Aunt Lily, who reported that Margo's favorite cousin, Donna, was up for the summer with her three children, while her husband came over on weekends from a construction job in Ohio. Late that night, the children asleep in the back seat, Margo coasted across the state line. Alerted to their arrival, Donna appeared from the cottage next door, the same frizzy blonde hair bouncing above azure-blue eyes. She helped Margo carry the drooping kids into the cottage, where earlier that day she'd made beds, and turned the water on— the welcoming ritual of years ago.

The next morning, dressed in old chenille bathrobes, Margo and Donna sat out on the front lawn as their own mothers once had, their rusted chairs turned not toward each other, but to the changing colors of the choppy lake below the bluff. Their kids shyly eyed each other for all of three minutes before Ginger, who was Polly's age, and the twins, who were a year younger, lured them off with tales of the tire swing that sailed out over the lake and the doghouse fort. As they emptied the coffee pot, Donna brought Margo up to date on family: who was having an operation, drinking too much, putting an addition on their house.

Later Margo paced around her tiny cottage—the galley kitchen, the two narrow bunkrooms once filled with cousins, her parents' bedroom, their clothes still hanging on hooks as if to witness and support her new resolve. She buried her nose in faded bath towels worn thin as silk, opened cabinets to run her finger over cracked and mismatched dishes, found old bottles of whiskey and gin, and cried over her mother's slanted handwriting labeling the shelves of sheets—twin, double, fitted, flat.

That evening, as the kids wound down, Margo sank into the cushions of the rusty glider on Donna's screened-in porch above the whispering lake. Drawn by the single candle's glow, june bugs and moths plinked against the screens and fireflies flickered in the night. When Donna snapped open a cold can of beer and held it to her forehead, one of Ben's habits, Margo began to cry. "Sweetie, tell me about it," Donna said, pulling her chair close to Margo's creaking glider. So Margo told her she was thinking about a divorce and why. Nodding, Donna said that's why she got her divorce.

"But you married again," Margo said.

"I found someone I could trust."

Margo had to ask. "Did Ben ever make a pass at you?"

Donna leaned forward to touch Margo's knee. "Oh, Margo, I told him to grow up. It never mattered."

When the kids were quiet in Donna's bunkroom, Margo crossed to her own cottage and carried pillows and sheets out to the sofa on the screened-in porch. It was too hot to sleep and for the third time since leaving home, Margo missed Ben—his quirky sense of humor, his gift for making any chore a game, and his messy apprenticeship to *Joy of Cooking*. She missed his hard chest heavy on hers; his thick legs nudging hers willingly apart. His tongue outlining her mouth. But as the night grew cooler, Margo pulled a sheet over her legs and images of Ben with other women appeared beneath a sky that continued to fill and empty with a trillion stars.

*   *   *

The next day, they straggled down the dirt road past the aunts' and uncles' cottages to the stony beach. Donna smeared the squealing kids with lotion while Margo spread blankets over the stones, then wandered down the rocky shoreline looking for old landmarks— the gnarled oak growing at the end of the crumbling stone boat ramp. She'd drawn both a dozen times. When the kids grew restless, Margo emptied a blue pail and announced the search was on. "We're looking for special stones. Stones that look like something else—a ball, a house." Polly, Ginger and the twins immediately bent their heads to the hot beach but Sam moaned that he didn't see any houses. So Margo knelt and raked the sand until she found a smooth, square stone, saying see, it could be a block, and Sam could paint a big, red S on it. "What for?" he wanted to know. His hand played with her bathing-suit strap in a gesture so innocent Margo desperately wanted to hug him harder than he would have understood. "For me," she said.

She set up a card table in the driveway and poked around for paints and brushes and her old painted stones. Stroking a red and black ladybug, Polly asked, "Has Dad seen these?" Sam picked up a stone umbrella. "When's Dad coming?" His voice was suspicious for the first time. "He's home working, stupid," Polly said. "You're stupid." Sam grabbed the ladybug and climbed into Margo's lap, his head hitting Margo's nose. Lord, was she going to cry all summer?

That night the children told Ben about the stones and he told her he missed her. "Stay a few more weeks so the kids have a real vacation. Then come home." The other things he said—I'm sorry and you know it wasn't personal and it won't happen again—had lost their power. She wondered what he'd told the marriage counselor when he'd canceled their appointment. "I need more time," she told him. He didn't ask "Time for what?" No doubt he pictured her slowly "recovering" while she painted rocks with the kids, pasted together peanut butter and jelly sandwiches, and at night drank beer with Donna, whom he no doubt hoped had kept his indiscretion a secret.

"Say hello to Donna," he said.

"I don't think so," Margo said.

*   *   *

"You new around here?" Mercer asked the third time Margo stopped by. She told him sort of, that growing up she'd spent summers at the lake. "Bet nothing's changed," he said, putting a draft in front of her. When he asked if she was here for long, she said, "I'm back for a while with my kids." Solid information in one short sweet sentence: no man; kids.

The Pirates were battling their losing streak on a silent TV. "Don't have to hear and watch them lose," Mercer said. A few seats away, Jake, the carpenter, was talking to someone in a suit and loosened tie about the new water system going through town street by street. "System coming your way?" Jake asked her.

"I'm out too far," she told him. "Over the state line."

"You're probably lucky," he said. "I'm not sure all the fuss is worth it." Then he and the man in the suit went back to talking taxes and assessments. She liked men to overlap like this, including her in the lazy ping-pong talk of an almost empty bar.

She arrived at Mercer's later and later in the afternoon when the kids were tired of the beach and happy to play at Donna's cottage. Mercer would pull her beer without a verbal exchange. Bartender's message: I know her. Soon it seemed she knew most of the men in the town's yellow pages: Jake and his assistant; the manager of the five and dime; a housepainter who drank too much too early; guys from Stop and Shop and the pharmacy; men who worked shifts at the grape juice plant on the outskirts of town; farmers, bankers, the veterinarian, two lawyers; and Mike, who owned Sullivan's Hardware. Mercer's was the place where Mike told people their special orders were in: Jake's hand-saw blade, the banker's outdoor sprinkler, Mercer's new rubber floor mats.

She was there the day they pried up the old mats behind the bar, tossed them out the door, then fit and laid down new ones. People hung around later than usual, lazily exhilarated to watch others work. Mercer pretended annoyance at all the fuss, pushing his dark hair back from his eyes. "They're just floor mats," he said when Jake and Margo stood on the rungs of their stools to admire the new black grid on the floor, but he called out "Drinks on the house" anyway.

Catching Margo's eye, Mike said, "Best mats we got in the store. Let me know if you need any."

"Wouldn't go well with sand, kids, and bare feet," she told him.

"Think not?" Sweat had darkened his shirt and made his face gleam and when he sat down next to her she could feel the heat of his arm where it rested next to hers. Deciding was as simple as that.

* * *

The kids wanted more stones so Margo organized another hike along the shore at low tide. The twins found identical forts, Ginger more alphabet blocks, and Sam pounced on a drum. It was Polly who found the perfect heart. "For you, mom," she said.

"Oh, Polecat, don't you want to keep it?" Margo cupped the warm stone in her palm. It was two inches wide, gracefully rounding to a flawless point and fragile as a wafer. Polly shook her head, red pigtails bouncing against her cheeks. "It's for you," she said. Sunglasses hiding her tears, Margo pulled Polly to her knees and hugged her. Kids know something, not always what, but something. Then Margo slipped the stone into the top of her bathing suit against her own thin heart.

* * *

"Out?" Donna asked in disbelief. "Around here?" Her dish towel paused on a plate. "You're not going to get into any trouble, are you?"

"What do you mean by 'trouble'?" Margo asked, elbow deep in the old porcelain sink.

"Well, groceries can't account for all the afternoons you've been gone."

"Are you saying 'no'?"

"Maybe I shouldn't have told you about Ben."

"Jesus, Donna." Margo pivoted on her submerged hands to read Donna's face.

"I'd hate something that silly to be the final straw," Donna said, then reading Margo's own look she said, "Never mind. I'm sorry." And waved her dish towel at the door. "I'll watch the kids. Go."

*   *   *

Margo put on jeans and a black V-neck T-shirt. She shook her hair free of its customary barrette; in twenty minutes the humidity would turn it into a washboard of tiny waves. Ben's disclosures in the past year had ruined her appetite and left her almost thin. Now she stood tan and pared down—and with an appetite for men. Before she left, she downed a shot of gin.

Lights pinpointed the pool tables in the front room where two men in Midas shirts were chalking up their cues. The bar was crowded, festive-looking without the dusty haze of afternoon muting the glow of neon. At the end of the bar, Mercer argued the flyball rule with two men. Neil Diamond was crooning from the jukebox and Margo knew if she listened too closely she might lose her nerve—or cry.

"Night out?" Mercer said, bringing her a draft. "You kill the kids or something?"

"Hit them with a stone," she said.

"She paints stones," he said to the guy a seat away from her and hitched his thumb toward the red pick-up—now parked in front of a bottle of Jack Daniels. She'd given it to Mercer a week ago. "No kidding," the man said. She'd talked to him twice before—he was from out of town, doing a government study on endangered lakes. Mercer swiped the counter with his bar towel and set the pick-up in front of him. An admirer of painted stones, he slid over a seat and bought her next beer. Mike never appeared. Anyway, she felt the need of a rehearsal.

The man's leg against hers as they planned how to leave the bar separately made her weak with longing. She waited at the abandoned icehouse, three blocks away, her front seat pushed back, eyes closed. She didn't know why exactly, but it was going to happen. She was eighteen again, except this time she knew what to do.

When he pulled up behind her, she clicked on her lights and led the way out of town, six miles on the winding, dipping lake road, alien territory by night. Her high beams caught the sharp angles of billboards, outlined farmhouses, and turned the flat landscape into an ocean of dangerous black water two feet from the road. She drove faster than usual, the headlights in her rearview mirror a constant reminder, casting an erotic, anonymous mask. A few more curves, then a left onto the hidden lane of beach cottages and another left to Uncle Ray's cottage at the end of the row.

She dropped her clothes on the floor. The sheets were icy and damp and she wouldn't let him turn on the lights because they might bring Donna wondering who was there. "The cottage is cold because it hasn't been used this summer," she said, shivering but not from the cold. "I live at the other end of the row."

Naked, he slid into bed and kissed her, probably because he didn't know what to say.

She came, he came—not in that order—but he worked hard to reverse it the second time, leaning into her spread legs. She smiled at the sheer pleasure of feeling another man's body. She liked his thick torso, the dark hair sprouting on his shoulders, the cocky arc of his penis, even limp. All of him different than Ben. Men must do that when lifting a woman's breast to their mouth, comparing as their tongue circles a nipple. Suddenly she remembered Ben saying, "You still have the nicest breasts." Now she knew what "still" meant. She bent anew to this new man and for another hour she felt like she owned him.

Her aunt's fridge was always stocked with beer so she brought two back to bed and opened the curtains to the lake beyond.

"Amazing," he said, sitting propped up against the headboard. "Where are we?"

"Doesn't matter," she said. "You're leaving for the west coast in two days."

An hour later, she gave him directions back to town. He waved and disappeared; no last names, nothing personal. She imagined telling Ben about tonight: the meeting in a bar, his car following hers, the cold damp sheets. She'd make him cry. Yes, she'd say, I can do this.

*   *   *

"So, are you going to see him again?" Donna asked. She was lying face down on a toy-strewn beach towel and didn't open her eyes. The kids were damming up the trickle of a creek with stones.

"Never," Margo said.

Donna's husband, Frank, had been here for the weekend, tactfully silent about Ben's absence, and grateful that Margo stayed with the kids so he and Donna could go to dinner and come home to a childless cottage. Evidently Donna hadn't told him why Margo was so amenable to sitting. Margo had watched him—how he admired the painted stones, brought Margo a cold beer, taught her to relax her knees when water-skiing. It was true: Donna's husband could be trusted.

"Was he married?" Donna wanted to know.

"Umm."

"How could you? After what you've been through?"

Margo propped herself up on her elbow. "It was a one-night stand, not an affair. And by the way, my first."

"I know that," Donna said, opening one eye. "But not your last."

"Meaning what?" Margo said.

Donna turned over and used a Barbie doll dress to shield her eyes. "Well, there's a first time for everything. And there's a last time. But you seem—intent on the middle."

"There wouldn't have been a first time if Ben wasn't such a prick." Margo lay back down and closed her eyes. "You're right. It's probably not my last."

When Ben called to say he missed her, she heard it like she heard him say he was cutting the grass, cleaning out the garage. Then she handed him over to the kids.

What would have happened if she had discovered Ben in the "middle" of an affair? She never had the privilege of issuing ultimatums that he must never see X or Y again. He was the prodigal husband returned before she had time to consider if she wanted him back. She became a "watcher," suspicious of everyone, expert at recognizing other "watchers" whose husbands had been unfaithful, women with a painfully acquired and perfectly developed peripheral vision.

When Polly called her back to the phone, Ben said, "If you don't come home soon, I'm coming out."

"When you're done cleaning the garage," she said, "start on the attic."

"I mean it," he said.

"So do I," she said.

* * *

"Yo, Margo," the housepainter said, nodding to Mercer and sliding onto the stool beside her. His long arms were speckled with tiny pale blue dots. "Where do you paint those stones? You live in town?" He swung around as he spoke, his knees brushing her leg, his hand dangling near her lap. She imagined him leaving blue dots on her skin. Not in town, she told him, and when he asked if she wanted to take a drive out of town she said no thanks.

"Stars are out," he said, nudging her arm.

"Every night," Margo said. She could handle him, but there was a shrewdness about him, as if he knew what she was up to—and of course he did. Anyone looking for an affair or a one-night stand learns to send and receive signals—you either are or aren't available. It's all in the tone of voice, steady eyes behind the banter, the touch you accept by simply staying still as someone's arm rests next to yours, as someone's leg applies a pressure you stay with—or release and thus decline. Pressure and heat. For instance, Jake wasn't available. Mercer wasn't. Mike was. She remembered Mike's arm against hers the day he and Mercer laid the new mats. Where was Mike?

She took her beer over to the pinball machine where Jake and a man called Trav were banging on the machine's corners with the heels of their hands.

Mike wasn't the next man Margo slept with, it was Trav—she called him Travis. She'd seen him once before at the bar and they'd nodded to each other, but tonight they moved from stools to a booth where he described the hassles of being the youngest foreman at the plant. He had intelligent, curious eyes, a full bush of a mustache, and quick nervous gestures she wanted to quiet in bed. Her breasts riding over the table, she leaned toward him and flat our suggested they meet at her place. She waited at the icehouse for him to pull up behind her and then led the second caravan out to her road of beach cottages, shifting into neutral at the state line and coasting in on blind desire.

It was different from the start.

In her uncle's cottage, between the same cold sheets, no lights, the moon out there floating in the same sky and water, they did not have sex; they made love. His mouth learned her mouth. Her hands his body. His fingers the wet folds of her skin. Willingly she drowned in wave after wave of that sweet unstoppable current trapping her legs, knowing somehow there would be other times. Later, she brought cold beer from her aunt's fridge and risked the flick of lights to see him for a few seconds, and for him to see her breasts, her flat stomach with its tiny stretch marks like strands of beads on a belly dancer. His tongue traced their line as she smoothed his dark brown hair away from his eyes, memorized the slight arch of his nose she'd sketch tomorrow, the wide mouth, his mustache exquisitely combing through her hair.

Sitting propped up against the old pine headboard, the entire length of their legs touching, they talked till three in the morning, exchanging the secrets and offerings of intimate strangers. Having improbably begun with making love, they laughed when they came to the exchange of last names. The cool precision of a one-night stand all shot to hell. And clearly, she wouldn't sleep with Mike.

"What do you do all day?" Travis asked.

"Paint. The kids and I paint stones." With only the moon for light, they took a shortcut behind the other cottages, through the damp grass, to her cottage and its narrow windowsills lined with painted stones. Finger to her lips, she told him the kids were at her cousin's next door.

"Stones," he said, moving from one windowsill to another. "Paint one for me. Give it to me next time." Words like heat to Margo's heart.

They lingered another hour at her uncle's cottage. She knew without asking that he was married. Finally, as they leaned together against his car, he promised he'd call her tomorrow from work. "The number's in the book," she said, then she gave him directions to the road to town. After she locked up her uncle's cottage, she lay sleepless for two hours on her porch, too hot for blankets, and in love. After one night? Infatuated, lovesick, brimming with emotion for which she knew no other word but love.

*   *   *

He never called.

Dreamily, she waited all day, painting the stone heart a searing red and bribing the kids with cookies and popsicles to stay at the cottage. That evening they drank beer on her porch instead of Donna's while Margo sketched Travis in charcoal.

"OK. Tell me about him," Donna said.

"His name's Travis," Margo began.

The second day, bewildered but still hoping, she again pleaded with the kids to stay home. When Polly sulked, she told her to get out her paints and shut up. Finally, Donna crossed the scribbly lawn to rescue them from her craft hysteria. She ushered the kids out onto the dirt road and turned and pushed her sunglasses to the top of her head, leaving a wise white forehead.

"It was supposed to be a one-night stand," Donna reminded her.

"It only started out that way."

"But that's also the way it ends."

"Don't say that," Margo pleaded.

"There's no such thing as 'the second night of a one-night stand.'"

"Third, fourth, tenth." Margo slammed the screen door. "Leave me alone."

"Look. You need me. And don't you forget it. Without me taking care of the kids, you'd be fucked. No, you wouldn't," Donna said, matter-of-factly. "You'd be nowhere." She pulled her sunglasses down, hiding her eyes. "We'll be at the beach."

*   *   *

It rained for the next three days. Tearfully, Margo apologized. "Baby, baby," Donna said, hugging her. Rimless gray clouds skidded low across the lake trailing sheets of solid water, but the heat never let up. The kids ran between cottages holding wet newspapers over their heads; Donna's dog peed on the Monopoly money; the toilet wouldn't stop running; Sam spilled Hummingbird Yellow on the rug. The phone rang. It was never Travis. When Ben called, she re-fused to talk, afraid her voice might give her away. She imagined Travis feeling guilty, going to confession—she made him Catholic because it was a Catholic town—looking at new carpeting with his wife, getting into an argument at the plant, avoiding the bar. She thought of calling him at work, filled with a despair from high school when boys called girls and girls waited to be called. For God's sake—hadn't the old rules changed?

*   *   *

Over the misery of the next few days, she realized how foolish she'd been to think she'd wanted a series of one-night stands. After the first, what had she been expecting? Accomplices to her revenge? The men on Mercer's bar stools like a row of sitting ducks? What else might she be deceiving herself about?

She had no answers a week later when, missing the men at Mer-cer's, she went back and slept with Mike.

Mercer brought her beer saying he thought maybe she'd drowned. Jake reported he was behind a week on the courthouse roof what with all the rain. And Mike said he'd sold more window fans in one month than he'd sold the last two years.

It took a while to find her uncle's fan, but she did.

The old fan whirred noisily while Mike and she made love that night and several times a week thereafter. One hot night, Mike brought an enormous fan that had four settings and turned slowly, benevolently, from side to side on a table in front of their bed. He'd come out to her uncle's cottage or they'd drive up the lake to the Harbor Inn. Sometimes they met at Mercer's. Donna's husband came on weekends when Margo gratefully repaid the babysitting. He and Mike never met. She stopped looking for Travis, stopped rehearsing what she'd say, which had gone from corny to cool. She painted Mike a stone fan with four-leaf clover blades. One night they lay facing each other, his hand curved between her throat and shoulder in a gesture so particular to him that she had to pull away. "Talk to me," he said. Instead she asked him to list all the things he sold in his store, shelf by shelf, and closed her eyes to picture irons, toasters, coffee pots, plastic tablecloths, shelf paper, ice cube trays, thermoses, shower curtains, toilet seats, screw drivers, hammers, wrenches, nuts, bolts, nails, chains, fireplace tools, grates, seeds, garden hoses, stepladders, and on and on. She and Ben owned one of everything Mike named.

*   *   *

When Ben asked when she was coming home, she said in time for Teacher's Institute and to get the kids ready for school.

"You're not seeing someone?" he joked.

"Wait till you see the stones."

*   *   *

Labor Day weekend, the night before her departure, Mike came out to her uncle's cottage one last time. Thunder and lightning promised to make it memorable and his shirt was soaked in the short run from his car to the cottage door. They set the fan to high and afterwards wound the cord around it and put it in the trunk of Mike's car. They planned to meet at Mercer's for old times. Margo gave him a half-hour's start and drove down to the beach to watch the lake get manic.

The oak tree was swaying in a wide arc, its branches almost touching the crumbling boat ramp where she sat, her windshield wipers clearing views that lasted only seconds, but even this brief clarity felt welcome. So this was her last night with Mike. She'd miss him, but at least with Mike no one was hurt—with Mike it was nothing personal.

*   *   *

The approaching holiday and county boat show had doubled the usual weekend crowd. Behind the bar, Mercer and his brother sloshed glasses, served up drafts, and passed change over the heads of seated customers. The Pirates were slogging through the sixth inning of a double-header, and the jukebox was putting out non-stop. Mike waved and she gradually inched her way over to the stool he'd managed to save for her.

Then she saw Travis—seated on the other side of Mike.

Mike's hand rested for a moment on Margo's back as he said "This is Trav," and Margo and Travis said "We've met before, how are you?" Travis peeled the label off his bottle and glanced quizzically across at Margo as Mike went back to discussing the vacant selectman's post. How soon could she leave? When Mike left for the men's room, saying order him another beer, Margo watched in the mirror as the door closed on his back.

Days, minutes earlier, she hadn't expected to see Travis again, but here he was. She hadn't wanted to talk to him, but now she did. And so she leaned across Mike's place toward Travis. At the exact instant he leaned toward her. Their heads hit so hard that tears welled up in her eyes, blurring all the rum and scotch and vodka on Mercer's shelves into a sparkle of stars. Real stars.

Laughing, embarrassed, they cautiously leaned together again, both speaking fast. Margo wanted to know why he hadn't called and he wanted to know why she'd lied about being in the phone book— if 'Ainsley' was even her real name? "I called information ten, twenty times with every possible spelling. I drove back and forth on that goddamn road, I came into Mercer's twice on breaks at the plant." Travis took a long swallow of beer. Foam rode his mustache till he brushed it away.

Her fingertips tingled. "Don't make excuses, please," she said, her voice shaking. "I'm in the book."

When she signaled Mercer for another beer, Travis said, "Like hell you are." He asked Mercer for a phone book and pushed it along to her. And then she knew. That night in the dark, a little drunk, and driving on the winding beach roads, he hadn't known they'd crossed the state line into New York. When you follow a car you watch the car.

"I live in New York," she whispered. "I'm in the New York book."

"Jesus." He shook his head. "We couldn't have driven that far."

"It was dark. I live right across the state line."

"Let's leave. We have to talk," he said, digging into his pockets with the quick nervous gestures she remembered from another time.

"Let me think." She stared at the silent TV where a batter warmed up with three bats to the mournful notes of Jimmy Buffet's "Margaritaville."

"You or me first? Meet at the icehouse . . ." Travis said.

"I don't know," she said, but she did.

"You want to, don't you?" Travis asked, spinning a coaster across Mike's place. It spiraled to a stop in front of her.

She put her finger to his mouth, to the silk of his mustache. "I'm leaving tomorrow."

As they stared at each other, out of words, she reached into her jeans for the flat stone she'd carried since they met. She slid it across to him. The tiny perfect heart. "I painted this for you—the next day. Waiting for you to call."

Travis outlined the stone with his finger and then he looked at her as his hand closed around it. "Call me," he said. Mike was making his way toward them. "We'll write. You'll be back next summer?"

"It's only a stone," she said.

"Not that night, it wasn't," he said.

When Mike cupped the back of her neck—for only seconds, but long enough—Travis's gaze met hers and he had the grace not to say more.

It was time to leave, time to say good-bye to all of them. She leaned across the bar and waved to Mercer, who pointed to the red stone pick-up and said next time make it a white '68 Thunderbird. She and Mike had said their real good-bye earlier, so now he covered everything by telling her to drive safely. "Send me a postcard here at Mercer's," he said.

"Travis," she said and he nodded, his thumb ripping down the label on a new Schlitz.

She ran to her car, past the rain-streaked windows of the pharmacy, Trilla's Beauty Shop, Sullivan's Hardware, her T-shirt feeling like another skin. The icehouse stood sentry to the winding wet drive along the lake, where rows of ripe grapes seemed heavy with consequence. She took her foot off the gas at eighty. Christ. It was dangerous to feel so sick with love, so humble about desire.

Donna's light was on. As she pulled onto the rough beach road for the last time, the rain was still steady although the storm's center had moved further east, taking with it the last high drama of thunder and lightning. Wet and crying, she sagged onto the old glider as Donna handed her a box of Kleenex and went into the kitchen for two beers.

Margo held the sweating can to her forehead, a gesture she'd forever associate with the heat of this summer. Then she told Donna about Travis. "If only I'd acted like a woman, not a girl. If only I'd called him."

Donna switched off the porch light where she'd been folding laundry and threw Margo a dry T-shirt. "Oh, Sweetie. But then what?"

"All that time I spent with Mike—"

"I know, I know. But think about it—then what?"

Margo clutched the soft bundle of T-shirt against her chest and rode the short, small tracks of the glider in silence. Then what? She closed her eyes. Well, if only she'd called Travis till she got him. She imagined Travis returning the next night and the next—hours spent beside the old whirring fan. Then one afternoon, feeling guilty, they would have taken the kids twenty miles up the lake for ice cream. He'd have painted a cluster of grapes or a handlebar mustache. Donna would have invited him to try out the glider, have a beer. He would have liked Donna's husband and the four of them might have played poker or pinochle. The kids would have called him "Uncle Travis"—and Ben, if he heard his name, would have said it was an uncle he didn't remember meeting. Given a few more nights with Travis, she might have wanted to spend the rest of her life with him.

She opened her eyes and breathed out a long shivering sigh. "You mean it might have been a different story?"

"It's better this way," Donna said. "Now you can go home and—"

The glider squawked as Margo rose. "Go home and what? Jesus, Donna, whose side are you on?" She banged the screen door behind her and, ducking under branches, ran to the edge of the bluff. Below, the lake crashed and roared. Then Donna's strong arms were around her, rocking her. "I just want you to have what you want," Donna said.

"I don't know what I want," Margo told her.

"You will," Donna said. "You almost do."

Then they were laughing, running back to the porch, where Donna rummaged again for dry T-shirts. Margo pointed into the night. "So often I fell asleep on that porch imagining what I'd tell Ben: about the summer's men, my Aunt Grace's cottage—"

"Don't forget the fans."

"Waiting at the old icehouse," Margo said, taking the dry shirt Donna handed her. "He'll probably know you were in on it."

"For sure he won't take you for granted anymore."

"Ever," Margo said. But it was a disquieting word.

"And now we both need to pack a ton of rocks. Or rather stones," Donna said, kicking a cardboard box near the door—it moved an inch. "Couldn't you have painted shells instead?"

They went in to look at the sleeping, sweaty kids layered on two beds. Margo bent over Sam and Polly to kiss their moist faces, then she turned, saying "Oh, Donna, it seems so selfish to think—" But Donna shook her head. "For years you've put up with Ben's screwing around. Think of yourself. And remember: whatever you decide, the kids will manage. They're tough."

Out on the porch, Margo hated to leave and stood there, staring through the rain-washed screens, across the muddy path to her own dark cottage, a newspaper over her head.

"We'll save our good-byes for morning." Donna said, hugging her shoulders. "Good night, dear Margo." Then she gave Margo a push, perhaps harder than necessary, and sent her into the rain.

*   *   *

Everything was packed, ready for tomorrow's trip, except the painted stones lining the windowsills. Margo poured the last inch of gin over two ice cubes and went from room to room gathering stones that had come alive with detail: a blue house with two gold windows and a rose trellis, the TV with six black knobs, a suitcase with a fat handle. Why didn't she feel better about her own offerings for Ben—the lurid details of her summer's sweet revenge?

Suddenly, standing there with her hands blessedly full of stones, she saw his confessions for the gifts they were. Ben told her of his affairs so they could begin again. Was that what she wanted? She'd almost evened the score, but what would keep Ben from pushing it higher?

Earlier tonight, as she watched Mike drive off, she'd told herself that their affair was nothing personal—but "affair" didn't begin to address the particularity of knowing another person: how Mike laced his shoes, never buttoned his shirt cuffs, followed *Doonesbury*, drank tea with milk but coffee black, read detective novels, liked soft pillows and hard mattresses, knew Sullivan's stock backwards and forwards, fought athlete's foot, believed in bonds. And even if you could love two people at once, time for an affair doesn't drop out of nowhere; it gets subtracted from something. Now, if Ben were to have another affair, she wouldn't imagine him in bed. Instead she'd see him discussing various balsamic vinegars, learning to like German opera or country, or smartly unstopping some woman's sink. And there it was: one night or a lifetime—it should all be personal, personal was the point of everything.

In her bedroom, Margo stopped at the mirror over her dresser and leaned forward to search her eyes for a sign from her heart. Her steady gaze told her that maybe being taken for granted was a good thing—a privilege you bestow on the other person, and being able to take their loyalty for granted was the gift you hoped for in return. She would tell Ben only one thing about her summer: how in the end she understood that each of his confessions was a gift—a gift she couldn't give because his had been given one too many times. Her summer had been for herself. It had set her free.

As she wrapped the stones with sheets of the summer's news, she pictured the kids unpacking the box for Ben tomorrow, basking in his surprise and praise as he unwrapped each separate stone—the house, the suitcase, the frog.

"Hey, you did a lot of painting this summer," he will say to the kids. "We'll have to find a good home for these." Then he will look to Margo and ask which stones are hers.

Unable to speak, she will point to the pick-up, the lamp, the tent.

"The heart," Polly will say, sifting frantically through the paper, telling him about the perfect heart. She'll describe finding it on the beach and giving it to Margo. Sam will point to his scarlet fire engine to show Ben the exact color that Margo chose for it.

Still hoping, Ben will pile the last of the crumpled newspapers on the table. He will look for the heart in the bottom of the box and then he will turn to her. Sam and Polly will both cry, "Mom, where is the heart?" Finally, Ben will understand, he'll know she didn't bring it home.

from *Wouldn't You Like to Know:*
Very Short Stories (2010)

Appetites and Addictions

I. Doing My Man

Her hands break my heart. I used to rent *The Rose* once a week and fast forward to the frames where the camera also loves her hands. Toward the end of the film, there she is, Mary Rose, our Janis Joplin stand-in, at what should be her moment of triumph—she's come home to play the sold-out football stadium in her hometown, arrived with stage sets and lights, backup bands, roadies and groupies, the whole damn show. She can outdazzle the most popular girl, easily win away the handsome quarterback, oh she can sing.

But where is she—she is in a fluorescent-on-fire phone booth screwing the top off a bottle of bourbon, the bourbon a translucent liquid like air and by now as necessary to her as breathing. Her slender fingers are so practiced in the hold, turn, release of the bottle's top—hold, turn, release—that she can do it with trembling fingers, she can do it with her eyes closed, with her mouth touching, moaning into the phone.

Her mouth is wet, glistening, the liquor stings as her tongue catches everything, and we follow her long swallows, but it is still her hands that the camera loves. Hold, turn, release. The pressure of her thumb and three fingers is so sure and graceful that not one revolution is ever lost. The pads of her fingers touch just above the top's rim, as if in boundaries the rim is everything. Oh Rose, you could have had it all.

You could have declined that needle, played to that rim for a while longer. Over and over, around and above that rim. You had a taste for love.

My fingers know all about it.

I hold him and turn and turn, back and forth, holding, turning, releasing. I am breathing him in, swallowing him. Closing him down. My fingers can break his heart.

II. Next Comes Soup

Not right after, no, but soon, I leave him where I did him and go to the kitchen to shift and clatter my pots and pans. Another satisfying sound that has to do with appetite. Sweet butter, a virgin oil, and chopped onions are sizzling away in a heavy pot before I have to decide, Which soup? This might be about soup. This might be about me and my man.

I consider black bean, or roasted eggplant and garlic, or a warm Vichyssoise, or I could just as easily slide the pot off the burner, turn down the gas, and have him do me again. I stop stirring for one long moment to think about this. I think about this scenario the way I sometimes think about falling asleep with his fingers inside me, my back curved into him, my bottom leg straight, my top leg bent at the knee and pulled in toward my damp breasts, pulled impossibly high.

The dense smell of onions softening in foaming butter keeps me with the soup.

Soup—what soup?

The butternut squash glows on the windowsill. I palm the round base of the squash and peel its narrow throat. Then I hold the long moist throat and peel its hard curve. Chicken broth floats the onions for seconds before I bury them under a peeled tart apple, all that chopped squash. Not quite too late I add cumin, turmeric, cardamom, and thyme. This is going to take a while, this soup. Later, I'll blend it smooth and serve it to my man with a cold dollop of sour cream and a baguette we'll acquire on a stroll to the corner bakery. For now he's not exactly waiting, but he's still in bed.

So. I'll adjust the heat, turn the flame low under the soup. Then I'll stand beside the bed. "I'm making soup," I'll say. And he'll say, "Hmmm, soup." I'll hold my fingers to his nose and he'll close his eyes and breathe the onions in. I'll tell him apples and coriander and cumin and squash. "Maybe add a bit of ginger," he'll say, opening his eyes.

He'll pull me down, press my fingers to his mouth, and his mouth will slowly open, opening me all over again. His wet sharp teeth and firm tongue will nibble the length of my fingers, swell the cup of my palm, ply the silent art of appetite. He'll teach me all of his. I'll teach him all of mine.

A View: *Office at Night*

They don't seem to be working, though up to a few minutes ago she was filing papers. A man (whom we assume is her boss) sits reading a page at his desk, holding it beneath a green banker's light. Her plump right arm bends to encompass a generous bosom and her right hand rests on the edge of the open file drawer. Perhaps seconds ago she turned toward the man at the desk. Her face is vulnerable, intent. She is waiting. A piece of paper, partly hidden by the desk, lies on the floor between her and the man. We are led to believe that Edward Hopper is in a train, passing by on the El.

A voluptuous curve—perhaps the most voluptuous curve in all of Hopper's paintings, almost to a surreal degree—belongs to this secretary in the night-blue dress in *Office at Night*, an oil on canvas, 1940. What word, in 1940, would have been used to describe those rounded globes beneath the stretch, from rounded hip to hip, of her blue dress?

If it weren't for that piece of paper on the floor, we might believe the museum's prim description of this painting. It says: "The secretary's exaggerated sexualized persona contrasts with the buttoned-up indifference of her boss; the frisson of their intimate overtime is undermined by a sense that the scene's erotic expectations are not likely to be met."

Indifference? Wrong. The man is far too intent on the paper he is reading—and he is not sitting head-on at his desk. He is somewhat tilted—toward the secretary. His mouth is slightly open as if to speak. His left ear is red. It is. It is red.

And what of their day? Her desk faces his in this small cramped office. He must have looked up from his papers to say to her, seated behind her black typewriter, that tonight they must stay late. Did she call her mother, or two roommates she met while attending Katharine Gibbs, to say her boss asked her to stay late? On other evenings, she would have finished dinner, perhaps been mending her stockings or watching the newsreel at the cinema's double feature.

But here she is tonight, looking down at the paper on the floor. Was it she who dropped it? It is true that her dress has a chaste white collar, but the deep V of the neckline will surely fall open when she stoops over, perhaps bending at the knees over her spiffy black pumps, to retrieve the page. Another paper has been nudged toward the desk's edge and shows a refusal to lie flat in the slight breeze blowing the window shade into the office. Other papers are held in place by the 1940s black telephone, so heavy that in a forties noir film it might serve as the murder weapon.

Perhaps this story began at an earlier time. It might already be a situation, causing the young woman, just this morning, to choose to wear this particular blue dress. We are all in the middle of their drama. She will bend before him. Someone will turn off the lights. They will leave before midnight. Perhaps it won't turn out well. But for now the blue dress cannot be ignored.

Ice

"Jesus, Keaton, how can you expect us to drink here anymore if you don't furnish ice," Roger called from the kitchen. He and the Inspector were peering into Keaton's fridge. Belatedly, Keaton remembered ice.

"Damn trays are frozen in place," the Inspector said. A biochemist, he knew his trays and had the odd habit, for only being twenty-five, of slowly nodding his head in agreement to most observations. They called him the Inspector. His contribution of tonight's bourbon was sitting on the counter. Sour, smoky vapor from the open fridge was billowing into the room.

"The trays are probably empty anyway," Roger said, his new beard giving authority to his complaint. "Anybody fill the trays last Saturday?"

Keaton knew "anybody" meant Keaton. His friends were pissed and he didn't blame them. It had been a whole five months since Carmel moved out, and Roger and the Inspector started coming over Saturday nights. Their women lived out of town; Roger's was getting a PhD in medieval studies at NYU and the Inspector's lived in Paris. They weren't into bars and Keaton wasn't into the bar scene. They were into ice.

"Let me look," Keaton said. He dumped black pawns onto the chessboard and joined them in the kitchen. His fridge was ancient, with one outside door and a metal freezer section inside with its own little door above the place for keeping things merely cold—the kind you see on porches in rural West Virginia. Edges of the freezer were round and white with frost, and the metal door was three inches from closing.

"Hey, we warned you about ice the last time," the Inspector said, then looked around in further accusation to ask, "Have you been feeding Nietzsche?" When Carmel was clearly gone, the Inspector brought Keaton a white rat from his lab for company. It rustled and squeaked beside Keaton's computer as he wrote software for medical diagnostics—but by Saturday he needed human company. Roger, an architect, had insisted Keaton shift his furniture around to exorcise Carmel's presence—he'd instructed Keaton to slide their bed under the eaves, and the couch in the next room no longer sat snugly in front of the fireplace. It had helped a little, but after a week Keaton put the bed back in its original spot.

"Maybe we should go to my place?" Roger said, tugging on his beard. "Inspector?"

Panicking, Keaton pleaded, "Hey, guys, don't leave." He banged the heel of his hand against a buried ice cube tray.

"Well, he looks like he's getting fed." The Inspector had retrieved Nietzsche's cage from Keaton's office and set him next to the chess board, where he chittered away, fat and white.

"Or we could go to your place?" Roger said to the Inspector. "You could rescue Nietzsche?" The Inspector nodded, still inspecting Nietzsche for signs of neglect.

"You guys are jerks," Keaton said.

"Who's the jerk," Roger drawled, in his Texas twang.

"Enough," the Inspector said. He gave Nietzsche's cage a pat, then returned to the kitchen. "Pull the plug and turn off the fridge."

Roger felt behind the fridge for the plug, his tie hanging down like a plumb line. The fridge died with a clunk.

"There's nothing in here going to spoil that fast," the Inspector said, dismissing cans of tuna fish and sardines, Chinese leftovers in white take-out boxes with little metal handles. "We're going to do a fast defrost." He poked around in the silverware drawer for a butcher knife, then began chipping away at the ice around the trays.

Resigned, Roger poured three glasses of bourbon and took a sip. He made a face. "This particular year definitely needs ice."

"I know, I know, I brought it," the Inspector said. He was now wielding the knife like a dagger. "This job needs an ice pick."

"I have an idea," Keaton said. He headed into the bedroom to look in the boxes Carmel said she'd be back for. Her silver hairdryer was in here somewhere. As he fished among her fossil collection, ballet shoes, and books, he wondered how she was drying her long, thick hair and pictured her sitting between some new guy's knees—then stopped. He would not cry. The dryer was in the second box.

"Carmel's," Keaton said, waving the dryer, and closing the bedroom door so Roger couldn't see that the bed was back in its old place.

"Man, you got to get over that woman." Roger turned Carmel's dryer on to fast and high and directed a hot stream of air into the tiny compartment. Keaton sniffed, remembering Carmel's apple shampoo, the annoying mist on the bathroom mirror.

Solemnly, the Inspector watched things melt, then sopped up puddles with paper towels. Keaton threw out gravel-gray cheese, a lime hard as stone—jars he didn't have the stomach to open. When he pushed the last of Carmel's chutney to the back of the shelf, the Inspector spied her name and the label's date and insisted on opening it. "You can't throw that out," Keaton said, so the Inspector passed it under his nose, then tossed it into the garbage. Meekly, Keaton found a sponge and began wiping down the shelves.

"Now we're humming," Roger said, the butcher knife in one hand, Carmel's dryer in the other.

Citing bacteria, the Inspector soaped a sponge, then set to wiping the stove burners. To show he was trying, Keaton scratched around the kitchen floor with a broom.

Finally, the frost was retreating from the dryer's assault, and Roger was able to pull one ice cube tray free. "Empty." Disgusted, he handed it to Keaton and gave Carmel's dryer to the Inspector. More chunks of frost broke free, and Keaton threw them in the sink. Guiltily, he attacked the week's—maybe two weeks'—stack of dirty dishes. Five minutes later the Inspector turned the dryer to low and announced his arm was tired. He looked at Roger, then Keaton. "Your turn."

"OK. Let's get this over with," Keaton said. With Carmel's dryer back on high, he pointed at the last of the frost and finished it off, a white tide going out. A bit of pressure and two more trays lurched free. Amazingly, one tray actually had six fat cubes in it. Roger plopped them into the glasses of bourbon and made a toast "To ice."

Finally, the freezer door was capable of closing. Like kids, they all tried it. Roger plugged it in and Keaton turned it on. Then he filled the ice trays with cold water

"Guess we'll stay," Roger said, moving to the chess board. The Inspector pinged Nietzsche's cage and told him he could stay too.

"You two play," Keaton said. "I'll sit the first one out." As Roger made a move—pawn to king four—Keaton sat back and closed his eyes. He and Nietzsche would settle in and listen to the fridge hum as ice began to form, grateful that water turns to ice.

Dud

I've watched it three times and each time I reach the same conclusion: this movie's a dud. It's a dud in spite of the medium-big stars playing network mogul, reporter on the story, mafia patsy, and the TV talking head who spouts the evening's news—the Peter Jennings type. My job's making the trailer. Dark and crowded with expensive equipment, my editing room is plastered with posters of *Casablanca, Citizen Kane, Unforgiven*—ghosts more alive than the dud running on my screen. Yesterday the boss pulled his glasses down his nose and said over their tops, "Eddie, there's a lot riding on this trailer. No market surveys. We're only doing one."

Today I take a hike down the hall to tell the boss what he must have suspected. For the past two days he's been running through the latest New Age western, a movie John Wayne would have shot dead. The boss hits the pause button and nods for me to make it fast.

"It's a dud," I say. I tell him I've pieced together ten prelims for the trailer and it's not coming out sweet.

He pulls his tiny glasses to the end of his nose. "Eddie," he says, "who paid you to be a movie critic?" He says with movies, a dud is a dud. It's a luxury big directors and rich studios have—making duds—but we don't have that luxury here, he says. There's no way the trailer can be a dud.

"Great logic," I say. "The movie's a dud, but the trailer can't be a dud."

He tells me do a preview that will bring the people to the box office before word gets out, before the real critics call it a dud. He pushes his glasses up, already back to work before I've left the screening room.

"Eddie," he says. "Rearrange. Deceive. But if you want to keep your job, don't use the word 'dud.'"

I go back to the editing room where it's waiting like a corpse. What with two sets of alimony and child support payments, keeping my job is top priority, so I need a resurrection. I run the dud through again, ready to stop at any even slightly promising moments. I make myself forget the plot. The dud doesn't have a plot. I hit the switch and take it in. It's me and the dud.

I look for sex, action; I look for bodies and blood; I look for weapons.

There's a spot near the end of the movie where they're having a fractious meeting and someone pulls a gun and shoots in order to get everyone's attention. Believe it or not, that's the only role the gun has in the story. I write "112:34 to 112:59" to let the cutter know to start with these frames. Then I think: OK, I have a gun. Now it's got to go off big. I try to recall any falling bodies, any blood. There's a scene right at the beginning where the talking head slips on a banana peel and ends up flat on his stomach with a bloody nose, a fat lip. I rewind fast. I look for the banana peel. Bingo! I can actually show the fall happening after the gun goes off and there are sixteen seconds where the banana peel does not show. One clip done—a body almost dead from the gun going off. Chekhov would be proud.

Sex. I fast forward to the network mogul's office where he is yelling "No, no, no," into a high-tech laser phone. He's trying to drown out his wife, who's called to complain about another fancy dinner party he is going to miss. He looks frantic to get off the phone. His

Chinese takeout just arrived and he has a fetish about eating food hot. I write "15:15 to 15:32."

Inspired, I fast forward to the nude scene in the hot tub, where the talking head and the reporter are refreshing themselves after screwing. A phone beside the hot tub is ringing but they ignore it. I do not. I reverse the order and feed forty seconds of hot tub, wet flesh and ringing phone into ten seconds of the mogul screaming "No" into another phone. Who says they have to be the same call. I'm feeling lucky about this dud.

Next, I remember a low-key chase scene in the shopping mall where the reporter is hysterically hunting for the right trench coat for her first big story. I splice it together with the mafia patsy's shakedown of a liquor store in a seedy part of town. I relocate the liquor store in the mall. So it's a slight change of neighborhood, but hey. Time flies as I make notes of where to cut and splice, cut and splice.

When I finish, it's a winner. My dud has a new story. My dud almost cons me into thinking the movie's worth seeing.

Why did I think this would be so hard?

Who says the story you tell has to be the story that happened?

Cut and splice. It's what I do every night warming a bar stool at O'Toole's: exaggerate, lie, edit. Hey, Eddie, someone will say, and then I'm off on another story before I head for home. It's what I do most nights when I can't sleep. It's what I do with my life.

Driver's Test

We are in the slow lane traveling west on the Pennsylvania Turnpike. We're moving west *and starting over*—my husband's words. He is driving as if his mind is already somewhere else; I'm collecting skid marks.

We were still talking to each other when we started out from Baltimore, when I first wondered out loud what story lay behind a startling set of black curved tracks before us on the road.

"Don't think about it," he said. It is something he's said too many times before: about our lost calico in grad school, my grandmother's singed quilt, Molly's red tricycle he insisted I give to the abashedly grateful neighbor on the next street.

So I didn't think about it—out loud. I left him to his driving and I allowed myself to imagine what made some car or pickup jam on its brakes hard enough to lay those black satin ribbons on this road. They had unraveled for over fifty feet, a desperate curve whipping twice across the line dividing two lanes on this divided four-lane interstate until they stopped abruptly. What made them stop? Did the brakes work, do their job, stop two thousand pounds of glass and metal as they were supposed to? The car halting just short of an uninterested bull moose ambling across the pavement in search of marshy grass, or just short of some other disaster? Perhaps one vehicle met another, say, the wall of a semi whose driver had been too long on the road, or the wandering sedan of some solitary person momentarily asleep at the wheel?

Now we're in Pennsylvania, dangerously drifting along the country's first superhighway built when fast meant fifty miles per hour. Our Honda is packed tight with my dissertation books, necessary clothes in duffels, and my husband's hard drives, computers, monitors—all the expensive electronics of a man in touch with the world. The white CorningWare casserole and transparent glass lid we almost left behind are rattling on top of boxes in the back seat, clattering softly in their Corning way—a sound that could never be mistaken for any other.

Starting over. We're *fleeing* to a place where Molly never lived. A place where we'll have to apply for new licenses, be photographed in faces we no longer recognize, retake our driving tests. Learn some other state's permitted speeds, right-turn-on-red law, animal hazards—their Rules of the Road.

Maybe skidding should be part of the test.

Skidding should be required so you're ready for it—if and when it happens, so you'll know what it feels like when front wheels lock, when you are careening sideways down the road, so you'll know how the only thing you're in control of is the futile pressure of your right foot on the puny, helpless brake. That way, the first time you are told to *hit the brakes*, the first time you hit those brakes with the full desire and intent to stop, stopping doesn't matter. The bored instructor could make a game of saying *now*, somewhere safe in a mowed abandoned field or an empty parking lot so large that contact with anything else is out of the question.

When I break the silence to explain this new test to my husband, my voice is animated for the first time in eight months and catches even me by surprise.

As I describe the test, he turns to me, and his wide profile thins to sharp cheekbones and angry gray eyes. When I tell him *Imagine your foot hard on the brake*, when I say *Please, just try*, he fails.

At the next rest stop, I wait till he has disappeared into the Men's and then I gather up the Corning casserole and its offending, murmuring lid and abandon it on a distant picnic table. As we pull out, its blue-white glow grows fainter in the dark.

Once again, we are bored by the landscape of Ohio's I-80 because it is the Ohio we remember from grad school, and once again, we are surprised and then dismayed by Indiana—the state, in spite of maps, we always forgot—somehow expecting to leave Toledo and an hour later find ourselves on Chicago's South Side.

The sun is going down in Indiana when my husband lets me drive. He doesn't want to, but he's tired so he questions me intently. "We could find a place for the night," he says, solicitously, but without looking at me, rubbing his eyes. "We don't have to keep on. Though it would be nice to get in two or three more hours."

"I'll drive," I say. Finally we pull over to exchange places. We don't touch as we pass behind the car—we could be strangers in a used-car lot.

Our doors slam shut and I hitch the seat up, adjust mirrors automatically, even though I've rarely driven since the accident, the word *accident* so inadequate for the amount of loss. The drama of medics, sirens, glass, and blood. And skid marks.

I am a collector now.

The next skid marks are short and conjure up a scurrying profligate animal who safely braved these lanes. Another set of marks is so precisely there that surely measurements of length and gradients and curve were carefully taken and had their day in court. Oddly, the next skid marks almost meander to the shoulder before they shoot straight up a steep bank, gouging out dark dirt lanes where a car must have finally stopped, its driver sweating, shaken at what she'd felt the car do without her. Something she'd never forget even sober, and thank god no one was hurt. This time.

When I glance over at my husband, his head is already bobbing above his rhythmic chest. He's not afraid of sleep, or dreams.

I practice, applying pressure to the gas pedal till we are going 85, then 90, then stepping on the brakes to slow us gradually back down.

When it happens he feels it.

He wakes up as I am laying down our own black silk path of rubber. We're sliding sideways then straight, there are no other lights on the highway.

"What happened, what?" he whispers, sensing that to cry *stop* would be foolhardy. He isn't sure there wasn't a disaster I just avoided as he peers behind us in the night.

Bracing himself—himself—on the dash, he turns to me. "Please, if it's about Molly," he says, please, he's ready to talk. But he's too late. Oh, we'll survive this skid, but not much else. He's left his marks and now I'm leaving mine.

Put to Sleep

Jackson's father calls at 5:00 a.m. "I'm depressed," he tells Jackson, "but that's not why I'm calling." Jackson's father, who turned ninety-two a month ago, says he just wants Jackson to know he's going to put Bucknell to sleep.

"Dad, you can't do that. Bucknell is a great dog," Jackson says. Bucknell, an Irish setter, has been a lifeline for Jackson's parents for the past eight years; he was named for the college whose football team Jackson's father's team could never beat. Jackson takes the phone from the bedroom, where his wife is sleeping soundly, to his drafting table in the next room. "What does Mom say?"

"She says she won't have to worry about me out walking Bucknell on ice or keeping track of dog food. Sending Gus out to find those special real-meat dog bones." Jackson's mother stopped driving a year ago when she turned eighty. Now Gus shows up twice a week to drive Jackson's parents on errands—the dentist, the doctor, and the butcher shop for Bucknell's bones.

"Bucknell's not sick, is he?" Jackson says. He pictures Bucknell drooping over the foot of his parents' bed, snoring noisily through dreams of hunting swift wild animals he's never seen, while Jackson's father is plotting to murder Bucknell. "Give Bucknell to Gus," Jackson says.

When his father counters with "Gus has us," Jackson says, "I'm coming to get Bucknell. I'm bringing Bucknell back home with me. Then we'll talk about depression."

"Nothing to talk about. Depression's depression." His father hangs up.

It isn't light yet when Jackson pulls into his parents' drive. Bucknell's stuff is on the porch, ready to go, in two plastic bags. Jackson's mother is watching Bucknell lope around the dewy yard. She wrings her hands in front of her herbal apron, her eyes are red, but the story has been that Bucknell is his father's dog. Dry-eyed and resolute, Jackson's father appears and makes a gesture that could be hello or goodbye. He doesn't acknowledge Bucknell, who is prancing around, pushing a slobbery tennis ball into his crotch.

Jackson loads up the car. When he calls Bucknell's name, the setter bounds down the walk with his breed's reckless stupidity and sits in the passenger seat, happy for the unexpected ride. His wet nose makes a prism of the window. He barks at anything that moves.

Back home, as the sun begins to rise, Jackson puts Bucknell's plaid blanket in the living room near the unused fireplace, his dog dish in the kitchen, his water bowl beside it. Puzzled, Bucknell pads around behind Jackson, sniffing as he goes. Jackson tells him everything will be all right. Jackson doesn't know what to tell his wife, who is still asleep. She sleeps through everything.

An hour later, over breakfast, his wife voices her displeasure with the unexpected guest. Hearing his name, Bucknell thumps his tail. He hovers carefully at a distance, well-trained not to beg at the table. Jackson tells his wife about the new depths to which his father's depression has sunk.

"I'd be depressed at ninety-two," she says, his wife, the psychiatrist.

"I don't find that medically helpful," Jackson says.

"Well, we do seem to have a dog now," she says. She's already dressed for the day, her long hair pulled back from a wise, high forehead and coiled into a bun.

Jackson leaves with Bucknell, to buy him fat fake bones and a few meaty real ones. They are meant to keep Bucknell occupied while, in the office adjoining the library, his wife sees her patients. She tells Jackson there are personal details that patients shouldn't ever know. They might be freaked out if they heard a dog bark, or even knew they had a dog, never mind a child or children, which Jackson fears they will never get around to planning for. "Freaked out" are Jackson's words. "Interrupted transference" are hers.

"The world has dogs in it," Jackson tells her. "The world is full of children and dogs." She doesn't answer. In her world, dogs do not bark.

All day Bucknell obligingly lounges by Jackson's drafting table as he sketches dazzling new kitchens, designs cunning granite countertop arrangements for upwardly mobile tract-home McMansions. While he and Bucknell take long walks in the burgeoning woods across the street, he tells Bucknell about the importance a well-designed kitchen plays in the family dynamic. Bucknell makes proper use of these walks, stopping at trees and fire hydrants, staking out new territory of his own. That night, Bucknell jumps onto the bed, clearly intending to sleep with them.

"Not on the bed," Jackson's wife says, tying her silk pajama bottoms with a double knot.

So Bucknell lurks around the edges of their king-size mattress, a solid, alert presence. At 5:00 a.m. still on Jackson's father's schedule, the dog starts to pace around and sniff. Even with his eyes closed, Jackson feels Bucknell watching them sleep, feels the breeze from his wagging tail.

* * *

It's been three weeks. Bucknell now wakes at 6:00 a.m. He and Jackson watch Jackson's wife sleep. Her hand is tucked beneath a freckled cheek, partially covered with fine, long hair. Jackson smoothes it back and tucks it behind her ear. She opens one eye. Bucknell senses their movements and quickens his pacing. From her side of the bed Jackson's wife says, "Somehow, it's like having your parents in the room. Patrolling our sleep, curtailing our sex life." And Jackson thinks, *If it's the dog, enough of that.*

The next day, Jackson goes over to talk to his father about his depression. They sit around the red and chrome kitchen table, bought in the forties. Jackson's father is wearing a tie with his sweater. Jackson's mother sets the kettle to boiling. "Look at your dad moping around. He misses the dog," she says.

"Dad was depressed *before* I took the dog," Jackson reminds her. "He was going to put Bucknell to sleep."

"Your mother doesn't believe in depression," his father says. "Tell that to your wife."

"You miss Bucknell," Jackson's mother says to his father, her tone accusatory. Jackson's cue.

"Look, I can bring Bucknell back," he says.

"I told you I'll have him put to sleep," his father says. "I'm too depressed to have a dog." His bald head glows in spite of his depression.

Jackson schedules an appointment with his father's doctor, who puts his father through a variety of tests. They wait for the results and Bucknell goes through a lot of bones. He now sleeps on the bed with Jackson and his wife, snuffles through satisfying predatory dreams, still wakes too early. "Tell me about the dog," Jackson says to his wife one evening before she turns off the light on her side of the bed.

"It would probably take six months of sessions to unravel the dog," she says into her pillow.

"Bucknell's only eight, so we must have four or five dog years ahead of us to do it," Jackson tells her. Then it occurs to him to ask: "Sessions for whom?" But his wife is already asleep. Bucknell's tail vibrates on the mattress like a drumstick.

Electrolyte imbalance is what the doctor tells Jackson's father. "Your depression is easy to fix. Two miracle drugs will do it." A week later Jackson's father calls again at 5:00 a.m. As Jackson shuffles into his study, Bucknell jumps down from the bed to follow. Jackson's wife probably thinks the slight movement is Jackson. In a booming voice, his father says he's coming by for Bucknell.

"To do what?" Jackson asks, but his father hangs up. Jackson waits in the kitchen with a wide-awake Bucknell.

"I'm taking him home," Jackson's father says through the screen door, as if he had never threatened any dire alternative. Bucknell lopes around his flannel knees in ecstasy. "Gus is going to stop by Petco and fill the trunk with dog food," Jackson's father says. He scratches Bucknell's ears in a way Jackson never thought to.

"Aren't you glad I took Bucknell in," Jackson says, handing over Bucknell's blanket, dog bones, leash, dish, and water bowl. Gus waves from the car.

Jackson is to get no credit from his father. "You two ought to get a dog," his father says as Bucknell tugs him down the walk.

"You know we don't want a dog," Jackson says.

His father shakes his head in disgust. "That wife of yours coddles her patients too much. Treats them like kids. You ought to have some kids." Bucknell barks as they all drive off.

What Jackson doesn't know yet is that a year later when his father calls at 5:50 a.m. Bucknell will already have been put down. His father will have told his mother he was taking Bucknell to Jackson but instead instructed Gus to take them to the pound. "Doing the hard job," his father will say.

There are things Jackson does know. It is still early. Jackson's wife is still sleeping, and the newspaper hasn't come. Jackson can avoid patients and designing kitchens for a few more hours. Dogless, he goes back to bed, turns his pillow over, and pulls up the quilt. His wife slumbers on beneath the light touch of his hand on her back. Jackson puts himself to sleep.

My Honey

For the second time he calls me honey, this famous author, our dinner guest. My husband does not or pretends not to notice. My cousin's eyes widen but she continues to smile. We became acquainted with this famous author after my husband wrote a favorable review of his recent controversial book on another famous author, earning his gratitude and the suggestion that he come to dine. Now, seated nearest him, I pour more Graves into his glass, watering his legendary love for the grape. We will need another bottle for sure. To his dwindling credit he brought two superb bottles of Graves—and he clearly intended them to be shared with him this very evening. I loathe the word "shared." Lately, my eighteen-year-old daughter has been sharing too many of her strong opinions with me. Tonight's opinion was just how late she could stay out with my car. She says it's her freckles that keep me thinking that she's a child.

It is a good Graves. When he gestures with his glass to mine and says, "Honey, do see to your own lovely self," I forgive him.

Talk has circled around to unsuspecting authors' waning reputations and their latest recycled books. He assures me that he intends to read mine. When he calls me honey for the fourth time, I put both hands flat on the table, a gesture my husband, for some reason, finds enormously sensual, and I lean forward toward our guest. "Please," I say politely. "Please do not call me honey."

My husband appreciates my gesture, knowing he's the only one who views it that way, and there's no doubt that later tonight we'll make love. He does not, however, appreciate the request I just made to our famous author. My husband clears his throat as our guest rolls right over what I said, as if I, too, merely cleared my throat. More wine slides down, and soon my husband suggests we move to the living room with glasses and sit by the fire to counter the chill in the air.

There is where the famous author calls me honey once again. At this point I drop the famous from my thinking.

Perhaps if I'd been seated across the room, or petting a cat on my lap, or stirring up the fire—anything but sitting next to this man—I would not have thrown my glass of wine at him. Thrown is not quite accurate, it just sounds more dramatic—but what I did was lift my glass, gracefully turn my wrist, and douse his head with his very good Graves.

Douse. He is very wet.

Everyone but me goes into action. The author sits up straight, blinks. Droplets fly. My cousin appears with a pink towel. My husband appears with the famous author's jacket.

They are all talking at once. "God damn . . ." the author murmurs from behind the towel. My cousin announces that she is going to make a pot of strong coffee. My husband, holding out the author's jacket, apologizes profusely for my bad behavior and says he imagines that the author would indeed like to take his leave.

The author shakes his head, his hair still weeping wine, and, looking thoughtfully at me, he says, "No, I'll have a double scotch."

Can the evening move on from there? Well, somehow it does, and my daughter is only an hour late with the car. She's read the famous author's books and joins us in the living room, where she introduces herself and her freckles, then sits across from us on the parsons bench. Her jeans have holes at the knees. Clearly she suspects I won't make a scene about her late arrival in front of everyone and she is right. One scene per evening is what I allow myself.

Now the famous author is famous again because my daughter thinks he is. He is also enjoying his double scotch as he asks her about the guitar case she arrived with, college applications, and her favorite authors. He is openly gratified that she has read his book, and then I hear it. My cousin hears it. My husband hears it. My daughter hears it too. That "Honey."

My daughter leans forward, arms on her knees, and says, "Whoa. Wait a minute. Did you just call me 'honey?'"

The famous author laughs. "Of course not," he lies. "Heaven forbid."

We let him lie. That daughter of mine sits back, arms crossed, and smiles. That daughter of mine with her strong opinions, her tantrums and her tears, she has real power. That daughter of mine can do anything she wants.

from *Ways to Spend the Night*

(2016)

Grief

Harris was walking his usual route to work, up Beacon Street and past the State House, when half a block ahead he saw their stolen car stopped at a red light. It was their missing car all right—a white '94 Honda Accord, license plate 432 DOG, easy to remember—and it was still pumping out pale blue exhaust, portent, Harris recalled thinking, of a large muffler bill and so much grief.

He quickened his pace to get a look at the driver leaning against his door, the driver's fingers drumming impatiently on the wheel as if he had better things to do with his time and Harris's car than wait for the light to turn green. Or maybe the police cruiser idling two cars behind was making him nervous.

Harris ran back to the cruiser and rapped sharply on the window, passenger's side. It scrolled down at a snail's pace. Pointing, Harris told the cop, "See that car two cars ahead? The white Honda. That's my car. It was stolen two weeks ago. See it? That's my car."

As the light turned green, the Honda pulled away with the rest of the morning traffic. Bursts of adrenaline shot through Harris— the first thing he'd felt in the year since his wife's death.

The cop looked after Harris's disappearing Honda and then back at Harris as if trying to decide if he was a nut. "OK, Mister, get in," the cop said. For once Harris was grateful for the respectable-looking briefcase his wife had given him on their twenty-fifth anniversary.

Harris yanked on the door handle but it was locked.

"No, in back," the cop said. "Get in the back."

Harris threw his briefcase onto the backseat and slid in behind what was surely a bullet-proof window between him and the cop, taxi-style. Siren blaring, they crept down Beacon Street in a low-speed chase and swung right on Tremont. Cars parted for them reluctantly—giving up feet not yards.

Thirty seconds later they were bumper to bumper with Harris's stolen car and the cop was strongly suggesting on his loud speaker that the driver pull over. Harris was sitting forward, his nose inches from the scratched plastic divider. "That's it, that's my car," he said.

"You wait here," the cop said, as if Harris had foolishly been planning to accompany him on the dangerous stroll to the stolen car. Unbidden images came to Harris's mind. He pictured a stash of cocaine or a weighty little handgun the new owner had tucked under the driver's seat or hidden among their maps of New England. If the thief had noticed all the hiking guides, he probably wondered why Harris needed a car.

Now the cop was standing outside Harris's car, legs spread in cop-stance, no doubt asking to see the driver's license and registration. Good luck. The registration was in the glove compartment where it belonged, but hidden—his wife's idea—inside a paperback mystery involving root vegetables. The cop car's siren and flashing lights had drawn a business-suited crowd, which gathered at a safe distance from any anticipated mayhem.

Knowing Boston, Harris had never hoped to get their car back—and still road-worthy. He'd merely expected to come home to a message from the police on his answering machine saying they'd found his car trashed and wired on the campus of Tufts or MIT or abandoned in a bad part of town. The day after his wife died, he'd driven an hour west on I-90 until he came to a rest stop with a phone booth. He'd pulled the folding door shut against the outside world, and he'd called home over and over to hear her voice say, "Hello, please leave a message. We don't want to miss anything." Then he'd saved the tape and recorded a message of his own.

"No license on him," the cop said as he dropped into the front seat. "Says he left the registration with his sister cause she's trying to sell the car for him." He punched 432 DOG into a black box on the dash. Seconds later, like a fax—maybe it *was* a fax—out scrolled a sheet of paper with not much written on it, but the cop studied it thoroughly. He verified Harris's name, address, and when he'd reported the car missing. Then once again he told Harris "Wait here" and approached Harris's stolen car, where he motioned for the driver to get out. The crowd drew back.

The driver's Red Sox jacket had a ripped sleeve and his jeans were faded to a pale blue. Short and stocky, he was this side of forty, a limp ponytail hanging off a bald rump of a dome.

The cop spun him around and told him to lean against the car, his legs spread apart, then he patted Ponytail down movie-style before clamping handcuffs on his wrists. Satisfied, the cop pointed to where Harris sat waiting and gave Ponytail a slight nudge toward him. Soon Ponytail was peering in at Harris on one of those fake freeze frames Harris would trust in any movie from that moment on. His gaze was cool, not giving anything away. Real static hissed on the cop's radio as the dispatcher asked if the cop wanted backup. "Nah," the cop said through the front window, "I'm bringing him in."

Somehow Harris couldn't picture himself and Ponytail locked in, side by side, in the back seat of this cruiser. He tried to roll down the window but it wouldn't budge.

The cop nodded for Harris to get out—what else could his nod mean? Harris gathered up his briefcase and waited for the cop to open the door. Harris's peripheral vision assured him that Ponytail and he were not going to do anything rash like make eye contact a second time.

"The car's all yours," the cop said. "Keys are in it."

All three of them looked at Harris's car, helping the police cruiser hold up traffic. Their bottleneck was doing a bad job of channeling three lanes of angry drivers into two.

"Thanks," Harris said. Then, "You mean I just drive it away?"

"Anywhere you want," the cop said. "I can't take custody of him and your car at the same time. He's coming with me. I guess that leaves you with the car." His mustache twitched with humor, impatience, and pride.

"Sure thing," Harris said, something he knew he'd never uttered before in his life. "Well, see you around." Feeling a bit ridiculous, Harris took possession of his car. He moved the seat back and adjusted the rearview in time to see Ponytail disappear into cop-carland, the cop's hand on the back of Ponytail's neck to make sure his head cleared the doorframe. The cop pulled out and around Harris, no siren, but his lights still flashing.

Slowly, Harris drove back to his apartment and parked in front, in the same spot from which his car had been stolen. For the first time, he assessed its state—then set to gathering up Dunkin' Donuts cups, McDonald's cartons, and candy wrappers, and stuffed them into a white Dunkin' Donuts sack. The paperback mystery—*Roots of All Evil*—was still in the glove compartment, and just as his wife had predicted, had disguised the registration well. The walking guides and maps were still under the seat; there was no handgun. And when Harris got home after work that night there was no wife to tell the story to.

*   *   *

Three days later, he was matching socks and watching the six o'clock news when the phone rang. He hoped it wasn't the solicitous new tenant from the upstairs apartment, a woman whose roast lamb and braised chicken tempted Harris to emerge from his solitary gloom—a gloom he always returned to well-fed but even more despondent. She had probably noticed his car in the street and wanted to hear how he'd got it back, perhaps help him celebrate. He didn't know how to tell her that more than the car was still missing. When he said "Hello," he felt instant relief that it was not the woman upstairs, but a man's gravelly voice. "You got my TVs," the voice said.

Harris told him he had the wrong number.

"No I don't," he said. "I want my TVs."

Harris hung up and went back to sorting socks. Mostly black, they were draped over the back of the couch, side by side, toes pointing down, the way his wife used to line them up. Now, fewer and fewer of them matched. The phone rang again. It was probably the guy missing his TVs, and Harris thought, "Let him."

*   *   *

Next night, about the same time, the phone rang. Harris was sitting on the couch beside the leftover socks, again dreading the cheerful voice of the woman upstairs. A man's gravelly voice said, "They're in the trunk of your car."

"The TVs?" Harris said.

"See, I knew you had them."

Harris matched the man's TVs with his own stolen car. Ponytail. Knowing Boston, what had made Harris think Ponytail would be arrested, indicted, convicted, and put away? The cop never suggested to Harris that he should press charges, a failure pointed out by his cynical colleague in the accounting firm where Harris spent his days.

"The cop probably dropped your Ponytail-guy at the next corner," Rentz had said. Clearly, Ponytail wasn't calling Harris now from some jail. Lord, Harris didn't need this. "Look—"

The man cut him off. "You got your car back safe and sound. No harm done. I just want my TVs."

"How did you get my number," Harris asked.

"Information," the man said. "AT&T."

"Someone's here," Harris said. "Can we talk about this another time?"

"You'll talk TVs tomorrow?"

"Tomorrow," Harris said, and hung up, picturing Ponytail carless, standing in some phone booth near a bus stop or subway, figuring his chances. Harris put a Stouffer's lasagna in the oven and headed out to visit his car.

The car was where he'd parked it when he got it back four days ago. In the beam of his flashlight, he unlocked the trunk and found three TVs wedged in tight, just like the man had said. Harris had to admire the way he packed. With a sharp pang of regret he recalled his annoyance that his wife insisted on packing up the car for their camping trips. She'd assemble everything outside by the car, eye it thoughtfully, then begin with the large items first—the tent, the kerosene stove. At the end, there'd be no extra space, but nothing left behind.

The TVs weren't new, but newer than Harris's, with large blank screens. All of a sudden he felt very tired.

The next night he waited for the call, not sure what he'd say. He turned the news on with no sound. The back of the couch was free of socks, the socks put away. Who said they had to match? When the phone rang Harris was ready with a gruff hello, but this time it was the woman upstairs calling to say she'd just slipped a stuffed free-range roasting chicken into the oven and it was far too much for one person. It would be ready in about two hours. Cornbread and onion stuffing, she said, and quite a bit of tarragon. Harris' wife had always used sage and rosemary. For what must have been the fifth or sixth time, Harris thanked her and said he'd bring a bottle of wine. He imagined the new photographs his upstairs neighbor would show him, her son's gourmet peppers, or alarming images from her daughter's latest assignment with Doctors Without Borders—a daughter who had his neighbor's same pale hair and deep-set, discerning eyes. He could hear his neighbor's stories of Sip, her cat, who carefully coated his trousers with hair, her hints about a new movie she'd like to see at the theater down the block. He wouldn't tell her, and she couldn't know, that his wife and he had held hands in every movie they ever saw—her hand in his, their fingers changing pressure in her lap of wool, or denim, or silk. Often now, his hands felt empty. His neighbor couldn't know he was afraid, no, terrified, that in a moment of high emotion or fright at the images on the screen, he might reach for her hand—her perfectly good, but achingly unfamiliar hand.

"I'll bring a bottle of white wine," he said, because he didn't know how to say no. Then he clicked off the silent news and hauled out his briefcase. Two hours was enough time to get through tonight's office work

Ponytail called five minutes later.

To Harris's surprise, he found himself taking part in complicated, delicate arrangements to give back the TVs. Of course, this was after Ponytail explained that they had once been in dire need of repair, but now they were ready to be returned to their impatient owners. "I pick up and deliver," he said. "This won't take long. You got any TVs, toaster ovens, anything giving you trouble?"

"Just the TVs," Harris told him. They said goodbye.

Ten minutes later Harris was driving to the appointed place, wondering if he really would go through with this maneuver. Lately, he didn't feel prepared for anything. He probably wouldn't be meeting

Ponytail if his wife were at home waiting for him, worrying. They would have talked it over, together come up with a plan. It saddened him that he didn't know what she would have wanted him to do.

As arranged, Ponytail was standing on the corner of Government Center, near the subway stop, only a few blocks from the spot where Harris had been given back his car. Neither of them had suggested Ponytail come to Harris's house. Though the September night was warm, Ponytail's hands were tucked into the front pocket of his Red Sox jacket. This made Harris a little nervous. He pulled to the curb and beeped his horn twice. Ponytail glanced at Harris's car, and then, as if to shield himself from a brisk wind, he slowly turned full circle to light a cigarette behind cupped hands. Clearly, he was looking for a trap, and somehow his caution made Harris feel a little better. Finally, Ponytail sauntered over and leaned down as if to make sure it was Harris, then casually he flicked away his cigarette and tugged on the handle of the passenger door. It was locked; Harris had made sure it was locked before setting off. Ponytail didn't seem to find the locked door strange and stepped back with a nod. Harris, embarrassed by his own unaccustomed display of caution, got out. His car idled in a light cloud of blue exhaust.

Across the Accord's roof, Ponytail squinted at him. "Like I said on the phone, this won't take long. An hour maybe." He took his hands out of his pockets and placed them flat on the car's roof—as if to offer Harris, with this gesture, his assurance that he was not going to do anything rash. No doubt he was counting on the same from Harris.

"Okay," Harris said, thumping the car's roof with the flat of his palm. "Let's do it." Once again, adrenaline was pumping through him as it had when he first spotted his car. He slid behind the wheel, leaned over to unlock the passenger's door. Ponytail got in, the first passenger to ride in his car since his wife died. Although he'd never thought of his wife as a passenger. Ponytail's knuckles were white and his fingers drummed on worn denim knees.

"Where to?" Harris said, belatedly thinking he should have told someone—maybe the woman upstairs—where he was going.

"Get onto Storrow and head up Route 1." Ponytail buckled his seatbelt and slouched against the door, eyeing his side mirror, his ponytail a wisp on his solid shoulder. Stealthily Harris rubbed the back of his neck, unable to imagine securing his hair with a rubber band, unable to feel a ponytail swishing against his collar, surprised even to consider it.

Once they were on the open road, Ponytail said, "Hear that rattle? Oil needs changing."

Harris glanced down at the dash which was reassuringly dark. "A light usually comes on if—"

"Them lights don't know nothing."

"So, you think it's the oil?" Harris said.

"I was gonna do it."

"Yes, well, thanks," Harris said.

"You probably know about the muffler," Ponytail said.

Harris told him he did. Then, "You been repairing TVs long?"

Ponytail thought for a moment. "Nah. Not too long. What do you do?"

"Mostly tax returns," Harris said.

"Repairing tax returns long?" Ponytail said.

Indeed, Harris thought, but only said "Not too long." They settled into silence as the neon of small roadside businesses flashed by. After a while Ponytail told Harris to turn off Route 1 and take the overpass, then make a right at Cappy's liquor. Three streets over they were in a neighborhood of two-story houses, lanky trees, and sloping cracked sidewalks. Aluminum siding glowed in the evening's dusk, and one house had a horizontal freezer on the front porch, another house an old-fashioned gas oven. Harris had seen such things on porches before, but now they seemed strange and menacing.

"OK, first stop coming up," he said, trying for a little light-hearted humor. But it turned out—and why was he again surprised?—that all the TVs were going to one house. Ponytail's house.

"I said it wouldn't take long," Ponytail said, as if he was doing Harris a favor by consolidating the deliveries. They pulled into a narrow driveway bordered on one side by a chain-link fence. Lights were on in the downstairs of the house. A green pickup on cement blocks loomed off to the side. Now it was Harris's turn to think about a trap as Ponytail got out and slammed the car door. A jungle gym took up most of the small back yard.

Harris guardedly emerged from his car. Clothes flapped on a clothesline in the skinny side yard next to the driveway: blouses or shirts, workpants, kids' clothes, socks, and a long red dress or robe of some shiny material that caught the light from the street lamp. Ponytail followed Harris's gaze. "Damn dryer's broken," he said. "Wife's been nagging me to fix it. I keep forgetting to order the part." At the fence, beneath a window, he gave a sharp whistle.

Harris backed up fast till he was flat against the car door with thoughts of taking off, TVs and all. Why on earth was he here?

As if on cue, a woman came to the window and peered out through the screen. She was jiggling a kid about two on her hip. Absurdly, Harris found himself noticing that her blonde ponytail was fatter than her husband's.

"Hey," Ponytail called out to her, his thumb jabbing the air in Harris's direction. "He's gonna help me put the stuff in the garage." Another kid, not much older, butted his head under her arm.

"Bring in the clothes when you finish," she said without acknowledging Harris, then smartly wheeled the children away.

"Let's get to it," Ponytail said.

His voice startled Harris, who had been imagining what it would be like to park in this driveway, to live in this house. With studied efficiency, Ponytail heaved up the garage door and turned on the light. "They're going in there," he said. With a jerk of his head, he indicated four sawhorses covered with boards at the rear of the garage. This makeshift table sat under a large, neat wall-board display of tools—most of which Harris didn't recognize—and three small blue cabinets of tiny drawers labeled *Screws* and *Nails* and *Nuts* and *Bolts*. To one side, Harris could make out the sturdy shapes of five microwaves still in their shipping boxes and four spiffy new leaf blowers. Ponytail swiped the table with a rag—it was a kind of "no comment" gesture, and Harris was grateful for it.

Together, they hoisted the first TV out of the trunk. Hobbling sideways, they carried it up the driveway, arms wrapped under and around it, foreheads almost touching across its top.

"Set her down—right—here," Ponytail panted, wiping his face on his jacket sleeve. The TVs were heavy. After the second one, Harris was sweating and huffing; his arms burned. He flexed his fingers and bent to wipe his face on his shirt sleeve, out of shape from no exercise, no long hikes for over a year. They trooped back to the car for the next delivery.

"Done." Ponytail patted the last TV. Carefully, he spread a brown tarp over the TVs and microwaves, then turned off the light. Harris stood to the side while he pulled down the garage door.

"Well—" Harris said, and because he didn't know what else to say, he turned toward his car. It had probably been parked on and off in this same driveway for three whole weeks. The candy wrappers must have been from the kids. Beyond the fence, the shiny robe or dress was fluttering back and forth. It was actually a bathrobe, and Harris could see now that the hem was a little ragged and one of the elbows had a hole in it, but it was still of use. Without thinking, he walked past his car to the clothesline and reached up to undo the clothespins holding the robe in place. The robe was red; it was light and slippery as he folded it over his arm.

Ponytail touched his shoulder. "Hey man, you don't need to do that."

*   *   *

On the way home, Harris forced himself to drive slowly even though the upstairs neighbor was waiting for him. She'd want to know all about his getting the car back, so over dinner he'd recount how he'd spotted his car in traffic, and his surprise that it was still road-worthy. He'd tell her about the telephone calls, the tense drive up Route 1, the wife and kids at the window, the garage full of companionable leaf blowers, microwaves and TVs. He'd tell her how, as he was pulling out of the drive, Ponytail had slapped the side of his car, hard, and Harris had jumped like he'd been shot, but Ponytail only wanted to tell him "Remember to check the oil." Then maybe somewhere along toward dessert, Harris would tell her more about his wife.

Breathe

For L. S.

Beginning with the very first fire at the unused Rotary Hall and the police report of suspected arson, Paul was fascinated and secretly collected every newspaper clipping he could find. As each story hit the evening news, he took in the wailing sirens of 2:00 a.m. alarms, the purple lakes of smoke hovering above the town, the surprising choice of scene: an old harness factory, the boarded-up house on Third and Main where drugs changed hands like candy.

His mom would come in from peeling or slicing in the kitchen, and his dad would be kicked back in his recliner, one eye on the sports page, while tiny cobalt flames from the night before raged and died on the TV screen.

"What's this world coming to?" Paul's mom said more than once, a knife or potato peeler suspended in the air. She worked the ER at Community Hospital four days a week, taught biology to nurses in training, and Paul guessed she knew exactly what the world was coming to.

"They'll find him sooner or later," his dad would say. Then he'd tell Paul to get the new glove from his ninth birthday and they'd head out to the street so Paul could practice his pitch. He was always surprised at the pinpoints of light, the heat in his father's eyes.

"You gotta try and make the team, and that requires lots of practice," his father said their last time out.

Paul was tempted to tell his father about a mean kid named Jeremy, who practiced his throwing arm on birds and flowers and occasionally on Paul or Billy Fraily. It used to be Jeremy started all the fights, but now Paul started a few on his own. He could tell when Jeremy was working up to a fight and all Paul had to do was point at the purple birthmark covering Jeremy's entire left cheek. "Your kids are going to have bigger birthmarks than that. It's in your genes," Paul told him, adding that sometimes it looked like a badge but more often like rotten grapes. Right now Jeremy was first team pitcher.

"What if I don't make the team?" Paul asked as his father placed Paul's fingers on the ball for a breakaway pitch. His father's eyes had narrowed.

"You're my son. You got to learn survival."

His father was big on survival. It had to do with Vietnam and his trouble sleeping, and why he kept saying no when Paul asked about getting a dog. "Come on, Frank," his mother said last week. "Every boy needs a dog. You're worse than when you came back from the war." His father had shrugged and said he'd learned to sleep light over there because too many guys were on drugs. "When those guys sat on watch I was on watch with 'em. Couldn't trust 'em." He said he'd get on the radio to them at odd times to keep their ears in practice. He said it might be years before he'd sleep OK. Till then, he didn't need anything moving around at night, or any damn dog triggering his nightmares. The slightest noise and he'd be reaching for his gun, so he didn't want guns in the house either. He'd said it again to Paul yesterday: "No dog. They eat dogs over there."

"Frank!" his mother said.

"No dog."

                    *   *   *

Every time a fire was reported on the evening's news, Paul dreamed about it the following night. He didn't think of these dreams as nightmares. His news clippings came from Mr. Felco, their next door neighbor, because Paul's father said he didn't want any world news coming into the house—especially bad news about what the US military was or wasn't doing. Mr. Felco sat in his wheelchair all day filling out racing forms and watching reruns of movies and soaps. Mr. Felco's wife died last year, so Paul ran errands for him after school, took out garbage, washed dishes, and stacked his day-old newspapers on the back porch, where he'd tuck the front page into his jacket. Headlines grew larger when the police and fire department figured out the fires were no freak of nature. *Arson* is a short word, so they used it often, far more than *incendiary* or *conflagration* or *pyromaniac. Firebug,* was Mr. Felco's word. Paul snuck his mother's pinking shears to cut out the columns of stories and photographs. Then he rolled back the faded rug beside his bed and threw out the collection of dog pictures he'd cut from magazines. They didn't look much like dogs anyway: too sleek or fluffy, or deeply wrinkled or with ankles as thin as a garden hose, more like exotic animals, not pets. Dogs that wouldn't know what to do with a stick or a ball. He wanted a dog-dog. He lined up his new clippings in rows under the rug's edge. At night, when he walked back and forth, they crackled like dry leaves catching fire. Sometimes, he could feel their heat through his socks.

*   *   *

Paul was at school when the police came.

His father had gotten off work and was probably starting a second beer while brewing mugs of Theraflu for Paul's mother, who was home sick. Her eyes were red when she told Paul. She said she didn't even get to change out of her bathrobe or tell his father goodbye—they came and went that fast. Too fast, Paul hoped, to find his stash of clippings. "You wait," she said. "Where do they get off—blaming him for those fires? They'll find out they've got the wrong guy."

"When?" Paul said.

"Don't worry," his mother said, hands on his shoulders in a gesture his father often used. "Soon. He'll be home soon. I bet in time to see you pitch your first game of the season."

"No way," Paul said, thinking *What first game?* Especially with Jeremy still practicing on birds. He wanted his father home, but how can you fear and want the exact same thing?

"Now go do your homework. Aren't you writing that report on genes?" She gave him a little push, saying maybe coach would fill in with extra practice time. After seeing him off, she got back on the phone, her voice shaky, talking bail and bonds.

Paul locked his door, took off his shoes, and walked back and forth on the border of his rug.

Then, lifting the frayed top edge, he slid out the first account from nine months ago—the old harness factory on faded, yellow newspaper, itchy with rug hairs. He placed his father at the scene of each fire, reconnoitering the territory like he'd do for his job at the gas company, measuring streets for gas mains and repairing faulty pipes. Maybe arson was in their genes? Like his father's red hair and sharp green eyes, his long big toe. His mother had blonde hair, and a million freckles mostly on the left side of her face, but as far as Paul could tell she hadn't shown up in him yet.

He knew this for sure: his father would hate jail. It would be too much like the army—counting heads, sitting around, waiting for something to happen and dreading it at the same time. His father said that of all the things you learned to kill in the army, what you wanted most to kill was time—something he hoped Paul never had to learn.

He pictured his father lying on his back on some narrow cot, hands folded behind his head, eyes closed. Maybe he'd be thinking about their pitching practice, or better yet, their fishing trips when he taught Paul how to breathe underwater, how to wade the creeks without making a sound or causing a ripple larger than a small trout would make catching flies. "Called survival. At times, we hid in those putrid rivers so long you could feel yourself rotting from the toes up. But at least it meant you were still alive." After one really bad nightmare his father woke screaming, and while Paul shivered in the hallway, his father had described to Paul's mother the stretchers full of arms and legs they collected after devastating firefights. Bodies half-burned, parts strewn everywhere and how the guys tried to put them back together. Someone filling a body bag would call out, "I need an arm" and someone else would yell "Black or white?" and, depending on the reply, "Can't help you there." Or "I got two—right or left?" But even Paul knew two legs or two arms didn't mean they got the person put back together right. If the genes were wrong maybe the body parts would fight it out. An arm could get rejected or rot.

A week later, Paul asked his father what a body bag looked like. He said that he'd watched *War and Pieces* with Mr. Felco but they didn't seem to use body bags in that war. In that war bodies were carted away or just left to the weather.

"'Peace,' not 'pieces,'" his mother said. *"War and P-e-a-c-e."*

His father sat there at the dinner table, not answering, his head in his hands. Paul's mother moved to knead his father's shoulders, saying that he should talk to someone. And to Paul she said, "You have to stop listening so hard." Why, he'd wondered, when listening hard had kept his father alive.

He put his clippings away and smoothed down the rug, leaving room for news of his father's arrest. Bottom line, he wanted his father home. Even if it meant his father would be complaining about nightmares, or keeping tabs on all the walks Paul gave up to the other team, or saying no to a dog. Paul wanted him home because he had questions he needed to ask.

*   *   *

His father never did get out on bail even though his case didn't come up till two months later. In all that time, his mother refused to let Paul visit. "County jail's no place for kids. Write him letters," she said. She brought home letters his father had written to him asking for reports on school and stuff, and sure, Paul wrote back, but he knew a letter wasn't the way to tell him about their secret collection of clippings.

When school let out for the summer, the third side of Paul's rug was almost full with news of his father's arrest and upcoming trial. Paul didn't walk on that side. Headlines had gotten smaller again and soon the articles were buried on the inside pages with ads for ladies' underwear, recipes, and world news. Mr. Felco had gotten more interested in the papers so Paul had to wait a few days before he could bring them home. This week he'd begun a collection of matches and was up to six books, mostly from Arlene, his mother's friend from work, who came over after shift to talk and plot while she moved from room to room, still in her white uniform, leaving nail files, half-smoked cigarettes and matches in her wake—matches from Rita's Place, The Bombshelter, Sweet Licks.

Because his mother wouldn't let Paul go to court for the trial, he had to catch it on nightly news. Each day after school he went next door to old Mr. Felco, who said, "Yo, Paul," when Paul walked in. He'd learned "Yo" from TV. Paul did his homework at the dining room table while Mr. Felco zapped the tube and said what he always said: "The people who write these soaps understand the true state of the world, more than those bozos down in Washington." Today he added, "Those generals weren't too good to boys like your dad." And then he hit the remote.

As music for *Heaven's Bounty* soared into the room, he said, "*Heaven's Bounty* did arson ten years ago." Paul said that was before he was born. Mr. Felco said too bad he missed it cause he didn't think they'd sold out yet to reruns.

An hour later, Paul joined Mr. Felco for *Cradle to Grave* till his mother called to him through Mr. Felco's screen door. Her eyes glistened and her nose was rawly red. It was plain his father had been convicted. Mr. Felco didn't ask any questions, just told her to send Paul over anytime.

Walking home, his mother squeezed Paul's face into the belt of her coat. "Don't you believe it," she said. Her chest heaved above his head like a storm, and he thought, *But what about all their clippings?*

Arlene was bustling around. She put glasses in the freezer and mixed up a pitcher of margaritas while his mother went up to the bedroom to call his grandfather who was in the Veterans Home with Alzheimer's. She said she better prepare him for hearing his name on TV since Paul's father was a "Jr."

Paul was asking Arlene about her dog—a golden retriever not good at retrieving—when his mother returned. Slumping into a chair she reported that her father-in-law said he was leaving the Vets Home and going right out to enlist tomorrow. "He's forgotten every awful war experience he ever had. Jesus, but look what it took." When Paul asked how soon he could see his father, she said as soon as he got to where they were sending him and visiting hours were set.

All evening, a parade of neighbors came and went like they did when old Mrs. Felco died, except no one seemed to know what to say with his father not here, but still alive. Two people brought casseroles, no one sent flowers.

*   *   *

A week later, the judge handed down his father's sentence. On the way home from Mr. Felco's, his mother explained how the judge took into account all the fires the army had encouraged his father to set in Vietnam, and how the US had used napalm to burn the country bare. Arlene was making Bloody Marys. Her earrings sparkled on the table. She and Paul's mother were still in their court clothes—white blouses, skirts, high heels.

"Paulie," Arlene said, ruffling his hair, "it's been a hard day. Now you go watch TV and let your mom and me talk."

As Paul listened from the next room, his mother told Arlene how his father had learned to do terrible things in the war. Paul could tell she was crying as she said he'd talked about it more in the past month than he ever had before. It was all coming out. How six radio operators had died in his arms. When his operators died, he held their guts together and felt their lives drain away. All that blood. Eventually he wouldn't let himself get close to any of them. He'd learn only their last names and would tell them "Stay two steps behind me, one on my right and one on my left." A new recruit the guys named Firebird insisted on reading his letters to Paul's father. He'd say, "But you got to hear this, Daddy Rabbit," when his father refused to listen, and in the end he said they always got through to him. "The worst," he'd told her, "was sending out two men on reconnaissance. There'd be no eye contact. Everyone knew they were going to die." How to choose was a terrible decision, he'd said. Every two months, his CO would put him down for R & R but afterwards they kept sending him back in. He finally started turning down the medals. He couldn't cry anymore. "He never put any of this in letters," she said. "It's all been inside." She stopped talking and the kitchen was silent except for the sound of ice cubes sliding back and forth in glasses. Over Arlene's murmur, she continued. She said the first month he'd been home they'd watched a TV movie about a street gang and, he'd nodded calmly at the screen and said, "They look like they'd be hard to kill."

"Oh, sweetie," Arlene said.

"I don't want to be a nurse at home too," his mother whispered. Paul had to strain to hear her say, "And Paul will never have a sister at this rate. Some guys from his company who stop by every year or so never had any kids. Couldn't. Things happened over there we'll never know."

"Lucky your house is paid off," Arlene said,

"Could we not jump to the bright side yet," his mother flared.

Paul had to ask, had to know. He carried a pillow in front of him, pressed against his heart. "Did the judge say anything about genes?"

"Dammit, Paulie. You were listening again," his mother said, wiping her eyes with a dish towel. "So you know we weren't talking genes. Where do you get genes?"

"But you said my red hair came from Dad, that genes got passed down."

"Paulie," Arlene said. "Don't think about—"

"He just does. He thinks. He's that kind of kid. So wait," his mother said, holding up her flattened hand to Arlene. Then she pulled the pillow from Paul's arms and sent it flying. She put his face between her cold hands. "War isn't in your genes. Sending men to die isn't in your genes," she said, with a fierceness Paul found terrifying.

Arlene put her hand on his mother's arm and shook it. "Please stop, stop that talk." She pushed his mother into a chair and put the pillow on her lap. To Paul, she said, "I'll bet you're hungry. I am even if you aren't." She handed Paul an empty cereal box to throw away and set to washing the morning's dishes with a great clatter. Water whooshed into the sink; knives and forks collided. Steam rose. "I brought a casserole," she said. "Heat it up."

Their gas stove was ancient and had to be lit with a match. Paul watched as his mother struck a match, efficiently, purposefully, but then she stood there transfixed by the tiny flame.

Hands dripping water, Arlene backed up three steps and blew it out. "Frank probably used a lighter," she said.

"And kerosene," Paul said. "In the army they used napalm, but I don't think he could get it here."

When both women swung around to look at him hard, he hurried out of the kitchen saying it was almost time for the news.

*   *   *

His father was the big story on local TV. "Frank Cronin, who a week earlier was found guilty on five counts of arson, was sentenced today," the announcer said. They showed his father being led away in handcuffs. His head was down and his suit jacket flapping. Paul bet his pockets didn't have any matches in them. On TV, Paul's mother and Arlene bobbed behind him. His mother had her hand out as if to keep him steady and Arlene was wearing sunglasses though anyone could tell it was about to rain.

"Oh, Paul, you shouldn't have to be seeing this," his mother said, her voice catching, as she patted the cushion beside her on the couch. Paul settled into her arms, his eyes on the screen.

Next, they showed before and after pictures of the abandoned Rotary Hall, the druggie house, and the harness factory as they told about the suspicious nature of the fires, the witness who had spotted his father's pickup, his fingerprints on the can of kerosene. The pictures of the harness factory were old. Black and white. Drifts of snow covered the bottom of the windows. One picture inside the factory showed boys Paul's age wearing flat caps and short pants like Babe Ruth's baseball uniform.

"Why aren't they in school?" Paul asked. His mother was big on school.

"Look at their clothes, Paul. The short pants, long heavy socks. Horses pulling the wagon. That picture was taken at least a hundred years ago," his mother said. "Those poor kids. It was way before child labor laws." Her voice was almost normal—like when she was helping with his school reports on bacteria or the human eye or talking about work—and he knew she'd be OK.

*   *   *

At the playing field, Jeremy called, "Hey, Paulie, your pitching's getting worse." He was throwing a hard ball at his captive catcher, Billy Frailly. "I hear your dad won't be home for a while."

Paul could have told him that.

"And there ain't been a fire since he got arrested. My dad said 'What more proof do they need?'" Wheeling, Jeremy blazed a hard fast ball at Paul, who stopped it with the heel of his gloveless hand. Billy Fraily snickered.

Paul didn't throw the ball back to Jeremy; he walked it over to him, his hand numb with pain, and slammed the ball into his glove. Aiming well, he poked Jeremy's cheek hard with his index finger.

"That's not a birthmark," Paul told him. "That's a deathmark."

That evening, when Jeremy's mother called Paul's mother to complain about Jeremy's torn shirt and bloody nose, Paul figured it was time to act.

The next day he strapped on his father's old army belt and pack, his tin canteen and rode his bike up and down the streets. Wavering heat mirages rose from the pavement as Paul scouted the town for what his father saw. He pictured him on his lunch break, wolfing down a sandwich before going out on reconnaissance, like he did in Nam. He'd feel the grime of black lines smudged under his eyes, the damp rustle of leaves from trees whose names he didn't know taped to his helmet or woven into a net, his feet deep in muck. His father would remember as if it were only yesterday. He'd drive slow and deliberate, squinting the town's blocks into long terraced stretches of rice paddies capable of hiding whole hordes of tiny submerged Viet Cong. He'd be looking for sagging huts—"They were that country's landmines, those deserted villages," his father once said. The matches in Paul's pocket felt puny for the job they had to do, the man they had to save. He imagined headlines—once more in big type: **ARSON AGAIN.** Then in smaller type: **Convicted Arsonist in Jail.** What would Jeremy's father and the police make of that?

His search ended beyond the high school football field, at the town cemetery. Bordered by a low stone wall, the cemetery hadn't been mowed the whole summer because the town voted down new taxes. Wild grass grew high and yellow like the jungle his father described burning, burning after the tremendous silence from fire raids and their momentary vacuum of air. His father said in Nam the sun's heat was so fierce that even the insects flew at half speed. He said there were twenty-seven species of poisonous snakes they forgot to mention at Fort Bragg. He said that sometimes Vietnam was deathly beautiful.

Paul propped his bike against a broken wooden gate and waded in through the tall grass and weeds till he found a flat tombstone just right for laying out his supplies. Knife. Matches. He'd have to leave fast. Carved words read:

> *Elmer Wissle, 1894–1918*
> *Beloved Husband and Father*
> *And His Country's Fallen Son.*

Wissle's gravestone was flaking at the corners and covered with scraggly brush, not getting the care it deserved. Eight tall trees flanking the sides of the graveyard would give his fire height. He hoped his father would be able to watch it on the news. He hoped his father would notice all the lessons he'd given Paul about survival.

Paul used his father's army knife to cut and rake together a pile of dry grass, then reached wider to gather twigs from recent thunderstorms. The matchbook was from Sousa's Bar and Grill. He would not *Close Before Striking.* He felt dizzy from bending over but when he looked up the sun's glare forced his eyes back down, and its afterimage became a ball of fire as he struck a single match. The flame wavered and descended almost to his fingers before he blew it out. It didn't smell like anything his father described. The sun's image faded to a tiny dot, so this time he put two matches together for a stronger flare. Holding his breath, he lowered his cupped hands toward the heap of twigs. Flame to fire. His eyes were wet with sweat and longing. What did it take for someone to start a fire? What did it take for his father to start a fire? To go to war?

He blew the matches out.

He couldn't do it, not even to help his father survive. *Why?* Was it because he wasn't being tracked and hunted to ground, to riverbed, or being haunted in his sleep, or maybe there was no one and nothing out there he'd learned to hate enough to kill?

He swept his supplies into his father's backpack. The water in the canteen was warm. He drank it all. Suddenly, the heat of the afternoon contained a sound he'd know anywhere. It was the rattle made by his father's pickup, the clanking of the tailpipe his father gleefully tolerated, saying that after Nam it was pure luxury to let people know he was coming.

His mother was still in her nurse's uniform. Her face gleamed with sweat and her long hair was ratty from the wind. After slamming the door, she walked over to his bike, then looked around, calling his name.

He shouldered his father's backpack and went out to meet her.

As he lifted his bike into the back of the pickup, she said she'd been hunting for him for over an hour, that Mr. Felco was beside himself trying to comfort her with stories of foiled kidnappings from his soaps. Arlene had talked her into scouting out the town before calling the police. "It's lucky I spied your bike. What on earth were you doing in there?"

What could he say? He tucked his father's backpack near the bike and brought the canteen with him into the truck.

"You're feeling pretty bad about all this, aren't you Paulie?"

He had to say something anything or he would cry. "I want a baby brother," he said. "Or a dog."

"A dog," she said. "You know your father—"

"I want a dog." He didn't back down.

*   *   *

"The dog I could do," she told Arlene later when they'd come home from the Animal Rescue League. All three of them had gone to the store for dog food and a dog bed Arlene predicted the puppy would never use. Paul stuck it in the closet and settled the puppy on his second pillow. The dog was brown with big ears and a skinny tail. It would probably never get its picture in a magazine. "I'll tell your father we have a dog," she said. "The time has come."

Things settled down. Soon, instead of Paul's father, people in town were talking about the missing councilman presumed to be accompanied by the missing twenty thousand from the county building's safe. Three weeks later, his mother put on pink lipstick and drove them to the state penitentiary two hours away in Gardner. It was a minimum-security prison, which meant Paul's father could walk around with them when they got there. "Visitors," his mother said into a microphone as if they were ordering fast food take-out. Low gray buildings were strung together with gray airless breezeways. All the rooms were painted gray or green and dimly lit.

His father's hair was very short and not as red. He was thinner. Paul and his mother stepped into hugs they couldn't seem to leave. They all must have planned not to cry.

"Tour, who wants a tour?" his father said. His room was small and neat, with a photograph of Paul and his mother that used to be on the mantle, now on a shelf with books on narrow gauge railroads, famous rivers of the world.

When Paul's mother said she had packages in the car that she needed to clear through the front office, his father suggested he and Paul take the tour first. Paul knew she was giving them time alone.

A guard unlocked an iron door to the outside. Paul's father nodded to another man in similar clothes who was being pulled toward a cement bench by a young girl in a bright yellow dress. As they walked around the grounds, his father put his hands on Paul's shoulders and steered him like a train. Saving his questions for later, Paul told him about not making the A team in little league and about the new dog. He said it was still in the puppy stage and that his mother said there must be a word for training dogs. It wasn't toilet training she said.

"House training," his father said. "We'll tell her when she comes back." He said to let Mr. Felco know he hadn't missed one episode of *Cradle to Grave* since he'd been in prison.

Paul repeated what Mr. Felco said the afternoon his father was convicted: that *Heaven's Bounty* did arson ten years ago.

His father stopped steering Paul and they coasted to a stop. "Haven't given up on your old man, have you?"

Paul squinted up at his father then looked around to see if anyone could hear. "What were you going to burn down next?" It took his breath away to say it.

His father hesitated, looking Paul in the eye—his green eyes to Paul's green eyes. "Hey, Paul. What is this? Research time?"

"I bet I can guess," Paul said.

"It wasn't like I had a mission," his father said. "Or any big plan like the Big Brass claimed they had for Nam, but sure as shit didn't."

"The cemetery," Paul said. He studied his father's face.

His father threw Paul an imaginary pitch. "No, not the cemetery." He said he had too much respect for the dead. And when he got out of this place, he said he was going to take a trip with other veterans, guys like himself, go back to Nam, visit one or two of their cemeteries, look up some of the soldiers they'd been fighting against. Like a pilgrimage. Maybe take Paul and his mother when Paul was older. When he set to steering Paul again, Paul's shoulders felt lower and weak with relief.

His father talked while he steered. "It was like the war, Paulie. Sooner or later, it had to end."

*   *   *

Paul took photographs of the puppy to show his father. "Now that's a dog," his father said. Kids in the neighborhood came by to teach the dog to play run-and-fetch-it. Jeremy watched from the sidewalk, the front wheel of his bike nudging the edge of their lawn, his birthmark flaming with puzzled heat.

The dog still wasn't house-trained—"Your father said that was the word we were looking for," his mother told him—and Paul's rug was evidence enough. The clippings grew yellow and damp. His room smelled. He stopped walking around in his socks.

A week later, the dog barked. Standing in front of the door, it barked again. A sharp, urgent bark. "About time," his mother said, watching from the doorway as the dog lowered his flat backend into a squat, ran a few steps in the grass, then raised his leg to the oak tree.

It happened a second time, same day. "Home free," his mother said. "It's probably safe to send your rug out for a good cleaning."

Paul threw away the clippings and it felt like he'd put out a fire and was coming up for air.

On their last fishing trip, before the harness factory fire, Paul and his father had been up to their knees in a narrow creek, forlornly casting silver loops of fishing line, swatting flies. The day's heat was keeping the trout deep and sluggish. Giving up on fish—but only on fish, Paul realized now—his father had waded over to the bank and broken off a tall, hard reed. He blew air through it, tickling Paul's neck, to show Paul that it was hollow inside.

"You can hide under water for hours with one of these," he said. "We could hear them on the banks looking for us and we'd be hunkered down, five six men, with our reeds only an inch above the water."

His father broke off a second reed and squatted low in the warm lazy current. He held out his hand to Paul, who crouched down beside him, buoyant in the shallow water. Then he put the reed to Paul's lips and said, "Lean your head back and let yourself sink under the water, slowly, slowly, don't make a sound. Now breathe. Breathe in and out through the reed. Breathe." And Paul did.

Reading in His Wake

"At last," my husband said, when I had locked up for the night and come to bed.

"You knew I would," I said.

"But I didn't know when." Propped up in the recently rented hospital bed, he peered more closely at my chosen book. A novel by Patrick O'Brian. "Wait, no, no," he said. "You must begin at the beginning."

"But I like the sound of this one," I said, drawing out the swish of *The Mauritius Command*.

"Ah, but you want to be there when Aubrey and Maturin meet."

"I can always go back," I said, only slightly petulant, aware that at another time we'd never see again I would have been reading favorites, Trevor, Atwood, or Munro. Or tapping into the wall of biographies across from our beds, Marshall's *The Peabody Sisters*, or Ellmann's *James Joyce*. Continuing through the poetry at the top of the stairs: Rivard, Roethke, Ruefle, Solomon, Szymborska.

His eyes gleamed. "But Aubrey and Maturin meet at such an unlikely place—especially to begin the series. They meet at a concert. Italians on little gilt chairs are playing Locatelli." He stopped, out of breath. "Never mind."

"So what's the first one?" If I was going to do this, give him this gift, so to speak, I must do it right. He named *Master and Commander* and, ignoring the irony, I did as commanded and retrieved *Master and Commander* from his study next door. Carefully I settled in beside him, our old queen set flush to his new bed, and embarked. In running commentary over years of hurried breakfasts and long dinners, he'd extolled to me Patrick O'Brian's sheer genius; how in the first novel he delivers to the reader in dramatic scenes of tense negotiation a detailed account of everything that Jack Aubrey must buy to outfit a ship circa 1859.

Four pages and an "introduction" later, I said, "I see what you mean. A most prickly meeting. Maturin delightfully pissy because a rapt Aubrey, from his seat in the scraggly audience, is audibly 'conducting' the quartet a half beat ahead."

"Don't forget their terse exchange of addresses as if for a duel," he said laughing and coughing. I looked toward the oxygen machine, then at him. He shook his head.

Relieved, I slid the damp shoulder of his nightshirt into place. "Conflict on page one," I said, making us both happy.

Fifty pages later, when I murmured "Mmmmmm," he said "What? Tell me." He turned on the pillow with an effort and put aside his own O'Brian, *The Truelove*. So I read for him, ". . . the sun popped up from behind St Philip's fort—it did, in fact, *pop* up, flattened like a sideways lemon in the morning haze and drawing its bottom free of the land with a distinct jerk."

"'. . . distinct jerk,'" he repeated.

I said again, "'. . . drawing its bottom free of the land with a distinct jerk.'" A shared blanket of satisfaction settled over us and we went back to our books, companionably together, and companionably apart.

When I stopped reading to bring him a fresh glass of water to chase his myriad pills, he wanted to know where I was now. I slipped back into bed and tented the book on my flannel chest as I described how Mowett, an earnest member of the square-rigged ship's crew, is explaining sails to a queasy Maturin, and here my husband smiled wryly in queasy recognition of feeling queasy. I took his hand, and went on to describe how Maturin affects interest, although he is exceedingly dismayed to be getting this lesson at the appalling height of forty feet above the roiling seas. "Meanwhile, the reader is getting the lesson, too—and drama at the same time. Here," and I read, "The rail passed slowly under Stephen's downward gaze, to be followed by the sea . . . his grip on the ratlines tightened with cataleptic strength."

"It makes me want to start all over again," my husband said. Then, not to be seen as sentimental, he held up his book to show he'd just finished the most recent O'Brian. It slipped to the rug and we left it there.

"You could read Dave Barry now," I said, acknowledging the only good thing about our new sleeping arrangement. My husband used to read Barry's essays in bed, laughing so hard the bed would shake, shake me loose from whatever I was reading. Annoyed, I'd mark my page and say, "OK, read it to me." The ensuing excerpt was a tone change and mood swing one too many times, because I finally banished Dave Barry from the bed after his column titled "There's nothing like feeling flush," which had my husband out of bed and pacing with laughter. In it, Dave Barry refers to an article published in the *Scottish Medical Journal*, "The Collapse of Toilets in Glasgow." Barry writes, "The article describes the collapsing-toilet incidents in clinical scientific terminology, which contrasts nicely with a close-up, full-face photograph, suitable for framing, of a hairy and hefty victim's naked wounded butt, mooning out of the page at you, causing you to think, for reasons you cannot explain, of Pat Buchanan." We said it again and again. It answered everything: "for reasons you cannot explain."

"Do you want a Barry book?" I asked. He didn't answer. He was either sleeping or wishing I would shut up.

*   *   *

When we were about to leave for radiation, he was still bereft of a new O'Brian. I found him standing in his study, leaning on a walking stick from his collection, now no longer an affectation.

"The Ws are too high," he said, stabbing the air with his stick. "It's Wodehouse I'm after."

"Why Wodehouse?" I said. Jeeves, the perfect valet and gentleman's gentleman, would be totally disapproving of how my husband's shirts went un-ironed and how his trousers drooped on his thinning hips. "I'm almost finished with Trevor's *After Rain,* it has that startlingly dark story about . . ."

"I think I'll read Wodehouse," he said, his jaw set. Out of breath, he slumped into his desk chair and pointed again, "But I can't reach him." On the shelves behind where my husband was pointing ranged the 200-plus books he'd edited at a Boston publishing house, and the four he'd written, the last novel, *A Secret History of Time to Come,* included by the New York Museum of Natural History in a time capsule that would outlast us all. "We have too many books," he said.

"That's what you always say," I said. Hitching up my skirt before the wall of English and European fiction, I mounted the wobbly wooden ladder we swore at on principal every time we retrieved an out-of-reach book. Waugh, Winterson, Wodehouse. I called down three titles before he nodded at the fourth. *The Code of the Woosters.* "Why Wodehouse?" I asked again on my descent.

"Ah, you haven't read Wodehouse yet. Arch, mannered humor. You'll see." Then, as if anticipating my early mutiny against O'Brian in deference to Wodehouse, his eyes narrowed, and he instructed, "Keep with the O'Brians for now."

We left for the hospital, armed with our respective books. On the way, I mentioned that Raymond Chandler, also English, and Wodehouse had both attended the posh prep school Dulwich

College. "Pronounced 'Dul-ich' but spelled 'Dulwich,'" my husband said, surprised by Chandler.

Our bookish, competent doctor always wanted to know what we were reading. My husband waved the Wodehouse at him. "It has a blurb by Ogden Nash," he said, and read, "In my salad days, I thought that P. G. Wodehouse was the funniest writer in the world. Now I have reached the after-dinner coffee stage and I know that he is."

"Woodhouse," the doctor said, making a note on his prescription pad.

"W-o-d-e. I hope he's still funny," my husband said, peering at the doctor over his glasses. "I'm way past the after-dinner coffee. I've reached the medicine stage."

*   *   *

A week later, we were again side by side, my husband's bed rising smoothly and electronically to a barely comfortable position I tried to match with pillows, despairing of the difference in height. I'd finished *Master and Commander* and put it in a safe place because the doctor had meticulously written his home phone number inside its cover. *Post Captain* was next. My husband's long fingers, thin and bony, were oddly free of books because he was listening to the tape of O'Brian's latest Aubrey/Maturin, *The Wine-Dark Sea*. His eyes were alertly closed beneath the Walkman's earphones curving over his new, silky growth of hair.

When he stopped listening to take his pills, I asked him to recall what he'd liked best about *Post Captain*. I closed my eyes against a hysterical welling up of water. And when he'd told me, I thought yes, yes, after years of reading and rereading, arguing, damning and praising, I knew now almost exactly what he would say. Although I didn't tell him this—but tested more. I badgered him about the repetition of one battle scene after another, asked him to name his favorite title in the series, asked him if Maturin ever dies. I moved on to Ford's *The Good Soldier*, didn't the narrator's equivocation grate on his nerves? Yes and no. Who was Dante's best translator? Yes, yes. And what did he think of the poem in *Pale Fire?*

"Stop it," he said, his voice stronger than it had been in days. "Enough."

*   *   *

The next evening, when he had finished both sides of the first tape, he told me to look in his desk for a second Walkman. "Why" didn't matter. "Now, listen to this tape," he said.

"You're still seducing me with literature," I accused him.

He took the tape from his Walkman and inserted it into mine.

"No. No. I can't," I said. "I'll get the plots mixed up." Already I was awash in the unfamiliar world of sloops and frigates, admiring of royals, baffled by masts and yards, and dipping in and out of *A Sea of Words: A Lexicon and Companion for Patrick O'Brian's Seafaring Tales*, chastely beside me on the bed. In love again.

"Here," he said. "Listen."

I donned the earphones and, because he was watching, I closed my eyes. Across the tiny gulf between our beds, his hand found my hand as a calming voice began, "A purple ocean, vast under the sky and devoid of all visible life apart from two minute ships racing across its immensity."

Until my husband's hand slipped from mine, until his breath failed, until I called 911, until the ambulance arrived to provide our last voyage together, on that last evening I sailed precariously in two different seas, astride two listing vessels, keeping a third in view against a dark horizon, reading in his wake.

Home Depot

"James. James, what is that big ugly orange building?" my father-in-law says to me, peering out the sliding door past our scruffy four by four deck.

There is no hiding anything from Henry—especially anything that large. "Home Depot," I say.

My in-laws arrived after dark last night, and by then we'd closed the door to the deck and pulled shut the drapes. This is their first visit since they moved to Miami last winter. As usual, Henry was up at the crack of dawn. An hour ago, the coffee grinder pulverized the beans to powder. Dressed in a white golf sweater and ironed khakis, he's still staring at Home Depot. I'm in my ratty plaid bathrobe.

"It's so close to your house," he says. "Isn't this a residential neighborhood?"

I don't take the bait. I treat Henry's questions as if they are statements I don't have an argument with. Wait till he sees the New and Used Gun Emporium, the three tattoo parlors, and all the fireworks stores that flank Home Depot. Seabrook is famously just over the Massachusetts state line. There's a long stretch of road leading into town where one side of the road is austerely Massachusetts and the other side a bustling, sleazy New Hampshire. No doubt Henry will want a tour today and will soon learn that we are just a mile from the Seabrook Nuclear Power Plant. Its unmistakable silhouette will surely lead to penetrating questions about the federal government's security measures and the town's evacuation procedures. Maybe my in-laws will leave early. But they are, after all, concerned parents. Ten years ago, in my mid-twenties, my parents died within a year of each other, and I miss them: my father's sweet skepticism and my mother's discerning grace. I regret that Maida never met them. Maida who changed her name from Margaret in college, though her puzzled parents still call her Maggie. Maida who never changed her last name to mine. Not a complaint, I tell myself, merely an observation. I am surprised, however, that her parents still don't know the real reason we invited them to visit: that Maida and I are embarking on a trial separation. One of us will be moving out.

Joining Henry on the deck, I give him the only good news. "Look closely down through the locust trees? There's a tiny creek—more like a marsh, actually a wetland—behind the house." I point with my coffee mug to the stand of trees hiding the low, fertile waters. "It separates us from Home Depot's parking lot." They often seem to build on wetlands—Seabrook and Medford, Mass.

Upstairs, the ladies are beginning to stir. Pipes are clanging and closet doors need oiling. Margaret/Maida would be pissed if she knew I thought "ladies."

Henry is bending over the railing, his keen attention now focused on the marsh. "That's probably where all the mosquitoes are breeding. They feasted on us when we unpacked the car last night. Which reminds me that Pony said to ask if you have any Benadryl lotion."

Pony is a nickname I refuse to use when addressing my mother-in-law.

Henry elaborately scratches his arm, and I resist scratching my own three newly acquired bites. "The city sprays a couple times a year," I tell him.

He shakes his head. "More chemicals leaching into the water table. Well, maybe you can get the neighbors to sign a petition." Before they moved, Henry was an alderman in his tiny Indiana town, a town with no Home Depot within two hundred miles. He was also the author of no less than twenty-three petitions.

"Maybe," I say. My own petition is pending with Maida, so I work harder to be a better son-in-law by asking, "A petition for—?"

"A tall fence. Get your neighbors to sign a petition asking Home Depot to put up a fence to hide their store. That way you won't have an orange landscape and what looks like a used-car lot in your backyard. And shady customers won't be thinking they might just wade across that buggy marsh and help themselves to a free computer or TV."

I snort into my mug—being one of Home Depot's best customers. I know the layout of the store so well I could work there: where the safety flashlights are shelved—not with flashlights; which floor surface will need a subfloor, something the literature only obliquely mentions; how to steer their heavy flat-bed carts up and down the aisles in a straight line.

"Those big chains are pretty open to local petitions," he says. "I could help you with the wording. The last petition I drew up was to block a detour that was going to cut into the nesting habitat of the Lesser Prairie Chicken."

*   *   *

Evidently Henry has missed the serious pick-ups skulking in every driveway on our street, half of which are owned by contractors. We are the only people for blocks who drive a car. I feel guilty putting it off onto the neighbors, but I do it anyway, saying, "If the neighbors ever signed a petition it wouldn't be for a fence between us and Home Depot. Hell, their petition would be for a bridge."

"A bridge?" He turns and looks at me, light dawning on his flat face. I nod. It occurs to me that I could use his help, but I don't know how to ask. He sees me hesitate, then with a tightening of my robe, I am on my way upstairs to look for Pony's Benadryl and take a hot shower that I wish Maida would interrupt.

Too late. Her long hair is pulled into a tight knot I like to cup in the palm of my hand, before I set it loose to shadow her full breasts or brush my stomach. She's made our bed with military corners and is already dressed in jeans and a pullover.

"Your father's up," I tell her. When I tug on the zipper of her jeans she pulls my hand away. Reluctantly. Or maybe that is my imagination. She's still holding my hand, when a burst of loud static erupts, like a goose looking for its goslings or mate: *URRRKKKKKK.* Then: *"Ernie to building four with the plane saw. Ernie to building four with the plane saw."* Static again, *URRRRRRKKKKKKKKKKKKKKK.* Then silence. Downstairs, the glass slider lets out a squeal as Henry opens it and steps back out onto the deck.

Maida and I exchange the warmest glance we've shared in weeks.

I open our upstairs window to hear what Henry will hear. That ear-piercing *UURRRRRRKKKKK.*

Sure enough, he calls out as if I'm still listening to him no matter where I am in the house, "Do you two hear that all day?" His voice is so loud that Home Depot's Ernie-with-the-plane-saw also probably hears him.

Maida rolls her eyes. "I was hoping it would rain."

It is raining, a hard, hard rain, I want to say, but don't.

"Your turn to go down there. I've just been," I say to Maida. "Be sure to tell him that their PA system shuts down after four."

With a polite cough, Pony emerges from the guestroom where my computer is being held hostage. The walls still sport a border of gleeful carousels so it must have once been a nursery. Last spring, Maida put "strip the border" at the top of our to-do list, but I said to let it be, that it reminded me of my happy childhood, at which point she'd shrugged hugely, though she didn't ask if I was joking or serious. I actually don't know myself. But the horses and lions still prance near the ceiling while I write software programs for a sedentary living.

Pony does not meet my gaze, actually my dismay that she is in full make-up and pearls, which means she has probably been up a while and heard our early morning argument. I wonder if she heard Maida's accusation that if we hadn't gotten married we might still be together. "So getting married was a bad thing," I asked her, though I knew she was referring to the terms of our engagement, terms I've been trying to rewrite. We agreed "No kids" three years ago when we set the wedding date. But now I wanted kids. More than one kid. Sons and daughters. Brothers and sisters. Siblings. Like my two sisters and brother. Their children my kids' cousins. An only child, Maida emphatically shakes her head at my talk of even one kid. For the past year, I have felt a longing in my loins that is not sexual, it curls up around my heart and leaves me breathless, my arms aching to hold a child. At Home Depot I watch as fathers explain electricity or cement to a son or daughter. I watch kids tag along behind carts loaded with plans and lumber for swing sets, sand boxes and elaborate tree houses. I smile and watch kids whine and cry, piss, and spill gooey purple-colored liquids. It is called "Home" depot, not "House," for a reason. Brilliant marketing that clearly has had an effect on me.

I want help from Henry and Pony, so I locate the Benadryl and present it to Pony as if it were a magic potion. "Good of Henry to remember," she says. It is true. Her right eye is swollen and red.

URRRRRRKKKKKKKK. "*Betty. Forklift to trees and shrubs. Betty: Forklift to trees and shrubs.*" *URRRRRRRRRRRRRRKKKKKKK.* Maida probably likes the idea of Betty behind the wheel of the compact forklift, Betty in overalls, pressing the gas pedal with her steel-toed boots. I like the idea of Betty on the forklift too, steering a careful path through flooring, cabinetry, kitchen appliances to arrive at large flowering shrubs, but I also suspect Betty is underpaid with four kids at home helping to spend her paycheck. To give Maida credit, she probably imagines representing Betty pro bono in a lawsuit claiming wage discrimination, so her sympathy is certainly more useful than mine.

"What makes you think you'll be a good father?" Maida asked during this morning's argument. When I told her that wanting to be a good father would go a long way, she said "Then go have your kids." An odd injunction, as if the rest of it was "And then come back." But we both know once gone I'm gone for good.

I shower in hot, hot water, and for the hundredth time berate myself for not knowing that children would one day matter to me. For not knowing that love could seep away from our marriage into a reservoir whose mysterious tides could not be reversed. *URRRRRRK-KKKKKKKK.* I laugh because I can't tell if I'm crying. And then I dress for a Saturday of in-law entertainment.

Downstairs, Pony and Maida are cooking breakfast. I would offer to help but instead I admire their practiced moves. Maida is sautéing mushrooms for an omelette or quiche. I imagine Pony instructing a six-year-old Maida in the culinary arts, and I picture her chubby fingers dipping into a bowl of pink icing. I try to picture Maida teaching our son or daughter how to mince garlic but—and this is telling—I just can't.

Henry is standing in front of the fridge, perusing our magnetic photographs from trips to British Columbia, Labrador, and Morocco. "Travel, not toddlers," Maida had chanted after the recent chaotic visit of my best friend who'd had his second child in three years. Sleepless, we helped them repack their car with carriages, diaper pails, stuffed animals, snacks, and bottles. We'd just returned from Bella Coola and were already acquiring maps of Slovenia. "Travel, not toddlers," I repeated after her, but with a sharp pang I'd never felt before. There was no going back. My next daydreams were of a toddler strapped to my back, rounded arms around my neck, another older toddler holding my hand as we navigated a particularly steep spot on our hiking trail. Maida following behind, identifying the calls of birds, carrying the newborn in a sling, beneath breasts alive with rich milk I'd tasted twice.

URRRRRRRRRRRRRRKKKKKKKKKK. *Thibideaux to outdoor lighting. Thibideaux to outdoor lighting. UUUUURRRRKKKKKK*

"That's Battle Harbor," I say to Henry who is peering at a photo of twin outhouses. I describe the tiny island off the coast of Labrador, where the indefatigable and noble Dr. Grenfell built one of the first hospitals. But Henry's gaze has moved past the photo to my list for Home Depot: screen for bathroom; caulking; half-inch washers.

"I see you're a regular customer," he said, a note of surprise in his voice.

Yeah, I think, *I'd use the bridge.*

*   *   *

After breakfast I suggest to Henry that a trip to Home Depot might be a good way to pass an hour. He is game, but Maida objects. "Dad doesn't want to follow you around while you moon over BBQ grills and lawn chairs." Pony waves her hand as if we've left already, assuring me she will go another time. *You might not have another opportunity,* I want to say, but we still haven't broken our news. The Benadryl helped her eye, but given what we are going to tell her and Henry, no doubt both eyes will be red by evening.

Henry insists on driving. We turn right out of our drive and go to the end of the long street, away from the disconcerting view of Home Depot. There he turns right to the light, passes a tattoo parlor, the fireworks stores, a vacuum cleaner repair shop, then takes another right which leads us to Home Depot's expansive parking lot.

I point out it is the long way round. As usual, the parking lot is alive with cars and pickups and the static voice instructing employees where they and their forklifts or plane saws are needed next.

We are greeted at the door by a man Henry's age wearing the familiar orange vest. His name tag says "Fred" and his greeting is so warm that if he wasn't decked out in the store's uniform, my father-in-law might have thought they knew each other. Even so, he shakes the man's hand and assures him we are happy to be here. Afterwards Henry mutters, "I wonder what hardware store he used to own. How can he be so happy?"

I snag a shopping cart and ask Henry if he wants to tag along with me. I show him my list, he nods and we're on our way. He shuffles after me, impressed, I can tell, by how well I know my way around the aisles of wheelbarrows and power tools, through nuts and bolts to a wall of washers.

While I am hunting for the right size and thickness, Henry says he thinks he'll wander around some on his own. "I didn't know they had a gardening section," he says. "Thought it was all construction stuff." I tell him my list won't take long and I'll look for him there. Today, with Henry accompanying me, I easily resist the temptation to buy a leather tool belt, which anyway would always look too new around my waist. Every once in a while, a contractor comes in with his still on. It is always supple, broken in, stained a golden sienna from sweat and grime. I envy that weight as if it were another set of balls capable of anything. They sell a miniature tool belt for kids, with almost as many loops and rivets as the grownup belt. I will treat my girls the same as I treat my boys and vice versa. But I can't imagine who their mother will be; I am still in love with Maida but I suspect that love can be replaced by longing. I think she is not in love with the me that wants children.

Today, a harassed-looking father is hauling his wailing kid down from a red rolling ladder. The father clearly smells the poopy diaper.

I note that the kid has the father's big ears, and my left hand involuntarily goes to my own left ear, which sticks out even further than the right. Maida used to say "The more handles the better."

I find the right size washer, then hunt for Henry. He is not in gardening, and I imagine he is standing impatiently near the car, peering past the roofs of too many pickups, trying to identify our house through the trees. He is probably hoping he can't see it, but he will be disappointed. Undaunted, perhaps energized, he will move on to plotting where the fence should go, drafting the first lines of the petition, for which he will expect me to gather signatures by going door to door up and down our neighborhood.

He's not at the car. Now my hope is that he hasn't decided the marsh can't be all that soggy or deep and, adventurer that he is, hasn't also tried to wade back to my house. I can't remember if he is wearing his golfing shoes, or if golfing shoes have cleats.

I return to garden supplies, though I fear failure. But there Henry is, lounging at the check-out counter, tucking a silver credit card into his wallet.

"You're not going to believe this," he says, and he's right. He tells me that Pony has always wanted an outdoor water fountain, but nothing cutesy like a fish spouting water, or a cupid pouring water from a chubby jug, and absolutely nothing that gurgles. He says he has found the perfect fountain. "Japanese design, a surprise for Pony. The neighbor's grandkids will love it." He says it will be delivered the week they're back by a Home Depot from two towns over.

He is right; the fountain is beautiful. Oblong granite stones interwoven in two towers three feet high, water cascading from one stone to another. Elegant even. Mesmerizing. A girl about six or seven, in frazzled pigtails, is holding her hand very still in the waterfall. She doesn't notice us. Henry points to her shoes, which are soaked, and we both smile. I love him for his enthusiasm and Pony for her taste. He is happy. On our way out, he wants to know if I think his daughter would want an identical fountain. I tell him, "I'll bring her by and let you know. Or maybe you should ask her." He nods distractedly and I suspect he is hoping to say goodbye to Fred, but Fred is no longer on greeting shift.

Pony and Maida have rearranged the living room—something I've wanted Maida to do with me for months. The couch and two chairs now allow more intimate conversation. Pony is polishing an end table and Maida is moving a lamp nearer the couch. "Perfect," Pony says, and looks to me for approval. I tell her she's read my mind, as if I am the son she knows only too well. Suddenly I am surprised that I am missing them already. Maybe Henry and Pony should adopt me, or I them. No, they have already adopted me, but now what? A wave of grief washes me onto the couch where I sink with the knowledge that they are not going to be the grandparents to my children. The cushions feel like quicksand. No one notices because Henry is extolling the virtues of Home Depot to his disbelieving daughter, his attentive wife.

* * *

His secret purchase gives lunch a festive air that cannot be dispelled by our own looming secret. As we open the second bottle of Pinot Grigio, it occurs to me that Maida's parents might be expecting the opposite of what we have to say because they talk of friends' grandchildren, family reunions. Maida must sense this because she hurriedly begins to gather up our empty plates.

As she serves a peach pie Pony made an hour ago, she says, "James and I have something to tell you."

"Oh, we thought so," Pony says, and rises to give Maida a hug, her pearls swinging against Maida's long hair.

Maida catches her hand, ducks her head to loosen the pearls from her hair. "It isn't what you think," she says.

Henry and Pony's eyes widen, parents' frightened eyes; they look to Maida then to me, and finally to each other for comfort. I wonder why Maida thought we needed a visit for this news, a couple's visit.

"James and I—we're separating," Maida says.

"Oh, Maggie, dear," Pony says, and Henry's bewildered gaze seeks mine. Our bond over Home Depot is stretching, stretching.

"I'm moving out," Maida says. And here she looks at me. She knows that "moving out" is new, and I thought still undecided.

Henry says, "Please don't do anything too hasty," and Pony's "Are you sure you want to do this" isn't a question, but rather her clear and tearful dismay.

I refuse to break down. I push back my chair and stand up, announcing that I'm going to put the lawn mower to work. "Henry, Pony." I duck my head at them, sad, because they belong to Maida. "You all will want to talk."

And what will Maida say? *James has decided he wants to have children, and I do not.* Or *You knew I never wanted to have children.* It is true that Maida said this all through law school and our courtship. Her parents probably never believed her. And I didn't know my own wants. I cry as I put my shoulders to the task of pushing the mower around our green puddle of a lawn, wanting kids trailing after me, squabbling over the rake, throwing fresh grass high into the summer air.

Has she already found an apartment? I think I suspected this. Over the roar of my lawnmower, the music begins again: *URRRRRRRKKKKKKKKK* It will be me here, starting a new life. Falling out of love, hoping to recover from a broken heart and waiting for the bridge to Home Depot. As I take a wide arc, the orange building comes into view, and I recall the ride home with Henry, who was still aglow with his purchase of the fountain for Pony and the neighbors' grandkids. Maybe he was planning how he would take

Maida aside and ask if she wanted one too, imagining his own grandchildren gleeful over the twin fountains—one here and one in Florida. He pulled out of the Home Depot lot onto the bustling highway, and as he took the first, then the second, then the third left turn of the trip onto our long street, he said, "You're right; it is the long way round."

Hindsight

Clare and her oldest friend from college had been planning this visit for the past three months. But only yesterday, her arms full of towels and pillows, Clare realized that it was too soon for her husband's study to become a guest room. First she needed to talk through her anguish and anger at finding him there, slumped over his desk beside the empty vials of pills, finding his folded note that said "Clare."

Today, Brenda was driving her rental car down from Maine, where she'd been camping with her youngest son and his girlfriend—still college kids. The couple would be staying behind in Castine for another week. That had been the plan, so Clare was startled to see three people outside of her back gate—Brenda, but also Brenda's son and a girl—looking irritable, and unwashed.

She tried to hide her dismay as Brenda said "Oh, Clare," and folded her into strong arms. Nate hung back for a long moment, then stepped forward to introduce a shyly nodding Rebecca. The girl was runner-thin—noticeable in spite of the wrist-length sleeves of her Kinks T-shirt. She had long red-blonde hair and red-rimmed eyes as if she'd gotten sunscreen in them, or had been crying. Nate's gangly arms and height mirrored his father's dark, messy good looks. Brenda's sunburned face was already peeling beneath her frown. Their car was crammed with backpacks and camping stuff, beach chairs, empty water bottles, soggy coffee cups, straw sun hats; the Volvo's engine—even off—sputtered in the humid August heat.

Clare ushered them past the patio's wilted ferns and roses into the cooler house, where Brenda instructed Nate to pile everything in the mudroom to be sorted out later. When the kids trudged outside for more, a distraught Brenda apologized for appearing with the unexpected guests. "Nate broke up with her so their backpacking plans for Maine are out."

"And now?" It was all Clare could offer.

"Oh, Clare, I knew you'd be upset, which is why I didn't call. Rebecca wants to go home. I'll put them both on a plane in the morning." She groaned and dropped onto the couch. "This week has been hell. Black flies. Cold water. The kids breaking up." Her blotched face attested to her motherly anxieties and her ample figure to the appetites that tried to assuage them. Closing her eyes, she promised to say more when the kids left to dump the rental car. "Did you mention Bloody Marys?"

*   *   *

It was a drink Stewart had loathed, but Clare gratefully mixed up a pitcher—shades of dorm room Sundays. After college they had kept in touch. Brenda and Cabot moved to Seattle, writing of the surprise of a third son, and Clare and Stewart relaying their own surprise at not having children. Clare was absorbed by the demands of arts administration and her increased ministrations to Stewart. For a while, his position as a civil engineer specializing in bridge work had served him well—when he was deep in plans, calculating the statistics of tensions and stresses or working on elaborate digital models. Between projects. Stewart's bouts with depression became a larger and larger part of their marriage. Clare found herself obsessively buying season tickets to the theatre and Red Sox games, making travel plans to view yet another of the world's great bridges. The sixth-century Anji Bridge in Zhaoxian or the Ponte Vecchio in Florence. Stewart would explain to her the religious beliefs, the military conquests, or the march of technology that made them possible. Travel was out of the question when his depression grew more pronounced—days spent in bed and nights in constant weeping before he agreed to several month-long stays in the hospital. And then his suicide.

Brenda was the only friend Clare had wanted to talk to, though they agreed that she should not come out for the memorial service, but later. She needed time alone with Brenda, to cry, to remember Stewart's virtues and complain about his faults, and to talk about her anger at being left. How long had he been rehearsing his final goodbye? Had he been wondering what to write as they talked of next year's opera festival in Santa Fe, or her brother's knee operation—something Stewart said was probably in his own future. Had he lain beside her at night, perhaps after making love in their practiced and satisfying way, unable to sleep, composing his letter.

My Dearest Clare,

Please believe me that I've stayed as long as I could—for you. You, our life together, kept me here longer than anything else could have. Don't look for signs in hindsight because there won't be any. I have to leave.

All my love,
Stewart

It was too courtly, infuriating in its reticence. How dare he claim full responsibility for his decision to end his life. Making it his story. Leaving her with what? Maybe she'd driven him to it in some way he did not want her to discover. If only—if only what? If only he'd loved her more?

*   *   *

She carried Bloody Marys and the pitcher of refills out to Brenda, who was fanning herself with a magazine on the patio. As the sun slipped from the high brick walls, the afternoon had grown blessedly cooler, so they sat amidst the geraniums and ivy on rusting iron chairs, aware that any minute, Nate and Rebecca would be back from dropping off the car.

"Tell me fast what happened with the kids," Clare said.

Brenda glanced at her watch, then began by saying that soon after Nate and Rebecca started dating he discovered she was into cutting. "Little nicks to draw blood. Or pin pricks. When he learned she was bulimic, he was already in love and desperate for her to see a therapist, afraid she might commit suicide." She stopped short— "Oh, Clare"—and leaned forward to touch Clare's arm.

Clare shook her head, willing herself not to cry. "Go on," she said. "It's OK. No, it's not OK, but you know what I mean."

Brenda's eyes searched Clare's for just that meaning.

"Please go on," she said.

The patio gate squeaked. Brenda held out her glass for a refill. "Ice is heaven," she said. The kids were back.

*   *   *

They couldn't go to Clare's favorite restaurant because Rebecca was a vegan. A bulimic vegan. Clare didn't want to think about Rebecca's tastes—any of them, going down or coming up. Dinner conversation was sparse, awkward, and Clare noted with sadness that Rebecca's fork was empty half the time it rose from her plate. Walking home after dinner, Nate and Rebecca seemed desperate to be with someone other than themselves. Nate told Clare more than she ever wanted to know about landscaping. How soil had its own form of

DNA, that pedestrians' muddy shortcuts were called "desire lines." Rebecca walked silently beside Brenda, occasionally looking over her shoulder at Clare and Nate. When Brenda asked about school, snippets of Rebecca's talk about her courses floated back—the politics of gender, her class on iconic architecture.

Back home, in a waif-like voice that unexpectedly pierced Clare's heart, Rebecca said she'd like to turn in early and so Clare gathered up sheets and a pillow for the living room couch upstairs. She wanted to shake Rebecca or take her in her arms and say "You have a whole life ahead of you," but it was something she wasn't quite convinced of for herself. Rebecca's curved back, her thin shoulders as she tucked in the sheets, looked too taut and fragile to touch. Her polite help with the pillowcase was painful. Clare left to find more pillows. Brenda would sleep in Stewart's study—it had become a "guest room" after all. Nate was given blankets for the couch in the family room downstairs, where Brenda and Clare were once again unable to talk.

Tomorrow, if they couldn't change their tickets, Clare would insist the kids go off somewhere—the MFA, the waterfront, Paul Revere's house—anywhere. She and Brenda deserved time off from the banal drama of this failed youthful romance.

Brenda had changed into a cotton flowered bathrobe and, feet up on the coffee table, balanced a mug of strong black tea on her stomach. Every so often Nate tilted his dark head toward the stairs as if to listen—for what, Clare wondered. His voice was thick as he relayed how Rebecca didn't believe he was serious that their relationship was over. He actually said "relationship." "She keeps making plans for a bike trip we were going to do next summer." Then wistfully, "I think I'll go up and say good night. See how she is."

Please stay a while, Clare wanted to say.

Brenda rose to brew another cup of tea, then in a low voice continued the story of Rebecca's life. That her father died when she was ten so they moved in with grandparents while her mother kept books for an auto body shop. Rebecca went to Barnard on a full scholarship, and Nate to Stanford, where his freshman year was consumed by long distance calls pleading with Rebecca to go for counseling. In the spring he gave her an ultimatum and she promised things would change. Then on this trip to Maine Nate said that tiny dots began appearing on her arms again. "She wore long-sleeved T-shirts the entire week in Maine, even though it was close to 100." Clare had noticed those long sleeves when they arrived. Who knew?

Brenda sighed. "Rebecca hasn't called home at all, not even when Nate told her it was over. This was Nate's first real romance. They don't realize that they'll get over it. He feels grief-stricken—" Brenda stopped.

Nate stumbled halfway down the spiral stairs to lean over the railing. "Mom, Rebecca said a strange thing. She said to come get her in the morning if she doesn't wake up."

"Why wouldn't she wake up?" Brenda asked, annoyance setting hard the corners of her mouth. "Do you want me to talk to her?"

"No, I'll go." Nate disappeared up the stairs only to reappear a moment later. "Mom. Mom, I think you better come upstairs. Please. She took all her pills." He waved three pharmacy vials, their tops off, empty.

"Oh God," Brenda cried. Then she was up the stairs, holding her robe high, her glance back at Clare beseeching.

No, Clare thought, *this can not be happening.* Rebecca's orange plastic vials were identical to those Stewart had saved up the last four months. Where had he kept his precious hoard of death?

Rebecca was bent over in a shroud of pale blue sheets on the edge of the couch, her thin arms holding her concave stomach. Clare had never seen arms that thin and helpless. Nate's arm around her shoulder looked too heavy for her to bear.

When Brenda asked if she'd taken all the pills, she nodded, eyes vacant and glazed.

"Up, up!" Brenda said, shaking Nate's shoulder "Get her to the bathroom, she has to vomit up the pills. Right, Clare?"

In a rerun of her call six months ago, Clare dialed 911, awash in anger that such questions hadn't been necessary when she came home to find Stewart slumped at his desk—his neck unearthly cold—his plans more sincerely made.

As calmly as she could—was her address in police records?—Clare answered the dispatcher's questions and listened to instructions. "If she is throwing up, don't flush. They might want to see what's there." Next was what had she taken and how much.

Speaking over the wet sounds of Rebecca's retching, Clare read off the labels: "Lithium, Xanax, Tylenol. Nate, how much?" He was kneeling in front of the toilet beside a heaving Rebecca, holding back her straggly wet hair in one hand, her forehead in his other. He repeated Clare's question and Rebecca shook her head, unable or unwilling to say how many pills had gone down. When 911 asked how much was coming up Clare forced herself to look at the floating dinner, the revolting debris of wild mushroom risotto and partially digested pills. "Hard to tell," she said. Meanly, she couldn't help thinking that the bulimic Rebecca must find this part easy.

Then the 911 voice said, "If nothing more is coming up, get her walking and keep her walking."

Minutes later, paramedics came to the door, black bags in hand, stretcher ready. Rebecca's name and age?

"Lord, I don't know." Helplessly, Clare turned to Nate who was walking a limp Rebecca around and around the living room. Her thin white nightgown hung on the sharply flat body of a child. Poor Rebecca surely didn't know Clare's name either. She must feel so alone with her shredded heart.

The paramedics walked her out, one on each side of her. "Better to walk," they said. Was there a note? No note, Clare said, thinking that a suicide *gesture* doesn't require a note. Brenda was the last through the door. "I shouldn't leave you," Brenda said, but she was moving down the stairs. "Go," Clare said. "Go."

Clare flushed the toilet twice, wiped down the seat, and threw Rebecca's sheets into the laundry. She tried to keep at bay unbidden images of Stewart being taken away on a stretcher, his face covered shockingly in a shiny body bag, no longer an emergency. In that way, except for his note, he simply disappeared. In the weeks that followed she became obsessed with knowing what it meant. She'd found accounts of a note carried in a locket where once a picture had been; a note torn in two by a sister who wanted to keep a father's dire prediction about a younger brother secret from him; another thrown away by a cousin who only valued stock certificates. Then there were the notes of Virginia Woolf, Rudolph Hess, Yukio Mishima, Kurt Cobain, and books of collected suicide notes: the improbable *To Be or Not To Be* and *I'm In the Tub, Gone. Let Me Finish* was a Christmas bestseller in Germany. One suicide note said *I'm annoyed that I will miss the O. J. Simpson trial.* And another was a list that ended *Buy eggs; Shoot Sam [the cat], Shoot self.* Was a note better than no note? Some experts said that suicide runs in families, though whether it was psychological or something genetics didn't yet understand wasn't clear. For several months after Stewart's death, Clare had regretted that they hadn't had a child, but would she ever have stopped worrying about her child's future when her own husband had been such a tenuous guest on this earth?

* * *

The emergency room entrance of Mt. Auburn Hospital bristled and glowed with the lights of three parked ambulances as policemen directed yet another siren's arrival. In the waiting room, Brenda wept and blew her nose, saying this must bring it all back for Clare. No, Clare thought, it was never really gone. Down the hall, Nate hovered outside Rebecca's bay and from time to time went to the cafeteria for coffees. They called Rebecca's mother, but she wasn't home. An hour later, Doctors assured them that the charcoal had worked, that Rebecca would recover just fine. If she had walked in at that moment, her white hospital gown dragging on the tiled floor, Clare would have slapped her silly.

Exhausted, they went home at 4:00 a.m. and slept till eight. After checking in with the hospital, Clare suggested she make omelets while Brenda tried to reach Rebecca's mother again. "I almost don't know where to begin," Brenda said, and Clare told her "Just dial."

When Brenda returned, Clare set her to grating a sharp cheddar. It disappeared in short furious strokes as Brenda said, "You're not going to believe this, Clare, but after everything I described her mother said, 'I suppose I should send flowers.'" She stopped grating, clearly expecting an equally appalled reaction from Clare, who instead yanked the grater out of her hands and clunked it into the sink. "That poor woman is probably in shock." Her voice was too harsh, even to her own ears. "It's not yet 6:00 a.m. in Seattle. We didn't think of that."

A chastised Brenda rinsed the grater automatically and dried it. "I told her that what she needed to do was make plane reservations. She's probably totally baffled by Rebecca."

"And maybe I'm still baffled by Stewart's death," Clare said. Why, why hadn't she been a strong enough force to keep him here? He had known that would be her question: Don't look for signs in hindsight. Damn Stewart. That is not an answer.

"Oh, Clare, I am so sorry for all of this."

"Brenda, look at me. What is 'all of this?'"

"Everything. These last few horrible days. Stewart."

"We haven't even talked of Stewart," Clare said. She turned the heat to high.

"But at least you understand what made him do it. His difficult last years." Brenda put her hands on Clare's trembling shoulders.

"Is that what you think? That I understand. You're relieved that I understand?" She pulled free of Brenda to splash whipped eggs into the hot skillet. How could Brenda have arrived at this point? There had been no bridge to here, no arc from one side to the other.

"That came out wrong," Brenda said.

"What I want to know is why I'm so fucking angry," Clare said. "Go home."

Brenda's shocked look was far more satisfying than her sympathy.

"You heard correctly," Clare said. "Not sad. Not heartbroken. Yes, that. But angry, too."

"Oh, Clare." Clumsily, Brenda pulled the skillet from Clare's hand, and slid it off the burner. "His note, I'd hoped—"

"Maybe it was the best he could do," Clare said. And maybe the best she could do was make all these false starts—talk and hope for some coherent story to emerge that would pull it all together. "I'm sorry. Please don't go," she told Brenda. Not yet.

*   *   *

The next day, Clare sat outside the state mental hospital in Newton, waiting for Brenda and Nate. They'd brought Rebecca magazines and books, a bouquet of irises. Massachusetts state law dictates that anyone who attempts suicide must go through evaluation before being released, so Rebecca had been delivered by ambulance to a facility locked down floor by floor. Their visit had been difficult to arrange because they weren't family. When Rebecca's mother called to say she'd be here by the weekend, Clare pictured her getting on a plane for the first time and flying east, her eyes closed the entire way. She'd get a cab to the hospital, bewildered by Boston's one-way streets and the unfamiliar grid of suburbs. Clare probably should offer her a place to stay, but she simply could not do it. The hospital would have lists of nearby hotels and B&Bs. Brenda and Nate were leaving tomorrow. Nate had resisted, but wisely Brenda had persuaded him to go home. His summer job was waiting. Friends. His own life. And Clare insisted that Brenda go with him. "He needs you," she said.

In truth, Clare wanted to be done with all of them. She felt drained of sympathy, almost inhuman. And now this final good-bye to Rebecca was taking longer than expected. She craned her neck to look at the depressing row of barred fifth floor windows. All this could have been me, she thought, driving back and forth to Newton. Bringing the daily crossword to Stewart; buying biographies for Stewart; planning a trip to see the Rockville Bridge in Pennsylvania, one of the world's most beautiful structures. Or the Akashi Kaikyō Bridge in Japan. The Mackinac Bridge in upper Michigan. She would have been desperate to anchor Stewart in the world—to be his anchor—to search for literally what on earth would make him care enough to stay alive.

The sharp tap on the window startled her before a depleted Brenda sank into the passenger's seat. Nate's eyes were red, his shoulder wet.

"The doctors say she'll be able to return to school in a month," Brenda said. "I don't know how well they understand the situation—the pressure of Barnard, her clueless mother. But they'll meet her soon enough."

"Yes," Clare said. She hadn't seen Rebecca since the paramedics walked her to the ambulance. It was unlikely she'd ever see her again. She'd already forgotten Rebecca's last name. It was all dissonance. Her head ached.

Behind them, Nate was rummaging in his backpack. Moments later, he was on his cell phone with a friend, his recounting of the events of the past two days impossible to ignore. His voice quavered with excited grief as he relayed details of the drama—their break-up, her pills, the wavering Rebecca walking, walking. He should have known, he said. How had he put it together so quickly? Clare wondered. Become the center of the story. This kid.

She tried to tune him out.

His cell phone snapped shut. "Mom, I really should stay till her mother comes, explain about breaking up."

Clare's exasperation flooded the car as she burst out, "Nate. It wasn't your fault. What is wrong with Rebecca is beyond what you can do." She pulled too sharply into traffic, horns blared.

"But who's going to tell her mother what happened?"

"The doctors," Brenda said, but her voice lacked conviction.

Clare dreaded the next few hours. "You don't really know what happened," she said.

But clearly he thought he did, because he was punching a new number into the phone.

"Stop. Enough," Clare yelled. She swerved to the curb, just missing the fender of a black Mercedes, and pulled hard on the brake. Brenda's hands flew to the dash, her shoulders rounded high with fear. Abruptly Nate clicked shut his phone.

Searching his surprised, hurt gaze in the rear view, Clare said she refused to be a party to the next ten calls he was going to make between Newton and Boston. "Can you please wait until we get home? Can you please give Rebecca some privacy."

*   *   *

That evening, Brenda was shy with Clare, wary, but they got through the awkward dinner and retired early. Only after the taxi was called the next morning did Clare and Brenda grow misty-eyed, thick-throated as they made plans for another visit. "We never talked about Stewart," Brenda said. "It's what I came for."

"You'll come back soon," Clare said. "And I will still be here."

Then they were gone.

Methodically, she collected towels and sheets, straightened chairs, restoring each room to its normal use. In Stewart's study, she put the folding bed away, removed the vase of wilted flowers, the tray of toiletries on his desk. Then she stood in the doorway, remembering that lonely, lousy night six months ago, the day of Stewart's death. After friends and neighbors left, she gathered up coffee cups and wine glasses and carried them to the kitchen, where she'd poured a glass of his favorite single malt. She recalled how its smell of peat and Scotland left her trembling with grief. Then she took Stewart's note to his study, certain of what she needed to do: retrace his last moments before he'd swallowed his pills.

She sat where he'd sat—in his old leather swivel chair at his rosewood desk. Sipping from his favorite glass, she forced herself to imagine his last movements, his folded arms, his sloping shoulders, his lowered head. Oh Stewart, why?

She leaned back in his chair to be him. She felt his intent expand her rib cage, she felt his urgency push against her heart. His Namiki Vanishing Point fountain pen still rested on his desk. The empty pharmacy vials were an orange cluster, and a fine white powder still dusted the old-fashioned green blotter where he had scattered the pills. An empty water glass had been pushed toward the lamp. He had folded the note once and written "Clare." His handwriting was steady, precise, so he must have worn his reading glasses.

Now, standing in this doorway months later, she understood what he'd done—unable to stay, Stewart had left her behind. She was alone with what he had given her—and taken away. This was her story. Eyes closed, Clare watched him take off his glasses as she'd watched a thousand times before. Finally, he had cupped the pills in the palm of his hand. He'd lifted the glass, and then—as simple, or as complex, as that—he'd swallowed their life.

Ways to Spend the Night

The first day after Carson and his wife checked into Hayes Cape Cabins they had an argument. Now Carson was holed up in the office, Meadowlark, cabin 1, listening to the ever-disheartening evening news and Juliet was knitting and sulking in Gull, cabin 9. All of the cabins were named for birds. It was late October and not exactly meant to be a vacation. When a dark green car turned onto the sandy drive leading up to the cabin office, Carson and his wife still weren't on speaking terms.

The car, its huge engine thrumming, was a large American model Carson didn't recognize—the kind that in a head-on collision always ended up intact and on top. Belatedly, he realized that Mr. Hayes, the cabins' absent owner, had neglected to hang a NO next to the VACANCY sign advertising efficiency cabins with cable TV.

Carson could see the silhouettes of two people, a man and a woman, weighing the various amenities of Hayes Cape Cabins against those advertised a few miles back. How could they resist the pots of straggly geraniums squatting on each cabin's steps, or the unlikely cabin aviary, or the enchanted forest of dark looming pines? Why were they here?

The stuffed chair where Carson sat had been molded over the years by Mr. Hayes, who was off in Florida assessing the damage done by Hurricane Ivan to his Tampa Bay trailer park. Hours after their arrival, Mr. Hayes had shown up at their cabin door, somewhat abject, to ask Carson and his wife if they would "mind the store" for him. His nephew, who did the yearly repairs, was unable to come early. Clearly, Mr. Hayes had counted on them to agree—and of course, they had. It gave them another reason to avoid accusations and too-glib confessions of infidelity and betrayal.

Through the thin trunks of the pines, Carson thought he saw the flame of Juliet's red hair in the window of Gull, but he couldn't be sure. This morning, when he had summoned courage from a place still unexplored and said, "We have to talk," she'd said, "Not yet," and stalked out for a mile walk in the woods, on a path worn down years ago by a heartier Mr. Hayes.

Carson slouched further into the gully of Mr. Hayes' chair to avoid being spotted peering through the window. He considered going out to tell the couple "No vacancy," but it was too obvious that the place was as deserted as an amusement park under quarantine. Besides, keys to all the cabins except cabin 9, Gull, dangled in plain view. If they came in, he'd have to explain the situation: that he didn't own these birds, and couldn't rent them out with the owner away. Please leave, he willed. You don't really want to witness my wife and me killing each other.

The passenger door opened and a woman's shiny black high heels sank into the sandy path. Wobbling, she stood on legs that could not be ignored. Her long blouse, maybe it was a short dress, glowed pinkly in the day's weak light. The woman's hair seemed to be pink, too, but surely that couldn't be so. She gazed around expectantly, then set the office bell to tinkling.

"I heard about cabins like these, but I've never actually seen them before except on TV," the woman said in a low, sandy voice. Her smile was beguiling, in spite of—no, because of—gleaming, slightly buck teeth that rested on her lower lip like Chiclets. It com-

pletely disarmed Carson, who guessed her age as somewhere between twenty-five and fifty. Sadly, anyone could peg him and Juliet
at a precise forty-five.

The woman gazed at the tell-tale keys then tiptoed over to the
window looking out on the semi-circle of cabins. "They are like doll-
houses. Tiny porches. Windows on either side. Exactly what I hoped
they'd be."

Carson could only nod. Just before Mr. Hayes left, he shuffled
around the office showing Carson and Juliet where things were:
cabin keys, outdoor floods, emergency phone numbers, everything
in its place with the sense of order that by seventy Carson supposed
one finally achieves. Lastly, Mr. Hayes thumped a large, dog-eared
reservation pad. "No more reservations on the books, and hardly a
soul comes by in the off-off season." When Juliet stepped forward
to peer at the reservation page, Carson admired her wariness, which
Mr. Hayes chose not to notice. Instead he described the devastation
the hurricane had wreaked on his trailer park. Why, Carson wondered, did people build trailer parks in areas constantly threatened
by hurricanes? Trailers became missiles the moment the wind came
up. "If you hadn't been guests here several times before," Mr. Hayes
told them, "I'd have shut the place early. Gone to Florida to clean
up the mess and stayed there to hassle the insurance adjusters."

The woman with the Chiclet teeth tapped the window with a
pink fingernail and pointed at the cabin furthest back from the road,
Sandpiper, cabin 5. "I think we'll take that one."

"Ah, Sandpiper," Carson said, as if approving her choice. How
to explain that it was only by chance—a result of an argument—
that Carson was even in the office. "The thing is—"

When a loud horn sounded, the woman turned and minced,
birdlike, out the door. Seconds later she was in tow behind an enormous man who wouldn't have fit into Carson's Toyota. His solid
chin and neck were shades darker than the proverbial shadow and

matched his sunglasses. Carson had read somewhere that men with high testosterone levels and an extremely active libido possess beards that begin growing with their morning coffee.

"Thought I'd speed things up," the man said. "I bet Lolly here already got her cabin picked out. Don't you, baby?"

"I do." The woman—Lolly—pointed at Sandpiper.

"We're not—" Carson began, then stopped. Did he really want anyone to know that he and Juliet were alone in this deserted aviary?

"Sandpiper. That right, Lol? Sounds like a bird."

Lolly nodded, happy and somehow sad at the same time.

The man tugged the registration pad out from under Carson's fingers, signed it, then handed the pen to Carson. It said "Sadow Construction." Then he pulled out a flat wallet and flipped a platinum credit card onto the counter.

The credit card machine, connected to the phone by a shiny black leash, was a mystery that Carson didn't want to try and solve in public. Juliet, he was sure, would have the patience to figure it out. He pushed the credit card back across the counter. "If you will stop by tomorrow, Mr. Sadow—"

"Not Say-dough. It's Sadow—rhymes with shadow," Mr. Sadow said. Then he held out his hand for the key. Unhappily, Carson surrendered it.

* * *

"I was forced to decide on the spot," Carson told a smoldering Juliet.

Her back was to him as she peered out their window at Sandpiper. Carson had already noted that Mr. Hayes' "minding the store" wasn't exactly the precise set of instructions it had once seemed.

"They're here. It's done," he said. "Unless you want to knock on their cabin door and explain that your husband made a mistake."

"Which one?" Juliet asked. She didn't expect an answer and he didn't have one. When she asked "So who are they?" Carson said he didn't know, but Sadow was in construction in Connecticut.

"What a tank of a car," she said. "And that blouse, or maybe she thinks it's a dress. I hope you realize that now we can't leave."

"Leave?" he said in wonderment. Together?

Juliet wheeled around. Had he said "together" out loud? "We just got here," he said. "We have over a week to go."

"You're the one who said 'leave' last night," Juliet said. Then, dismissing that, she asked, "So how long is the green car staying?"

When Carson admitted he hadn't asked, Juliet said, "I'm going to find that damn NO for the VACANCY sign. Surely Mr. Hayes needed one in high season." And she was gone.

*   *   *

Their most recent argument happened the evening after Mr. Hayes left when Carson and Juliet had snooped inside the other cabins. "The only perk of this job," Juliet said, rattling a handful of keys. The slanted evening light transformed her curly red hair into a flaming wide-brimmed hat. She was slim, and had once been pliant in his hands. "Aren't you curious about how different they are?" Juliet said. No—and well, yes, Carson thought, remembering her sister Deidre, then followed her to Osprey, cabin 2.

"Curiosity" had been one of his lame excuses for Lisa, the new person in human resources at the software firm where he worked. Their affair hadn't lasted longer than the summer, though it added to the fraught atmosphere of his marriage. Now he and Juliet were here to repair unacknowledged and, Carson feared, unknown wounds.

The cabins were arranged around a sandy semi-circle of a lane, each with its own tiny porch and a parking space for one car. Pushing open the door of Osprey, Juliet set the game in motion. "OK. On a scale of one to ten." Mold dappled a corner, and twin beds held down wall-to-wall puce carpeting that surely had fleas. Carson gave it a weak two. Tern, cabin 3, sported an old-fashioned wooden crib and high chair with robin decals. "Vintage decals," Juliet said. "But it's still only a five." Cabin 4, White Owl, was empty except for a rickety wooden stepladder and three red buckets strategically spaced on the floor. "Less than zero," Carson said. Sandpiper, cabin 5, was the most attractive, with a faded hand-hooked rug and lumpy quilt. Everything in cabins 6 and 7, Plover and Warbler, even the photograph, *Provincetown Dunes*—was identical. Blue Heron, cabin 8, had wicker furniture, a blue-checked tablecloth, blue drapes, and pale blue chenille bedspreads.

"Deidre and I had the exact same bedspreads growing up," Juliet said. "God, how I miss her."

It was an arrow to Carson's heart that Juliet assumed she missed her sister more than Carson did. Lord knew he missed Deidre in his own flawed way. She was the real secret of his storm.

Blue Heron also had a Bennington pitcher that Juliet, over Carson's objections, carried back to Gull to fill with dried flowers. Carson's objections continued when Juliet pushed the couch into a corner, unplugged the TV, and dragged two reading chairs in front of the window. It felt too cozy to Carson, who also feared the reason they were here. "Let's leave," he had blurted out.

"Leave? Leave!" Juliet echoed in amazed outrage, her arms now resting on the reading chair she'd just pushed into place. "You're the one who signed on as Keeper of the Birds." Before collecting her knitting and flouncing into the tiny bedroom, she placed her foot on the chair and sent it flying back into the middle of the room, where it bumped against Carson's weak knees. "We're not leaving. But it's your move."

*   *   *

Toward morning, he woke sweating beside a snuffling Juliet, the word they used for her indelicate snoring. Suddenly, with a vengeance, Carson's nightmare from the last hour blossomed in his mind. In it, Deidre, Juliet's sister, was dying in Mass General Hospital. Juliet was off somewhere and Carson had gone to visit Deidre alone. When he tiptoed into room 312, Deidre was wearing a red sequined gown that kept snagging on her white hospital blanket. Holding out her thin arms to Carson, she'd announced that she'd made a miraculous recovery and was ready to resume their affair, and oh, how she'd missed him. Her room too had undergone a transformation. Red brocade drapes merged night with day. A wall of bookcases was filled with Carson's favorite biographies. A slim hospital bed sat beside Deidre's own bed, the back cranked up at an angle that in the dream Carson found faintly erotic. "Oh, that," Deidre said waving her hand at the extra bed. "I've ordered a queen-size and a hot tub. We won't have to wait long." Carson remembered being terrified that Juliet was going to appear any moment and discover their affair, and sure enough, her high heels were soon clicking down the hall toward them. Frantically, he'd tried to crawl under Deidre's hospital bed, but it was too crowded with stuffed animals and her sleeping husband Brad, who also looked stuffed. When Juliet arrived at Deidre's room, she was carrying armfuls of his clothes and seemed oblivious to Carson's feeble attempt to hide. Leaning down to peer at him, she said, "I put your suits on hangers" in the same efficient manner she'd moved their daughters out of the house and into college dorms and their first apartments. Awkwardly, he'd backed out from under the metal hospital bed and stood up as Juliet leaned over to kiss Deidre's damp forehead. Then the two sisters watched in their usual complicit amusement as Carson struggled to fit his suits into the room's narrow metal closet. He realized that they must have flipped a coin for him.

With a tiny dance step and wave Juliet left, taking with her a wilted bouquet of red roses and dragging a stuffed Brad behind her. Whispering his name, Deidre held out her red-sequined arms to Carson and at that point he'd woken up, chilled and sweating, pathetically relieved that it had been only a dream. He'd peered around Gull's bedroom, felt the bed flat, double, normal, and filled with his sleeping Juliet.

But Carson's relief drained away as he faced the dream's kernel of truth. It was his affair with Juliet's sister—not his stupid affair with Lisa—that he regretted most.

It all started when . . . were words he wished he could turn into a complete sentence, but they went nowhere. Juliet at work. Deidre staying with them during her brief separation from Brad. Her chicken soup ministering to a wretched cold that kept Carson bedridden. Wine in the middle of the day. A conversational impasse. Reaching for her, his hand between her thighs. In the two years that followed, he'd found in Deidre something that was not lacking in Juliet, but in himself. Deidre he could take from, and she was generous toward his childish ardor. Juliet simply didn't see the wimp he was; or maybe she refused to see it. He also discovered that he could love two people at once.

It ended when—here too words failed him. He felt such guilt when Juliet opened her arms to him, when her hands opened him. Nor could he ignore Deidre's sisterly horror at what they were doing, even as they made plans for their next meeting. The toll taken by the emotional chaos of assignations and deceit had been too high: holidays the families spent together when they dared not touch; colognes and perfumes they didn't allow themselves to wear for each other; his pure terror the afternoon when Deidre was late and hadn't called, and he suspected Juliet knew. He and Deidre still loved each other even as they brought it to an end. Relieved of love.

Later, weak and dying, Deidre had made him promise that he would never tell and had made the same promise to him. They'd been alone in her hospital room, Carson seated on her white hospital bed, the back tilted up, her cold hand beneath his. Her voice was whispery, faint. "For Juliet to know, I would have to be here to get railed at, punished—and I won't be. I would have to be here to beg forgiveness and I won't be. Please, I have to trust you." She closed her eyes. He'd tasted tears without salt. She was purest water, air, and soon she would be fire.

*   *   *

"Bad news," Juliet said, coming through Gull's screen door. "The 'NO' is missing." She stood peering out Gull's window, framed as if by one of the book jackets she designed for the post-modern novels—by kids—her publishing house promoted. Evening light made a silhouette of her tense back, her wiry hair riding the crest of her strong freckled shoulders. Carson felt heat. How long since he'd buried his hands in that wiry hair, pulled her to him, kneaded her scalp hard enough to transfer its musky sweet oil to her breasts.

"Here she comes. Lordy, they must think we're the welcome wagon," Juliet said seconds before Lolly scratched at their screen door. Her pink skirt-blouse had been exchanged for a pea-green jumpsuit. And now her hair looked slightly green.

"Hi there," Lolly said, her nose close to the screen, white Chiclets resting on her full bottom lip. "Hope I'm not interrupting. Hard to believe we forgot a corkscrew."

Even in their small cabin, Lolly resisted standing still. "Oh, I'd love to knit," she said, picking up the red mohair scarf that hung from two needles. "Is it hard to learn?"

Juliet said buy some needles and she'd give Lolly a lesson. Juliet had taken up knitting a year ago—her therapist's suggestion—for stress. Carson understood why Juliet would knit through editorial meetings and the disturbing news from the Middle East, but he resented how Juliet also knitted during their arguments, as if they would otherwise be a waste of time. And somehow he couldn't picture Lolly working away on pink or blue booties.

"Size 10 needles," Juliet said, handing over their corkscrew. At the door, Lolly waved a familiar little wave. Smiled her Chiclet smile.

Catching his eye, Juliet said, "Promise me there won't be any more guests," and Carson promised.

*   *   *

The next morning, he went to the office to do his own search for the NO to add to VACANCY, and again was amazed at Mr. Hayes' sense of organization. There were photograph albums of a young Mrs. Hayes with a parrot and several cages of birds. Account books lined one shelf. On a bottom shelf, *Playboy*s were sandwiched between *Sports Illustrated* and *Cape Cod Living*. The girls in the airbrushed centerfolds looked more like life-size, rubber sex dolls than real women with real pubic hair. He felt a stirring. Juliet's red hair sprouted a feathery path he used to lovingly traverse with his tongue from her belly button down. Before Lisa. Carson feared Juliet would soon declare, "OK, tell me about her," because he no longer knew what to say—only what he was not allowed to tell.

The office door tinkled. Sadow had come by to return the corkscrew. In spite of the gray day, he still wore sunglasses, and it seemed likely that his beard was intentional. A disguise?

He set the corkscrew on the counter and asked if the whale watches in Provincetown actually watched whales. "Maybe they're really party boats? Singles stuff. I mean, do you have to go on a whale watch with other people?" Outside, the green car's motor was humming with purpose. What purpose?

"Probably, to make it cost-effective," Carson said, adding that he hadn't been on a whale watch for years.

"Money always talks," Sadow said, slapping the counter hard enough to make the corkscrew bounce.

Please leave, Carson wanted to say. "Afraid of your own shadow," his father had teased him till he was ten and could pretend he wasn't. "I like my shadow," he'd said. "It's what else might be there that I can't see."

After Shadow-man left, Carson called Juliet to say he was headed to Snow's in Orleans for a NO and did she need anything? Not a thing. Had Lolly come by for that knitting lesson?

"She doesn't exactly seem like the baby blanket type," Juliet said.

Driving down Route 6 he felt as if he'd been let out of jail.

* * *

Two hours later, Carson had the "NO" ready to hang when an ancient Honda coughed its way to the office. Doors slammed and a young man emerged, haggard, thin, with a frayed collar beneath a real beard. He went around to the driver's side to offer assistance to his very pregnant wife. She in turn opened the back door to reach in and release from a car seat a howling, swaddled baby with the largest mouth Carson had ever seen. Two tiny front teeth. He wondered if the Sadows had children. Children with Lolly's irresistible teeth.

The office door tinkled again. The young mother, her cheeks glistening with sweat, held her baby tight with love and puzzlement.

Their domestic little group filled the office and made Carson feel inordinately happy. He knew he was grinning as he quoted an unbelievably low rate and described the perfect cabin, Tern, number 3, complete with crib and highchair, and a microwave for bottles. The man said, "Great. Great," then, sheepishly, as if it had been an afterthought, the man said, "Uh, we have a dog . . ."

"A dog. Not a problem," Carson assured him. "I love dogs."

A low-slung spotted mutt emerged from the back seat, and Carson wished it had been larger, more like a guard dog. Its fur and skin were splotchy. Was that smell the baby or the dog? It lay down in the middle of the office floor, and had to be coaxed to leave. "Arthritis. He's old," the young man said.

Carson helped the couple move in to Tern, carrying bags of baby supplies and dog food—all the while hoping the Sadows would find the baby's wails annoying enough to leave. They didn't look as if they'd had much experience with children or crying babies.

"Enjoy your stay," he bellowed through Tern's door, which set the baby howling even louder. They were the Beeks, Ginny and Jeremy. And little Oliver Beek.

*   *   *

"You promised no more guests," Juliet accused him when she returned from her walk and heard the racket coming out of Tern. With long swishes, she unlaced her hiking boots and pushed into her clogs. "You're dangerous in that office. You've turned into someone who can't say 'no.'"

Ignoring this, he explained that the couple had spent their honeymoon in Tern, and that she was pregnant, so how could he turn them away. "Their name is Beek. They belong in this aviary." Somehow the young family made him feel unaccountably safe. Forced to put a name on it, Carson would have said safe from Shadow-man's menace, from something in the shadow of the Sadows' lives.

Juliet's red hair couldn't be tamed by the new Cape Cod baseball cap she pulled on. "I'm taking the car and I'm going to have a divine dinner and a bottle of vintage Bordeaux. And you march right back to that office and choose a key. Six cottages are empty—including the one with the stepladder and buckets. You clearly have a knack for sleeping anywhere."

*   *   *

That night Carson slept alone in Osprey, cabin 2. All night the baby howled and the dog alternated between whimpering and barking. Carson looked for a light in any of the cabins. Dark. A solid loneliness lay on his heart—shocking in its abrupt appearance, swooping down to take his breath away. Midnight. He wanted to go home. He wanted to go home not with Juliet, but to her. To their past collective life of books and morning sex and cooking smells, their companionable togetherness apart.

Around 2:00 a.m., unable to sleep without nightmares, he rose, pulled on his jeans, and stood on his cabin's tiny porch. Throat-thrumming wails were still coming from cabin 3. How can a baby cry that long? Was it teething? Surely Juliet was awake, too.

He crossed the dewy grass and crept around the side of Gull to Juliet's open window. Juliet was sleeping on her side, naked. He had a fleeting thought—benevolent almost—of her in the arms of another man as the moon made an alabaster figure of her rounded shoulder, her deep, deep waist, her solid hip and thigh. What could lead us back, Carson thought, to simple loyalty and love? Juliet's narrow ankles were primly crossed and caused his heart to lurch, his mind to gently part them.

*   *   *

For the next two days they took turns with the car. One day he went to the used bookstores in Wellfleet, then on to an abandoned P'town, whose summer entrepreneurs had whacked the tourists for their dollars then followed their bank deposits out of town. But he loved the rakish atmosphere they left behind. Real artists and writers, real fishermen, real fish stews. Two other days he took long walks on the ocean beach at McGuire's Landing and out to Indian Neck on the Bay where a gull with a broken leg limped around doing just fine. He missed Juliet's piss and vinegar. Last night, when he'd gone back to Gull for clean clothes, Juliet was sitting in the dark, which startled him. "What are you doing?" he said. Could she knit in the dark?

"Thinking," she said. And to his "About what?" she said "You'll know eventually. Turn out the light when you leave."

*   *   *

For the next few nights, he moved from Osprey to Plover to Blue Heron, occasionally crossing paths with young Beek carrying the dog into the trees to do its business. Twice, Carson had stepped in shit. The dog waggled its long tail when Beek passed Carson on the way back to Osprey, where the young mother must be close to despair. At night, Carson used his pillow to drown out the intermittent cries of the wailing baby. Maybe it was acquiring a full mouth of adult teeth. A day later Sadow hunted him down to say that the baby's crying disturbed Lolly. "Its crying goes right through her," he told Carson from the front seat of the green car. When Carson suggested they might want to cut short their stay, Sadow told Carson it wasn't an option.

What if they all stayed and stayed? A call to Mr. Hayes informed Carson that, due to the hurricane, phone service in that area was temporarily unavailable.

When Carson couldn't sleep, or wouldn't sleep, he imagined what it was like to be Mr. Hayes, to putter around the property or wait in his little office for the next cast of characters to check in. Instead of sheep, Carson dredged up Cape birds: grackle, swallow, killdeer, kestrel, flicker, blue jay, robin, crow, kingfisher, shrike, mourning dove. He recalled his dismay at learning it was "mourning" not "morning." When Deidre died, Juliet had been so bereft at losing her that Carson's affair with Deidre felt like a burden he couldn't endure another day. It was why he'd fallen into the meaningless affair with Lisa. He remembered his alarmed relief that she'd succumbed so easily, and then so easily spun him loose when the summer ended. He'd wanted to be found out. He needed to regret an affair that never mattered. Most of all, he needed to lay his heart almost bare. But getting to the place where their hearts were on the table was a reservation neither he nor Juliet could make. Instead, Juliet was out with the car, and he was roaming around the property, pruning the geraniums, poking into sheds, looking under the cabins, inspecting drains as if he were a prospective buyer.

*   *   *

This was how he knew exactly where the shovel was when Jeremy Beek came looking for him. He was cleaning leaves off a wooden canoe that he'd discovered in the trees behind Osprey. Deep circles under Jeremy's eyes testified to the non-vacation the couple was having. When he asked if Cozy Cape Cabins owned a shovel he might borrow, Carson said sure he had a shovel and retrieved it from the shed behind the office.

"My wife's good about people. She knew you'd be sensitive to our—ah—situation. Dozer died in his sleep last night. He's been her dog since she was ten. Do you think Mr. Hayes would mind if we buried him here off in the woods?"

Carson longed to be sensitive. Dozer wouldn't take up much space. A biodegradable dog. Minutes later, he found himself following Jeremy into the woods, far off the path. Every now and then Jeremy stopped to kick at the underbrush, study the ground. Finally he started digging beneath a stand of young oaks and old pines. He was stronger than he looked, and soon, only sweating slightly, he had carved a shallow rectangle in the pine-needle carpet. The end of daylight savings had stolen the afternoon's sun, and dusk was turning the forest floor a dark purple. Carson stood watching because it didn't feel right to leave. The shovel was meant for snow. Finally he told Jeremy, "Here, I'll finish. You go and get—ah—Dozer."

Jeremy wiped his brow on his sleeve; he seemed glad to know he'd have company for the burial, and loped off toward the cabins. Now that night had fallen, Carson was surprised to see they were hidden from view. The dirt was porous and dry, easy to cut away and lift, although Carson's aching shoulders reminded him he hadn't done hard labor for years.

He might have stopped when he had deepened the grave by two more inches, but he didn't. The rhythm had become a mesmerizing physical pull. Suddenly, he shivered against the dark he remembered as a child. He couldn't look up to find the moon, for fear of what else he'd find. He dug and dug and dug. Dirt flew out of the dark into the dark. It was strangely satisfying to rend the earth in preparation for a permanent goodbye. Cremation and memorial services don't allow for the physical work of loss. He would have liked to shovel out a portion of Deidre's grave or begin to fill it in.

Jeremy returned with a flashlight and Dozer wrapped in a blue baby's blanket. Standing at the side of the grave, peering in, he seemed taken aback by how deep and wide and long it was—with Carson in it. "Yes, well," Jeremy said. "Dozer will be able to stretch out."

Carson flung his last shovelful of dirt and hoisted himself out; the grave's dark interior had felt ten degrees cooler than the evening's air.

"Ginny insisted I use this blanket," Jeremy said. He knelt down, one knee at a time, and lowered the stiff Dozer into the hole. When he held out his hand for the shovel, Carson surrendered it. Quickly, Jeremy worked to cover the round mound that had been Dozer. "Goodbye, Dozer," he said, tears in his eyes. And in Carson's eyes— Jesus Christ—over a dog he'd only seen a few shit-on-his-shoes times.

When he got back to Osprey, Carson cried full out. He didn't put a name to why. Later that night, no moon, he couldn't sleep. He needed Juliet. Clutching his pillow to his chest, he was creeping from the too-soft bed in Goldfinch to Gull when he was stopped by Shadow-man, who cleared his beard-covered throat and held up a flat, wide palm. "Wait."

Carson threw up his own hands, dropping the pillow. What time was it?

"Whoa, man," Shadow-man said, his voice low and, to a terrified Carson, threatening. "You always travel with a pillow?" Sadow picked up the pillow and punched it before handing it back. Carson thanked him and pretended he'd been headed to the office. Following him, Sadow said he and Lolly had some good news for a change. Lolly's brother and sister-in-law were able to get away from their party goods store and would be arriving the next night. He pointed back over his shoulder. "Plover is next door to us. They'll take that one."

Carson fumbled with the office key, threw wide the door, and dumped his pillow on Mr. Hayes' chair. He felt belatedly brave. "I'm sorry. I can't—"

"Wait a minute." Sadow had followed him inside, his gaze roving around the dim messy office. "Something's not normal here." He worked his shoulders in round rolling motions. "That NO VACANCY sign for one. It went up since we got here. And last I counted you got seven empty cabins."

"Repairs have been scheduled," Carson said.

Sadow scratched his beard. "You never asked for money, a deposit. Never ran our Visa card through the machine."

"If you're unhappy here—" Carson dusted off the credit card machine with his sleeve.

"You don't own this place, do you." It wasn't a question. Sadow slapped the counter. "What were you and Beek up to tonight? I saw you with that shovel."

"Look, why don't you just go dig up the dog. Remember the dog?"

"Dog!" Sadow snorted, and pulled out his cell phone.

Unaccountably, Carson leaned over the counter and knocked it out of his hand.

Tongue between his teeth, Sadow shimmied around the desk and hit a switch on the wall that Carson had never noticed. Lights flooded the cabins with the brightest glow Carson had seen outside of Fenway Park. Of course. Sadow was in construction so he'd know where electricity came from. If he wanted to he could probably turn off the water, put the cabins up on blocks, and haul the whole shebang away.

His eye on Sadow, Carson dialed Gull and Tern and pleaded with Juliet and Jeremy to come to the office. Sadow waited, his cell phone back in hand.

Minutes later Juliet appeared in jeans and a sweat shirt. No bra. Hair a burning tangle. "Carson, what is going on?"

Sadow stepped forward to tap her shoulder. "Where's the owner?"

When Juliet said "Florida," Sadow rolled his eyes.

The Beeks arrived running. "What? What?" Jeremy cried, "We saw the lights come on." Ginny's eyes were red and shiny. Oliver was wailing until Lolly appeared at the door and reached for him. He quieted the minute she began murmuring, her cheek against his fuzzy head. "Oh, Lolly, bless you," Ginny Beek said. Jeremy hadn't changed his shirt.

"Tell him," Carson said to Jeremy, "what—who—we buried."

Jeremy's face sagged as he dug into his pocket and pulled out a limp dog collar with two rusted tags. "Dozer," he said, his eyes tearing up. He shrugged toward the glowing woods and Carson. "He helped me bury Dozer."

"Look, Sweetie," Lolly whispered to Sadow as Oliver slept in her arms. "He's sleeping for me."

Juliet's left hand wormed its way into the back of Carson's waistband and hung there, a weight that left him breathless with longing.

"Dozer. That old dog." Sadow put his cell phone away and patted Oliver's head. All he wanted, he told Juliet, was an extra cabin, and he explained why.

"Why not," Juliet said. "You want Plover?" She gave the key to Lolly, who tucked it into Oliver's blanket. Sadow turned off the floods.

"I'm going to bed," Juliet said. One hand was holding back her fire-red hair. "Carson. Come to bed."

Once there, her voice cracked. "Oh, Carson. You helped Jeremy bury his smelly dog." She started to cry softly.

Carson knew she hated the way she cried, her nose leaking more water than her eyes. Unexpectedly, he joined her, snuffling into her hair. Juliet eased her arms out from under his to lean back, her hands now gripping his trembling arms.

"My sister told me everything," Juliet said. "So, I know."

"Jules—" Carson tried to pull away but she held on tight.

He knew it was true—from his nightmare—that his affair with Deidre was clearly a matter of record, but he hadn't been ready to know it. Even though his dream of Juliet's visit to the hospital to deliver his clothes had been so straightforward.

Then Juliet told Carson she wanted him back. "Deidre didn't trust you. But she said I should. So I will, if you tell me to." And so he told her.

* * *

They saw fourteen whales on the whale watch. One breached so close to their boat that they could see the barnacles on its teeth. Spray misted the air. The young Beeks from Tern sat in the bow, their baby quieted first by Lolly and then by the boat's engines.

Juliet and Carson stood side by side, hips touching, arms resting on the rail, Juliet's head from time to time dipping to Carson's shoulder. Last night, Juliet had fitted herself around Carson and told him that they would be going on a whale watch with the young Beeks from Tern, the Sadows, and Lolly's sister and brother-in-law, who were now staying in Plover. She said it was a trip in memory of Lollypop, the Sadows' daughter—whose leukemia, a year ago last fall, burned through her eight-year-old body in a race she couldn't win.

Now, as the whaling boat sliced through the water into open seas, Lolly never left the railing. Sadow never left Lolly, who held tight to a Barbie doll suitcase full of Lollypop's ashes. Lolly's sister and brother-in-law cried as they took videos and photographs and wrote down everyone's address. Lolly's sister had Lolly's Chiclet teeth. When they were out of sight of Provincetown, Lolly let the ashes loose to fall. But the very lightest ash drifted up and over Lolly, over Sadow, and over Carson and Juliet standing next to them at the rail. Carson rubbed the tiny gritty flakes into his cheeks, his lips, touched his finger to his tongue. Juliet's eyes were closed, ash soft on her lashes. Carson took her face in his hands and pulled her to him as he'd done in their cabin, in Gull, in the morning's first light. He hadn't needed to say anything more. Facing her, his fingers in her hair, he'd kneaded her scalp hard, lingering in its slight indentations, releasing the holy oil of grace, then going there.

Acknowledgments

I want to thank my children for being in my life and sometimes in my stories: Kate, who, when my writing friend, Anne Brashler, asked what it was like to move back and forth between warring divorced parents, said, "It's like—feeding the piranha"—and a title was born; Derek, who recognized a story when he lived it, and would say "Sit down, you aren't going to believe this"; Wayne, who passed along tales of his college roommates' antics and his own misadventures; and my stepson, Cameron, a superb writer who publishes his own stories. And always my gratitude to my late husband and lasting love, writer and editor Robie Macauley, who once surprised me with tickets to a Buddy Rich show, where I met up with Rich for the third time and gave him a copy of my first story collection that included "The Next Time I Meet Buddy Rich."

Thank you also to my readers—first in Chicago many years ago, and then in Boston. I have almost always belonged to a writing group, and when I moved to Boston, I created a new group from classes I taught and writers I met. Countless stories and books later, several of us are still together, and so to Kate Wheeler, Thomas McNeely, and Stephanie Reents, my enormous thanks for your companionship, dedication, and generous reading of my stories.

Other fellow writers and editors have offered support and friendship over many years, and so my thanks also to Jackie Davis Martin, Bobbie Ann Mason, Margot Livesey, Steve Yarbrough, Ewa Hryniewicz-Yarbrough,

Sue Standing, Pablo Medina, John Skoyles, Ladette Randolph, Elizabeth Libbey, Lisa Diercks, Bill Beuttler, Alexandra Marshall, James Carroll, Megan Marshall, Kassie Rubico, Sarah Miley, Gish Jen, Anne Bernays, Greg Harris, Emilia Dubicki, DeWitt Henry, Bill Henderson, Don Lee, Douglas Whynott, Kim McLarin, Jessica Treadway, John Trimbur, Maria Flook, Julia Glass, Jabari Asim, Stephen Tapscott, Robert Dulgarian, Lynn Potts, Michael Anania, Gene Wildman, James Park Sloan, Richard Bausch, Tom Bracken, Sharon Dilworth, Dawn Raffel, Lynn Reynolds, Colleen Mohyde, Nancy Heffernan, Jeanne Stanton, Laura Zigman, Sue Miller, Douglas Bauer, Virginia Pye, Eve Bridburg, Christopher Castellani, Mameve Medwed, Mary Bonina, Lynda Sturner, Megan Sexton, Robert Shapard, Tara Masih, Bill Henderson, Sherrie Flick, Ellen Langer, Nancy Hemenway, Askold Melnyczuk, Alex Johnson, Barbara Sofer, Donna Gordon, Rita Doucette, Ken Rivard, Randall Brown, Victoria Large, David Lynn, Thomas Kennedy, Gladys Swan, David Rivard, Patricia Spears Jones, Peter Wyman, Enid Powell, Laurie Levy, Rochelle Distelheim, Meg Pokrass, Robert Scotellaro, Grant Faulkner, Lynn Mundell, Kim Chinquee, Louise Crowley, Thomas Christopher Greene, Sharon Stark, Richard Jackson, Phyllis Barber, Mary Ruefle, Nance van Winckel, Victoria Redel, Melissa Pritchard, Jewel Parker Rhodes, David Jauss, Patricia Smith, Christopher Noel, Ron Carlson, Christopher Merrill, Steve Bergman, Leslie Epstein, Colleen Mohyde, Manil Suri, Lawrence Cole, Abigal Beckel, Kathleen Rooney, Elizabeth Peterson, Katie Howdeshell, Toni Lee de Lantsheere, and Charles de Lantsheere.

My appreciation also to friends and early supporters of my work who are no longer with us: Ralph Angel, Toni Cade Bambara, Anne Brashler, June Brindel, Francois Camoin, George Core, Alice Cromie, Daniel Curley, Stanley Elkin, George Garrett, Justin Kaplan, Roberta Pryor, Helen Rees, Thalia Selz, and Robley Wilson.

A special thank-you to editors Gerald Costanzo at Carnegie Mellon University Press and Victoria Barrett at Engine Books. Cedering Fox of WordTheatre brought many of my stories to life in staged readings in Los Angeles, New York City, and London; she also recorded two of my Pushcart Prize stories, "Grief" and "The Kiss," for WordTheatre CDs. Anthony Russo, artist and illustrator, whose work often appears in the *Boston Globe* and the *New York Times*, gave his voice and art to several of my stories on his YouTube channel, Cronogeo. Finally, my immense gratitude to editor and poet Wyatt Prunty, who chose my new and selected collection for Johns Hopkins University Press, where my editors, Catherine Goldstead and Hilary S. Jacqmin, gracefully saw *Fabrications* through to publication.

*   *   *

I am grateful to the editors of the journals where some of these new stories, in slightly altered forms, first appeared.

"A Fabricated Life," *New Jones Street*
"Brochures," *Missouri Review*
"Doors," *StoryQuarterly* and *Ghost Writing: Haunted Tales by Contemporary Writers*
"Her Elvis Presley Wedding" (first published as "Knots"), *Elm Leaves Journal: The Dirt Edition*
"Hitchhikers," *Five Points*
"Off Stage," *Elm Leaves Journal: The Dirt Edition*

The other stories in this collection were originally published in the following works:

Getting to Know the Weather, copyright © 1985 by Pamela Painter. Published by the University of Illinois Press, Champaign, IL. Reprinted 2008 by Carnegie Mellon University Press, Pittsburgh, PA.

The Long and Short of It, copyright © 1999 by Pamela Painter. Published by Carnegie Mellon University Press, Pittsburgh, PA.

Wouldn't You Like to Know: Very Short Stories, copyright © 2010 by Pamela Painter. Published by Carnegie Mellon University Press, Pittsburgh, PA.

About the Author

Pamela Painter is the author of four story collections: *Getting to Know the Weather*, which was the recipient of the 1986 GLCA New Writers Award for fiction; *The Long and Short of It; Ways to Spend the Night*; and the flash fiction collection *Wouldn't You Like to Know: Very Short Stories*. The coauthor with Anne Bernays of *What If? Writing Exercises for Fiction Writers*, she was a founding editor of *StoryQuarterly*, and served as guest editor after moving to Boston. Her stories have appeared in the *Atlantic, Five Points, Harper's, Kenyon Review, New Flash Fiction Review, Ploughshares, SmokeLong Quarterly*, and *Threepenny Review*, among other magazines and literary journals, and have been reprinted in numerous anthologies. Painter has received grants from the Mass Cultural Council and the National Endowment of the Arts. She has been the recipient of three Pushcart Prizes, as well as *AGNI*'s John Cheever Award for Short Fiction. Her stories have been recorded for National Public Radio and for the HarperAudio CD *Love Hurts*, and appear on artist Anthony Russo's YouTube channel, Cronogeo. Her work has been presented by Wellfleet Harbor Actors Theater and staged by Cedering Fox of WordTheatre in Los Angeles, New York, and London. Painter is a founding donor of the Flash Fiction Collection established in 2020 at the Harry Ransom Center, The University of Texas at Austin. Since 1996, she has taught in the Writing, Literature & Publishing Program at Emerson College.

Fiction Titles in the Series